The Dream of the Iron Dragon

A Novel by Robert Kroese

Book One of
The Saga of the Iron Dragon

Contents

Note on Old Norse and Old English Pronunciation

For the most part, the same set of symbols is used to represent words in modern English, Old English, and Old Norse. Modern English, however, uses *th* for both the voiced *th* sound (as in *this*) and the unvoiced *th* sound (as in *thin*), whereas in Old English and Old Norse, these sounds are represented by two separate letters: *ð* for voiced; *þ* for unvoiced. Thus the Old Norse word for *time* is *tíð*, pronounced like *teethe*, and the Norse god of thunder is *Þórr*, pronounced *Thor*.

For quoted speech, I did my best to use the correct Old Norse and Old English spellings, respectively. For characters' names, I sometimes substituted *th* for *ð* or *þ* for easier reading.

Robert Kroese

Scandinavia and Northern Europe

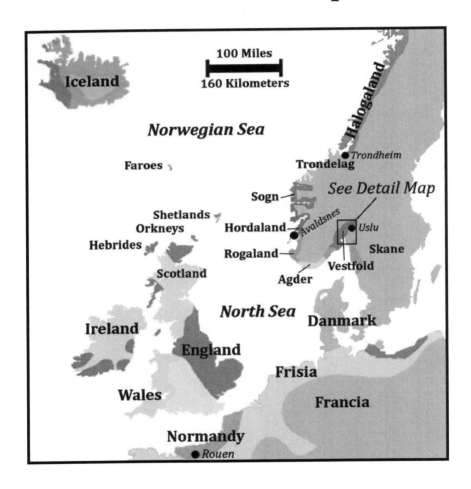

Southern Norway Detail Map

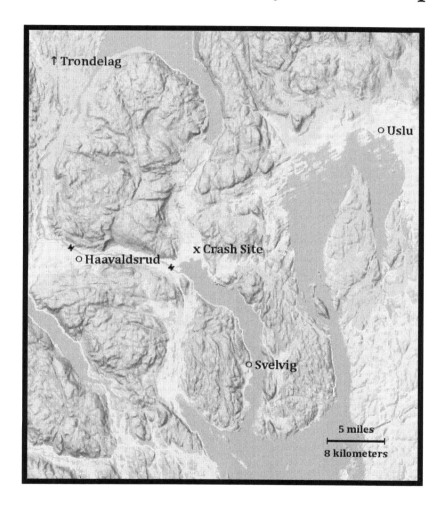

PROLOGUE

U nited States Air Force Colonel Emily Rollins ducked out of the chartered helicopter and walked briskly to the police car parked across both lanes of Route One. The air was cool, and the sun hung low in a clear blue sky. She handed her credentials to the red-cheeked, blond officer standing in front of the car. The man made a show of inspecting her ID and then handed it back to her. "Over there," the man said, in crisp English. His nametag read STEFÁNSSON. "He's waiting for you."

Rollins looked in the direction Officer Stefánsson had pointed. There was nothing but a field of black volcanic rock dotted with dull green lichen—the sort of landscape you could see anywhere in Iceland. She'd been to this country once before, on vacation. The whole country was like an alien planet. In the distance arose a mountain of white: the largest glacier in the country, called Vatnajökull. Her hastily conducted research on the plane from Andrews Air Force Base had revealed that the name meant "water glacier." Some things were better left untranslated.

Walking a few steps into the lava field, she still saw no sign of the man she was supposed to be meeting. A black Audi was parked on the side of the road, just past the police car. Her contact had to be around here somewhere. She turned to ask Officer Stefánsson for better instructions, but he was busy pointing an angry French tourist in a rented Toyota back toward Reykjavik. She sympathized: Reykjavik was a five-hour drive, and this was the only road into Vatnajökull National Park. It would be closed for the foreseeable future.

Rollins picked her way carefully among the rocks, eventually spotting a brown-haired man in a drab tweed jacket standing about a hundred yards away. She hadn't seen him before because he'd been crouched over something in the field. He waved to Rollins, and she waved back. He hunched over again, almost disappearing among the lichen-covered rocks. That was Major Alan Hume of the Royal Air Force, her British counterpart. Rollins made her way toward him.

"Come here often?" Rollins said as she approached the man. It was a dumb joke, but it was part of the routine they went through every time they met at a field site.

Hume stood up and smiled at her. "We're supposed to be keeping a low profile, you know."

"You can have low profile or you can have fast," Rollins said. "I know you Brits don't like to make a spectacle of yourselves, but we Americans have places to be."

Hume chuckled good-naturedly and shook Rollins's hand. "Good flight?"

"I hate helicopters," Rollins said. "They're unnatural. Speaking of which, nice work on the cover story."

"What, the bit about the snowmobile helmet?"

"I meant the Russian Cosmonaut stuff."

"Oh, that! Well, yes. Had to do some thinking on my feet."

"And they bought it?"

"The folks at the newspaper? Hook, line and sinker. The snowmobile helmet thing was their idea. The only thing media people like more than getting a scoop is making up a bullshit cover story. Did most of the work themselves. They've got everybody convinced this bloke was a scam artist, trying to make a name for himself. You know, one of these flat Earth, ancient astronauts types."

"What happened to him? The guy who found it."

"Oh, we took care of him."

"Took care of...?"

"Christ, Emily. We don't do that anymore. We found him a nice place in the Virgin Islands."

"He's not going to talk?"

"Unlikely. We've a plan in place to thoroughly discredit him if he does."

"And no one else knows?"

"Just the newspaper people. And I've got them scared shitless they're going to start an international incident if they make a peep. Icelanders aren't keen on being in the middle of a new Cold War."

"What exactly did you tell them?"

"Experimental Soviet spy plane was shot down by the Americans over the North Sea in seventy-eight. Soviets denied it was their plane, Americans denied they shot it down. The usual bollocks. I told them Putin himself was in charge of the program. Nobody wants it brought up now, what with the Yanks and the Russians about to go at it in Ukraine. Old wounds, sleeping dogs, et cetera."

"You're a little too good at this, Alan."

"Don't I know it. Would have been a used car salesman if I were a bit more honest."

"Where is it?"

"In the boot of my car."

"Is that safe?"

"Safer than lying out here in a field."

Emily nodded. "Have you found anything else?"

"Not yet. A field team is flying in tonight."

"Then what are you doing out here?"

"Killing time."

"Can I see it?"

"Of course."

They started walking across the field back to the Audi.

"How long will the road be closed?" Rollins asked.

"As long as it takes. We're in talks with the Icelandic government about rerouting the road to the south."

"Permanently?"

"If this site turns out to be as big a deal as we suspect, yes."

"You've found a single artifact."

"We've found an artifact in *Iceland*, Emily. What are the odds they took the trouble to set up a decoy site in Iceland? Who would even think to look there in the first place?"

"You're sticking with the decoy theory then?"

"It's the only thing that makes sense. They were trying to hide the location of their actual base of operations."

"Okay, but why would they set up their base in Iceland of all places? Sparse population, remote, resource-poor, high latitude...."

"Hell of a place to hide a space program, eh?"

"It makes a perverse sort of sense, I suppose. Pick the worst possible site because no one will look there."

"Not only that, but this whole area was covered by ice until about twenty years ago. The rest of the facility might still be under the glacier."

"Hold on. You're saying...."

"I think they knew, Emily. I think they knew the glacier was going to advance, covering their tracks."

"Climate modeling?"

"That's one possibility."

"For heaven's sake, Alan. Not the time travel thing again."

"It explains everything. The advanced technology, how they knew about the glacier, the lack of—"

"The tech isn't that advanced."

"For the tenth century it is."

"You've dated it?"

"Not yet, but I assume it's of roughly the same vintage as the other pieces."

They'd reached the car. Hume pulled the key fob from his pocket and opened the trunk. Inside, lying on a layer of newspapers, was a roughly spherical object a little larger than a basketball. Under a layer of mineral deposits, a yellow-white shell of hard material was visible. On one side was a shaded, translucent visor. The headline of one of the newspapers beneath the object read: *American hiker finnur fornu rými hjálm.*' Below it was a picture of a grinning man holding the round object in front of his chest.

Emily pointed to the headline. "I'm assuming that says...?"

"American hiker finds 'ancient space helmet.'"

"Jesus Christ."

"The story is less committal. Anyway, the correction went out this morning. Well-executed hoax, nothing to see here."

After glancing at Officer Stefánsson to make sure he was otherwise occupied, she reached into the trunk and picked up the artifact. It was surprisingly light.

"Do you ever wonder if this is worth the trouble?" she asked, turning the thing over in her hands.

"Looking for the artifacts?"

"I meant the elaborate secrecy. Who are we hiding this stuff from anyway?"

Hume shrugged. "It started during the war. We wanted to keep it away from the Germans and the Soviets. Now, who knows. Force of habit, I suppose. So what do you think?"

Emily peered through the visor, trying to imagine a face looking back at her. Had it ever been worn? By whom?

"I think," she said, "this is a thousand-year-old space helmet."

CHAPTER ONE

The survey ship *Andrea Luhman*'s antennas picked up the signal about 3500 astronomical units out from the Finlan Cluster. Traveling at its current rate of nearly a tenth of light speed, *Andrea Luhman* would approach the nearest star in the cluster, M-341698, in just under three weeks. At that point, the crew would have a decision to make. They would analyze the sensor data and pick the star system in the Cluster that seemed likeliest to contain a planet capable of supporting human life. Based on that choice, *Andrea Luhman* would alter her trajectory relative to M-341698, using the star's gravity to bank toward their destination.

That had been the plan, anyway—before *Andrea Luhman*'s pattern recognition algorithm siezed on the tightly focused microwave transmission repeating the first seventeen numbers of the Fibonacci sequence in an endless loop. Now things had changed, and Lieutenant Michael Carpenter, the man currently overseeing this leg of *Andrea Luhman*'s voyage, had to decide whether to stick to the plan or take action in response to this new data. The signal repeated:

0, 1, 1, 2, 3, 5, 8, 13, 21, 34 …

Carpenter sighed. This decision was above his pay grade, which was part of the problem. The captain and the rest of the crew were in stasis, with three weeks of hibernation left. If he revived them now, it would throw everything off. Food and oxygen calculations, work assignments, stasis schedules. There was no clear protocol for something like this. Distress signal? There were procedures for that. Enemy contact? Everyone on board knew those protocols by heart. Contact with a previously unknown alien intelligence? Sixty-eight pages of guidelines. But it was hard to be sure which of these procedures to follow in the case of a signal of unknown origin broadcasting numbers according to a well-known mathematical algorithm. And still the transmission continued:

... 55, 89, 144, 233, 377, 610, 987

And then it started over again at 0.

The approximate source of the signal was easy enough to pinpoint: by using directional antennas and comparing the relative strength and doppler shift of the signal at two moments several hours apart, the ship's computer had effectively determined the source through triangulation: an uncharted planet orbiting a star about half a trillion kilometers from *Andrea Luhman*. The star had been considered for investigation when *Andrea Luhman*'s mission had been outlined, but it had ultimately been rejected in favor of the more closely grouped stars of the Finlan Cluster.

The numbers being transmitted meant nothing in themselves. But their mode of transmission—and the very fact that someone had gone to the trouble of transmitting them in the first place—implied several facts. Carpenter ticked them off in his mind:

Number One: this area of space wasn't as devoid of intelligent life as previously thought.

Number Two: somebody wanted to communicate Fact Number One. Also, given the tightly focused transmission, they wanted to communicate it specifically to *Andrea Luhman*—or at least a ship on this approximate course. It was highly unlikely the sender had actually spotted *Andrea Luhman*; at this distance, a radio signal would take almost five days to reach them. No, whoever was transmitting that signal had known—or suspected—a ship would be traveling from the Fomalhaut Gate to the Finlan Cluster.

And Number Three: the being or beings transmitting the signal either could not or did not wish to transmit any additional information. They could just as easily have transmitted a standard distress signal, but they didn't. That might mean the source of the signal was an uncontacted alien intelligence. Or it might just mean they wanted to say hi as *Andrea Luhman* shot past. Neither of these possibilities seemed particularly probable to Carpenter. In all likelihood, the senders were either human or Cho-ta'an. Whoever they were, they knew what *Andrea Luhman* was looking for, and they knew the crew wouldn't be able to resist investigating the source of the signal.

And yet, Carpenter hesitated. If he woke the captain, he knew what would happen. They'd change course to investigate the signal. If the senders were Cho-ta'an, then this was almost certainly a trap. *Andrea Luhman* was a scientific survey ship; it wasn't equipped to defend itself against a Cho-ta'an warship. In short, if Carpenter woke the captain, they were all probably going to die.

*****

"Hell, Carpenter. You woke me for this?"

Captain Nathan Mallick sat across a molded plastic table from Carpenter, his hands spread flat on the table and his eyes fixed on the squeeze bottle full of electrolyte solution in front of him. To Carpenter, it looked like the captain was staring the bottle down, and he had to bite his cheek to keep from laughing. Waking up from three weeks in stasis was no joke. The IDL's scientists had made great advances in the field of in-transit hibernation, but the protocol for emerging from stasis had remained essentially unchanged since the first trials twenty years earlier: take it slow and drink plenty of water. Of course, it didn't help to drink water if you couldn't keep it down. Muscle atrophy, dizziness and nausea were the main side effects. Mallick handled it better than most, which was probably how he'd lasted long enough in the IDL to become *Andrea Luhman*'s captain. Carpenter had never actually seen the captain get sick, but next to the squeeze bottle was the standard-issue IDL barf bag.

"Sorry, sir. The protocol isn't clear, and I thought—"

"Yeah, yeah, I know," said the captain, waving his hand. "You did the right thing. My head's still foggy. It's just... what the hell is it?"

Carpenter ran through the possibilities: the source of the signal was either human, Cho-ta'an, or... something else.

"Humanity's been in space for two centuries now and we've only encountered one other intelligent race—and that was eighty years ago. You think we've stumbled on another one?"

"I'm just listing the possibilities," Carpenter deadpanned.

"Fair enough," the captain replied, the faintest hint of a smile flickering across his face. "For now, though, let's assume they're human or Chota'an." He reached slowly across the table, picked up the bottle and squeezed a little of the liquid into his mouth. He grimaced. "We got any coffee?"

"I'll make some."

Carpenter started a pot of coffee. While they waited for it to brew, he stood in silence as the captain took a few more sips of the electrolyte solution. By the time Carpenter handed him a mug of coffee, some of the color had begun to return to the captain's face. Mallick took a sip of the coffee and sighed contentedly. He was beginning to seem like himself again. "Okay," he said. "Let's assume they're human. What are they doing on an uncharted planet this far from IDL territory?"

Carpenter held up his hands. IDL territory—also known simply as "human space"—was a vaguely defined, kidney-shaped area of space some fifty light-years long. The Sol system was roughly in the middle of the kidney; *Andrea Luhman*'s home port, Geneva, was one hundred twenty light-years toward the kidney's base. *Andrea Luhman* had left the confines of IDL territory a week earlier, after jumping from Geneva to the most distant gate, which orbited the star Fomalhaut.

"Come on, Carpenter," Mallick said. "I just got up from a three-week nap. Help me out here. Do some spit-balling."

Carpenter nodded. "Civilian craft gets knocked off course by an asteroid. Engines and radio are damaged. Can't get back on course, can't call for help."

"Any civilian ships unaccounted for?"

"Maybe they're smugglers. Unregistered."

"Seems like a stretch, but okay. If they're having mechanical problems, how did they manage to change course to land on a planet? And why?"

Carpenter shook his head. "Their new course intercepted the planet's orbit. They couldn't avoid it, but had just enough control to make a landing."

"The odds just went from slim to infinitesimal. If they had enough thrust to land safely, they could have avoided the planet altogether. They must have landed on purpose."

"Maybe the planet is habitable. They decided to take their chances rather than drifting in deep space."

"So our unregistered smugglers hit the lottery. The IDL hasn't found a new habitable planet in seven years, even with *Andrea Luhman* and four other ships like her scouring the galaxy, and these idiots find one by accident?"

"I'm spit-balling, Captain. What do you want from me?"

Mallick laughed. "Sorry. Continue. Why are they broadcasting the Fibonacci sequence?"

Carpenter held up his hands again.

"Yeah, I don't have a clue either," Mallick said. "So let's consider the other possibility."

"They're Cho-ta'an."

Mallick nodded. "More likely that a Cho-ta'an ship ended up here than a human ship went off course. We don't track all the Cho-ta'an ships. And we know the Cho-ta'an have their own exploration program. Who knows how many habitable worlds they've discovered that we know nothing about?"

"We have no records of the Cho-ta'an being anywhere near this area of the galaxy. The nearest known Cho-ta'an jumpgate is a hundred lightyears from here. It's one of the reasons we picked this region."

"You really think the IDL has a complete registry of Cho-ta'an gates?"

"No."

"Me neither. We know the approximate locations of sixteen gates, but we don't know how many gates they have altogether. They could have a gate within a lightyear of here and we'd never know."

"There's another possibility," Carpenter said, rubbing the stubble on his chin with his thumb.

"What's that?"

"Maybe they hacked the Fomalhaut Gate."

"You think the Cho-ta'an used *our* gate to get here?"

Carpenter shrugged. "Occam's razor. The simplest explanation for running into another ship way out here? They used the Fomalhaut Gate."

Mallick frowned. "The gates use quantum encryption. And even if they could somehow get through, there'd be a record of the transit."

"There are ways around any kind of security. And you know the dirty secret about those gates as well as I do. They're black boxes, modeled after the Cho-ta'an gates. The IDL still doesn't fully understand the physics behind them. We know they work, but we don't know *how* they work."

Mallick scowled at him, but Carpenter shrugged. As much as Mallick—and the IDL brass—hated to admit it, the fact was that no human really understood how the jumpgates worked. It was only because of luck that they had the technology at all: in the year 2143, an IDL warship intercepted a radio signal originating from what turned out to be an unfinished Cho-ta'an jumpgate. The ship eliminated the Cho-ta'an and took control of the gate. A research team was dispatched with the goal of deciphering the technology and reverse engineering the gate. The team, led by a physicist named Chris Turner, succeeded at the latter task, but made little progress on the former. Turner theorized that the gates made use of a hidden dimension—now known as Turner Space—to create shortcuts between two points in conventional space, but he died before publishing any conclusive findings.

Mallick said, "We know the gates open a wormhole between two points in space, allowing instantaneous travel over light-years of conventional space."

Carpenter chuckled. "That's *what* they do. Not how. Maybe the Cho-ta'an know how the gates cause a wormhole to open, and they're using that knowledge to exploit our gates against us. Our security precautions prevent the gate activation mechanism from turning on. But if the Cho-ta'an can bypass the mechanism, they could use the gates. Without us ever knowing."

"Like hotwiring a car."

"Exactly."

The captain took another sip of coffee, his brow furrowed in thought. Carpenter knew this couldn't be the first time Mallick had heard about the possibility of the IDL's jumpgates being hacked, but like most IDL officers, the captain didn't take the possibility seriously. The reason was obvious: if the Cho-ta'an could slip through the IDL's jumpgates, the war was already lost. The IDL tended to focus on problems it could do something about. True to form, the captain changed the subject.

"Doesn't explain the transmission though," he said. "Could be a trap, but why? *Andrea Luhman*'s a sitting duck. If the Cho-ta'an wanted to take us out, there are easier ways. Our only defense is the assurance that we're not important enough for the Cho-ta'an to waste a ship chasing us."

"And why not a distress signal instead of the Fibonacci numbers?"

"Too obvious," Carpenter said, half-joking. "They know we'd never fall for that old trick."

Mallick ignored him. "And whatever they gain by luring us off course, it would seem that they have more to lose by revealing their position. I assume you've already sent the coordinates to Command?"

"Of course," said Carpenter. "It'll be weeks before anyone receives the transmission though. Maybe it's a rogue element."

"Meaning what?"

"Meaning that the Cho-ta'an have this secret base out here, and they detected *Andrea Luhman*. Somebody on the base is an IDL sympathizer, and they managed to jigger a transmitter to send us a signal."

"An IDL sympathizer? Is there such a thing? Has a Cho-ta'an ever come over to our side?"

Carpenter shrugged. He'd never heard of it happening.

"Seems more likely, if they have some kind of base on that planet, that the whole thing is off the books."

"You mean not sanctioned by the Cho-ta'an High Command? An outpost run by some rogue faction?"

"Exactly. Could be the Fractalists."

"I thought they were a myth."

"That's what the Cho-ta'an tell us," the captain said. "But they would, wouldn't they? It's of utmost importance to them to maintain a monolithic front. Wouldn't do to let their enemy know about their dissident factions."

"But even if the Fractalists exist... are they sympathetic to humanity?"

"No idea. We may have to wake Stauffer. He knows all about this shit. Of course, this is all academic if we can't get there. How far out of our way is it?"

"Not far, relatively speaking. We'd have to pull three gees for a few days to decelerate and change course, but we could do it. I haven't had time to work out a course, but I ran some quick calculations. We could be in orbit in less than a week."

Mallick winced. "Three gees is rough."

"It'll be rougher the longer we wait."

"I hear you," said the captain. "What do you think?"

"Our mission is to look for habitable planets. Some place humanity can hide out and regroup if this war keeps going the way it has been."

"And?"

"And I think up to a few hours ago, our best chance was the Finlan Cluster. Now the situation's changed."

"Agreed. Even if that's a Cho-ta'an base, our odds are better than bouncing around the Finlan Cluster. Whoever's down there, we need to check it out."

*****

Mallick and Carpenter spent some time going over *Andrea Luhman*'s roster. *Andrea Luhman*'s landing craft could hold four, and Mallick's position was the more brains the better. It was a given that Mallick would be in the landing party and that Carpenter would stay with *Andrea Luhman*.

The ship had a crew of fourteen, mostly scientists, who remained in stasis during the voyage. They agreed on reviving the ship's engineer, Carolyn Reyes, as well as the resident expert on Cho-ta'an culture, Johannes Stauffer. If it really was a contingent of Cho-ta'an transmitting that signal, they'd need Stauffer's knowledge of the aliens' language and culture. The short, slightly built Lieutenant Reyes was not the most physically intimidating member of the crew, but she was probably the smartest and was definitely the coolest under pressure. Mallick and Carpenter differed in their choices for the fourth member of the expedition. They considered—but ultimately rejected—Chad Rogers, a mathematician and information systems expert. Even if the math-centric Fractalists were the source of the signal, it was doubtful that *Andrea Luhman* had been summoned to provide assistance with a particularly tricky equation.

Carpenter next suggested their chief of security, Gabe Zuehlsdorf, but Mallick thought Thea Jane Slater, a biologist, was a better choice. Mallick argued that if they were walking into a trap, they were almost certainly doomed. Having a security expert with them was unlikely to help. Additionally, Slater had training as a pilot, so she could relieve Mallick if necessary. In the end, the captain overruled Carpenter. Gabe—the only member of the crew who was routinely addressed by his first name, due to his unwieldy surname—would remain in stasis for now. The four members of the lander mission would be Mallick, Reyes, Stauffer and Slater.

Prior to intercepting the signal, *Andrea Luhman* had been decelerating toward the Finlan Cluster at half a gee. Now Carpenter had changed course and upped their deceleration to a full gee. The captain had told him to give Reyes and Stauffer a couple of hours to adjust before ramping up to a full three gees. Coming out of stasis was hard enough without finding your weight had suddenly tripled.

Reyes seemed to know immediately that something was wrong. Whether she somehow knew that she hadn't been under for the full six weeks or she noticed something in Carpenter's demeanor, she started asking questions before he'd even gotten her upright.

"Where are we?" she murmured. "What's happening?"

"Easy," Carpenter replied, cradling her shoulders with his right arm. With his left hand he pressed an oxygen mask to her face. Her stasis suit was wet with the warm translucent goop that filled the chamber. "Captain will brief you in a couple hours."

"Captain's up?" Reyes asked, her voice muffled by the mask.

"Just relax," Carpenter said. "I gotta check on Stauff—" He almost stopped himself in time.

"Stauffer? Is it the Cho-ta'an? Have they made contact?"

Carpenter sighed. The captain had told him not to say anything, but it was clear that Reyes wasn't going to let it drop. "Just a signal," Carpenter said. "Uncharted planet. Somebody is sending us the first seventeen numbers in the Fibonacci sequence. Captain wants to check it out."

Reyes nodded slowly but didn't say anything more. She was either too stunned to think of any more questions or too busy fighting nausea to concentrate. Carpenter betted on the latter.

"You gonna be all right?" he asked.

Reyes nodded again.

"Okay, I'll be back in a few."

*****

The five of them met around the plastic mess table. As there were only four chairs, Carpenter stood. The captain had just briefed them on the situation. At this point, they didn't know much more than what Carpenter had told Reyes. Currently they were waiting for Stauffer to expand on the single word he had uttered in response.

"Fractalists," he had said, and then turned aside to vomit into a bag. As the rest of them knew next to nothing about the semi-legendary Cho-ta'an cult, they had little choice but to wait for Stauffer to recover. Stauffer, a tall, balding man in his late forties, was an unlikely choice for a space exploration mission. He had barely met the physical requirements but was selected because of his encyclopedic knowledge of the Cho-ta'an.

Whatever was known about the Cho-ta'an, Stauffer knew it. He was fluent in the predominant Cho-ta'an language and had literally written the book on human-Cho-ta'an interaction. The book was short and mostly theoretical; aside from a few notable and abortive diplomatic meetings, the only contact between humans and Cho-ta'an thus far had been military confrontations.

The very first human contact with the Cho-ta'an was in 2125, when a scout ship called *Ubuntu* was destroyed by a Cho-ta'an warship in the Tau Ceti system, less than twelve light-years from Earth. Coordinated attacks on human vessels started some three years later, indicating that the aliens possessed a means of faster-than-light travel. The Cho-ta'an underestimated the humans' resolve and inventiveness, however: the governments of Earth, along with a collection of multinational corporations, quickly formed the Interstellar Defense League, which gradually beat back the Cho-ta'an. Eighteen years after the *Ubuntu* incident, an IDL warship took control of an unfinished Cho-ta'an jumpgate, and another eight years after that, the IDL finished construction on the first of its own gates.

After a lull in hostilities of twenty-six years following the initial IDL victories, the Cho-ta'an attacks resumed. For the past twenty years, the Cho-ta'an had been sending warships further and further into human space, gradually conquering or rendering uninhabitable every human-occupied planet. In the past decade, the Cho-ta'an had even started building jump-gates well into human territory, allowing them to advance even faster. So far they hadn't destroyed any of humanity's eighteen gates, but it was hard to say whether this was because of the IDL's formidable defenses or because the Cho-ta'an hoped someday to use the humans' gates for their own purposes.

All efforts at diplomatic overtures since the *Ubuntu* incident had failed. The Cho-ta'an didn't respond except to launch more attacks. It was clear that they had no interest in sharing the galaxy or in any sort of peaceful resolution. Their scorched-planet tactics and overall strategy made it clear that their goal was the extermination of the human race. And over the past eighteen years, they'd made considerable progress.

Sixteen of the nineteen habitable human worlds had been either taken over by the Cho-ta'an or so thoroughly polluted by Cho-ta'an bombardment that they were now essentially uninhabitable. Earth was one of the latter. The cradle of humanity had been one of the first casualties in the war with the Cho-ta'an. Only three human worlds—sparsely populated, barely habitable and spared thus far only because of their remoteness from the Cho-ta'an homeworld—remained, and these were in the process of being evacuated. Soon all that remained of humanity would be aboard several hundred starships. Most of humanity would wait in stasis aboard hastily constructed sleeper vessels. If the war didn't turn around soon, the human race would last only as long as it took for the Cho-ta'an to hunt these ships down and destroy them—a few years, at most. Given the Cho-ta'an's larger numbers and superior military strength, a reversal seemed unlikely. Even if *Andrea Luhman*'s mission was successful and they located a habitable world that was unknown to the Cho-ta'an, it would only be a matter of time before the Cho-ta'an found them.

"Fractalists," said Stauffer again, as if testing himself.

"I thought they were a myth," Slater replied. Tall, dark-skinned Slater was the youngest member of the crew. If by some chance the source of the transmission was neither human nor Cho-ta'an, they'd want her along.

"No," said Stauffer evenly. "That's the official story, but most experts on Cho-ta'an culture believe they exist. Or did exist. The Cho-ta'an military command is pretty effective at weeding out these dissident sects. The Fractalists are obsessed with mathematics, like the old Pythagoreans on Earth. They consider the Fibonacci numbers to be sacred. And they would know that a ship like *Andrea Luhman* would have somebody on board who would know that. They're identifying themselves."

"Why?" asked the captain.

"Impossible to say. Clearly they wanted to get our attention. If they have anything else to say to us, they're not ready to do it yet."

"They want to talk to us in person," Reyes offered.

"Perhaps," Stauffer replied. "Or it could be a trap."

They all turned to look at Stauffer, whose expression was unreadable.

"Look," he went on, "obviously we're going to check out the source of the signal. What choice do we have? And on a professional level, I'm very excited at the possibility of actually meeting a Cho-ta'an. But I'd be remiss if I didn't give my honest assessment of the situation. Whoever's on that planet, their reasons for being there have nothing to do with us. They're Cho-ta'an, which means they're most likely hostile to the IDL and humanity in general. They probably detected our transit by accident and now they're sending an innocuous signal with just enough information to lure us to them, presumably for the purpose of eliminating us as a threat and/or seizing *Andrea Luhman*."

The room was silent for a moment. "I have to admit," said Mallick at last, "I didn't see that coming, from you of all people."

Stauffer shrugged. "My knowledge of Cho-ta'an culture hasn't blinded me to what they are: a militaristic civilization bent on humanity's destruction."

"To be clear," Slater said, "you're arguing that this is probably a Cho-ta'an trap... and that we should check it out anyway?"

"Precisely," said Stauffer. "The potential upside outweighs the overwhelming likelihood that we are going to die."

CHAPTER TWO

I t took fifteen days for *Andrea Luhman* to reach the planet's gravity well, the first three of which were spent at three gee acceleration. Several hours after *Andrea Luhman* changed course, the signal abruptly stopped transmitting, and at first Mallick thought the senders had changed their mind about their invitation. But then it started up again, two hours and thirty-eight minutes later. The signal repeated its sequence three more times over the course of seventeen seconds and then stopped again.

"Conserving power?" Carpenter asked.

"Maybe," the captain replied, sitting next to Carpenter on the bridge. "Or just keeping a low profile. If they've detected us approaching them, they know we've gotten the message; no need to broadcast it to the whole galaxy."

Four days into the new course, the signal stopped completely, and once again Mallick began to wonder whether he'd made the right decision. At this point, though, it would make more sense to continue toward the unknown star, even if this turned out to be a wild goose chase. Worst case scenario, they could arc around the star and, with a few more days of uncomfortable acceleration, get back on their way to the Finlan Cluster. They'd have lost a few weeks, but that wasn't much in the scheme of things.

But when Mallick awoke the next day, he found that the signal had resumed its previous schedule—seventeen seconds on, followed by two hours and thirty-eight minutes off. The gap in transmission was just under eight hours long. Another eight hours (and three transmissions) later, there was another long gap.

It was Reyes who figured it out. "They've switched to a ground transmitter," she said, standing behind Carpenter and Mallick. "Must have been using a satellite before. The planet has sixteen-hour days, and the transmitter has line-of-sight to us for only half that. So they transmit once at dawn, once at noon, and once at dusk, so to speak. Three transmissions per day."

Mallick looked to Carpenter, who nodded. She was right, of course.

Another pause of just under eight hours followed. Then the signal was broadcast three more times, with gaps of two hours and thirty-eight minutes between. This cycle continued for the remainder of *Andrea Luhman's* journey toward the planet. Fifteen days later, it coasted into a high orbit. They'd pinpointed the location of the signal to within ten meters.

The planet was—to put it mildly—a disappointment. If it weren't for the mysterious signal, Mallick would never have given it a second look. The planet was small, pulling about point six gees. Its surface seemed to be made up of volcanic rock and ash—mostly silicon, iron and magnesium. A meteorological probe indicated a thin atmosphere of methane, ammonia and a few other trace gases. The surface temperature averaged a brisk negative-thirty-degrees Celsius. Hardly a candidate for the last refuge of humanity. There was no sign of any large structures or activity on the surface, and Mallick began to wonder if the Fibonacci broadcast hadn't been triggered by some automated process left in place years or even decades earlier.

Still, at some point someone—human, Cho-ta'an or other—had been here, and that was worth looking into.

*****

The landing craft descended orthogonally to the planet's surface, the thin atmosphere providing minimal resistance. The lander used liquid hydrogen for fuel, and the planet's atmosphere had enough water that if necessary it could refuel by pulling the water out of the air and separating it into hydrogen and oxygen using its proton reactor as an energy source. This probably wouldn't be necessary: the planet's gravity was a just over half of Earth's, so the lander's engines spent little fuel on the landing. It landed on a smooth volcanic plain about two hundred meters from the transmitter, which was a nondescript metal tower some twenty meters high. While Carpenter tracked them from above, the four expeditionary team members donned their EVA suits and exited the vehicle.

"Where to, Captain?" asked Reyes, over the suit's radio.

Mallick pointed to the transmitter. "Might as well start there." He took a few slow steps toward the tower, taking his time to acclimate to the suit, the rocky landscape and the reduced gravity. Reyes followed him. Stauffer and Slater brought up the rear, moving in long, slow bounds.

"What do you think, Reyes?" the captain asked, as they stood looking up to the tower.

"Looks like Cho-ta'an construction," Reyes said. "Aluminum, like most of their structures. And they use these funny clamps instead of screws. That's a directional antenna on top. Definitely the source of the signal. The second signal, that is. Tower hasn't been here long. Hard to say what this atmosphere would do to aluminum, but I'd expect more corrosion if it had been here for more than a few years."

"So, relatively recent Cho-ta'an construction. Anything else?"

Reyes shrugged, but the gesture was all but lost in her bulky suit. "Nothing I can see."

Stauffer, towering over the diminutive Reyes, concurred with her conjecture. None of the others had anything to add.

"Well," said the captain, "we didn't come all this way to stare at a damn radio tower. Unless they're screwing with us, whoever sent that signal has to be around here somewhere."

"Captain," said Slater, "look."

Mallick turned toward Slater and saw that she was pointing at the ground. The terrain was mostly volcanic rock, but there were patches where powdery dust had settled. Slater was pointing at one of these. It had a boot print in it.

"Cho-ta'an?" the captain asked.

"Affirmative," said Slater. "Or a very big human, with unusually elongated feet. She took a few steps away from the tower. Here's another. They lead this way."

"Seems almost too easy," said Reyes.

"Tell me about it," said the captain. "But we're committed now. If we're walking into a trap, we might as well get it over with. Come on." He walked past Slater, taking the lead.

*****

The trail ended after about a hundred meters at a horizontal hatch almost two meters in diameter, made of a dull gray metal with a bluish-green tint. Barely perceptible on the surface were lines that spiraled out from the center, marking an iris-like opening. The hatch was raised several centimeters above ground level, giving the impression they were looking at the top of a cylinder, the rest of which was buried in the rock. There was no visible latch or any sort of control panel. Mallick did the only sensible thing he could do: he knocked.

First he tried stomping on the hatch with his boot, but between the rubbery surface of the boot and the weak gravity, he doubted he was making enough noise for anyone inside to hear. He tried with the butt of his fist as well, but that didn't work any better. Finally Reyes handed him a rock about the size of a softball. He made three tentative taps on the hatch and then stepped back. The others had felt the vibrations through their feet. If anyone was inside, they must have heard it.

After several seconds, the hatch silently spiraled open. The expedition team members stood in tense stillness for a moment, as if waiting for some alien beast to spring out and devour them.

"I guess they know we're here," said Slater, stating the obvious.

Mallick took a step forward and looked down. When he suffered no ill effects, the others stepped forward as well.

The hatch had opened to reveal a vertical shaft about fifteen meters deep. The shaft appeared to be a perfect cylinder, with walls constructed of the same bluish-gray metal. A series of metal rungs led to the bottom, where a roughly human-sized opening led to another tunnel or an underground chamber; it was impossible to say which. The illumination seemed to be coming from a series of palm-sized white discs that lined the shaft in a spiral pattern, spaced about half a meter apart.

"You getting this, Carpenter?" the captain asked. Their suits were all equipped with cameras, and the video feed was being transmitted to the lander and then relayed to *Andrea Luhman*.

"Aye, sir," said Carpenter over the radio. "What is it?"

"That's what we're going to find out," Mallick said.

"You're going in?" Carpenter asked.

"I don't see we have much choice. In for a penny and all that. We may lose you down there, though."

"If you leave one man on the surface, their suit will act like a repeater," Carpenter's voice said. "The suits' transmitters are designed to provide redundancy."

"Copy that," Mallick said. "Something tells me nothing's getting through that hatch, though. If that thing closes after us...."

"You might be cut off completely, yeah."

"And possibly trapped," said the captain. "All right, Slater. You stay up here. You're our link to the lander."

"Seriously?" Slater said. "You wake me up from stasis to make contact with an alien civilization and I end up being a human antenna?"

"On the plus side," the captain said, "if this is all an elaborate trap, you've got much better odds than the rest of us. You get low on oxygen, you jump back in the lander and head back to *Andrea Luhman*. We need somebody to fly the lander back anyway."

They could read Slater's body language even through her suit.

"Look, Slater," Mallick said. "I get it. This isn't what you'd envisioned when you signed up for this mission. But we don't know what's down there. Somebody's got to stay topside, and other than me you're the only one certified on the lander."

"I understand, Captain. I'm not arguing with you. Just... disappointed. Anyway, get going. I'll be up here waiting."

"Try to maintain line-of-sight to us as long as you can," Mallick said.

"Got it, Captain. Go."

The captain nodded and turned back to the shaft. "I'll go first. Stauffer, you're next. Reyes, you bring up the rear. Take your time and don't crowd each other. As far as I'm concerned, the biggest danger is still the environment. A tear in an EVA suit and this whole expedition is over before we even know what we're here for. Wait for me to give you the go-ahead before you come down."

"Aye, Captain," the others said together.

"Okay, let's do this," Mallick said. "For the record, this is Captain Nathan Mallick of the IDL exploratory ship *Andrea Luhman*, transmitting from the surface of this beautiful ball of rock, where the temperature outside is a balmy negative twenty-one degrees Celsius. We're about a hundred meters from the transmitter tower, looking down a metal shaft about fifteen meters deep. A hatch has opened, apparently in response to me banging on it with a rock. At this point we don't know who built this thing, what's down there, or who opened the hatch. This could very well be my last transmission." He paused a moment to look at the others. "Did I miss anything?"

"I think that pretty much covers it, Captain," Stauffer said.

"Great," said Mallick with forced enthusiasm. "Here I go."

Mallick lowered himself into the shaft, continuing to narrate his way as his feet hit one of the rungs and he began to climb slowly down. It took him nearly three minutes to reach the bottom. He gingerly set one boot and then the other on the metal floor. Turning around, he saw a man-sized arched doorway leading into a square room about five meters in diameter. In the far wall was a heavy-duty metal door, also man-sized. A small window at eye height revealed nothing beyond but darkness.

"What do you see, Captain?" Reyes said, causing Mallick to realize he'd ceased his play-by-play.

"Room about five meters square, with walls of the same metal. Door in the far wall. Looks like it could be an airlock. I'm guessing this is some kind of foyer or entry room. There's something strange, though. Rather, there's something unusually ordinary."

"Sir?" said Reyes.

"Stauffer, how tall is the average Cho-ta'an?"

"Two point two meters, sir. The tallest specimen we've recovered was almost two and a half meters, if I'm remembering correctly."

Mallick nodded, trying to imagine one of the tall, lanky Cho-ta'an standing where he stood. He reached up and touched the top of the arched doorway with his fingertips. "I don't think we're dealing with Cho-ta'an," he said. "The doors are too short. This place was built by humans, or somebody about the size of humans."

"I'd still wager it's Cho-ta'an who sent that signal," Stauffer said. "But maybe somebody else built this structure."

"Point taken," Mallick said. "I'm heading into the foyer." He ducked as he walked through the archway to keep his helmet from brushing against the metal. Whoever built this place, it wasn't Cho-ta'an. But humans had never been to this part of space, as far as anyone at IDL knew—and these doorways were too low even for a tall human in an EVA suit. So... some other race entirely? Or some rogue human element? Probably the damn Chinese, Mallick thought, and couldn't help chuckling. It would be just like the Chinese to build a secret facility with doorways too low for most people in the IDL. He kept this thought to himself. Since the rebellions in their mining colonies in 2219, the Chinese had been too preoccupied to worry about deep space exploration, and these days they were nominally allied with the IDL against the Cho-ta'an menace.

"The room is illuminated by overhead panels," he said, looking up at the ceiling, which was less than a meter from the top of his helmet. "Circular. Same as in the shaft, but bigger. Door in the opposite wall is definitely an airlock. There's a window in it, but it's either very dark on the other side or the window has been obscured. There's a control panel. Again, it seems to be at a height that would be more suitable for humans than Cho-ta'an." He approached the panel, which was a metal disc that extruded about two centimeters from the wall. Several circular buttons of various colors were arranged in a spiral pattern. Each button had a symbol or set of symbols etched into it. The symbols, composed of interlocking swoops and zigzags, were no language Mallick had ever seen.

"Can you see this, Stauffer?" Mallick asked.

"Yeah, I've got your video feed on my heads-up," Stauffer said. "Hard to make it out, but those characters don't look like Cho-ta'an iconography. And that spiral pattern, that's just weird."

"That's your professional opinion? It's 'weird?' Could it be a Fractalist thing?"

"Could be," said Stauffer. "But frankly I've never seen anything like it. Maybe if I could get a first-hand look…."

"I hear you," said Mallick. "Okay, come on down. No obvious threats down here, and I seem to be at an impasse."

"Roger, Captain," said Stauffer.

"Remember," said Mallick, "take it slow."

Stauffer made his way down the ladder. Mallick waited as he lowered himself to the metal floor and then joined him in the small entry room. Stauffer, who was a good five centimeters taller than Mallick, had to bend to get through the archway. The captain moved aside so he could get a look at the control panel.

"Definitely not Cho-ta'an design," said Stauffer. "None of this is. But…."

"It doesn't look human either," said Mallick. "Yeah, I thought the same thing. Okay, Reyes, come on down."

A few minutes later Reyes joined them. She at least had no trouble getting through the doorway. The two men moved aside to let her take a look at the panel.

"Any ideas?" Mallick asked.

"Not really," Reyes said, moving about to look at the extruded disc from all angles. "It's not like any control panel I've seen. These symbols... too abstract to interpret. And the colors could mean anything. I'd just be pressing buttons at random. My suggestion? Stick with what worked before."

Mallick nodded. "Slater, can you read me?"

Slater's voice came over his helmet speakers, distorted but audible. "Aye, Captain. You're breaking up a little, but I can still hear you."

"All right," said Mallick. "I'm going to try knocking on the airlock door."

"Copy that," Slater said.

Mallick turned to face the other two. "Ready?"

The other two nodded. Mallick pounded three times on the window with his gloved fist.

For a couple of minutes, nothing seemed to happen. Mallick put his palm on the window and debated knocking again.

"They have to know we're here," Stauffer said. "If they heard you banging on the hatch outside. I don't see any cameras, but—"

"Shh!" Mallick hissed. "Did you hear that?"

Neither of them answered. Had he imagined it? A sound like a click of metal? It occurred to him that the atmosphere was too thin to transmit sound waves. So if he really had heard something, it was either over the suit's speakers or....

He felt his chest tighten. "Slater, do you copy?"

No answer.

"Slater, this is the captain. Respond if you read me."

Still no answer.

"Where'd she go?" Stauffer asked.

"Nowhere," Mallick replied after a moment. "I think the hatch closed." He'd heard it only because his hand was on the airlock door. The sound had been transmitted through his glove. "Look alive, people. I think our hosts are—"

Just then, the door slid open, revealing another small room. It was round, with walls of the same bluish metal. An identical door was in the far wall.

"Airlock," Reyes said. "We're being invited in."

"That's one way to put it," Mallick said. "We don't seem to have much choice in the matter. Come on." He stepped into the airlock and the other two followed. Once they were all inside, the door slid shut. A moment later, they heard a faint humming noise.

They spent the next two minutes watching the atmospheric readouts on their suits. When the humming ceased, Mallick's display indicated twenty-one percent oxygen, seventy-eight percent nitrogen and just under one percent carbon dioxide, with a pressure of one point one atmospheres. The temperature was eighteen point four degrees Celsius.

"A little high on the CO_2," Reyes said, "but it should be breathable."

"Helmets stay on for now," Mallick said. "We don't know what kind of pathogens are in this air."

"Copy that," said Reyes.

"One thing is clear," Stauffer said. "We're definitely dealing with Cho-ta'an. These readings match what we've found on the Cho-ta'an ships we've salvaged. Whoever built this place, the Cho-ta'an have it now."

He had barely finished speaking when a voice somewhere overhead said, "Please remove your suits and leave them on the floor. You will not need them. The air is safe to breathe." The voice didn't sound quite human—it had the low, raspy intonation of a Cho-ta'an—but it spoke with no discernable accent.

Stauffer and Reyes looked to Mallick. After a moment, Mallick unlatched his helmet. There was a hiss of air as the pressure equalized, and then he removed the helmet. He took a deep breath and exhaled.

The others hesitated, watching the captain as if expecting him to turn green and fall to the floor.

"We're going to have to trust these people," said Mallick. "If they wanted us dead, we'd already be so."

Reyes nodded and unlatched her helmet. Stauffer did the same. He breathed deeply through his nostrils.

"Strange smell," he said. "Metallic."

"Maybe this is what the Cho-ta'an homeworld smells like," Mallick said. "Anyway, a weird smell isn't going to kill you. Just try to breathe naturally. If you start hyperventilating, the CO_2 could be a problem."

As soon as they had removed the bulky EVA suits, the door on the other side of the airlock slid open to reveal another room, not much larger than the airlock. It too had no windows and only a single door in the far wall. Mallick walked into the room, followed by Reyes and Stauffer. When they were all inside, the door they had come through slid shut.

"Please close your eyes and raise your hands over your head," said the voice. Stauffer raised an eyebrow at the captain.

"Decontamination," Mallick said. "Do it." The others nodded. He closed his eyes and raised his hands over his head. Warm, dry air blasted him from all sides, filling the room with a deafening roar. After about two minutes, it stopped.

"Put down your arms and open your eyes," said the voice. Mallick and the others did so. The door on the far side of the room slid open. On the other side was another room, somewhat larger and furnished with several oversized chairs. In the middle of the room stood three tall, gaunt, grey-skinned figures with elongated heads and large, pure black eyes. It was the first time any of the crew had seen a live Cho-ta'an.

CHAPTER THREE

"Enter, please," said the Cho-ta'an in the middle, who was a bit taller than the others. The Cho-ta'an were wearing utilitarian gray uniforms. The two on either side wore some type of sidearm in shoulder holsters. The Cho-ta'an were hermaphroditic, each of them cycling through male, female and asexual phases every few years. Those in the military and other strategically important roles were known to use hormone supplements to remain in the asexual phase indefinitely. As far as Mallick could tell, these three were all asexual. Other than the slight difference in height, the three looked identical to him. A black plastic case resembling a briefcase rested on the floor next to the middle Cho-ta'an.

The three humans entered the room.

"Welcome," said the Cho-ta'an in the middle. Mallick thought it was the same voice that had spoken to them over the speakers. The Cho-ta'an went on, "Thank you for coming. As my real name would be difficult for you to pronounce, you may refer to me as Aaron. These are my associates, Richard and Olivia." He indicated the Cho-ta'an on his left and right, respectively. Neither of them reacted in any discernible way.

Mallick had to stifle a chuckle at the mundane names the Cho-ta'an had chosen, as well as the ordinariness of the reception. He'd encountered more fanfare the last time he'd visited the IDL academy. As Mallick had never been much for fanfare, he followed suit.

"I'm Captain Nathan Mallick of the IDL exploratory ship *Andrea Luhman*. These are two of my crew members, Carolyn Reyes and Johannes Stauffer. What is this place?"

The three Cho-ta'an were quiet for several seconds, and Mallick began to wonder if he'd violated protocol by pushing for information too quickly. The IDL had guidelines for meetings with Cho-ta'an, but they were mainly theoretical. Only a handful of diplomats had ever met with the Cho-ta'an, and only under strictly controlled circumstances. Mallick could only hope that the direct approach would yield the best results.

"Your question is more complicated than it may seem," said Aaron at last. "As far as we can tell, this facility was built several hundred years ago. We are not certain of the original purpose. As you have probably surmised by now, it was built neither by Cho-ta'an nor humans, but by another race altogether. Currently the facility acts as a sort of sanctuary for our sect."

"Then you are Fractalists?" Stauffer asked. Whether Stauffer was simply following his lead in his directness or he was acting out of his knowledge of Cho-ta'an culture, Mallick didn't know.

"I am aware that is how we are known in your language," Aaron said. "Having taken the time to learn English, I find the term distasteful and inaccurate, but it will do for our purposes. Yes, we are what you call Fractalists. I assume that you are aware of our plight?"

"To be honest," Mallick said, "we weren't even sure you existed."

"The High Command has done its best to suppress the release of information about our sect," Aaron said.

"They consider you a threat." It was a statement, not a question.

"We *are* a threat," Aaron said. "Cho-ta'an society is premised on absolute conformity. It's the basis of the Cho-ta'an leadership's claim to racial superiority over humanity. If they acknowledge we exist, their *casus belli* evaporates. So we are quietly persecuted and gradually exterminated. It is, ironically, due to the High Command's insistence on keeping our persecution unofficial that we have been able to survive as long as we have. We are not without resources, and our exploratory arm has settled numerous remote outposts in an effort to continue our work and evade the threat presented by the High Command. Sadly, we have lost contact with all the other outposts. It is believed that this facility is the only one that remains."

"Is that why you sent us that message?" Mallick asked. "You want our help against the Cho-ta'an High Command?"

The Cho-ta'an Aaron had identified as Olivia shifted perceptibly in response to this question.

"No," Aaron said, seeming not to notice. "Not directly, anyway. In fact, we took a great risk in sending that signal, and the decision to contact you was not by any means unanimous. Several on our ruling council believe that we have signed our own death warrant. And an even larger faction has argued that our actions have made us traitors to our own kind." The two Cho-ta'an on either side of Aaron remained stock still.

"Why?" Mallick asked. "Are you planning on sharing information about the High Command with us?"

"No," said Aaron. "I'm sorry; I don't mean to be coy, but it's better if I show you. It is not my job to convince you to do anything, but rather to present you with an option. Any conclusions about what I show you and the resulting choices must be yours. Do you understand?"

"I think so," said Mallick, trying to read the alien's indecipherable features. The other two Cho-ta'an remained silent, and it seemed to Mallick they were watching Aaron as closely as they watched the humans. "Before we go any further, I have a request. One of our crew remains on the surface. We have been unable to reach her on our radios because of the density of the rock down here. Would it be possible to send her a message letting her know we are okay?"

"I'm afraid I cannot allow that," Aaron replied. "We are monitoring the crew member on the surface, and she appears to be in good health and in no danger. That is all the assurance I can give you at present."

"Understood," Mallick said. "May I ask one more question?"

"You may ask."

"The IDL was not aware of any Cho-ta'an presence in this area. From what you've said, it sounds like the High Command is equally in the dark about this outpost. So I gather that you didn't use a Cho-ta'an gate to get here."

"You are wondering whether the Fractalists have their own jumpgates."

"Yes."

"That is not a question I will answer."

Mallick nodded, expecting as much. It seemed unlikely that the Fractalists had the resources to build their own gates—and that left only one possibility: Carpenter had been right. The Cho-ta'an had hacked the IDL's gates. And yet, if they were capable of launching a surprise attack on the IDL headquarters, why hadn't they? Perhaps, Mallick considered, it was only the Fractalists—and not the Cho-ta'an High Command—who possessed the secret of bypassing the IDL's security.

Aaron continued, "What I must show you is some distance from here. Approximately three kilometers, if I am remembering the conversion from our units. We will need to take vehicles."

"Three kilometers?" Stauffer asked. "Underground? How big is this place?"

Aaron's face contorted into something Mallick took as a frown. He didn't answer except to say, "We should not waste time. If you are willing to see what I have to show you, we should leave now."

"We're ready," said Mallick.

"Very good," said Aaron, bending to grab the handle of the black case at his feet. "Please follow me." He turned and walked to the door. He waved his four-fingered hand in front of a panel to the right of the door and the door slid open. Aaron bent down to walk through the doorway and the three humans followed. The two other Cho-ta'an silently brought up the rear.

They found themselves in what appeared to be a small clearing at one side of a forest. The trees were leafy and green, but of no species Mallick had ever seen. Some twenty meters overhead hung a dark green canopy through which filtered sporadic rays of sunlight. After a moment of vertigo, Mallick realized what had happened: the airlock was also an elevator. They had descended some unknown distance into the planet. The trees appeared to be real, but the sky they mostly obscured had to be an illusion: an azure backdrop with an artificial sun. Mallick had never seen anything like it. Even the most luxurious artificial habitat designed by the IDL paled in comparison. Whoever had built this place, it was someone with great technological prowess and vast resources. At the far end of the clearing, about twenty meters away, were two four-wheeled vehicles. They resembled automobiles of human design, but at a slightly larger scale to accommodate the Cho-ta'an.

"The species in this garden are all native to the Cho-ta'an homeworld, Yavesk," said Aaron as they strolled through the clearing toward the vehicles. "Originally it was filled with alien species, but by the time we found this place, it was overgrown and in ill repair. Many of the plant species were dangerous to Cho-ta'an, and in any case the atmosphere was not breathable by our kind. We vented the whole place and re-pressurized it according to our needs."

"It's beautiful," said Reyes. "If I may ask, does it serve a purpose other than aesthetics?"

Aaron emitted a noise from his throat that Mallick took to be a laugh. "It provides some of our food and oxygen, yes," he said. "But you must understand that for Fractalists, there is no division between aesthetics and practicality. Our entire purpose is the study of what you would call aesthetics, so anything that assists in this purpose is necessarily practical."

They had reached the vehicles and Aaron stopped in front of one of them. "We will be taking these vehicles to the artifact," he said.

"The artifact?" Stauffer asked, raising an eyebrow. But the Cho-ta'an again acted as if they hadn't heard them. Mallick shot Stauffer a cold glance.

"I'm afraid these are the largest vehicles we have," Aaron said. "Richard and Olivia have been selected by our ruling council to come along. As you are our guests, I will leave it to you to determine how you wish to divide the group between the two vehicles."

Again Mallick had to suppress a laugh at the mundanity of the situation. They'd traveled a billion kilometers to get to an ancient alien structure built inside a previously unknown planet, and they were making decisions about carpooling. "All right," said Mallick. "Well, I'd like to keep my team together, if that's okay. Looks like there's enough room in the front vehicle for the three of us and one Cho-ta'an. So perhaps Aaron should ride with us and Richard and Olivia can ride in the other vehicle."

One of the Cho-ta'an—Mallick thought it was Olivia, although he couldn't tell them apart—seemed about to protest, but remained quiet. The two shorter Cho-ta'an spoke briefly in a language Mallick couldn't understand and then made their way to the second vehicle.

"Very good," said Aaron. He walked to the front car and opened the doors. Mallick got in the front seat and Aaron sat next to him, resting the black case on his lap. Reyes and Stauffer got in behind them.

"Please take us to the artifact site," said Aaron, and the car began to move. He turned to Mallick. "There may be listening devices in this vehicle, but we will have to risk it. As you may have surmised, Richard and Olivia are members of a faction that dissented with the council's decision."

"If I had to guess," Mallick said, "I'd say you're not very popular with this council of yours."

"That would be an accurate summary," Aaron said. "I am the leader of a faction that believes a Cho-ta'an victory in our war with humanity will ultimately be disastrous for the Fractalists. When your ship was detected, I lobbied aggressively to send the signal. Contacting the IDL had been discussed prior to this, but only as an academic possibility. The appearance of your ship forced us to make a decision. My arguments carried the day only because I was better prepared for the possibility. I had theorized that the IDL might send a ship into the Finlan Cluster."

Mallick made a note of Aaron's words: *when your ship was detected*. It was virtually impossible for the Cho-ta'an to have "detected" the passage of *Andrea Luhman* 3500 AUs away, even if they were looking for it. Unless the Fractalists had developed surveillance technology that transmitted faster than light speed, the only way they could have known *Andrea Luhman*'s position and trajectory was if they had dispatched a probe to spy on the Fomalhaut Gate. That lent even more credence to the hacking theory.

"You think that when the High Command is done with us, they're going to go after you more aggressively," Mallick said.

"That is not in doubt," said Aaron. "The question is a matter of the appropriate response. Of course, until the discovery of the artifact, this question too was academic."

"You believe this artifact puts you in a position to affect the outcome of the war?"

"I will allow you to draw your own conclusions once you've seen the artifact. Allow me to be clear, though, Captain Mallick. I am not your friend. I am not even your ally. I have seen what your IDL has done to our settlements, and I will not weep if your race is erased from the galaxy. Fractalists believe, as do all Cho-ta'an, that our race is superior to yours. Our point of disagreement with the High Command is only in how we should go about demonstrating that superiority. Fractalists believe that the Cho-ta'an have no need of violence in our quest to displace humanity throughout the galaxy. Unfortunately, that belief is being sorely tested right now. Our ideals tell us that violence is counterproductive, but our eyes tell us that soon our sect will be hunted to extinction. I represent what you might call the more pragmatic wing of the Fractalists. For now, we have the upper hand. But make no mistake: we are in a precarious position. Whatever you decide, you must do it quickly and decisively. Any display of hesitation on your part will be interpreted as weakness by the others. If they think you do not have the will to do what must be done, they will seize the opportunity to act."

"Are you saying my crew is in danger?"

"Your crew has been in danger since you set foot on this planet," Aaron said. "I did not know until I saw you with my own eyes whether you would even be allowed inside the facility. And I do not know whether there might be armed partisans waiting for us at the site."

"It might help if we knew more about this artifact. What is it?"

"It is something that was left by the previous occupants. More than that, I will not say."

"Who were these previous occupants? Who built this place?"

"A race biologically similar to yours, but somewhat more advanced technologically, at least in some respects. We call them… well, in English it would be something like 'Izarians.' Cho-ta'an archaeologists have known of their existence for some time, but they seem to have very little trace of their civilization. It was long believed that this race essentially exterminated themselves. They built weapons so powerful that a war between two competing powers ultimately destroyed them all and most remnants of their civilization."

"And is that what we're going to see? Some kind of weapon?"

Aaron did not respond.

While they talked, the two vehicles made their way along a narrow, winding path through the forest. Occasionally Mallick glimpsed other Cho-ta'an, who were raking leaves, pruning branches, or performing other ordinary-seeming tasks. As the humans passed, the Cho-ta'an stopped to gawk at them. Again the juxtaposition of the strange and the mundane made him shake his head. The whole experience was surreal. If he didn't look too closely, he could imagine he was watching one of the 3D simulations that had been made of Earth before the Cho-ta'an bombed it. Is this what the Cho-ta'an homeworld, Yavesk, looked like? As an IDL officer, he had access to a lot more information about the Cho-ta'an than the average person, but his knowledge of the Yavesk was limited to generalities about climate, population, and geology. The only pictures he had seen had been taken from the edge of the Cho-ta'an system by probes before they were destroyed by Cho-ta'an defenses. He'd never thought much about what the Cho-ta'an homeworld was like, but if this underground forest was representative, it was much more Earth-like—and beautiful—than he would ever have imagined. On some level he had assumed that anyone capable of doing what the Cho-ta'an had done to Earth must have originated from some cold, ugly, brutal place, a place where the concept of beauty existed only as a sterile abstraction. The design of Cho-ta'an ships reflected a certain aesthetic sense, but he'd never imagined the Cho-ta'an knew of places like this. Had the Cho-ta'an found this place populated with alien vegetation and simply aped the builders, filling it with more familiar species? No, the forest had an intentional beauty to it. It was not a random collection of plants; it had been designed with a particular aesthetic in mind. Aaron had said the Fractalists' purpose was aesthetic. Was this inclination a Fractalist aberration, then? Were the Fractalists persecuted for their appreciation of beauty? As much as he wanted to believe in an idealistic notion of the Fractalists, Aaron's words were fresh in his mind: *I will not weep if your race is erased from the galaxy.* He had a thousand questions to ask Aaron, but the situation seemed tense enough without grilling their host about the destruction of Earth.

In any case, they seemed to have more immediate concerns. They had left the open forest area and entered a dimly lit tunnel that was just large enough for the vehicles. After a hundred meters or so, they emerged into another open area, much smaller than the forest and devoid of vegetation. Gone too was the illusion of being outdoors. The ceiling was high, but dotted with the same circular, luminescent panels they had seen on their way in. The chamber itself was roughly circular and about twenty meters in diameter, with walls of volcanic rock. Directly ahead of them was a group of forty or so Cho-ta'an, who appeared to be talking amongst themselves. As the front vehicle approached, the conversation stopped and the aliens turned to face the newcomers. It was difficult to read the aliens' expressions, but Mallick was confident in his judgment that they were displeased.

As the vehicle slowed, Aaron continued to stare straight ahead. "This facility is made up of natural volcanic chambers that have been enlarged and made airtight," he explained flatly. "When it became clear that the other Fractalist outposts would soon be destroyed, we began digging tunnels to connect to other chambers in order to expand the volume of usable space. Our soundings indicated the presence of a large void some thirty meters in that direction." He pointed toward the gathered crowd. "So we dug through the rock. What we found was an artificial vault that was sealed off from the rest of this facility. It appeared that someone— presumably the original builders of this place—had built a room that was completely inaccessible. Eventually we did find a hatch like the one you entered through, but it was buried under three meters of rock that had been camouflaged to look like the rest of the surface."

"I think I get the idea," Mallick said. "These Izarians went to a lot of trouble to hide this thing. This 'artifact.'"

"They intended to make it impossible to find. It was only through a fortuitous series of coincidences and a lot of effort that we uncovered it.

And as you see, although the original guardians are long gone, there are those who still believe strongly that it should not be disturbed."

"But you disagree."

"I know what will happen if the war continues as it has been going. Follow me." Aaron opened the door and got out, taking the black case with him.

"All right, folks," Mallick said. "I don't know what we've gotten ourselves into, but stay cool and follow my lead." He got out of the vehicle and the other two followed. Aaron, leading the way, stopped a couple meters in front of the group. The Cho-ta'an directly in front of him raised his left hand and spoke something in a low growl. Aaron responded similarly. A heated exchange followed—one that was completely incomprehensible to Mallick.

The three humans waited nervously behind them, as Olivia and Richard brought up the rear. Mallick turned to Stauffer and said quietly, "Are you following any of this?"

"The dialect is difficult," Stauffer said. "But it's pretty much what you'd expect. These guys really don't want us to see whatever's back there."

They listened for another moment. If anything, the exchange was getting more animated.

"Are they going to get violent?" Mallick asked.

"Hard to say. I'm hearing the word 'traitor' and 'genocide' thrown around a lot."

CHAPTER FOUR

Mallick nodded grimly, forcing himself to take a deep breath. If things got violent, there was little they could do, being unarmed and on enemy territory.

Finally, the group parted, making room for Aaron.

"Let's go," Aaron said to the humans. "Do not waste time." He turned and walked through the opening in the crowd. Mallick went after him, followed by the other humans and Aaron's two watchers. Soon Mallick saw where Aaron was headed: a roughly circular opening in the cavern wall that had been carved out in front of them. The tunnel, which curved slightly to the left up ahead, was dimly lit by small glowing disks like the ones they had seen elsewhere in the facility. Aaron ducked his head and climbed into the tunnel, which was barely large enough to accommodate him. The humans had a somewhat easier time of it. The group traveled twenty meters or so through the tunnel before coming out in another chamber. This room was roughly dome-shaped and significantly smaller than the one they had just left, maybe seven meters in diameter. The walls looked like natural volcanic rock, but the floor had been ground smooth. A circular stone pedestal about two meters in diameter and a meter high dominated the room. On either side of it was an armed Cho-ta'an. Their hands were on their weapons, and they visibly tensed as Mallick entered the room. Aaron said something to them, but they didn't relax until the other two Cho-ta'an entered the room.

Aaron moved to the left to allow the humans to see the pedestal—or rather, what was on it. Resting on the smooth gray stone was a framework of the same bluish metal that they had seen on the walls of the corridor on the way into the facility. The framework formed a cradle in which was nestled a cylindrical object made of a dull gray material. The cylinder, about two meters long and half a meter wide, was comprised of three segments of equal size, which were only discernable because of the rings of rivets holding them together. An access panel had been removed from the middle segment, exposing the artifact's innards. Light discs overhead revealed bundles of translucent conduits inside. A flat, curved piece of the same dull gray material—the access panel cover—lay on the ground next to the pedestal.

"What is this?" Mallick asked. Reyes and Stauffer remained silent, regarding the oddly archaic-looking device.

"Surely you can devise a hypothesis," Aaron said, still holding the black case in his right hand.

"My guess, based on superficial observation and the manner in which we were brought here," Mallick said, "is that it's a bomb. You found it here? Is it a nuke?"

"It was left by the previous occupants. As for what it is, we have our own theories, but I would prefer not to bias your examination."

"Our examination? You want us to look at it?"

"That is why you are here, yes."

Mallick looked from Aaron to the other two Cho-ta'an. Their expressions were unreadable. "What about these two?" he asked. "Are they going to give us any trouble?"

"They have been instructed to stand down," Aaron said. "Please, feel free to examine the artifact as you see fit. I only ask that you hurry. The situation here is… volatile." He glanced at the Cho-ta'an he had called Olivia.

"All right, Reyes," Mallick said. "You're up."

"Sir?" Reyes asked.

"You're the closest thing we have to a bomb expert. Take a look, tell us what you think."

"Yes, sir," she said, and moved closer to the pedestal. It came almost to her ribcage. She rested her fingers on the surface. "Can I…?"

The two armed Cho-ta'an shifted nervously.

"Go ahead," Aaron said. He barked something to the two guards and they took a step back.

In the low gravity, Reyes had no trouble pulling herself up onto the pedestal. She tested the strength of the framework and, finding it solid, leaned on it and looked through the opening at the top of the device. She tapped the button for the LED flashlight on her wrist cuff and spent the next few minutes peering at the workings of the device.

"Well?" Mallick said at last. "Is it a nuke?"

Reyes shook her head. "It has some superficial resemblance to a fission bomb, with a primary charge meant to drive one element into another, but the warhead isn't big enough. You need a minimum amount of fissile material to reach critical mass. Whatever effect is achieved by detonating the primary, it isn't a fission reaction."

"So what does it do?"

"Impossible to say," Reyes said. "It's clearly a bomb, but of a sort I've never seen before."

Mallick noticed that Aaron nodded slightly at this.

"Did we pass?" Mallick asked. "You could speed this along by telling us what we're looking for."

"Your findings correlate with our own," Aaron said. "We have spent nearly a year examining this device, and we have not been able to ascertain any more than your engineer. The primitive casing is deceptive. The technology inside is mostly foreign to us."

Reyes climbed down, landing lightly on the stone ground.

"You've known about this thing for a year and you never took it apart?" she asked. "Or even took it out of this room?"

"The matter is politically sensitive, as I've indicated. And we lack the expertise at this facility to conduct a thorough analysis. But we have mapped the interior with imaging devices, and our scientists are at a loss." The other two Cho-ta'an remained silent, watching the humans.

"If you don't know what this thing does," Mallick asked, "why did you bring us here?"

"On the contrary," Aaron said. "We know precisely what it does. We just don't know how it does it."

Mallick suppressed a smile, thinking about his conversation with Carpenter about the jumpgate technology. It was oddly reassuring that the Cho-ta'an had their limits as well.

"You have additional information," Stauffer said. "Something you haven't shared with us."

"That is correct," Aaron said. "I wanted you to see this first."

"All right, you've got our attention. What else is there?"

"I apologize for the low-tech nature of this demonstration," Aaron said, kneeling down and setting the black case on the ground. He touched a button and the top opened on a hinge, revealing a stack of papers inside.

"Sometimes the stark nature of a physical photograph is the best means of communicating. He pulled a folder out of the stack and opened it to reveal several dozen photos. They were square, about twenty centimeters on a side. He handed several of them to Mallick.

"What are these?" Mallick asked, frowning at the pictures.

"Photos taken from low orbit around a now-uninhabited planet that we believe was the Izarian homeworld."

Mallick looked from one picture to the next. They showed the remnants of what once must have been a heavily populated city. Many of the structures still stood, but virtually all of them had been severely damaged. They were pitted and worn down, as if they'd been subjected to an immensely powerful sandstorm. There was no identifiable vegetation or other life; anything that once grew on the planet was now dead.

"Are you saying a bomb like this one destroyed this city?"

"Not just that city," said Aaron. "All these as well." He handed Mallick another stack. Mallick gave the others to Reyes. Stauffer looked over her shoulder.

"These show the area surrounding the city," Aaron said. "Our scientists have determined the region was once covered by forests not unlike the artificial one we drove through to get here. Now it looks like this." The photos showed nothing but a bleak, rocky landscape.

"Okay, so somebody nuked this planet," Mallick said. "Or hit it with something like nukes. It's horrible. So what?"

"Look closer," Aaron said. "Look for the pattern."

Mallick stared at the pictures, growing impatient. Why wouldn't Aaron just tell him what he was supposed to be seeing? All he saw was destruction on a massive scale.

"These striations," Reyes said, staring at the picture in her hands. "It's a blast pattern." She knelt down on the stone floor, placing the picture in front of her. She placed another picture to the left of that one, and another above it. Mallick now noticed that on the edge of each photo was a set of figures in the predominant Cho-ta'an language. Only Stauffer was fluent, but all IDL officers received some basic training in the language—enough to identify numbers, at least. Reyes was arranging the photos according to location.

When she'd finished, she took the stack from Mallick as well. After a minute of shuffling photos around, she had assembled an eight-by-eight grid. Three large clusters of buildings, connected by some sort of highway, were now evident. Faint lines ran parallel across the landscape from the upper left to the lower right.

"How large are these cities?" Stauffer asked.

"Each of these photos depicts one *vokaut*. Roughly thirty-six square kilometers. Many of those buildings were over a kilometer tall. Our best estimate is that each of these cities housed between three and five million Izarians."

Stauffer let out a low whistle. "That's a lot of people."

"Are those striations really the blast pattern?" Mallick asked. "They're parallel."

"Almost parallel," Aaron said, handing him another large stack of photos. "The epicenter of the blast was roughly eight-hundred kilometers to the southeast. If you look closely, you will see that the lines are slightly closer together at the bottom righthand corner." He paged through the photos until he found the one he was looking for. He handed it to Mallick.

Mallick held the photo so that Stauffer and Reyes could see it. It showed nothing but the faint lines radiating outward from a central point.

"Jesus Christ," Stauffer said. "You're saying a *single bomb* did this? When?"

"Our best guess is around three hundred years ago."

"Who dropped the bomb?" Mallick asked.

"Our understanding of the belligerents is fragmented. Apparently, however, these weapons were used by both sides. The Izarians once spanned several planets within a few lightyears of their homeworld, but now they all look like this. All Izarians—all life—has been extinguished."

"This makes no sense," Reyes said. "These buildings are all still standing. And they're all equally damaged, regardless of distance from the epicenter. No explosive works like this."

"It's not an explosive, per se," Aaron said. "We believe the device works by creating a chain reaction that temporarily weakens the covalent bonds between molecules. From the fragmentary descriptions we've found, it seems to turn solids into liquids, for only a few nanoseconds. Long enough to kill any living organism and weaken structures. The effect spreads outward from the epicenter, affecting any matter in its path. The range appears to be unlimited."

"Unlimited?" Stauffer said. "What do you mean?"

"The chain reaction travels until it runs out of matter."

"It's a planet killer," Mallick said coldly. He felt a sinking sensation in his gut. "They liquefied the entire fucking planet."

"And you're saying this thing, this artifact," Reyes said, gesturing at the cylindrical device, "is one of these planet killers?"

"We know the artifact is of Izarian design. We know they went to a lot of trouble to hide it. And there is something else. We translated the words on the casing. We couldn't make sense of them at first. We assumed they were technical in nature. But then we realized they were a poem. Roughly translated, it reads, 'The sea gives us birth, and to it all will return.' Our linguist tells me that 'sea' can alternately be translated as 'water' or 'liquid.'"

"A prophecy," Stauffer said.

"Or a threat," Reyes added.

"If this thing really is a planet killer bomb,' Mallick said, "why was it left here on this remote outpost?"

"We believe it was hidden here to be used as a last resort. Probably they had several such hiding places. There may still be more bombs out there, for all we know. The outpost was hurriedly evacuated at some point, and the refugees never made it back."

Stauffer frowned. "If this planet is such a good hiding place, how did you find it?"

"The Fractalists have devoted considerable resources to researching the Izarians. Our research was largely suppressed by the High Command, which wishes to maintain the story that the Izarians never existed. But our scholars persisted in secret, and clues we found led us here. When persecution of our sect intensified, many of us fled here."

"Using a jumpgate that had conveniently been constructed not far away," Stauffer said.

Mallick shot a glare at Stauffer, but Aaron acted as if he hadn't heard him.

"Why are you telling us all this?" Mallick asked. "Are you expecting the IDL to act as a go-between for you and the High Command?"

"No," Aaron said. "We expect you to take the bomb."

The chamber was eerily quiet for some time. Finally Mallick spoke. "You're *giving* us the bomb?"

"Our sect faces certain extermination," Aaron replied. "This is not the path we would take if we had any choice. But the future of the Cho-ta'an rests with the Fractalists. If we are wiped out, the race is doomed."

"So you're going to give us the ability to destroy the Cho-ta'an homeworld to save yourselves?" Stauffer asked.

Mallick winced at Stauffer's directness. Still, somebody had to ask the question, one way or another.

"Yes," Aaron said, with only a moment's pause. "There is no sense in denying it. We are giving you the power to kill billions of our own."

"Surely you could negotiate with the High Command," Mallick said. "If they knew you had this bomb…"

"If they knew we had this bomb, they would devote all their resources to exterminating us. As I've said, the only reason we are still alive is that the High Command does not consider us an immediate threat. Given the political situation here, there is a good possibility that they have already been warned by someone who disagrees with the council's decision to give you the bomb. There is no place for us to hide. The bomb is not safe here, and we lack the means to deliver the bomb to Yavesk ourselves. You must take it with you."

"So much for it being our choice, eh?" Mallick said.

"Allow me to rephrase," Aaron said. "If you do not take it, both the Fractalist sect and the human race are doomed. The choice remains yours."

Mallick looked from Aaron to the pictures on the floor and then to the device resting on the pedestal. He shook his head again. "You have to understand, we're on an exploratory mission. We're not military. Even if I could verify what you are saying, I don't have the authority to—"

"Do you imagine this is a ruse?" Aaron interrupted, his irritation evident in his voice. "With what conceivable purpose?"

"Trojan horse," Stauffer murmured. If he was hoping the idiom would slip past Aaron, he was disappointed.

"We wouldn't expect you to be foolish enough to deliver the bomb directly to the IDL headquarters," Aaron snapped. "We assumed you would examine it somewhere far from any civilian population. Though of course that's up to you."

"For what it's worth," Mallick said, "I suspect your motives are genuine. But you said yourself you've been unable to verify that this is one of the planet killer bombs."

"You have seen the evidence," Aaron said. "I will not attempt to convince you of anything. It is up to you whether you wish to take the artifact. Many here will be very relieved if you do not."

Mallick thought for a moment. Could this really be happening? A group of humanity's mortal enemies giving them a chance to win this hopeless war? It was almost impossible to believe, but the alternative seemed even less likely. If this was some kind of ruse, it was hard to see what the Cho-ta'an might gain from it. And they'd already paid a heavy price, giving up their location to the IDL.

"I'll need a moment to confer with my crew," Mallick said.

"Of course," Aaron replied. "But be quick about it. We will wait outside." He conferred with his two Cho-ta'an watchers, and then the one called Olivia spoke some orders to the guards. Aaron left the room through the tunnel, followed by Richard and Olivia. The two guards brought up the rear, leaving the three humans alone in the chamber with the strange cylindrical device.

"Well," said Mallick. "Did anyone else see this day ending with aliens handing us a device to destroy their own home planet?"

"So you believe them?" Stauffer asked.

"I believe they're sincere," Mallick said. "Whether that thing actually works is another question. You have any more thoughts on it, Reyes?"

"It's not like any Cho-ta'an tech I've ever seen," Reyes said. "Nor human, for that matter."

"What do you think, Stauffer?"

"I defer to Reyes's expertise."

"I meant more generally."

Stauffer shrugged. "I'll grant the Trojan horse scenario doesn't make much sense. Could be a red herring, though."

"You think this is an elaborate ruse to keep us from exploring the Finlan cluster?"

"Honestly, no. Would have been a lot less work just to shoot us down. Cho-ta'an don't generally resort to elaborate ruses when a simple show of force will get the point across."

"Agreed," said Mallick.

"In any case," Reyes said, pointing at the device, "if there's any chance that thing could help us win the war, I don't see that we have much choice. We've got to bring it to the IDL and have them check it out."

"Do you think they'd actually use it?" asked Stauffer.

Reyes shrugged, looking to Mallick.

"Most likely they'd use it as leverage first. But yeah, if things got desperate enough, they'd use it."

"So we'd be party to the deaths of billions," Stauffer said.

"Okay, don't go getting all philosophical," Mallick said. "That question is above our pay grade. All we've got to decide is whether to accept this…

gift or not. If we do, we're bound to get it to the IDL as quickly as possible."

"We have to do it," Reyes said. "Can you imagine trying to explain to Command why we turned them down? 'They offered us a weapon that could win the war, but we decided mapping uninhabitable planets was more important?'"

Stauffer nodded. "The mere existence of that thing turns my stomach, but Reyes is right. Humanity is on the verge of extinction. Trying to find alternatives to that is what this mission is all about. We don't get to turn up our nose at something like this because we find it morally distasteful."

Mallick sighed. "I figured you guys would say that. All right, we take the device back to the IDL."

"That assumes we can get it out of this cave and onto *Andrea Luhman*," Reyes said.

"One thing at a time," Mallick replied. "Can we get a message to Slater?" They had left their suit radios behind, but each of them also wore a wrist comm with limited range.

Reyes shook her head. "I've been monitoring the frequency. Way too much rock between us to get a signal."

"All right, keep an eye on it. We need to brief Carpenter as soon as possible. If we get stuck down here, the secret of that bomb—or whatever it is—dies with us. I'm going to tell our pal Aaron we're going to accept his offer."

CHAPTER FIVE

T he trip back to the lander was dicier than the journey to the artifact. Four more Cho-ta'an were summoned to carry the device from the chamber to the vehicles. The framework was not attached to the pedestal; each Cho-ta'an took a corner and lifted it along with the bomb. Whatever the bomb was made of, it was heavy: the four big aliens grunted and strained to move it, even in the low gravity. Getting it through the tunnel was an ordeal, requiring them to stop and rest twice. The two armed Cho-ta'an preceded the bomb and the others followed close behind.

The crowd outside was twice as big as when they had entered, and still more agitated. Many of those gathered shouted incomprehensible words at the humans as they passed, but they gave way to the armed Cho-ta'an in front. At least a few of those in the crowd seemed to be on Aaron's side; there was a fair amount of shouting back and forth within the crowd. The humans managed to get inside one of the vehicles before the assembled masses could unite against them.

The bomb was loaded onto the back of a truck while the humans waited in the vehicle. A tense exchange ensued as a large Cho-ta'an slipped in front of Aaron, blocking his way to the vehicle. Aaron attempted to brush past, but the Cho-ta'an grabbed his arm. Aaron jerked away, hitting the Cho-ta'an in the chin with his elbow. The Cho-ta'an moved toward him. A muffled gunshot rang out and the Cho-ta'an stumbled backwards. Gasps and screams went up as the crowd shrank back from the Cho-ta'an guard who had fired. Aaron threw the door of the vehicle open, got inside and slammed the door. He yelled something and the car began to move. More screams followed as Cho-ta'an dived out of the way of the vehicle. It made a sharp left turn and sped away, followed by the truck and the other two vehicles. Several more shots sounded, but then the shooting stopped as the crowd mobbed the two armed Cho-ta'an.

Aaron leaned back in his seat, closing his eyes and exhaling deeply.

"There seems to be a lot of opposition to your decision," Mallick said after some time.

"The ruling council is slightly more enlightened than the general population," Aaron said. "But this sort of demonstration is rare among Cho-ta'an. It reflects a profound lack of confidence in the leadership. Those on the council who favored giving you the planet killer will undoubtedly be removed from office shortly. It is quite possible the new government will find us guilty of treason."

The humans were silent. There was only one penalty for treason among the Cho-ta'an.

"You'll be leaving by a different airlock," Aaron said. "I've received word that more protesters are waiting where you arrived."

"On the surface?"

"No. Access to the outside is strictly regulated. Once you get above ground, you are safe. Relatively speaking."

Mallick decided against asking Aaron to expound on his qualification. For now, they needed to focus on getting out of this facility.

The convoy skirted the edge of the forest and then turned to go through a narrow tunnel. They came out in another open area that looked like a warehouse or loading dock. Stacks of crates and boxes lay scattered about the floor. In the far wall was the door to an airlock. The car holding the humans stopped just past the door, allowing the truck to pull up next to it. The humans and Cho-ta'an filed out of the vehicles. Other than them, the entire area appeared to be deserted.

Another heated exchange occurred, this time between Aaron and his two watchers. The tone was rancorous but desultory, as if the two were more concerned with getting their positions on record than with changing Aaron's mind. Aaron's demeanor reflected equal parts relief and exhaustion. Finally Olivia and Richard stepped back and Aaron made a gesture to the other Cho-ta'an, who lifted the framework from the truck. As they approached the airlock, the door slid open. This airlock was somewhat larger than the one they'd arrived through; there was plenty of room for both the humans and the bomb.

"Our suits," Reyes said.

Mallick cursed quietly to himself. How could he have forgotten something like that?

"Here," Aaron said, climbing onto the back of the truck. He opened a box and pulled out a helmet. He must have made arrangements for the suits to be loaded onto the truck before it arrived. At least somebody had thought this through.

"Thank you," said Mallick, taking the helmet from him. Aaron didn't respond, reaching into the truck to grab a suit. He handed the suits down to them and they began to put them on. When they were nearly finished, another vehicle emerged from the tunnel, moving toward them at high speed.

"Hurry," Aaron said. "This group may be armed."

"Into the airlock," Mallick said. "Let's go."

The three of them moved into the airlock as quickly as the bulky suits would allow. The door slid shut behind them. Their view of the cargo bay was blocked, but they heard the squeal of tires and muffled shouts. A blue light went on overhead and the hum of a fan started. The air pressure began to drop.

"Shit!" Stauffer barked. "I'm not sealed!"

"Take a deep breath," Mallick said. "I'll get to you as soon as mine are tight." The suits were designed to be put on and taken off by the wearer, but less experienced spacers often needed help with the harder-to-reach seals. Mallick took his own advice, filling his lungs with air. He finished fastening his own and then turned to Stauffer, only to find that Reyes had beat him to it. Stauffer was on the verge of panic, but she got his suit sealed before the atmosphere in the airlock was purged. It was quiet, but very little sound would travel without any air. Mallick wondered if this airlock doubled as an elevator, like the last one. If so, it moved too gradually to feel the change in acceleration.

His question was answered when the door on the far side slid open, revealing a stone chamber slightly larger than the airlock. The far end opened to the planet's surface.

"Thank God," Stauffer said. "No ladder."

Mallick nodded. This entrance went all the way to the surface, presumably to make it easier to load and unload supplies. He tapped the shared channel button on his wrist cuff. "Slater, do you read?"

There was a crackle of static followed by incomprehensible fragments of speech.

"Looks like we're in a cave," Stauffer said. "Still too much interference."

Mallick turned to Reyes. "Reyes, you have any idea where we are relative to the lander?" Reyes's sense of direction was legendary.

"Yes, sir," Reyes said, pointing. "Should be about two klicks that direction."

"Good. Go outside and see if you can direct Slater over here. We're going to need her help with this thing. Use a flare if you have to."

"Yes, sir." Reyes walked to the opening. The moment she exited, Slater's voice came pouring over the radio.

"—read me, sir? Where the hell are you? Carpenter's been trying to get a hold of you."

"Slater, this is Reyes. Do you copy?"

"I'm here, Reyes. Go ahead."

"What's your location?"

"I'm in the lander. O2 was running low, so I—"

"Good. You see a rock formation, about twenty degrees to the right of the lander's nose? Looks like a turtle on its back."

"I see it."

"We're about half a klick beyond that, and maybe another ten degrees to the right from your position. I'm standing at the edge of a lava field next to a rock mound about eight meters high. You should be able to set the lander down on the field."

"You can't get to me? I'm going to waste a lot of fuel moving the lander a couple of klicks."

"We've got some cargo," Reyes said.

"Cargo? What… Never mind, I'm on my way. Carpenter has been trying to get through to you guys for the past hour."

"Slater, this is Mallick. Patch me through to Carpenter."

"Can't. He's darkside now. Just lost contact before you called. Apparently he's got a bogey."

Damn it, thought Mallick. Another thing that had slipped his mind. *Andrea Luhman*'s orbit had taken it below the horizon. They would be out of contact until they rejoined it in the lander. "A bogey? You mean a ship?"

"Sounded like it. Unknown craft, coming toward us, fast."

"Did Carpenter give an ETA?"

"He said three hours. That was twenty minutes ago."

"All right. Get here as fast as you can. Captain out."

"What do you think that's about, Captain?" Reyes asked. "Cho-ta'an?"

"Must be," Mallick said. "Somebody here snitched to the High Command. It's pretty clear not all the Fractalists are on board with the idea of giving us a bomb capable of snuffing out the Cho-ta'an homeworld. Let's see if we can move this thing out of the cave before Slater gets here with the lander." He bent down to grab the framework while Stauffer and Reyes took the opposite side. They lifted on the count of three, barely managing to get the thing off the ground.

"Shit, that's heavy," Stauffer gasped.

"Just be thankful we're at point six gees," Mallick said. "Let's go."

Straining, the three of them managed to move the device just outside the cave before setting it down with a crunch on the hardened lava. Stauffer moved to wipe his brow, smacking his helmet with the back of his glove. Reyes laughed. "Smooth, Stauffer. Are you sure you haven't done this before?"

Stauffer chuckled sheepishly. "Moved a genocide device across the surface of an alien planet? Sure, I did it three times just last week."

"Look," Mallick said, pointing just above the rock formation Reyes had spoken of. The small silvery shape of the lander was approaching. A moment later, they heard the rumble of its thrusters. Mallick waved his arms.

"I've got you," Slater said. "Be there in a minute."

"Captain," Reyes said, still breathing heavily, "how could a Cho-ta'an ship have gotten here so quickly?"

"I've been wondering the same thing," Mallick said. "Assuming this place is what it seems—an outpost unknown to the Cho-ta'an High Command—then it's very unlikely the Cho-ta'an have a jumpgate anywhere in the vicinity. That leaves only two possibilities: either that ship started heading our way a couple hundred years ago or…"

"Or the Cho-ta'an hacked our gate," Reyes finished. "Which was the most likely explanation for how the Fractalists got out here in the first place."

"If the Cho-ta'an can use our gates," Stauffer said, "why haven't they used them to attack Geneva or any of the other IDL worlds?"

"The Fractalists hacked the gates," Reyes said. "The snitch must have told the High Command how to do it."

They felt the rumble of the engines though their boots as the lander descended in front of them.

"When?" Stauffer said.

"Probably around the same time we received the Fibonacci broadcast. Before we were contacted, the possibility of giving the bomb to the IDL was academic. They'd have kept their secret as long as they could, but if they wanted the High Command to intercede, they'd have had to broadcast their location and the key to getting through our gates."

The lander settled onto the plain.

"Nice work, Slater," Mallick said. "Did Carpenter say what direction the bogey was coming from?"

"Yeah," Slater said. "He said at first he thought it might have been an IDL ship, because their trajectory intersected with the Fomalhaut Gate coordinates. But they don't respond to a hail on any frequency."

"Hell," said Mallick. "So it's true. The Fractalists hacked our gates, and now the Cho-ta'an High Command knows how to do it too. This bomb better be the real thing, because otherwise we just lost the war."

CHAPTER SIX

Two hours later, they were back onboard *Andrea Luhman*, in orbit around the planet. Mallick took off his helmet and walked to the bridge while the others fought with their suits.

"Any more data on our bogey?" Mallick asked Carpenter, who was hunched over the controls.

"On an intercept course with the Fractalist planet," Carpenter said. "At the current rate of deceleration, they'll be here in just under an hour."

"Any idea what it is?"

"I'd assume Cho-ta'an, except that it seems to have come through our own gate."

"We think they've hacked the gates."

"Jesus."

"Yeah. Assume the bogey is a threat. What's our best evasive strategy?"

"Are we heading back to the Finlan Cluster?"

"No. Our mission's been preempted. We need to get to a secure IDL facility as soon as possible."

Carpenter raised an eyebrow. "What the hell is our cargo anyway?"

"A bomb," Mallick said. "Powerful enough to end this war. We need to get to Geneva. Or any other IDL facility. Someplace that can analyze this thing."

Carpenter nodded. "Then we continue our current orbit around the planet and break free at the optimal trajectory to reach the Fomalhaut Gate."

"How long?"

"About four hours. I can give you a more precise estimate shortly."

"Can that ship catch us?"

Carpenter frowned. "What do you mean, 'catch'? Ram?"

"Assume it has missiles."

"You think it's a warship."

"Figure it is. Can it take us out?"

"Hard to say. It'll have to follow us around the planet. If they drop into a tighter orbit, they could gain a few minutes on us. I can run some calculations, but my best guess is they'll be too far away for an effective missile strike. Even if they can close to a thousand klicks, we'll have plenty of time to deploy chaff. Of course, once we're clear of the planet...."

"It'll be a matter of acceleration," Mallick said.

Carpenter nodded. "We can do three point eight gees in a pinch. Any idea how fast those Cho-ta'an ships go?"

"Faster than three point eight. But the Cho-ta'an aren't built for high gravity, and they don't use stasis. Pulling anything more than three gees for more than a few hours is going to be an ordeal for them."

"It's not exactly going to be a pleasure cruise for us either."

"No, but we can keep most of the crew in stasis. How long until we reach the gate?"

"At three point eight gees?" Carpenter did some quick calculations on his screen. "Just under twelve days, if we spin around at the midpoint. But sir, you can't seriously be suggesting we spend twelve days at three point eight gees? Even in stasis, the damage—"

"I doubt it will come to that. Just get us around that planet, Carpenter. As soon as we're clear, give it all you've got."

Yes, sir."

*****

Almost an hour later, Carpenter's frantic voice came over Mallick's comm. "Sir, you need to see this! Hurry!"

Mallick ran to the bridge. He arrived in time to see a series of flashes erupting on the planetoid's surface.

"What the hell?" Mallick said, rubbing his bleary eyes.

"Missiles," Carpenter said. "Apparently nuclear. Looks like our mystery ship took out the Fractalist facility."

They watched as several more flashes appeared and then winked out.

"Jesus Christ," Mallick said. "Their own people."

"People they consider traitors."

"Well, it tells us one thing. The Cho-ta'an High Command isn't interested in seizing the bomb. For all they knew, there was another one of them hidden on that rock somewhere."

"They don't need it," Carpenter said. "They're going to win anyway. They just need to make sure the IDL doesn't get the bomb."

Carpenter was right. The odds were against the IDL even before the Cho-ta'an gained the secret of hacking the gates. Now victory was impossible without the bomb.

"The good news is that apparently the bomb is for real," Mallick said. "They wouldn't expend this much effort if they didn't believe we were a threat."

They watched for a bit longer, but the explosions had stopped. "How long until acceleration?" Mallick asked.

"Twenty-three minutes."

"Everything is dialed in?"

"Yep. In twenty-three minutes, the thrusters will come on at full. We'll pull three point eight gees until the program is manually overridden."

"Good. I want you in stasis by then. You and the others."

"You're staying up?"

Mallick nodded. "For a while, anyway. Somebody's gotta be conscious in case these crazy bastards do something unexpected. You've transmitted our new course to headquarters?"

"Yes."

"What else did you tell them?"

"Just what you said. That we've got a package to deliver, we're being pursued by a hostile ship, and we need a tech team standing by. Couldn't give them an ETA because I don't have a clue when we're arriving."

"All right," Mallick said. "I'll take over. Go get in your pod."

*****

Mallick sat in the acceleration chair, breathing deeply from an oxygen mask while clenching and unclenching his fingers and toes. Even with the stimulating vibrations of the chair encouraging blood flow to his extremities, he could feel his arms going numb. A fit human body could tolerate up to twenty gees for short periods of time, but three point eight gees was damned uncomfortable for anything more than a few minutes. Mallick had been at it for nearly three hours. He could only imagine what the Cho-ta'an were experiencing. Yavesk had lower gravity than Earth, and

Cho-ta'an biology was ill-disposed for stasis. That meant the entire crew of the Cho-ta'an ship was conscious and extremely uncomfortable. Mallick could only hope they gave up pursuit soon.

A crackling voice came over the ship's comm. It was in the Cho-ta'an language, but an English translation appeared on the nav screen:

Attention, human vessel. You have an object on board that is the property of the Cho-ta'an High Command. Cease acceleration and prepare to be boarded, or we will destroy you.

"You guys never were much for subtlety," Mallick grumbled.

His words appeared on the screen with a prompt:

Transmit? Y/N

"Belay that," Mallick said. "Attention, Cho-ta'an vessel. This is Captain Aaron Mallick of the IDL ship *Andrea Luhman*. This is an exploratory ship, not a military vessel. We have nothing that belongs to you. And I can keep this up longer than you can. Go ahead and transmit that."

A minute passed. Another transmission came:

Human vessel. This is your last warning. We will fire on you.

Mallick managed a chuckle. "If you were going to fire, you'd have done it already, you motherfuckers." He paused a moment. "Don't send that."

Five minutes passed and the missiles didn't come. After twenty minutes, Mallick allowed himself to believe it: they weren't going to waste missiles at this distance. They must have figured out that *Andrea Luhman*'s chaff would be deployed and dispersed before the missiles got within five hundred kilometers.

When the Cho-ta'an ship's acceleration rate began to drop, Mallick breathed a sigh of relief. For now, they were safe. He waited another ten minutes to be sure. The alien craft had dropped to two point four gees and was holding. Mallick reduced *Andrea Luhman*'s acceleration to a more tolerable two point eight gees and waited an hour to see if the Cho-ta'an would respond. Their acceleration remained at two point four. *Andrea Luhman* had won this round.

*****

When the Cho-ta'an ship had dropped nearly a light-second behind *Andrea Luhman*, Mallick decided it was safe to go into stasis. Even if the Cho-ta'an cranked up their acceleration again, it would be hours before they were in missile range. On the off chance it was necessary, *Andrea Luhman* would deploy countermeasures automatically.

When the ship's computer awakened him a week later, he braced for a warning of incoming missiles, but it didn't come. After he was certain there was no immediate threat, he allowed himself a few hours to acclimate and then did a thorough survey of their situation.

Andrea Luhman's velocity was now close to a tenth of light speed and increasing. The Cho-ta'an ship continued to accelerate at two point four gees and was now nearly a hundred million kilometers behind them. That was the good news. The bad news was that to use the jumpgate, *Andrea Luhman* was going to have to lose most of its speed. The gates were designed to accommodate ships traveling at no more than ten percent of light speed. That meant that the Cho-ta'an ship was going to have plenty of opportunity to catch up to them. The Cho-ta'an knew that, of course, which was why they'd let *Andrea Luhman* go so easily.

While he had been in stasis, a message had come through from IDL headquarters. It read:

New heading received. Tech team standing by. Request additional information. What is the cargo?

Mallick sent back their current heading along with the message:

Cargo may be an item of high strategic importance. Unable to say more at this time.

It was highly unlikely the transmission would be intercepted, and the Cho-ta'an would have to decrypt it to read it. Still, there was no point in being more candid in their transmissions. Even if he were one hundred percent certain what *Andrea Luhman* was carrying, the IDL would insist on conducting a thorough investigation of the artifact before altering their strategy—and at this point it wasn't at all clear *Andrea Luhman* was even going to be able to deliver it.

Mallick ran through the math three times. Carpenter was better at this stuff, but Mallick was pretty sure he'd gotten it right. If they went through the gate at double the maximum recommended speed, they might just be able to stay far ahead of the Cho-ta'an ship to avoid its missiles. But that strategy had its own dangers, and in the end Mallick decided it was too close to call. He needed Carpenter's expertise.

Carpenter wasn't thrilled to be awakened from stasis, and was even less happy to be pressed into performing complex calculations a scant hour later.

"Sorry, man," Mallick said, as he watched Carpenter punching numbers into the computer while trying to combat nausea. "If we weren't on the razor's edge here, I'd have gone with my gut."

Carpenter waved him off in annoyance. Mallick decided to shut up and give him some space. In less than an hour, they were going to have to make a decision about when to start decelerating, and how fast.

Forty-eight minutes later, Carpenter sat back in his chair and gave a defeated sigh.

"That bad, huh?" Mallick asked.

"To be safe, we're going to have to hit the gate at point three light speed."

"Will the gate even work at that velocity?"

"Oh, it will work. The question is whether we will hit it. *Andrea Luhman*'s a comparatively small ship, so we've got some margin of error, but still. This is like shooting a bullet through a keyhole a million kilometers away."

"And if we miss…"

"If we miss, the best-case scenario is that we end up traveling at a third of light speed in the wrong direction. Worst case, we hit the gate, destroy it and blow ourselves up in the process. And of course even if we avoid hitting it, the Cho-ta'an ship might still take it out, stranding us in deep space for the next twenty years. We're six light-years from the next gate."

"Or we could miss the gate and they could go through."

"Right. Then we'd have a Cho-ta'an ship traveling at interstellar speed inside the Geneva system. Assuming that's where we're headed. Which is another problem I was going to mention…."

Mallick groaned. That was a whole other consideration: *Andrea Luhman* would emerge into the Geneva system at whatever speed it was traveling when it entered the gate. Several ships went through that gate every hour. "What are the odds we'll hit another ship?"

"They've got shuttles running all day, evacuating civilians to the stasis ships. Those things don't carry enough fuel to make major course corrections. If we transmit an ETA within the next few hours, they might be able to clear us a path in time. But even if they do, the Geneva gate is too close to the sun for us to come in at over point one light speed. If we're lucky enough not to get pulled into the sun, we'll shoot right past it. It'll take us weeks to backtrack to Geneva."

"Okay, so we can't use the Geneva Gate. We need to find one that's not as busy."

Carpenter shrugged. "At the speed we'll be traveling, we stand a pretty good chance of hitting something, no matter which gate we use. Even the planets the Cho-ta'an wrecked have salvage runs. They're all in use."

Mallick thought for a moment. "Not all," he said.

Carpenter's brow furrowed. "You're thinking about using the Sol gate? Is it even active?"

"Sure," Mallick replied. "They still send probes through once in a while to monitor the system. But for all practical purposes, it's clear. And it's farther out in the system than most of the other gates, so we're less likely to get pulled into a gravity well."

"Could work," Carpenter said. "We try to lose the Cho-ta'an in the Sol system, ricochet around the sun and head back through the gate to Geneva. Hopefully at a less insane velocity."

"Exactly. It also gives the IDL some time to clear us a path, if we can give them a definite velocity."

"I like it," Carpenter said. "This could actually work."

"We've got another problem, though," Mallick said. "If the Cho-ta'an can hack the gates, how do we know they won't shut it down before we get there? Or change our destination? Hell, for all we know, they're capable of rerouting us through one of *their* gates. They might be tricking us into delivering the bomb right to their doorstep."

"I don't think we need to worry about that," Carpenter said. "If I'm right about how they're hacking the gates, they're controlling the gate mechanism itself, not subverting the control circuits."

"Meaning what?"

"Meaning I think they can control where the gate sends them. I don't think they can control the programming of the gate."

"So they could go wherever they want, but they can't remotely program the gate to send us somewhere else?"

"Right. I've been pinging the gate since I got up, and the responses are all nominal. No sign of meddling. I think the possibility of the Cho-ta'an screwing with the gate is the least of our problems."

Mallick nodded. "Okay, we'll assume the gate will work as planned, then."

"I'll run the numbers again with several different scenarios and try to figure out our best move." As Carpenter finished speaking, a light blinked overhead. "That's the halfway point," he said. "I'll cut the engines and spin us around."

"Good," said Mallick. "Tell the IDL what we're doing. I'm going to get some rest. Keep me updated."

*****

They spent the next several hours in free-fall, and it was a glorious relief from the crushing gravity they'd been tolerating. Unfortunately, it wouldn't last long. Soon they would need to begin decelerating to avoid missing the gate. At their current speed, a miniscule trajectory error could send *Andrea Luhman* hurling into deep space, dooming humanity to genocide at the hands of the Cho-ta'an.

The Cho-ta'an ship continued to accelerate at two point four gees, slowly closing the gap between them. Carpenter calculated that for *Andrea Luhman* to slow to twenty percent of light speed by the time it reached the gate, it would have to decelerate at just over one gee for most of the trip. That was certainly manageable; the problem would be that it would allow the Cho-ta'an ship to get within missile range well before they reached the gate. Carpenter woke the captain to tell him the bad news.

"What's the fastest we can go and be sure we'll make it through the gate?"

Carpenter sighed. "The aux thrusters just aren't precise enough for anything over point two light speed. No matter how closely I line us up now, I'm going to have to make minute adjustments when we're a few hours out. And there's a margin of error of a hundredth of a degree on any one of those adjustments. If we even brush the edge of the gate as point two light speed...."

"We're vapor, I get it."

"And that's assuming they maintain acceleration of two point four gees. If they increase their acceleration, it'll be even closer."

"I understand," Mallick said. "For now, get us to one gee and maintain it. No point in provoking them into an acceleration race. If they increase their thrust, we'll reassess."

"Got it, Captain."

The two ships maintained their respective acceleration rates for another six days. *Andrea Luhman* was now forty AUs from the Finlan Gate, traveling at just over point two light speed, with the Cho-ta'an ship less than an AU behind and gaining rapidly. Mallick began to think they were actually going to make it when Carpenter reported the Cho-ta'an ship had increased its acceleration to three point four.

"They're going to kill their entire crew," Mallick said, watching the readout in disbelief.

"Maybe that's the plan," Carpenter replied. "Put the ship on autopilot. Program it to fire all its missiles as soon as we're in range. The Cho-ta'an High Command would certainly consider it a small price for denying the IDL a planet-killer bomb. So what's the plan, Captain?"

Mallick's brow furrowed. "Assume they'll maintain this acceleration rate for the rest of the trip. Lower our deceleration rate to stay at least a second in front of them. If they get within that range, we're dead."

"If we try go through the gate at over point three light speed, we're probably dead too."

"That 'probably' is all we've got," Mallick said. "Do it."

When *Andrea Luhman* was less than an hour out from the gate, the Cho-ta'an ship cranked up its thrust again, reaching an acceleration rate of three point eight gees.

"I wonder if there's anybody left alive on that thing," Carpenter said.

"If there weren't, they'd be going even faster," Mallick said. "I think they've overestimated our defenses. If they were smart, they'd have gone all out. Sacrificed their crew to get within range. They must think we've got antimissile measures on par with the IDL warships, so they're playing it safe. Trying to stay alive to follow us through the gate if they need to."

"This sure doesn't feel like playing it safe. If I lower our deceleration rate any further, we might as well just figure on missing the gate altogether. Change course to the Perseid Gate."

"And get there in twenty years, after the war is over?"

"Better than blowing ourselves up."

Mallick thought for a moment. "How close will they get if we maintain our current decel rate?"

Carpenter punched some numbers into the computer. "By the time we reach the gate, they'll be within a hundredth of an AU. About point eight seconds behind us."

"All right," Mallick said. "Maintain current decel rate. No matter what those assholes do from now on, focus all your attention on threading that needle. We've done everything we could. Call me if you need anything. Otherwise I'll stay out of your way."

"Aye, Captain," Carpenter said.

"You've got this, Carpenter," Mallick said.

"Get the fuck out of here. Sir."

*****

At five minutes out, the Cho-ta'an still hadn't fired. The gate was finally visible on the nav screen display, a tiny dot of light only marginally brighter than the stars trillions of kilometers away. The insanity of what they were doing finally registered in Mallick's mind: in less than five minutes, they were going to try to fly right through the middle of that nearly microscopic dot, traveling at a hundred thousand kilometers per second. He pushed down the sick feeling in his gut, rejecting the temptation to second-guess himself. They had no choice. If they didn't make it through the gate, they were going to be killed by Cho-ta'an missiles. And humanity's chances at survival would die with them.

Carpenter sat next to him, arms folded, nervously chewing his lower lip. There was nothing more he could do to adjust their course. He'd been experimenting with the aux thrusters to see how finely he could adjust their attitude, but at this point it was better to leave the matter to the nav computer, which would err on the side of caution and could react a million times faster than he. If Carpenter's calculations were off, they'd find out soon enough.

The bright dot—which was in reality a massive torus nearly three hundred meters in diameter—grew steadily larger on the display. *Andrea Luhman* was transmitting its current location to the gate, and the gate had responded by firing its attitude jets to align its aperture with the ship's approach. The gate could be moved laterally as well, but the mass of the gate made this impractical. Adjusting approach vectors was ordinarily left to the approaching ship. Of course, the approaching ship wasn't usually traveling at nearly a third of the speed of light.

The nav display was now rather pessimistically indicating that less than two minutes remained until "impact." Apparently whoever had programmed the thing had never considered the possibility that someone might be piloting the ship toward an eight-thousand-ton hunk of metal on purpose. Mallick was about to give himself permission to feel relief when another warning flashed, indicating the approach of six nuclear missiles.

Before Mallick could even react, the display indicated four of the missiles had vanished.

"Holy shit," Carpenter gasped.

"The chaff worked," Mallick said. "Thank God. But…"

"Christ," Carpenter said. "The last two weren't aimed at us."

Two flares entered the forward-facing display, one from the left and one from the right. The two missiles converged toward each other as the gate loomed ahead.

"Here we go," said Carpenter.

Mallick nodded. Whatever happened next was out of their hands. The Cho-ta'an had hedged their bets, sending four missiles at *Andrea Luhman* and two at the gate. The gate had its own defenses, but they weren't designed to protect it from nukes traveling at point three light speed.

The gate grew steadily larger. Mallick had just enough time to noticed how perfectly centered *Andrea Luhman* was within the ring before a blinding flash filled the display.

CHAPTER SEVEN

The first thing Mallick was aware of was cold. The second was silence.

Opening his eyes, he found himself in near complete darkness. Only the dim emergency lights cast a faint glow on the floor. His body was held in the chair only by the restraint straps; there was no gravity. *Andrea Luhman* was in free fall, floating dead in space. The question was: where?

"Carpenter," Mallick said.

Carpenter, in the seat next to him, let out a low groan. "What happened? Where are we?"

"That's what I need you to find out."

"It's cold as hell in here."

"Everything seems to be offline. I'm going to revive Reyes and get her working on it. You figure out where we are."

"How am I going to…?"

"I don't know, look out the damn window."

It took nearly three hours for Reyes to get everything back online. A massive electrical surge had fused several circuits. Amazingly, Carpenter managed to figure out roughly where they were in the meantime—by looking out the window.

"We're definitely in the Sol system," he said, as the nav system blinked back to life. "That's Orion out the port bay."

Mallick nodded. He'd never seen Earth constellations before, but children were still taught about the shapes humans had identified in the sky thousands of years earlier.

"So we made it," Reyes said. Mallick could see her breath in the still-cold air.

"We made it," Carpenter replied. "The question is whether the Cho-ta'an managed to follow us."

"Figuring that out is priority two. Number one is slowing us down. The faster we can get back to that gate, the better."

"Primary thrusters are still offline," Carpenter said.

"Shit," Mallick replied. "Reyes?"

"I've checked everything I can from here," Reyes said. "We must have sustained some external damage. Probably got hit by a piece of debris from the gate."

"All right. You okay for an EVA?"

"Yeah, stomach's settled. I'll suit up." She had been fighting post-stasis nausea the whole time she was working on the ship.

Mallick nodded. "Anything you can do in the meantime, Carpenter?"

"I can get some thrust out of the auxiliaries," Carpenter said, "but even at max capacity we're not going to get much more than a fifth of a gee."

"How long will it take to get back to the gate at that rate?"

"You don't want to know."

While Reyes surveyed the damage to the outside of the ship, Carpenter continued to work on pinpointing their location. Mallick heard him cursing under his breath.

"What is it?" Mallick asked.

"Well, I found the Cho-ta'an ship," Carpenter said.

"Shit."

"Yeah, they followed us through. They're about a million klicks behind us. The good news is that either they've sustained some serious damage themselves or they're out of missiles. We're in range, but so far they haven't fired."

"Then we're in the clear. We just need to evade them long enough to get back to the gate."

"About that…" Carpenter said uncertainly.

"What?"

A pause followed. "I lost the gate."

"You *what?*"

"I'm not picking up a signal from the gate's beacon."

"Maybe it sustained some damage from debris we brought through."

"That's what I thought. So I did a full scan. I can't find it."

Mallick rubbed his chin. "If the Cho-ta'an ship has maintained its trajectory, it would be directly between us and the gate, right? Could be interfering with the scan."

"Yeah." Carpenter didn't sound convinced.

"You think it was destroyed when we came through?"

"Doubtful. And unless it was completely vaporized, I'd be picking up signs of debris. If it was in pieces, it would actually be easier to find."

Mallick thought for a moment. "Okay, this is academic. We know where the gate has to be. Do you have a firm fix on our location?"

"Not yet. The nav system is giving me gibberish. One of the sensors must be damaged. Going to have to do the calculations manually until I can figure out what's wrong."

"Do it."

They sat in silence for some time while Carpenter worked on his calculations. He was chewing on his lip and staring out the porthole when Reyes came in from her EVA.

"The ionization manifold's cracked," she said, walking onto the bridge. "Computer shut the subsystem down. Good thing, too, or we'd all have been vaporized."

"That bad, huh?"

"That bad. We're not using our primaries until we can get that thing replaced. And in this neighborhood, that's not going to happen anytime soon."

"So we're stuck with aux thrusters. Carpenter?"

Carpenter was furrowing his brow at his screen. "How long were we out?"

Mallick frowned. "What are you talking about?"

"That power surge, whatever it was, when we went through the gate. We both lost consciousness briefly. How long were we out?"

"I don't know. Seconds. Maybe a minute or two. Carpenter, I need you to focus. We're on aux thrusters only. What can you do to get us back to that gate?"

"That's what I'm trying to figure out," Carpenter snapped irritably. "I need to know how long we were unconscious."

Reyes started, "Ship's clock says—"

"Forget the clock. I don't trust it. Everything went down."

"Not life support," Reyes said. "Ventilation went down, but the stasis systems and health monitors kept running. They've got triple redundancy."

Carpenter rubbed his scalp thoughtfully. "How much time has elapsed since we went through the gate?"

Reyes navigated to the life support interface at her station. "Four hours, twenty-three minutes, sixteen seconds."

Carpenter shook his head. Clearly something wasn't adding up.

"That's ship's time," Mallick offered. "We're traveling at nearly a third of light speed. Temporal dilation is going to—"

"You don't have to explain temporal dilation to me, Captain." There was an edge in his voice. Mallick decided to let it pass. He'd never seen Carpenter like this.

"It's not just the gate," Carpenter said. "I'm not getting any radio signals. From anywhere."

"The Sol system is dead," Mallick said. "There may be a few thousand stragglers still trying to make a go of it on the burned-out husk of Earth, but for all intents and purposes there's no one here."

"You think humanity turned off all the satellites on its way out?" Carpenter asked, a bitter smile playing at the corner of his lips.

"What are you saying, Carpenter?" Reyes asked. "You're not picking up any satellites at all?"

"I'm not picking up *anything*," Carpenter said. "Not a single radio signal anywhere in the system. I've checked all three antenna arrays. They're working perfectly. There's nothing out there."

"Okay, calm down," Mallick said. "I thought you were trying to get our location. Why are you looking for radio signals?"

Carpenter laughed. "Because I found Earth. Except that it can't be Earth, because it's in the wrong place. Everything is in the wrong place. Jupiter, Mars… Hell, Cassiopeia is wrong. A star in Cassiopeia went nova around 1680 AD. Not only are the remnants of that nova missing, but *the star is still there*."

"It's gotta be a problem with the sensors," Mallick said.

Carpenter shook his head. "That's what I thought. So I checked them all. They're fine. You know when I said the nav system was giving me gibberish? Turns out it wasn't gibberish at all. The system just hadn't been programmed to properly display dates before 1970."

Reyes and Mallick exchanged glances. "You're not making any sense, Carpenter."

"It's a holdover from early operating systems," Carpenter said. "They had a limited amount of space to store dates, so they used January one, 1970 as a starting point."

"The Epoch," Reyes said. "I'm familiar with it."

"Yeah, so the whoever wrote this software assumed that it would never need to deal with dates before 1970. With good reason, obviously. After a jump through Turner space, the nav system has to recalibrate its value for the current time. The sensors look for patterns. Known astronomical objects. The system then deduces a date from the positions of those objects. With a few minutes of gathering data and crunching the results, it can provide a datetime value with accuracy within a millionth of a second. I couldn't make sense of the output it gave me, so I looked at the raw data. You know what the date is, according to *Andrea Luhman*'s nav computer?"

"I couldn't begin to guess," Mallick said.

Carpenter smiled without mirth. "March sixteen, 883 AD."

CHAPTER EIGHT

They spent the next hour checking and re-checking Carpenter's data. Everything—the positions of stars and planets, the missing gate, the lack of radio signals—pointed to a single conclusion: *Andrea Luhman* had traveled thirteen hundred years back in time.

"So the gate acted as a sort of time machine?" Mallick asked. "That's... difficult to accept."

Carpenter shrugged. "You've seen the data. Is there a better explanation?"

"We know the gates work by warping spacetime," Reyes said. "But we've never really understood how, despite the IDL spending vast resources to reverse-engineer them."

"But if the gates can be used for time travel," Mallick said, "why haven't the Cho-ta'an used them that way?"

"Maybe they have," Carpenter said, with a smile. "How would we know?"

Reyes shook her head. "If they could go back in time, they'd already have wiped us out. We assume that the Cho-ta'an understand the gates better than we do, but overall they don't seem to be more technologically advanced than we are. They've never even figured out stasis, for Pete's sake. What if the discovery of Turner space portals was an accident? What if the Cho-ta'an don't really know how they work either?"

Mallick nodded. "We have to assume they don't know the gates can be used this way. Or didn't, anyway. Some combination of our high speed and the damage to the gate from the missiles caused a malfunction that warped time as well as space."

"So you believe me?" Carpenter said.

"I don't see any alternative. We can't deny the reality in front of us. If the stars tell us it's 883 AD, we have to assume it's 883 AD. At least until we can come up with a better hypothesis."

"Something that can move stars other than time and momentum?" Carpenter said. "Good luck."

"As I said," Mallick said, "we have to run with it for now. The question is still: how do we get this bomb to the IDL?"

Reyes frowned. "The IDL won't even exist for another thirteen hundred years."

"Well, that gives us some breathing room, doesn't it?" Mallick said with a grim smile.

"Not enough," Carpenter replied. "The closest jumpgate is the Gliese Gate, and it's twenty light years away. At max thrust, the aux thrusters will burn through our hydrogen supply in less than a week. That means we'll top out at about one percent of light speed, so the trip to nearest inhabited world will take around 1500 years. Even if we could survive in stasis that long, we'd arrive two hundred years after the war is over."

They were silent for some time.

"What about the lander?" Reyes said at last.

Mallick shook his head. Carpenter answered before he could.

"The lander can manage pretty good acceleration, but it'll have the same problem. You'd run out of hydrogen before you left the solar system. I can run the math, but I suspect it would take even longer for the lander to get to the Gliese Gate than *Andrea Luhman*. On top of that, no stasis. The crew would all be dead less than a quarter of the way into the voyage."

They were silent again for a moment.

"Is there any way to repair the manifold?" Mallick asked.

Carpenter shook his head. "It's a precisely engineered piece of titanium alloy. Welding it would be just about impossible, and unless you could do it perfectly, it would result in thrust imbalance. It might last a few minutes or a few hours, but eventually it would blow up and take us with it."

"What if we just wait in stasis until the Sol Gate is built?" Reyes asked.

"Stasis isn't meant to be used for thousand-year stretches," Mallick said. "Maximum stasis time is ninety days, with nine days in between. By the time the gate is constructed, we'll all be over a hundred and forty years old. And with the tissue damage from that many stasis periods, we'd be lucky to live to half of that. Hell, our *grandchildren* will die before the Sol Gate is built. And while I don't remember the fertility status of everyone on board, let's just say we'd have to get rather, uh, creative to propagate four generations on board this ship."

Carpenter nodded grimly. "And something tells me the third generation of kids raised on this ship aren't going to have strong feelings about saving humanity. We'll be lucky if they don't mutiny and pilot *Andrea Luhman* into the Sun."

"Then we need to cast a new manifold," Reyes said. "It's the only way."

"How?" Carpenter said. "We don't have the space, the tools, or the materials."

"We have plenty of space," Reyes replied. "Tools can be manufactured. Materials can be gathered and fabricated."

Carpenter stared at her. "You must be joking. Do you have any idea how difficult it is to cast a solid titanium structure that size? It's a difficult task even on an industrialized world with the right equipment."

"It's difficult, sure. But we have the specifications and the expertise. If any group of people can build a manifold from scratch, it's the crew of this ship. Anything we don't know, we can look up. We've got terabytes of data on this ship. If you have a better idea to save the human race, I'd love to hear it."

Carpenter scowled but said nothing.

"It would take some time, but I don't see why it couldn't be done," Mallick said, rubbing his chin. "It's just an engineering problem."

Reyes nodded.

"We'd have to send a team down in the lander," Mallick said.

"Down where?" Carpenter said.

"Earth," Reyes replied. "It could be done elsewhere—Titan, maybe, or Mars—but then we'd have to worry about maintaining a pressurized atmosphere on top of everything else."

"Can you get us to Earth, Carpenter?" Mallick asked.

Carpenter shrugged. "I can get you anywhere with enough time. My hope was to arc around the sun and head back to the gate. Rough calculations indicated it's possible. With some modification to our trajectory, I could probably swing us past Earth. How long are we expecting this project to take?"

"Forging a twenty kilogram part out of titanium?" said Reyes. "Honestly, it could take months. Maybe years."

"Years?" Mallick asked, taken aback.

"I'll have to do some research, but the melting point of titanium is something like sixteen hundred degrees Celsius. You'd have to ask O'Brien about extracting and refining titanium ore, but there's a reason titanium is expensive. Don't get me wrong; it can be done. But it's going to take a lot of work."

Mallick nodded, rubbing his chin.

"It's not like we have anything better to do," Reyes said. "And what do you care? You'll be in stasis most of the time."

Mallick nodded. "Okay, I'll get O'Brien up. Get started on the research."

"Yes, sir."

"Let's just hope the laws of physics will cooperate," Carpenter said.

"We have to assume the anomaly was a one-time thing," Mallick said. "A fluke resulting from some combination of our velocity and the damage to the gate."

"So we're going to assume that the laws of physics don't work the way we thought, but assuming they'll keep working the way they always have?"

"Carpenter," Mallick said coldly.

"I'm not trying to be difficult, Captain. You're asking me to do precise calculations involving time, matter, and acceleration, and apparently none of those things are what we thought they were. Even your statement that it was a 'one-time thing' is wrong. If I'm right, that anomaly wasn't a one-time thing. It's something that happened a few hours ago, and also thirteen hundred years ago. And it will happen again in thirteen hundred years. That anomaly will occur—or has occurred—an infinite number of times. It's an endless loop."

"I get it," Mallick said. "I understand how unsettling this is. None of it makes any sense. But here we are, trying to make sense of it. And the only way I can do that is by boxing off whatever happened when we went through that gate and assuming reality is more-or-less the way it seems. Given that, I have to figure that in thirteen hundred years, the Cho-ta'an will be on the verge of wiping out humanity, and that delivering this bomb before that happens is our only chance. I know you want to wrestle with the philosophical implications of time travel, but now is not the time. Compartmentalize. Can you do that?"

Carpenter nodded. "I think so. But I have one more concern. A concern pertinent to our mission."

"Fine. What is it?"

"Well, if it really is 883 AD, Earth is inhabited. It's the Middle Ages down there right now. We'll be screwing with history."

"Shouldn't be hard to find an uninhabited island somewhere. But in the end, we're talking about the future of the human race. If we have to screw with history, so be it. Now do your job."

*****

Three days later, *Andrea Luhman* rounded the sun in a wide arc, putting it on a path to intersect Earth's orbit. It would then use Earth's gravity to decelerate and change course toward Jupiter. It would use Jupiter's gravity to further decelerate and redirect back toward Earth. Six weeks after its first swing, *Andrea Luhman* would enter Earth orbit.

Unable to anticipate the human ship's course, the Cho-ta'an followed at a conservative distance, allowing the gap between the two ships to gradually widen. It was impossible to know what the Cho-ta'an had deduced regarding the temporal anomaly. At the very least, they must have figured out that the gate was missing, which meant they would probably not expect *Andrea Luhman* to return to its entry point in the solar system. If they had noticed she was using only her auxiliary thrusters for deceleration, they might have determined that the ship was going to have a hard time attempting interstellar travel, but it seemed unlikely they would anticipate a stop at Earth.

"Stop" was a charitable description in any case. Even after rounding the sun, *Andrea Luhman* would be traveling far too fast to enter orbit around Earth. They were going to have to rely on the lander's more powerful acceleration to slow to Earth's relative velocity. It would be a tricky and dangerous maneuver, but it was the only chance they had.

Mallick had selected a landing party of four. Reyes, as the head engineer, would lead the group. Dan O'Brien, whose expertise in geology and chemistry would be vital in forging a new manifold, was another obvious choice.

The third member of the team was Thea Jane Slater, the biologist who'd also been part of the mission to the Fractalist facility. Her knowledge of biology might come in handy if the expedition lasted for more than a few weeks and the team were forced to forage for food, but she was picked primarily for her experience piloting the shuttle.

The final team member was Gabe Zuehlsdorf, *Andrea Luhman*'s security officer. Carpenter argued against Gabe's inclusion on the grounds that technical expertise was needed more than brawn, but Reyes figured she'd have enough to worry about without having to be concerned about wild animals and potentially hostile Earthmen. Gabe was an ex-Marine with wilderness survival and medic training. Just as importantly, from Mallick's perspective, Gabe was an amateur historian, the only one of the crew besides Johannes Stauffer who possessed substantial knowledge about Earth cultures of the ninth century. Stauffer was never a serious candidate: although he knew a fair amount about Earth history, his primary field of study was Cho-ta'an culture, and he'd be less than worthless in the wilderness.

Another member of *Andrea Luhman*'s crew, Justin Schumacher, a physicist, had also been revived—not to be part of the mission crew, but to consult on what had happened with the gate.

Once the three newly revived members of the crew had more-or-less acclimated, the crew was assembled for a briefing. As O'Brien and Schumacher knew nothing of the planet killer bomb and Gabe and Slater had been in stasis during the time travel portion of the adventure, the meeting was predictably chaotic. Mallick did his best to get everybody up to speed.

"Everybody clear on the details?" Mallick asked when he'd finished the briefing. He stood at the front of the room, while those most recently revived—O'Brien, Slater, Gabe and Schumacher—sat on the chairs around the table. Reyes and Carpenter stood in the back.

O'Brien, the wiry, sandy-haired geologist, nodded. "We're landing on Earth during the Middle Ages to build a forge to fabricate a spaceship part so we can carry an alien doomsday weapon across the galaxy to save humanity."

Chuckles went up from the group.

Slater frowned. "Well, it sounds ridiculous when you say it like that."

"Ridiculous or not," Mallick said, "it's what we have to do. That bomb is the only chance we have to win the war, and the only way to get the bomb to the IDL is to repair *Andrea Luhman*. The future of humanity rests on the four of you."

"Do we really think we've gone back in time?" Slater asked. "That's crazy."

"All the evidence we have points to that conclusion," Carpenter replied. "Constellations, positions of planets, background radiation, the lack of radio signals… every bit of empirical data we have tells us the date is March sixteen, 883."

"This is absurd," Gabe muttered.

"Which part?" Slater asked.

"The time travel part, for starters. Schumacher, you're the physicist. Tell me this is a joke."

"If it's a joke," Schumacher said, "it's a damn good one, and I'm not in on it. I haven't had time to look at all the sensor data, but it's pretty clear something is very wrong. Stars don't just jump out of position. If we deny the possibility of time travel, we'd have to allow the possibility of something even more bizarre."

"But how?" Slater asked. "How could something like this happen?"

"The gates open a wormhole between two points in space," Schumacher replied. "We can describe the phenomenon in great detail, but the mechanism is still a mystery. We stole the tech from the Cho-ta'an, and they may very well have stolen it from someone else. What we know of their scientific prowess indicates their knowledge of physics is no more advanced than ours."

Gabe stared at him. "You're saying we jump all over the galaxy in these damn things, and nobody knows how they work?"

"What I'm saying," Schumacher said with a smile, "is that it's a little late to start worrying about spacetime anomalies. The question isn't 'How did this happen?' It's 'Why hasn't it happened before?' Space and time are inextricably linked. If you travel from one point in space to another instantaneously, you're screwing with time, one way or another. We've just found a new way to do it."

"You think the effect could be replicated?" Reyes asked.

"Theoretically, sure. But it's going to be difficult, since the first gate won't be built for thirteen hundred years."

"What if it's never built?" O'Brien asked.

"What do you mean?" Slater asked.

"I mean, we've traveled to the past. We could change history. It was only happenstance that the *Ubuntu* ran across that Cho-ta'an mining site eighty years ago. Er, twelve hundred years from now. What if we alter the course of history, preventing that from ever happening? We'd never meet the Cho-ta'an, never get the gate technology. Hell, the war would never even start. Maybe we'll save humanity just by setting foot on Earth."

Schumacher shook his head. "We have to assume that temporal paradoxes are impossible. We can't change what's already happened. If we appear to change something, it's because our knowledge of what actually happened is limited. What you are going to do on Earth—assuming you make it there—has already happened."

"Another good reason we can't wait around for the Sol Gate to be built," Mallick said. "If a ship from the future had gone through the Sol Gate, the IDL would have a record of it. So if we try, we'll fail."

"Whoa," said Gabe. "So much for free will."

Schumacher shrugged. "Pick a number between one and ten."

"Huh?" Gabe replied.

"Humor me. Pick a number. Tell me what it is."

"Three."

"Good. Were you free to pick any number you wanted to?"

"Sure."

"Are you free now to have picked a different number?"

"Of course not. It's already done. I can't change the past."

"Right. So when you're making the choice, it's free. When you're looking back on it, it's not. Same rules apply here. If you go to Earth and smash a grasshopper, you were free to do so. If, however, I were to look at the complete catalog of all grasshoppers ever smashed on Earth, I would find that you have already done it. Or chose not to, as the case may be."

"That's a dodge," Slater said. "There's no catalog of smashed grasshoppers. For a real test, you need to use an event that we know has happened. What if… Gabe strangles William the Conqueror in his crib?"

"William the Conqueror wasn't born until 1028," Gabe said. "I'd have to strangle his great-grandfather. And I'd have to live to a hundred and forty to do that."

"Fine," Slater said. "Gabe goes to Earth and strangles William the Conqueror's great-grandfather. William the Conqueror is never born. The Normans never take over England. All of history is changed. England never colonizes America. America never lands on the Moon. Human exploration of the galaxy is delayed for decades. Maybe longer."

"Clearly that didn't happen," Schumacher said. "Therefore, we have to assume that if Gabe tried to assassinate William the Conqueror's great-grandfather, he failed."

"So he never had a choice."

"No, but there are lots of things we don't have a choice about. I'm not going to Earth, so obviously I have no opportunity to strangle anyone's great-grandfather. But does that mean I have no free will? Of course not. I still have thousands of other choices I can make. The fact that some avenues are closed to me doesn't mean I can't make choices."

"You're saying that if Gabe tries to kill William the Conqueror's great-grandfather, something will stop him."

"I'd say that it's a bad idea to try to do something that you know is doomed to failure."

"Our mission might be doomed to failure," Slater said. "That is, we might already have failed."

"True," Schumacher said. "But as there's no way for us to know at this point whether a group of people from the future landed on Earth in 883 A.D. to repair their spaceship, there's only one way to find out."

"I hate to bring this fascinating discussion to a close," Mallick said, "but it's time for Reyes and Gabe to suit up."

"Aye, sir," Gabe said, as he and Reyes got to their feet. They had been selected to detach the manifold and bring it inside the lander. The entire procedure was expected to take about an hour.

*****

Moving the manifold went as planned, and shortly after the manifold had been placed in the lander's cargo bay, O'Brien and Slater boarded the shuttle. Reyes and Gabe came inside, changed into their flight suits and followed the others into the lander.

Mallick stopped Reyes as she was about to climb through the hatch to the lander.

"I feel like I should say something," he said.

"Like what?"

"You know, a pep talk. About how we're all counting on you to save the human race or something."

"I know what I'm doing, Captain. It's an engineering problem."

"It's a bit more than that."

"There are things outside our control, sure. But there's no point in worrying about those. If we're careful and work together, there's no reason we can't do this."

"I was referring to the stakes. If you pull this off, you'll be heroes. If something goes wrong…."

Reyes shrugged. "I can't worry about it. I'm just going to do my job. So if there's nothing else…?"

Mallick laughed. "You really aren't scared?"

A smile played at the edge of Reyes's mouth. "Terrified, sir."

"Well, remind me never to play poker with you. Godspeed, Reyes. I'll see you in six weeks."

Reyes smiled and climbed into the hatch.

Six weeks. That was the plan. While the lander stopped off at Earth, *Andrea Luhman* would keep hurtling through the solar system, round Jupiter and head back toward Earth. Carpenter's estimate put them back in Earth orbit in six weeks. Hopefully that would give the ground team enough time to forge a new manifold. If not, *Andrea Luhman* would remain in orbit, its crew in stasis, until the mission team was ready to launch and rejoin them. If anything happened to the ground team, there was nothing *Andrea Luhman* could do about it but limp to the future location of the Gliese Gate at point two gees of acceleration. There was only one lander.

CHAPTER NINE

Sigurd Olafson lifted a chunk of sod from the pile and hefted it over his head with a grunt. The chunks were an arm's length on a side and a good eight inches thick, and he'd been at this all morning. Sigurd had fences to mend and sheep to shear, but the roof was the current priority: a recent thaw had revealed a leak that was letting water into the house. Sigurd had half-expected it: a blight had killed much of the grass on the roof the summer before, but he hadn't had time then to replace it. For now, the water was running harmlessly down a support beam to the wall, but over time it would cause the wood to rot, which was a much bigger problem.

Sigurd's arms began to quiver under the weight of the sod.

"Yngvi!" he shouted.

"Sorry, Father," the boy called from above him. A moment later, the burden was lifted from Sigurd's hands. Sigurd took a step back from the ladder and wiped his brow as Yngvi moved out of sight to place the turf in the damaged area of the roof.

"Daydream later, Yngvi," Sigurd chided. "We're supposed to be working as a team."

"I'm not daydreaming, Father. There are people on the road."

Sigurd frowned. "Who?"

"I don't know. Five of them. They have skis."

"Get down, boy. Let me see."

"Yes, Father."

The sky overhead darkened momentarily as Yngvi leapt over the ladder, landing on the grass behind Sigurd.

"Odin's beard, son," cringing as he watched Yngvi land. "I've told you not to do that. You're going to break an arm. And then what good will you be to me?"

"It's barely eight feet," Yngvi said, getting to his feet. "You're just jealous because you're too old to do it."

"Watch your mouth, boy," Sigurd said, but he smiled to himself. His knees hurt just watching Yngvi perform his acrobatics. The boy was sixteen and already stronger than most full-grown men. Sigurd could still best him in wrestling, but that wouldn't last much longer. Sigurd had been twenty-five when Yngvi was born, and he was now one of the older farmers in the area.

Sigurd climbed the short ladder to look over the roof of the house and saw why Yngvi had been distracted: there were indeed five men coming down the road. They were strangers, wearing colorful tunics and trousers. Strapped to their backs were skis, indicating they'd traveled some distance, probably from the north. Gabe watched for some time, waiting to see if the men continued down the road that led to the coast or turned down the narrow track leading to Sigurd's farm. When they turned, he sighed and climbed down the ladder. Yngvi lay on his back in the snow, soaking up the sun.

"We're going to have guests. Get some ale and bread. And see if there's any of that duck left."

"Are those men important?"

"Yes, unfortunately," Sigurd said. "Go."

*****

Yngvi brought out a tray of food and placed it on the stump they used as a table when eating outside. He returned to the house and got a keg of ale. He affixed the tap to the key while Sigurd cleaned himself up. "Fetch my sword as well, son."

Yngvi eyes went wide but he didn't speak. He ran back inside and returned with the sword, which was sheathed in a leather-clad wooden scabbard that hung from a wool belt. He handed it to Sigurd, who strapped it around his waist.

"May I stay?" Yngvi asked.

"Better if you don't."

"Are you going to fight them?"

"No, son."

"I won't say anything. I'll just sit and listen."

"It's not that, son. These men are here in part to gather information. I won't give them any more than I have to. You're free to listen, but do so from inside."

"Yes, sir," Yngvi said glumly. He returned to the house and closed the door. Sigurd sat down on a stump.

Yngvi's mother, Thora, had died three summers ago. The illness had come on her suddenly, eating at her insides and stealing her appetite. She wasted away over twelve weeks, eventually succumbing just before the autumn equinox. She had been a strong, fierce-minded woman, and it had cut Sigurd like a knife to see her reduced to a shell of herself. He spoke of her little, but was reminded of her every time he looked into Yngvi's penetrating, slate-gray eyes. Sigurd's neighbors urged him to remarry; he was wealthy by local standards, and there was too much work for him and Yngvi to do alone. There certainly was no shortage of pretty young girls in the valley. But Sigurd had no interest in those pliable, rosy-cheeked girls; he missed his beautiful, stubborn, infuriating Thora.

As the men approached, Sigurd's thoughts turned back to his work. If these guests didn't stay long, he and Yngvi might be able to finish the roof today. That was good: the sky promised snow in the near future. He and Yngvi had taken advantage of the brief thaw to carve up some chunks of sod from the valley floor. His house, like most in the valley, was constructed primarily of pine logs, but dirt and grass on the roof helped keep the heat in. That was not as much of a concern in the spring, but it would be good to give the grass a full summer to put roots into the layer of soil underneath.

The man in the lead walked toward Sigurd. He was a great strapping man with a forked, braided beard and a jagged scar that ran from his brow across his left cheek and down to his chin. As he approached Sigurd, he grinned and held out his hand.

"Welcome," Sigurd said, with feigned enthusiasm.

The big man clasped Sigurd's hand. "Sigurd Olafson," he said. "You have quite the reputation in these parts."

"As do you," Sigurd replied with a smile.

The man acted as if he hadn't heard him. "I'm Gunnar Bjornson," he said. "I'm here on behalf of King Harald."

"I know who you are," Sigurd said. "I remember your father."

"Ah, very good!" Gunnar said. "I didn't realize you were so old."

"Are your men hungry?"

"We won't dip into your stores," Gunnar said. "But if there's ale in that keg, I'll gladly accept some."

"Shall I get the benches ready for you?"

"I appreciate the hospitality," Gunnar said, "but we won't be staying long."

Sigurd poured a mug of ale and handed it to Gunnar. "You can tell your men they're free to drink as well. I'd suggest we go inside, but it seems more pleasant to me out here. Besides, as you say, you won't be staying long."

"You heard our friend," Gunnar said to the men. "Finish up and you're free to stand outside and have some ale." He took a long draught of the ale and wiped his beard with his sleeve.

"What can I do for you, Gunnar Bjornson?" Sigurd said, straining to keep his irritation in check.

"The question is what I can do for you. You have heard news of the alliances Harald has made with the villages in the north?"

"Alliances?" Sigurd asked, with an amused tone. "Is that what you call these arrangements?"

Gunnar met his gaze. "And I'm certain you've heard about the Danish raids."

"The Danes don't come this far inland."

"They would if we didn't stop them at the coasts."

"That is up to you. Send them our way if you tire of them."

"It's only fair that you help provide for a common defense."

"We have sent able-bodied men when needed, both to Trondelag and to Vestfold. With little to show for it, I might add."

"You're being modest, Sigurd," Gunnar said. "It is not every farmer who owns a sword like that. Is that a Frankish blade?"

"It is."

"Few Danes carry such a sword. Did you kill the king of the Danes by any chance?"

"I took this sword off a Saxon knight in East Anglia, as I'm sure you know."

"Oh, yes! I knew you had some business with the Danes. I'd forgotten which side you were on."

"I was killing Saxons," Sigurd said. "If there were Danes killing Saxons alongside of me, that's no concern of mine."

Gunnar let out a bellowing laugh. "Well said, sir. If some of your old friends decide to visit you here in Haavaldsrud, though, that will be of some concern to you, will it not?"

"Indeed. It will be the business of the people who live in this valley. Not yours."

"Don't be a fool, Sigurd. You can't live like this forever. A string of independent settlements, barely scraping by. Don't you see the way things are going?"

"I see well enough. If the sun is bound to move from east to west, it doesn't need my help. We appreciate your offer, Gunnar Bjornson, but the people of this valley have always provided for their own defense."

"The people of this valley are fools," Gunnar said with a snarl.

Sigurd's eyes narrowed. "Do you care to name any of these fools? Or shall I dismiss your judgment as idle talk?"

Gunnar smiled weakly, seeming to regret his outburst. "The farmers and fisherman in this area may believe themselves capable of standing up to the Danes, but you harbor no such conceits. You know what they tell me when I advise them of the danger they are in? They say, 'We leave such matters to Sigurd Olafson.'"

Sigurd shrugged. "I have neither vassal nor slave. If men listen to me, it's because they believe I have something of value to say. How many have you spoken to?"

"Just the heads of some of the larger households. I'll be making several more stops today. Harald wants to make sure the people are informed."

"Harald wants to rule all of Norway. Whether his subjects are properly informed is far down on his list of priorities."

"Harald *will* rule all of Norway," Gunnar said. "Over the past few years, he has consolidated his holdings along the coast. The jarls from Sogn to Halogaland have already sworn their allegiance. Only Hordaland and Rogaland in the south remain, and they are weak."

"The valley remains independent as well," Sigurd said. "Or have you forgotten why you are here?"

"We set out from Trondheim a week ago," Gunnar replied. "I've spoken to half a dozen jarls and scores of landowners. I have received oath of loyalty from several, and many more will come over to Harald's side when the time comes."

Sigurd laughed. "Then I congratulate you on your success and wish you the best in your future endeavors. Clearly you don't need my help."

"The Danes are going to strike," Gunnar snapped. "Maybe not this year. Maybe not the next. But they will. And what happens when they do will largely be the consequence of your actions. Good men will be killed. Your stores and your women will be taken, your storehouses burned. Do you really want that on your conscience?"

"You would have us submit to be looted by Harald to forestall looting by the Danes? No. We are free men," Sigurd said. "Our choices are our own."

Gunnar sighed heavily. "The people say you are stubborn as well. I don't expect to change your mind in one meeting. I only ask that you reflect on what you have already lost—and what you stand to lose." He glanced toward the house.

Sigurd's heart suddenly pounded in his chest. Fists clenched at his sides, he eyed the sword at Gunnar's hip. "Is that a threat, Gunnar?"

"You misunderstand me, Sigurd. I only mean to say that violence is the way of the world. It behooves you to plan for it."

"I don't need to be lectured about taking care of my family by a man who left his own father to die."

Gunnar regarded him coldly, fingering the hilt of his sword.

"Oh, yes," Sigurd went on. "I know who you are. When I was very young, I used to go down to the creek with some other boys to fish. Some days we would catch more than we could eat; other days we would catch nothing. But we never went hungry, because there was an old fisherman who would sometimes come down to the creek with a bag full of dried fish. He only came when the fish weren't biting. I don't know how he knew. Whenever he showed up, we knew we may as well give up for the day. But we kept our lines in the water, because we knew we wouldn't get any of the dried fish unless we kept at it. I thought Bjorn Odinson was old even then, but I remember hearing later that he had gotten married to a woman from the south and had a son. I was happy for him, because I didn't think it was right that such a kind man be alone. Years later, his wife drowned in an accident and his son, unable to bear his grief, ran away. This boy was only seventeen, but he showed great prowess as a warrior and there were rumors that he had gone to work for a chieftain to the west named Harald. Bjorn was quite old and feeble at this point; he died three years later. The son did not even return for the funeral, and, in fact has not been seen in these parts until very recently."

"You know nothing of my family," Gunnar said through gritted teeth.

"And you know nothing of mine. Or my people. Have as much ale as you like. I have work to do." Sigurd turned and went into his house.

CHAPTER TEN

Thea Jane Slater sank into her chair as the lander's thrusters fired. In the past few seconds, her weight had gone from zero to four times her ordinary weight: the lander was pulling over four gees. It was an unpleasant way to travel, but if the lander didn't slow below fifty thousand kilometers per hour, it was going to cruise right through Earth's gravity well and continue into deep space. If the lander came in too fast, it wouldn't get a second chance: it would run out of fuel before it could reverse course.

Carpenter had done the math and assured them they'd be fine. It didn't feel fine, though. To Slater it felt like her skull was going to collapse from the pressure. They could have disembarked earlier and slowed more gradually, but Mallick was concerned the Cho-ta'an ship might try to follow them down. By disembarking at the last minute and decelerating at the maximum possible rate, they hoped to be in orbit before the Cho-ta'an even knew they'd left *Andrea Luhman*.

Unfortunately, it didn't work out that way. The Cho-ta'an ship had been slowing for some time, probably to give themselves time to react in case the humans did something unexpected—like sending a lander down to Earth. Less than two minutes after the lander began to decelerate, Carpenter's voice came over the comm.

"Bad news, guys," he said. "The Cho-ta'an ship is slowing."

"How much?" Slater managed to shout through clenched teeth.

"They've flipped around. Looks like close to full reverse thrust. They're going after you."

"What the hell?" Slater replied. "Why?"

"I can only assume they've figured out what we're doing. They can see our thrusters aren't working and have deduced you're making a repair run."

"Can they catch us?"

"They're still several seconds back, and they've got to be pulling their hair out trying to calculate an orbital trajectory. I mean, they would be if they had hair."

"Damn it, Carpenter," Slater groaned.

"Sorry. Point is, you're in no immediate danger. It's going to take their full attention to avoid bouncing off the atmosphere or missing the planet entirely. If they manage to make orbit, we'll revisit the situation."

"Copy that," Slater said.

Slater closed her eyes, fighting to breathe. Her hands and feet had gone numb, and her eyeballs felt like they were pushing into her brain. Part of her wished the Cho-ta'an ship would just get it over with and take them out with a missile. But the ship seemed to have exhausted its missiles, and whatever other weapons it had wouldn't work at this range. In any case, as Carpenter said, the Cho-ta'an were going to have their hands full just trying to achieve orbit. Calculating an orbital trajectory was no small feat, and trying to do it on the fly was borderline suicidal. The Cho-ta'an had clearly decided the lander was a threat. How much they had guessed about the crew's insane mission was impossible to say.

Some twenty minutes later, the lander was arcing around the curve of the Earth at fifty thousand kilometers per hour, still decelerating at four gees. Gabe and O'Brien had lost consciousness; Slater envied them. She remained conscious, although it didn't really matter, as the lander was handling the course adjustments at this point. This was the moment of truth. If Carpenter's calculations were correct, the lander would descend into an orbit of thirty-six thousand kilometers, falling to Earth at the same rate as its momentum carried it past the planet's surface. That's all orbiting was: falling and missing the ground.

It worked, of course. Carpenter could be a pedantic jerk, but he knew his stuff. Slater breathed a sigh of relief as the thrusters cut out. It was such a relief not to weigh three hundred kilos anymore that she didn't notice at first that they were experiencing near full Earth gravity.

"Orbit attained," she gasped.

"Nice flying," Carpenter's voice said over the comm.

"All I did was hold on," Slater replied.

"It was enough."

Slater smiled. Behind her, Gabe and O'Brien began to stir.

"Ugh, my head," O'Brien groaned. "Are we in hell? Did we die?"

"No such luck," Reyes replied. "We're in orbit around Earth."

The word hung in the air like a spell. *Earth*. None of them had ever seen the cradle of the human race. There had never been any point in making the trip before. Earth had been rendered uninhabitable by the Cho-ta'an before any of them were born. Although they'd seen the vids, heard the stories of Earth's grandeur and beauty, it existed for them mainly as an abstraction. People talked about Earth the way people had probably once talked about the glories of ancient Rome. They thought of it more as an unattainable ideal than a real place.

But when Slater put a view of the vast blue-white sphere on the overhead display, all four of them gasped. It was like nothing they'd ever seen. Even Geneva, the jewel in the IDL crown, with its towering black spires jutting up from vast mountain ranges cloaked in pristine white snow, paled in comparison. It was like something out a dream. She found herself blinking tears out of her eyes.

"My God," O'Brien said, echoing her thoughts. "I had no idea."

They gaped in silence for some time as the white and azure swirls rolled slowly beneath them.

"What if...?" Slater began.

"What if what?" Gabe replied.

"What if we could save it? Earth. What if we can prevent the Cho-ta'an from destroying it?"

"Let's not go down that road," Reyes said. "You heard what Schumacher said. We have to assume paradoxes don't exist. It's a bad idea to try to do something you know is doomed to fail."

"Maybe it's not a paradox," Slater replied. "Maybe there's more than one reality. Maybe in one reality, we succeed in saving the Earth from the Cho-ta'an."

"Metaphysical questions aside," Reyes said, "how the hell are we going to do that? We're four people. And humanity doesn't even meet the Cho-ta'an for thirteen hundred years."

"Four people with encyclopedic knowledge of twenty-third century technology," O'Brien said. "Imagine what humanity could do with thirteen hundred years of preparation."

Gabe laughed. "You really think that's how history works? That we're going to land in the center of Constantinople, wow the natives with gyroscopes and pocket calculators, and then institute a thirteen hundred-year plan to defeat aliens humanity hasn't even met yet?"

"Doesn't sound a whole lot crazier than what we're actually doing," O'Brien replied.

"No, Gabe's right," Reyes said. "You're not talking about defeating the Cho-ta'an. You're talking about rewriting all of human history since the Middle Ages. That's a bad idea. Civilizations take time to adapt to technological change. There's no telling what kind of carnage we might unleash."

"Or prevent," Slater said. "The Black Death, the Inquisition, the Holocaust...."

"The Renaissance, the Reformation, the development of representational government," Gabe muttered.

"We're not having this discussion," Reyes snapped. "Not now. Feel free to indulge in fantasies on your own time. We have a mission to execute. We land, we fabricate a new manifold, and we get the hell back to *Andrea Luhman*."

Slater wanted to argue but thought better of it. They remained in silence for some time, watching the Earth slide beneath them. The thrusters had kicked in again, gradually decreasing the lander's velocity relative to the surface below. As the lander slowed, it would begin to fall toward the surface. The idea was to time the fall with the ship's deceleration so that when the lander hit the atmosphere, she would be traveling just faster than the rate of the Earth's rotation at the equator. If the ship were going too fast when it hit the atmosphere, she would bounce back into space. Carpenter had calculated a nice, gradual descent that would allow them to land somewhere near the center of the continent known as North America. Mallick's idea of an uninhabited island was nice, but the impromptu nature of their mission required a bigger spatial margin of error. Australia would have been ideal, but the lander's trajectory put it on the opposite side of the globe. Europe and Asia were considered too populated and technologically advanced—the crew didn't want to have to contend with Frankish knights or Mongol hordes in addition to the other challenges they'd face. So they'd decided on North America. Carpenter's flight plan would take them right to the center of the continent, a place once known as Colorado, known for its rich mineral deposits. The region was sparsely populated by tribes of preliterate humans.

"You there, Slater?" Carpenter's voice said over the comm.

"I'm here. Go ahead."

"Bad news. Looks like the Cho-ta'an ship pulled it off. Whoever's flying that thing has balls of steel. They've settled into an orbit about three thousand klicks below you."

"What's their velocity?"

"About 40,000 kph and slowing. They just slipped underneath you. That's the good news."

"I assume the bad news is that they're going to be coming around again in about an hour and a half."

"A little less than that, actually. Looks like they're trying to match your orbit."

"Damn it," Slater grumbled. "So now what?"

"Don't panic," Carpenter said. "You're going to have to increase your deceleration rate to enter the atmosphere before they catch up to you. I've done some back-of-the-envelope calculations, and it looks like three gees will do it."

Slater groaned.

"You'll survive. Assuming they aren't saving a few missiles for a rainy day, all they've got is railguns. Effective range of a couple hundred klicks, maybe. Much less in the atmosphere."

"All right," Slater said. "Should I crank the thrusters up to three gees now?"

"Yeah. I'll send you an updated flight plan in a few minutes."

They spent several minutes at three gee deceleration. Slater received the updated plan from Carpenter and plugged it into the nav system. A few minutes later, their deceleration decreased slightly.

"Are we still aiming for Colorado, Carpenter?" Slater asked.

"'Fraid not," Carpenter replied. "The North America route would give the Cho-ta'an time to catch you. You'll have to set down sooner, which will put you about seven thousand kilometers to the east. Looks like North Africa is our best bet. Climate's a bit inhospitable, but at least there won't be many people around."

"You're talking about the fucking Sahara desert," Gabe said. "Where are we going to find fuel to burn in the Sahara?"

"Relax," Carpenter said. "Top priority right now is evading the Cho-ta'an. Once you're on the ground, we can look for a more optimal place to set up shop. The good news is that I'll have line-of-sight with the lander for the next few hours." *Andrea Luhman* was already hurtling toward

Jupiter, but as long as it was on the same side of the Earth as the lander, they'd be able to communicate.

Slater heard a high-pitched whine that gradually turned into a dull roar. They had entered the atmosphere.

"Looking good, Slater. You're over the Atlantic now. In a few minutes... shit."

"What is it, Carpenter?"

"The Cho-ta'an ship. Damn, these guys can fly."

"What, Carpenter? What the hell is going on?"

"Okay, don't panic. They've entered the atmosphere, but they're still about a thousand klicks behind you. Railgun range in the atmosphere is a hundred klicks, max. And they'll have to be a lot closer than that to hit a moving target the size of the lander."

"How fast are they moving?"

"Faster than you. Man, this is going to be tight."

"Find me a mountain range," Slater said. "If I can put some mass between us before they get in range, they'll never find us. We'll just power down, throw the camo nets over the lander and wait them out."

"Good idea," Carpenter said. "Give me a sec." He was quiet for some time. "Okay, in a couple minutes you're going to see land. That's western Africa. As soon as you're over land, adjust your heading thirty degrees to port.

"What, no mountains in Africa?" Slater said.

"Too much empty space between you and any cover. Going to have to take you to Europe."

"Copy that," Slater said. A hazy brown strip was growing larger at the edge of her window. She trusted this was the coast of Africa, although it was too indistinct and remote to make out any features of the landscape. The sky was clear, but they were still twenty kilometers up and traveling over two thousand kilometers per hour. Soon they were over land, and Slater pulled the lander hard to the left.

"They're closing on you fast, Slater," Carpenter said. "Your best chance is to lose them in the Pyrenees."

"Pyrenees? Where the hell is that?"

"Mountain range between Spain and France. Can't miss 'em. How fast can you descend in that thing and maintain control?"

"About thirty meters a second."

"Do it. And increase your velocity, if you can. You need cover, fast."

"I'm on it."

She nosed the lander down and it began to descend at a sickening rate. Soon they were over water again—water of an impossible azure that Slater was vaguely aware was the Mediterranean Sea. Her knowledge of Earth geography was decidedly spotty, but every human child still learned about the cultures of the Mediterranean, where human civilization was born.

When they were only a few thousand meters up, land appeared on the port side again. "You should be seeing Spain on your left," Carpenter said as if in response to her mental question. "In about a thousand kilometers, you'll approach a mountain range. That's the Pyrenees. Get on the other side of them and then bank as hard as you can to the right. Find a valley and set the lander down as fast as you can. As long as you're in the air, you're a sitting duck. Those railguns will slice right though you."

"Copy that," Slater said.

Not much later, Slater spied a bank of clouds butting up against a jagged line of gray and white. At the near edge of the clouds, the foothills of the Pyrenees were visible. The lander was barely two thousand meters above them. Slater pulled up and leveled out. "I'm going to have to gain some altitude to clear those peaks," she said.

"Stay low as long as you can. The Cho-ta'an ship is within a hundred klicks now. If you stay below the clouds, they'll have a hard time spotting you from above. They'll have to follow you through the mountains, which should give you an advantage. I'd expect them to start firing at any moment. Take evasive action if you can do it without slowing down."

"Copy that," Slater said again. "Let's see what this beast can do." The lander groaned as she pulled the stick to the right. The lander wasn't built for tricky atmospheric maneuvers. Its profile was too exposed and its wings were too stubby, so that the aux thrusters had to be used just to keep it airborne. Her only consolation was that as clumsy as the lander was, the massive Cho-ta'an warship was worse. Those things were built for interplanetary combat, not flying through mountain ranges.

The lander's altitude remained steady. Slater saw the wisdom of staying close to the ground, but she also knew the one thing the lander was good at: falling. If the Cho-ta'an ship started firing, she wanted to have the option of cutting the aux thrusters and dropping like a rock.

She didn't have to wait long. To her left, a line of gray projectiles streaked past, missing the lander by less than ten meters. Cho-ta'an railguns shot streams of explosive projectiles about the size of a human fist. Each one of them possessed enough explosive power to tear a gaping hole in the lander. No sound accompanied the stream: whatever noise the railguns made was traveling too slowly to reach the lander, which was still flying almost double the speed of sound.

Slater pulled the yoke to the right, and another stream of projectiles shot past, even closer this time. The lander was now over the foothills. A blanket of gray clouds slid over top of them. The mountains ahead grew steadily larger.

"You need to descend, Slater!" Carpenter yelled over the comm. "Use the terrain!"

"I've got this, Carpenter. Trust me." She managed to keep her voice from cracking as she said it.

Slater waited until the stream of projectiles stopped, counted to three, then pulled sharply to the left. The lander groaned with the turn, and another stream shot past, this time on their right.

"Jesus, Slater," O'Brien gasped from behind her. "Cutting it a bit close, aren't you?"

"Cho-ta'an railguns take three seconds to aim between volleys," Gabe said quietly. "She knows what she's doing. Now shut up and let her concentrate."

Slater smiled grimly. She wished she had Gabe's confidence. Her knowledge of Cho-ta'an weaponry was entirely academic. She'd never been under fire before, but the IDL required all pilots to study basic evasive maneuvers. The training really hadn't amounted to much: her instructor had impressed on the class the futility of trying to evade a Cho-ta'an warship in a civilian craft. The goal of the training was simply to allow them to stay alive long enough to eject from the ship. That wasn't an option at present.

Slater pushed the yoke forward and she felt her insides jump as the lander dived under another volley. The green, tree-dotted hills below surged toward them. She pulled back on the yoke and the lander leveled out, barely a stone's throw from the treetops. Yet another volley shot past somewhere overhead.

Slater pulled the yoke to the left, following the course of a creek that ran along the bottom of a valley, then banked hard to the right to avoid a snow-capped mountain that arose directly ahead. Behind her, she heard O'Brien groaning with nausea.

The lander's left wing missed the mountainside by an arm's length. Adrenaline shot through her. She hadn't meant to cut it *that* close. But nobody behind her said a word. They had no choice but to trust her. Soon they would all find out whether that trust was misplaced.

The thought had barely crossed her mind when she heard a dull thudding from her left. It took her a moment to understand what had happened.

"We've been hit," Gabe said, loudly but calmly. "Nobody panic. Stay seated and get ready for a rough landing. Slater, you've got this."

Slater nodded, grateful for Gabe's vote of confidence but not feeling it.

"Slater, you okay?" came Carpenter's voice.

"Tore through the wing," Slater said. "Getting some drag, but no serious damage. Aux thrusters are compensating."

"They're getting really close," Carpenter said. "You're going to lose your cloud cover if you leave the range. Double back when you can."

She made a wide bank to the right around another peak. Another streak of projectiles shot overhead.

"This is no time to get conservative, Slater," Gabe said from behind her. "You don't get points for dodging the mountain if the railgun takes us out."

Slater nodded. Gabe was right. They weren't going to get out of this if she didn't take some risks. She pulled the yoke hard to the right and back as another volley shot past. The Cho-ta'an ship was now visible as a dot on the rear viewscreen, visible without magnification.

For a moment, her view was obscured by clouds. When they'd cleared, she found herself flying directly toward a mountainside. Traveling at over Mach two, they'd impact in seconds. The lander shrieked and groaned as she pulled as hard as she could to the left, aiming for a small gap between two peaks. Another series of thuds sounded to her left. Warnings flashed on the control panel.

"Shit!" she yelled. "We've lost the port aux thrusters. I'm not going to be able to bank. Can barely maintain altitude." She held her breath as the lander barely cleared the gap between the two peaks. The clouds cleared and soon they were soaring over the hills of southern France.

Well, that's that, thought Slater. *I did my best, but it wasn't enough.* No more mountains, no more cloud cover, no way to dodge the railgun. They were going to die.

"Slater!" Carpenter's voice cried over the comm. "You did it!"

Slater stared at the control panel, flashing furiously with warnings. "Did what?" she asked, unable to make sense of Carpenter's jubilant tone.

"Outmaneuvered them," Carpenter said. "The Cho-ta'an ship grazed the mountainside. They're losing speed. Altitude is dropping."

"Huh," Slater said. That was something, at least. The Cho-ta'an were going to die along with them.

"Can you pull up?" Carpenter asked. "I'll try to get you to a better location."

"No can do," Slater replied. "Banking is going to be a problem too. Even at max thrust, we're losing altitude."

"Shit," said Carpenter. "Well, you picked a great place to land, if you're trying to get the attention of all of Europe. You're headed straight for Paris."

"Can we land south of there?"

"Still pretty heavily populated, but I guess we don't have much choice. The sooner you can put her down, the better."

"Copy that." Slater reduced thrust and the nose of the lander began to tip forward. "Damn it," she growled, and engaged the thrusters again. "Uh, Carpenter, we've got a problem. Aux thrusters aren't coming on to compensate for lack of thrust."

"Oh," Carpenter replied. The simplicity of his response made her heart sink. Carpenter was never at a loss for words. He knew what she did: if the aux thrusters wouldn't fire, they'd have to keep the main thrusters firing to stay level. If they reduced thrust, they'd lose lift. The nose would drop, and they'd hurtle toward the ground. Slater remembered somebody telling her about a species of sea animal on Earth called a shark. Supposedly if the shark stopped swimming, it would die. *That's us*, thought Slater. *If we stop moving forward, we die.*

"Okay, here's the plan," Carpenter said. "You've got to lower thrust as much as you can and still stay level. Eventually the atmosphere will slow you down enough to make a landing. I'm going to try to find you a large flat area to set down."

"The low countries should work," Gabe said. "The Netherlands or Belgium. Or whatever they're called these days."

"I was thinking larger and flatter than that," Carpenter said.

"Larger and flatter…" Gabe repeated, puzzled.

Reyes smiled grimly at him. "He means the ocean, genius."

*****

An ocean landing wouldn't be a landing at all. It would be a crash—one they were unlikely to survive. Not that it mattered. If the lander sank to the bottom of the ocean, their mission was already doomed. They were never going to get off Earth.

It wasn't actually the ocean Carpenter had in mind in any case: it was the North Sea, the vast, rough, icy cold body of water that separated Scandinavia from the British Isles and the European mainland. It was certainly large enough, although "flat" was debatable. According to Gabe, it wasn't unusual for the North Sea to have waves ten meters high. Carpenter insisted the sea looked "relatively calm" today, whatever that meant.

Unfortunately, Slater couldn't reduce the lander's thrust by more than thirty percent without the nose dropping. Their speed was still falling, but not enough.

"You're going to overshoot the sea," Carpenter said.

"Is that good news or bad news?" Slater asked.

"Let's go with good," Carpenter replied after a moment. "You're headed toward Norway. Odds are fifty-fifty you'll find a nice snowy plain to set down in."

"And if we don't?"

"You'll hit a mountain. But at least it'll be over quickly."

Slater sighed. He was right. An instantaneous death sounded a lot better than drowning in the North Sea.

"The Cho-ta'an ship is down," Carpenter said. "It just hit the water about fifty klicks behind you."

"Any chance they'll survive?"

"Not a clue. The ship is sinking like a rock, though."

"Well, thank God for that at least." If they somehow survived the landing, at least they wouldn't have the Cho-ta'an to worry about.

They were now only five hundred meters up and still traveling over half the speed of sound. The sea slid beneath them like a tablet of bluish-black marble streaked with white. Snow-covered mountains loomed ahead. Soon they were once again over land—intricate swirls of rocky land that jutted into the dark mass of the sea. The coast was dotted with small, primitive structures, many of which had stone chimneys that emitted plumes of light gray smoke. Several small, square-sailed ships floated near the shore. Further inland, the snow-covered ground sloped gently toward a distant mountain range.

The mountains ran mainly northeast to southwest, roughly parallel with the lander's current course, so it was not inconceivable the lander would hit the ground before they reached the mountains. Even if it did, though, it would hit at over five hundred kilometers per hour. Soon they were close enough to the ground to see individual people, who stopped what they were doing to gaze at the strange silvery object hurtling through the sky. There wasn't much the crew could do but stare back.

They were moving gradually farther inland as they soared over the coast. Buildings were becoming more scarce, and the few people they saw seemed to be traveling to or from one of the coastal settlements. Many of these were using mules—and sometimes sleds—to transport loads of cargo.

After another few minutes, Slater could no longer see the fjords. For some time their view was dominated by evergreen forests, and then they were over mountains.

"Shit," Slater muttered. There was no way they were going to survive a mountain landing.

"Hang on," Carpenter said. "Bank left. Try to line yourself up with that valley."

"On it," Slater said, as the lander shot over a wide river valley. There was enough flat ground on either side of the river that they might still be able to make a landing they could walk away from. The lander groaned and shuddered as she pulled it to left. Soon they were above forest again. The tops of the taller trees nearly brushed against the bottom of the lander. A few klicks ahead, a wide swathe of pure white opened up—a snow-covered plain sloping gently down from the foothills.

"You see that white patch?" Carpenter asked. "That's your best shot."

"I'm going to overshoot it," Slater said, watching the line of trees approaching at the end of the plain, some ten klicks away.

"Not if you shut off the thrusters."

"If I shut off the thrusters, we're going to crash."

Carpenter didn't answer. He didn't need to. The lander was going to crash no matter what they did. The only question was where.

"All right," Slater said. "Preparing to cut thrust."

"You're going to need all the room you can get. Cut thrust as soon as you're clear of the trees."

"I've got it, Carpenter."

"Copy that. Good luck."

Carpenter's assessment was optimistic: they were still too high. If she waited until they were over the clearing to cut thrust, the lander would smash into the trees at the far end. "We're going down," she said. "Check your restraints. Eye shields on. It's going to be a rough landing." Behind her, she heard rustling and metallic clicks.

She waited until they were about three klicks from the clearing before cutting thrust. For a moment they were suspended in air as the nose of the lander dipped. They began to dive, and suddenly the trees were surging toward them. For a split-second, Slater wondered if she had cut the thrusters too soon. But then they were clear of the treetops. Ahead of them was nothing but pristine white. She closed her eyes and pulled the eye shield of the helmet down. The gel pack filled, pushing uncomfortably against her eyelids.

The lander's nose hit the ground.

CHAPTER ELEVEN

"I suppose most of you have heard Gunnar Bjornson's sales pitch," Sigurd said. "Or have at least heard about it. Nothing much has changed since the last time Harald Tanglehair made this play, except the urgency of the plea. It's the same deal he offered last time. And that is to say, it's no deal at all."

A few chuckles went up from the group. There were twenty-eight of them altogether, Twenty-six men and two women, representing nearly all the households in the scattered settlement known as Haavaldsrud. Only two were missing: old Hjalmar had injured his foot and was unable to make the hike down from his cottage, and Torvald Ulfson was off chasing down some missing sheep in the foothills, several miles away. The assembled met around a fire pit in a clearing not far from Torvald's farm, as they generally did on the first day of the new moon. It made a good meeting place as it was centrally located and easily accessible to most of the area's residents.

The air was cool and crisp this spring morning, and the group was huddled tightly around the fire pit, where a pile of pine logs sizzled and crackled, throwing off thick gray smoke. Sigurd stood near the edge of fire, his eyes stinging as a gentle breeze pushed the smoke toward him. Gunnar and his men had left early that morning, after speaking with several other prominent men in the community—all of whom were present here. They had spent the night in the house of a wealthy man named Oyvind, a relative of Gunnar's. Sigurd had seen Gunnar and his party turning onto the main road inland when he got up to attend the meeting.

"Harald has grown in strength since then," said a man slightly older than Sigurd, who stood at the back of the group, across the fire from Sigurd. The man was named Arnulf, and he knew of what he spoke: he'd lost two fingers on his left hand to a Dane's axe when his shield splintered during a battle in Vestfold seven years earlier. They had won the day, but at the cost of twenty-three men. Many more had been wounded. Sigurd himself had nearly been killed when a thrown spear missed his throat by an inch.

"Our numbers have grown as well," Sigurd said.

"Not enough to stave off Harald's army," Arnulf said.

"Our arrangements for mutual assistance with the neighboring villages remain in place."

"Those agreements were made to deter attacks by Danish raiders and bandits," Arnulf said. "There is no telling whether anyone will come to our defense against Harald. If it's true that the jarls in the north have sworn fealty to Harald, then we certainly can't expect any help from them."

"You would have us surrender without a fight?"

"Svelvig is less than a day's journey from here. You've heard the rumors as well as I: Harald is amassing a force there, under the command of Ragnar Ivarsson. I've heard reports that there are as many as fifty men there, and word is that more are on their way. Do you suppose this is a coincidence?"

"I don't put much stock in rumors," Sigurd said, "but it's never been a secret that Harald plans to rule all of Norway. It's been to our advantage that until now he's found more appealing targets along the coast. That said, if he does launch an attack from Svelvig, we are the first line of defense for the valley. I suggest that we make our own appeal to the jarls and villagers to the north. Two dozen men stationed at the bridge—"

"Two dozen men! For how long? How many able-bodied men do you think this valley can spare? Will we build our own garrison at the bridge? How do you think Harald will respond to that?"

"It is not an easy thing, to be sure," Sigurd said. "But this is not a deal that we will be able to back out of. It's not an even exchange by any stretch of the imagination. We'll be giving up our freedom in exchange for security."

"Freedom to do what?" Arnulf asked. "Die at the hands of Harald's army?"

Sympathetic murmurs went up from the group.

Sigurd frowned. "Arnulf, did Gunnar Bjornson come to speak with you?"

"That he did," Arnulf replied. "And it took all my restraint not to throttle him where he stood. What Harald was thinking sending that lout to win us over is beyond me. Few in this valley remember him, and that is to his benefit. But we must not confuse the messenger with the message. This is a matter of survival."

Sigurd was disheartened by Arnulf's sympathy to Harald's offer. He said, "Surely this is not the same Arnulf who killed three Danes with his axe and then, when the handle split, brained two more with the axe head?"

"One and the same," Arnulf said, with a grim smile. "Seven years older."

"And still two fingers short," said the young man next to him, holding up Arnulf's mutilated hand. "In a couple years, you'll need to take off your shoes to count that high."

Laughter went up from the group. Arnulf jerked his hand away in mock annoyance. "I can still wield an axe, you diseased whelp," Arnulf growled good-naturedly.

"And you're still worth five Danes," Sigurd said. "As are most of the men here."

Nods and grunts of agreement went up from the group. It was an obvious ploy, but Sigurd knew he couldn't go wrong playing on the men's sense of bravery and manliness.

"The bravado of men," muttered a hoarse voice to Sigurd's right. Two men moved aside to make way for Gunhild, the oldest woman in the community. Her husband, a fisherman and warrior, had died some twenty years earlier, leaving her a widow and the owner of his considerable land holdings. Although all free persons were considered equal under the laws of the Northmen, Gunhild's age, wealth and history of providing shrewd counsel gave her outsized standing in the community. If Sigurd couldn't rally Gunhild to his side, he would be fighting an uphill battle to gain the support of the others.

"You think we are unable to provide for our own defense, Gunhild?" he asked.

"I think there is no defense against violence in this world," Gunhild replied.

"What will you have us do, woman?" asked a dour fisherman named Jannik. "Lay down our arms and hope the gods protect us?"

"Not at all," Gunhild said. "I counsel no strategy. I'm only suggesting that you do no one any favors by lying to yourselves."

"In what way are we lying to ourselves, Gunhild?" Sigurd asked, his voice measured and respectful.

She pointed to Arnulf. "This man was a fierce warrior once. Perhaps he really was worth five Danes at one time. But his eyes have gone hazy and the fingers he has left are swollen with gout."

Arnulf's face went red with shame and rage.

"Gunhild," Sigurd chided gently. "It isn't necessary to—"

"It *is* necessary!" Gunhild cried. "You tell yourself these lies, and then you die and leave the weak amongst us to fend for themselves. You're still strong, Sigurd, but you have your limits as well. You all do. What happens when these unstoppable warriors are cut down? The young and healthy are taken away to be slaves, and the old and infirm are left to starve."

"What is your solution, Gunhild?" Sigurd asked. "Weakness will only embolden the Danes, to say nothing of Harald."

"As I say, I counsel no strategy. I will say only this, and then I will allow you to go on with your chest-beating and war cries: if you spurn Harald's offer, do so not because you are powerful, but because you would rather die than be subjects of that simpering buffoon. Do not confuse the messenger with the message, but observe that they sprout from the same root. A powerful man needs to make no difficult choices. Bravery arises not from strength but from perseverance despite weakness. The weak among us already know what we face if you lose. We will not have the luxury of a quick death on the battlefield. We are not afraid, for we are brave. And now you must do us the courtesy of acting out of bravery, not foolhardiness."

The group was quiet for some time.

"Gunhild is right," Sigurd said at last. "Arnulf, there is no doubt in my mind that you are still worth five Danes, but we must not deceive ourselves. We have only one Arnulf among us, and we may very well be outmanned six to one at some point. Harald has us badly outnumbered, and help from the north may not arrive in time to save us—if it arrives at all."

"Then we have no choice," Jannik said. "We must turn to Harald."

"If it's foolish to believe we can defend ourselves," said the other woman in the group, to Sigurd's left, "then it is equally foolish to believe Harald is our savior." The woman's name was Hella. She had inherited her father's pig farm. Over six feet tall and built like a bear, Hella had never married.

"Hella speaks wisdom," Sigurd said. "Allowing ourselves to be subjugated by Harald is a guarantee only of a different sort of defeat."

"We've heard your thoughts on the matter already," Arnulf said. "If no one has anything new to add, I suggest we vote and get it over with. I have a field to plow."

No one else spoke.

"All right, then," Sigurd said. "All in favor of taking Harald up on his offer?"

Several men raised their hands, Arnulf among them. It was less than half of the group, but Sigurd suspected Gunhild and a few others would abstain. Sigurd counted ten hands altogether. It was going to be close.

"All in favor of rejecting the offer?"

Several others raised their hands, including Hella and Oyvind. Sigurd noticed Jannik's eyes darting from one hand to another. Jannik seemed on the verge of voting against the offer, but in the end his hand dropped to his side.

"Looks like ten to nine," Sigurd said grimly. "It saddens me to ally with a man like Harald, but I will abide by the wishes of the community. We'll send a messenger to inform Harald of our decision. His men left only a few hours ago; a fast runner should be able to—"

"Hold on, Sigurd," said a young man named Sven, who stood in the middle of the crowd. "I stopped by Thorvald's house on the way here. Thorvald said he will not be party to any pact with Harald."

"Then we're at an impasse," Sigurd said, trying not to let his relief show.

"The law states that entering an agreement requires a majority vote," Gunhild said. "A tie means the agreement will not be ratified."

A few dissatisfied mutters arose from the crowd.

"What about Hjalmar?" someone asked.

"Hjalmar abstains," replied a young hunter named Njáll.

"He told you this?" Sigurd asked.

"Well," Njáll said, "his exact words were 'Fuck those people and their endless meetings.'" Laughter went up from the group. "I can run to his house and ask him to clarify if you think it's necessary."

"I don't think that will be necessary," Sigurd said with a smile.

"So that there's no question of the legality of our decision," Gunhild said, "I will change my vote. Sigurd, I'm on your side."

Sigurd nodded his thanks to the old woman. "Then we're at eleven to ten against. Does anyone else wish to change their vote?"

There were a few grumbles and mutters, but no one spoke up.

"Then Harald's offer is rejected. I don't suppose we need to send a messenger. He'll figure it out soon enough."

Several men laughed.

"Then if there are no more pressing matters to discuss…"

Sigurd trailed off as several men in front of him gasped as they looked up at the sky behind him. He turned to see what they were looking at: a small, silvery object glinting in the sun. The thing was moving impossibly fast; it was nearly overhead now. It looked to Sigurd a little like a duck, its wings pinned against its sides as it dived.

"What is it?" Hella gasped.

"Some kind of bird?" Jannik offered.

"It would be the biggest bird I've ever seen," Arnulf. "And it shines like it's made of—"

His words were drowned out by the rumble of thunder. Sigurd's heart raced with fear and excitement. The object disappeared behind the trees to the east.

"The gods are angry with us," Njáll murmured, looking fearfully to the sky.

"Not the gods," said another man. "One god."

Sigurd heard murmurs of agreement, but no one dared speak the name of He Who Thunders.

"It is the hammer, Mjölnir," Jannik said, "cast to Earth."

As if in response to Jannik's words, they heard a rumbling in the distance, echoing off the snow-covered mountains.

"We need to vote again," Jannik said.

"Don't be a fool," Arnulf snapped. "Nothing has changed."

"Nothing has changed? The god of thunder has thrown his hammer to the Earth!"

"Didn't look like a hammer to me," Arnulf said. "And if the Thunderer is angry at us for rejecting Harald's offer, he's got lousy aim."

"That's enough!" Sigurd barked. "Stop your cowering and foolish talk. We don't know what it was. It may have been Mjölnir, or a skystone, or something else entirely. We would be wise to put aside other business and investigate."

Grunts and murmurs of assent went up. Skystones were extremely rare, and Sigurd had never heard of one this size, but they were prized as a source of iron.

"Whatever that thing was," Sigurd said, "it seems to have hit the ground a few miles to the east, just north of the fjord. It must have been seen from many miles away. We have to assume the sentries at Harald's outpost at Svelvig saw it and will be taking an interest. We will need to be quick. I will lead the expedition. Who else can come?"

About half the men present raised their hands. Sigurd was pleased to see Arnulf among them. Jannik and Njáll raised their hands as well.

"Good," said Sigurd. "Go home and gather your things. It shouldn't take more a few hours to get to the place where the object hit the ground, but bring enough food for three days, in case we are gone longer. We'll meet where the path from my house meets the main road. We leave at mid-morning."

CHAPTER TWELVE

Carolyn Reyes dozed beside the fire, the flickering red light playing across her eyelids. This had always been her favorite part of these hunting trips with her father. She'd never been much for hiking or hunting; she'd rather sit in the cabin, reading a book and sipping hot chocolate. But these lazy evenings around the campfire made it all worth it.

Geneva, where Reyes had grown up, had no native life, but since being terraformed it had become home to several thousand species that had been introduced from the gene banks of colonization ships. Before life on Earth had been exterminated by the Cho-ta'an, biologists had assembled a library of DNA for tens of millions of Earth species. The vast majority of these remained on ice, as the process of reviving a species from a genotype was difficult, time-consuming and expensive. Additionally, suitable homes for most species had not been found. Geneva was one of the more welcoming worlds, and it had taken the HCC twenty years to give it an atmosphere that could support plant life. Even now, only a narrow strip near the equator was habitable; the rest of the planet was too cold to support life.

Reyes had been one of the lucky ones: her father was on the board of the HCC's settlement committee, so he'd gotten in on the first round of real estate picks. He hadn't gotten his first or even his second choice, but they'd ended up with a sizeable estate right on the bigger lakes. Much of the land was considered uninhabitable, as Geneva was a young planet by geological standards. Not enough time had elapsed for much topsoil to form; most of the ground was volcanic rock covered by a thin layer of silt. Genetically modified grasses had been introduced to help break down the rock, with minimal success. The problem was that the grasses proved unexpectedly tempting to the burgeoning deer population. The deer had no natural predators in the region (or on the planet, for that matter), so the settlement committee had set bounties for deer. As a result, deer hunting had become very popular of late, particularly on large estates like the Reyes's. Her father had built a small cabin about five klicks from the lake, and their family spent many weekends there. Her father and older brother hunted while Carolyn sat by the fire and read.

Those lazy days seemed to last forever, but now they existed only as hazy memories. Since enlisting with the IDL after engineering school, she'd had little time to read for pleasure. Even during her downtime, she was reading manuals and white papers. The IDL's efforts to stay technologically ahead of the Cho-ta'an were relentless. Taking into account the periods she spent in stasis, as well as the time dilation involved in interstellar travel, she fell further behind every day. As a young ship's engineer, she always felt like she was running to stand still.

Even now, sitting beside the fire, she felt a twinge of guilt. The IDL was working on a prototype for a new type of reciprocal ionic thruster that was small enough to be used for auxiliary thrusters. If it worked, it would be a huge advantage for the IDL's ships. Currently their starships had two separate propulsion systems: a reciprocal ionic thruster for primary propulsion and an old-fashioned hydrogen-and-oxygen system for attitude adjustments and axial movement. Using ionic propulsion for both would eliminate the need for ships to carry massive fuel tanks filled with chemical propellant. A ship like *Andrea Luhman* would be a prime candidate for upgrade—but only if the ship's engineer were up to speed on the technology. *I should get up*, she thought. But she was so tired. It had been far too long since she had just sat and relaxed like this, her surroundings silent except for the crackling of the campfire, the smell of smoke filling her nostrils....

No. There was no smoke. Why was there no smoke? The sound was unmistakable, and the light.... No, the light was wrong, too. Not comfortingly chaotic, but precise and insistent. The light was a warning.

She slowly opened her eyes. It was dark except for the red light flashing above. The sensation of restraints pressing against her flesh penetrated her awareness. No fire, and yet the crackling persisted.

Moving her right arm, she felt unexpected resistance, as if she were submerged in liquid. She looked down, but her eyes refused to focus on anything. Where was she?

The lander, she remembered. She was on a planet. Earth? No. Ridiculous. Shelve that thought for now. They had been flying over trees. Who was 'they'? Slater. Slater was the pilot. Why couldn't she see anything? And that goddamned crackling!

Foam, she thought. The crash foam had deployed. Which meant the lander had crashed. Upon impact, jets lining the walls had sprayed liquid into the cabin. The liquid reacted with the atmosphere, expanding and creating bubbles. Within a fraction of a second, the foam had completely filled the cabin and hardened to the consistency of soft rubber. A few seconds later, the foam had begun to dissipate, contracting and drying into discrete, pea-sized pellets. That was the crackling she heard. The visor of her helmet was still down, but the gel-packed eye shield had retracted.

Soon the level of the foam receded until it was below her knees. She saw now that a tall man sat in the seat in front of her. Gabe something. Next to Gabe was Slater, the pilot. Reyes turned to her left. Sandy-haired man, skinny. Something Irish. O'Hare. No, O'Brien. All three were unconscious.

The four of them had been selected for a mission. They had been picked to land on Earth and....

She stopped again. Land on *Earth*?

Earth was dead, destroyed by the Cho-ta'an. And yet, when she closed her eyes, she saw the fjords slipping underneath them.

The man in front of her stirred.

"Gabe?" she asked. "You okay?"

Gabe grunted. "Feel like I got hit in the head with a sledgehammer, but otherwise, yeah. You?"

"I think so. The foam...."

"The foam probably saved our lives. We must have rolled twenty times."

"Rolled..." Reyes repeated.

"End over end. You sure you're all right?" Gabe said, releasing his restraints and turning to look at her. "You know where you are?" He unstrapped his helmet and pulled it off, letting it fall to the floor.

"Earth?" Reyes suggested.

"Right-o. You know what year it is?"

"Twenty-two... no, wait. That's a trick question."

"Indeed it is," Gabe said, moving toward Slater's chair. His feet crunched in the dry pellets of foam. He leaned over Slater and touched the side of her face. "Hey, Slater," he said quietly. "You okay?" She didn't respond. Gabe unstrapped her helmet and gingerly removed it. A crack ran along the top of the helmet where the overhead support had buckled. He dropped the damaged helmet to the floor.

"Shit," Reyes said.

"I don't think it's too bad," Gabe said. "Maybe a concussion. Helmet took the worst of it." He pulled open one of Slater's eyelids with his thumb. "No retinal damage. Can you check on O'Brien?"

Reyes nodded, and then regretted it. A sharp pain had set in right behind her eyes. Excessive gee force would do that. If it weren't for the eye shields keeping her eyeballs from stretching beyond their limits, she'd likely be blind. She gritted her teeth and fumbled with her restraints. "Yeah, I'll take a look."

Gabe pulled a retractable blade from his belt and began working on Slater's restraints. Reyes got up from her seat, immediately stumbling in the foam and falling with a crunch at O'Brien's feet.

"Smooth," O'Brien murmured. Looking up, she saw him smiling at her. Dark circles had already begun to appear around his eyes, from blood vessels that had burst during the crash.

"A little... disoriented," Reyes said.

"Traveling thirteen hundred years back in time and then taking a ride in a blender will do that," O'Brien said.

Reyes leaned back against the cushion of foam. "So that really did happen? We're on Earth during the Middle Ages?"

"Only one way to find out," O'Brien said, moving to detach his restraints. He let out a scream and for a moment his body went limp. His eyes rolled back in his head.

"O'Brien!" Reyes said, moving toward him. "What's wrong?"

O'Brien's eyes flickered open, and a weak smile played at his lips. "Think I... broke something." His face had gone pale.

"Okay, try not to move. You done with that knife, Gabe?"

"Yeah, here." Gabe carefully handed her the knife. She cut through O'Brien's restraints and then handed the knife back to Gabe. O'Brien winced as she pulled off his helmet. "You hit your head?"

"No," O'Brien said. "I mean, yeah, probably. But it's my left side that's bothering me. May have broken a rib or two."

"Would you be more comfortable lying down?"

Gabe winced again. "I'd be more comfortable with about six shots of whisky."

"It hurts when you're not moving?"

"Is breathing a kind of moving?"

Reyes sighed, turning to Gabe. "What do we do?"

"Why are you asking me?" Gabe said, still examining Slater. "You're in charge of the doomsday bomb time travel spaceship repair team."

"You're the medic and our tactical expert," Reyes growled. "Now stop screwing around and help me figure out what to do." She'd gotten used to Gabe's teasing, but this wasn't the time. She was still addled from the crash, and she didn't need Gabe undermining her authority to make a point.

Gabe nodded. "Grab the medkit from the back. Get some smelling salts and see if you can get Slater conscious. I'm going to check out O'Brien."

Reyes went into the back and pulled out the white plastic case with the medical supplies. She grabbed a handful of smelling salt packets, shoved them into a pocket and then worked her way forward in the cabin, trading places with Gabe. Sitting down in the seat next to Slater, she cracked open one of the packets under her nose. Slater didn't stir.

"Jesus!" O'Brien screamed from behind them. Reyes glanced back to see Gabe with his hand under O'Brien's shirt.

Gabe turned to face her, shaking his head. "Three cracked ribs," he said. "Probably some internal bleeding, but hopefully that will stop on its own. If it doesn't...." He trailed off. "Hopefully it stops on its own," he said again.

Reyes cracked open another capsule and waved it under Slater's nose. "Slater," she said, loudly and firmly, "wake up." But Slater still didn't stir.

"This is bad," Reyes said, as much to herself as to Gabe. "This is very bad."

"Take these," Gabe said, putting a couple of pain pills in O'Brien's hand. O'Brien put the pills in his mouth and then sucked down some water from a packet Gabe was holding. Gabe handed him the packet and the pill container. "Hold on to these," he said. "Take them as you need them." O'Brien nodded.

"Half our crew is injured," Gabe said, turning to Reyes. "We can attend to their medical needs, but moving them is going to be just about impossible. The area we crashed looked pretty deserted, but anybody within twenty klicks must have seen us go down. Or heard it, at least. I'd guess we've got at most two hours before the natives start showing up."

But Reyes wasn't thinking about the wounded, or even their tactical situation. She was thinking about the mission. The reason they had come to Earth. Casting a new manifold was going to be difficult enough, but repairing the lander? Slater had barely been able to keep it in the air even before the crash. Even if it was reparable, it could take years to get it airborne again. And that assumed they'd have a safe place to work, undisturbed—which brought her back to Gabe's point.

"The locals," she said. "They'll be armed with what, swords? We've got pistols and there's a portable railgun in the back. We can hold them off."

Gabe laughed. "For how long? A day? A week? Even if our whole crew were conscious and in fighting shape, we'd have to sleep eventually. Don't get me wrong, there are worse ways to go out than holding off a Viking horde with a railgun, but it's not a long-term strategy."

Reyes cracked open another capsule under Slater's nose, and finally she began to stir. Slater moaned quietly and her eyes flickered open.

"Hey, Slater," Reyes said. "Welcome back. How do you feel?"

Slater gave a weak smile and raised her hand in a thumbs-up.

"Good," Reyes said. "It's only fair that you have to live through the aftermath of that shitty landing with the rest of us."

Slater smiled again. "Tired," she said.

"You may have a concussion. Try to stay awake."

O'Brien groaned.

"Help me get O'Brien out of his chair," Gabe said. "Might help to get some pressure off those ribs."

"Coming," Reyes said. "Stay awake, Slater. Use these if you have to." She handed Slater the rest of the capsules and then climbed into the back to help Gabe.

While O'Brien whimpered and moaned, they dragged him as carefully as they could to the rear of the lander. Reyes removed the cushions from his chair to create a makeshift bed. They laid him down on his back and covered him up to his shoulders with a blanket.

"Is that better?" Reyes asked.

"It's… not worse," O'Brien said, wincing.

"I'll give you a local to take the edge off," Gabe said. "Better to keep you conscious for now. We're going to have visitors soon." O'Brien winced again as Gabe touched the infuser to his side. Then he seemed to relax a little. Gabe put the infuser back in the kit and turned to Reyes. "Okay, chief," he said. "What's the plan?"

"You're our historian. What kind of people are we going to encounter here?"

"Not to put too fine a point on it?" Gabe said. "Vikings. Norsemen, if you prefer."

"So guys with swords and horns on their hats?"

"The horns thing is a myth. Unlikely they'll have swords, as the Vikings didn't have the technology to forge steel. Probably spears and axes. That's good news and bad news, of course. The steel of the lander's hull is superior to anything on this continent. It's priceless, if we can hold on to it."

Reyes nodded. "Any guess as to how many we should expect?"

Gabe shrugged. "You saw the landscape. It's pretty rugged. Sparsely populated, no major population centers. Scandinavia lagged behind the rest of Europe in political centralization, which could work in our favor. There aren't any big standing armies or security forces here. The Vikings were mostly opportunistic raiders."

"So...?"

"Our first encounter? Could be one, could be a hundred. But within the next day or two we're going to be getting a lot of visitors. So what's the plan?"

"Get the weapons," Reyes said. "We protect the lander at all cost."

CHAPTER THIRTEEN

Gunnar Bjornson stood on his skis at the head of the group, peering into the woods across the river. No one spoke for some time. Even the birds had been temporarily shocked into silence.

"Was it a skystone?" asked the man behind him at last. This was Leif, the dark-haired young warrior who had joined their party ten days ago in Trondheim. There they had met with Håkon Grjotgardsson, the jarl who administered Trondelag for Harald. Håkon had reaffirmed his loyalty to Harald and loaned Leif to them, insisting that he knew the terrain as well as any man alive. Leif was competent enough, but he was young and over-eager.

Gunnar shook his head. "You saw that thing. Its lines were like a ship's."

"A sky ship?" asked Leif asked dubiously, standing next to Gunnar. The other men waited dutifully behind. "Do even the gods possess such things?"

"I don't know," Gunnar said. "But I intend to find out. It looked like that thing hit the ground only a few miles north of here. The trees are sparse here, so we should have no trouble finding it."

"Is that wise, Gunnar?" Leif asked. "I understood we were expected at Svelvig tonight. The king himself will be arriving soon."

"I'm aware of our instructions, Leif," Gunnar said irritably. "Do you think Harald was aware a ship made of metal would be falling from the sky when he gave them?"

"Certainly not, sir. But we don't know for certain it was a sky ship."

"Whatever it is, I think we can assume Harald will grant us some leeway under the circumstances. Even if it is only a skystone, it's worth looking into. I heard of a skystone falling in Denmark that was made of pure iron. Enough to make twenty swords. Do you think Harald would forgive us a day's tardiness for twenty swords?"

"I should think so, sir."

"Then we head northeast, over the bridge. Figure on another day of travel."

"Yes, sir," the men murmured together. Gunnar steered his mount to the right. Leif and the others followed.

The bridge across the river was less than a mile ahead. The men removed their skies to cross and and then followed a narrow hunting trail that led through the woods. It was nearly midday when the group emerged from the woods into a clearing and started walking across the plain. Soon they began to see signs of impact.

"Look at that," Leif said, pointing at a gash in the ground that had been cleared of snow and the top several inches of soil. It was perhaps four yards wide and ten yards long. A great mound of snow and earth lay at the far end of the gash. Beyond this, the ground was unbroken for perhaps a hundred yards. Then there was another gash, somewhat shorter and more irregular in shape.

"Gunnar," said the man behind Leif, whose name was Thorvald. Thorvald was a mountain of a man, a hand taller than the others. He rarely spoke.

Gunnar turned to look where Thorvald was pointing. A dark gray object lay in the snow a stone's throw away. Gunnar walked toward the object. The others followed.

"What is it?" Leif asked, as the others approached.

Gunnar bent down to pick the thing up. It was a piece of flat material, perfectly rectangular, about the length of his arm and half as wide, and as thick as his forefinger. He lifted it easily. The weight and flexibility reminded him of birch bark.

"A shield?" Thorvald suggested.

"No place to hold onto it," Gunnar said. "I think it's part of the sky ship." He tried to tear the material and failed. "It's strong, and looks to be waterproof. Would be good building material. If you could shape it, it would make a nice saddle." He bent the panel as far as he could, but it sprang back to its former shape as soon as he let it go. Gunnar shrugged. "Here, Leif, you hold it."

Leif scowled but took the thing without complaint, tucking it under his arm. Gunnar knew he shouldn't antagonize the young man, but he couldn't help himself. They were ill-equipped to haul cargo; Leif would simply have to carry it.

They continued to the next gash in the ground. Before they reached it, they could see another gash after it, and another after that. The distance between the gashes grew gradually shorter as they went.

"It hit like a flat stone striking the surface of water," Ivar said. "It tumbled end over end, many times." Ivar was the youngest member of the group.

Gunnar nodded. He pointed at a gray thing sticking out of the snow to his right. "There's another one. Leif, go get it." The fifth member of the group, a man named Steinar, allowed himself a chuckle at Leif's expense.

Leif wordlessly walked to the flat panel jutting out of the snow and picked it up. He tucked it next to the one already under his arm. By the time he had returned to the group, Gunnar had pointed out another.

Leif sighed. "Sir," he said, "there's a limit to how many of these things I can carry."

"Perhaps," Gunnar replied disinterestedly, "but we haven't reached it yet." As he finished speaking, he pointed to another panel in the distance. Leif hung his head but went after the thing. He was carrying six of the gray panels by the time they spotted the silvery object in the distance.

"Amazing," Gunnar said. "It seems to be mostly intact. Follow me."

As they got nearer to the fallen object, Gunnar was more certain than ever that it was some sort of craft, fabricated by human—or human-like— hands. It was even shaped roughly like a ship, with a long middle and two tapered ends, although it was somewhat larger than even the biggest long ships. The main difference was the wings and tailfins, which made it look a little like a gigantic silver starling. The wings weren't quite right, though. They seemed to be fixed in place and were too small, proportionally speaking. Even if it were possible for a bird of this size to fly, it would need much larger wings to stay airborne. It was no surprise that such a craft would plunge from the sky; Gunnar could hardly imagine it getting aloft in the first place. Gunnar and his men were approaching from the rear left of the craft. He drew his sword, and the others followed, their weapons at the ready.

Gunnar reached the tail of the craft and stopped, listening. All was quiet. He motioned for Ivar and Thorvald to go around the left side while he, Leif and Steinar took the right. Gunnar crept along the side of the craft, unsure what he was looking for. Assuming he was correct about it being a ship, it had to have a door somewhere. Where would they put it? On top? In the stern? The metal exterior of the craft was incredibly smooth and uniform. Whoever fashioned it knew more about metallurgy than even the famed Frankish blacksmiths. Gunnar was not one for fanciful stories, but he began to wonder whether it was perhaps dwarves or giants who had built the craft. Might the door be enchanted somehow, making it impossible for a mere human to see?

So disconcerted was he by this possibility that Gunnar did not at first notice the man sitting with his back against the craft, looking right at him with a bemused smile on his face. Gunnar stopped and gripped his sword tightly in front of him.

The man spoke something that sounded like a greeting, but Gunnar could not understand him. Other than his drab, tightly fitting clothing, the man did not look in any way unusual. He did not look like a Norseman, but could easily pass for a Frank or Saxon. Gunnar noticed that the man was sitting on a sort of box that had been propped against the craft as a seat. In his hands, the man held a finely molded piece of metal. The main body was shaped like an oblong box; the man was holding it by a handle the protruded from the bottom. The man lifted the object before him, as if making sure that Gunnar saw it. He spoke again, in the same strange tongue. His tone was firm but not impolite. It occurred to Gunnar that the thing might be a weapon. It certainly didn't look intimidating.

"Who are you?" Gunnar said, hoping that the man might speak the Norsemen's tongue in addition to his own.

The man shook his head and said something else that Gunnar could not interpret. Something about this man was very strange, something Gunnar could not quite put his finger on. No, the problem was not that he was strange; it was that he was too familiar. This was no dwarf or giant, but merely a man. The language was clearly not Nordic, and Gunnar knew enough German to eliminate that possibility, but the words did sound vaguely Germanic.

"It sounds a little like English," Leif said.

"You speak English?"

"Some. I occasionally translate for foreigners who visit my jarl." Leif was still carrying the gray panels he had picked out of the snow.

"Put those down, you fool," Gunnar snapped.

Leif dropped the panels.

Gunnar saw Ivar peeking around the front of the craft. Gunnar held up his hand and Ivar halted where he was. Thorvald stopped just behind Ivar. The stranger glanced in Ivar's direction, but he didn't seem concerned at the prospect of being surrounded by armed men. Gunnar wondered if the stranger knew something he didn't. Were there more men hidden somewhere? There was nothing but undisturbed snow all around them. If there had been others in the craft, they were still inside.

The stranger continued to stare back at him with a slightly bemused look on his face. Gunnar wondered whether the man's calm demeanor was a bluff. Given the exotic nature of the craft, it was not inconceivable that he was protected by some powerful magic, but Gunnar tended to favor simpler explanations: the stranger was hiding his fear to unsettle Gunnar and his men.

Gunnar turned to Leif. "Ask this man who he is and where he came from."

Leif nodded. "I will try." He thought for a moment, and then spoke a few halting words.

The stranger regarded Leif curiously, as if he were a dog walking on his hind legs. After a moment, the stranger said something back to him. Leif frowned.

"It isn't English," Leif said, "but it's similar. It might be Friesian, or some dialect of Saxon."

"Can you talk to him or not?"

Leif spoke another series of halting words to the stranger. The stranger responded, speaking very slowly. He gestured toward the sky. He said a few more words, patting his chest with his fingertips.

"He says..." Leif started. "That is, I think he is saying that he comes from a place very far away. He calls himself Gabe."

"Good," Gunnar said. "Tell him my name. And ask him what this thing is." He gestured to the craft. "Ask him where he was going, and why it fell to the ground."

Another slow, halting exchange followed.

"He calls it a 'sky ship,'" Leif said. "His people are at war. Their ship was damaged in a fight. A battle."

"Then there are other ships like this one?"

Gabe seemed to understand what he was asking. He replied, and Leif translated. "He says there are others, but they are very far away. I think he means to say that they are not a threat to us."

"What about the enemy who damaged his ship? Could they not have followed?"

Leif and Gabe engaged in another halting exchange.

"The enemy ship fell into the sea. His ship is the only one in this area."

"Are there others inside the craft?"

Leif pointed at the craft and spoke several more words.

Gabe shook his head.

"He is alone?" Gunnar said.

"He claims to be," Leif said. "Or he doesn't want to answer the question. I can't be sure which."

"There are others inside," Gunnar said. "Count on that. Ask him what he intends to do now."

Leif spoke again, and Gabe replied, motioning at the panels at Leif's feet.

"He says he wants to… add these pieces to his ship?" Leif said uncertainly.

Gabe shook his head and spoke again. He gestured at other pieces of the ship that had fallen to the snow around them.

"Repair," Gunnar said. "He wants to repair his ship. Ask him how long it will take."

Leif spoke again, and Gabe laughed. He said something and then pointed at the sun.

"A long time he, said. He spoke the word for moon."

"Months," Gunnar said. "Maybe years. Tell him this land belongs to King Harald. If he wishes to stay here to repair his ship, he will have to request an audience with Harald directly."

Leif translated as best he could. Gabe shook his head.

"What's that?" Gunnar said. "He's refusing to ask for permission?"

Leif spoke again, and Gabe replied curtly. He patted his weapon as he did so. Leif did not need to translate.

"I tire of this," Gunnar said. "Tell him he has no choice. This land and everything on it is the property of King Harald. He can come with us to plead his case before the king or he can die."

Leif translated as best he could. Gabe seemed to understand, but he merely shrugged and patted his weapon again.

"Kill him, Ivar," Gunnar said.

Ivar took a step forward, brandishing his sword in front of him. The stranger calmly stood up, holding his weapon before him. A loud bang sounded, like an iron hammer hitting granite, and a tuft of snow exploded between Ivar's feet. Ivar gave a yelp took a step back. The others stared at Gabe in shock.

Gabe said something and patted the weapon again.

"What is that thing?" Ivar said. "I've never seen anything like it."

"He can't kill all of us," Gunnar said, keeping his tone pleasant to disguise the content. "On my mark, we all attack at once. Ready? Now."

The four of them lunged forward. Gunnar's foot came down on a patch of packed snow and slipped, causing him to fall to his knees. As he fell, a deafening boom filled his ears. Steinar, to his right, howled and fell backwards. Another thunderclap and Thorvald dropped his sword and fell forward, clutching his belly. With the third boom, Ivar shrieked and slumped to the ground. The foreigner now had his weapon pointed at Leif, who'd barely had time to draw his hunting knife. It was over before Gunnar could get to his feet. He backed away and sheathed his sword.

The stranger, still composed, said something Gunnar couldn't understand. Gunnar turned to Ivar, who was lying on the ground to his left, softly whimpering. Blood spread rapidly across the snow underneath him. To Gunnar's right, Thorvald and Steinar appeared to be already dead.

"You son of a whore," Gunnar hissed. "You don't know what you've just started." He backed slowly away from Gabe several more steps. Ivar, lying on his back, reached for him and tried to speak. Blood poured from his mouth, and he began to cough uncontrollably. The young man would be dead soon. Gunnar turned and walked away, ignoring Ivar's gasps for breath. Behind him, the stranger's weapon boomed again and Ivar was silent.

"What—what do we do?" Leif asked, walking behind Gunnar.

"Continue to Svelvig," Gunnar said. "If these people want a fight, we will give it to them."

CHAPTER FOURTEEN

"A re they gone?" asked Reyes's voice in Gabe's ear. She was still inside the lander. Gabe had left his comm channel open so she could listen in.

"For now," Gabe said quietly.

"You let some of them go."

"You expected me to hunt them down and execute them?"

"They'll be back in larger numbers."

"More will be coming either way. If they think we can't be reasoned with, they have nothing to lose."

"Understood. Thanks, Gabe. Let's hope we've at least bought some time."

"How are your patients?"

"O'Brien's sleeping. Slater's got a killer headache but seems okay otherwise."

"Welcome to the club," Gabe said. His head hadn't stopped pounding since the crash, and firing several shots from his pistol hadn't helped any. He sighed and wondered if he should do something about the three corpses lying in the snow in front of him. He decided against it, as he was the only line of defense between these barbarians and the lander. He couldn't afford the distraction. At least the cold air would keep them from rotting for a while.

Notwithstanding his pounding head and the three dead Vikings at his feet, Gabe felt good. The lander was probably irreparably damaged, and they were all eventually going to be killed by psychopaths with spears, but he was rather enjoying the fresh air and the view of the mountains. The air was cold on his face and hands, but—thanks to the temperature-regulating flight suit—he was comfortable. The sky was a deep blue and the sun was had just passed its zenith in the southern sky. *Earth*, he thought. They had made it to Earth. And not the burned-out husk of a planet that remained after the Cho-ta'an bombardment, but the Earth of the old vids and stories. If Reyes wanted to kid herself that they were still getting off this planet, that was her choice. Gabe intended to enjoy what time he had left.

He got to his feet, stretching and filling his lungs with the crisp, clean air. Following the path in the snow he'd made before Harald's men showed up, he made a wide circuit around the lander. Tactically speaking, the lander's position wasn't bad. There was nothing around them but snow in every direction for several hundred meters. On three sides, the plain was hemmed in by forest; to the west were mountains. The snow provided plenty of warning; he had heard Harald's men coming a hundred meters off.

King Harald, Gabe thought. That would be Harald Fairhair, although he probably wasn't known by that name yet. The lander's data banks contained terabytes of information, including thousands of Earth history books, but everything was still offline. Reyes had been working on getting the systems back online since the crash, but without any success. Her priority, though, was to get the external cameras working and maybe rig some kind of alarm system that would allow them to get some sleep. So far the lander remained essentially an inert hunk of metal.

Having completed his circuit of the lander, Gabe sat down again on the storage crate he'd been using as a chair. He stared at the wispy clouds veiling the mountains and wracked his brain for details about Harald Fairhair. Gabe knew quite a bit more about Earth history than the average person, but most of his knowledge of Harald could have been gleaned from his conversation with Gunnar's men: Harald was a Viking chieftain who, through a series of conquests, became the first king of Norway. As Gabe recalled, he was succeeded by his two sons, Eric Bloodaxe and Hakon the Good. More than that, he couldn't say. So much for his knowledge of history giving him an advantage in dealing with the natives. The average ten-year-old probably knew more about politics in the region than he did.

Gabe had never had much use for politics anyway. In his mind, there wasn't much difference between the Human Colonization Consortium carving up worlds for their political cronies and Vikings dividing the spoils of battle. Humanity hadn't really changed in thirteen hundred years; the only real difference was the scale of conquest. For a short while between the American Revolution and the colonization of space, there had been reason to hope that ideals had triumphed over tribalism, but that delusion had evaporated upon contact with the Cho-ta'an. For the past eighty years, most of humanity had lived under a de facto military dictatorship—a mostly benevolent dictatorship, to be sure, but a dictatorship nonetheless. The Interstellar Defense League was the only political power that mattered, and it was no more democratic than its parent organization, the HCC. When Earth was destroyed, democracy went with it.

It turned out that for all its virtues, Western Civilization was too fragile to be transplanted. Western ideals survived in some attenuated form, like vines clinging to a stone wall, hoping for an errant ray of sunlight, but all the great Western democracies had died. Some, like the Republic of Germany, existed as quasi-feudal mockeries of their former selves; others, like the United States, collapsed into a thousand competing factions. China and Japan lived on as nation-states, having come to understandings with the HCC that allowed them to create ethnically homogenous zones on several newly colonized planets. Several quasi-sovereign groups of Muslims also survived, the largest of which, the Interstellar Islamic Caliphate, was spread across seven worlds. New Jerusalem, constructed in orbit around Geneva, housed some three hundred thousand people of Jewish descent; it was the largest structure ever built by humans.

For all their differences, though, all these groups—the IIC, the Chinese, the Jewish state, as well as all the big interstellar corporations— were members of the Interstellar Defense League. The IDL's power was not absolute, and its members often fought among themselves, but the ever-present threat of the Cho-ta'an meant that the IDL always held the trump card. All other interests were secondary to preventing humanity's destruction. For the most part, the IDL played this card judiciously, but members of the Security Council were not above using the threat of Cho-ta'an attack to indulge their own grievances.

Having been born into such a universe, Gabe never felt like he had any other choice but to fight. He signed up for the IDL's Surface Attack Force, commonly known as the Space Marines, on his eighteenth birthday, and spent most of the next ten years on extremely dangerous assignments dreamed up by someone in the IDL brass who may or may not have been motivated by a desire to save the human race. Even when the motives of the operation were pure, the odds were fifty-fifty that the person who had dreamed it up was a paper-pusher who had no understanding of conditions on the ground, and on the off-chance the operation's architect was both competent and of pure motive, he still didn't give a rat's ass whether Gabe lived or died. Marines were expendable, by definition.

There was less political bullshit in the Exploratory Division, but it had its own problems. If he were perfectly honest, the whole division seemed like a waste of resources to him: the Cho-ta'an were never going to stop hunting them, no matter how far they ran. Any ship that was off looking for habitable planets was a ship that wasn't directly involved in the effort to push back the Cho-ta'an. But that too was a decision that had been made far over Gabe's head. He'd done his part for the war effort; it was time for something different. *Andrea Luhman* was his first assignment in ED. And whatever else could be said for his current predicament, it certainly was different.

Reyes cursed in his ear.

Gabe tapped Reyes's icon on his cuff. "What's up, Chief?"

"Everything is fried. I may never get the electronics back online."

"Can we get power at least? We're going to need life support soon."

"We've got a charge in the batteries, but they'll run down quickly if I can't get the reactor back online."

"Any chance of that?"

"Sure, but without the regulating software running, the safety override will shut it down after ten minutes. Then it'll be locked down for six hours. Hard to generate much power that way."

"I guess I don't want to know what happens if you disable the override?"

"Meltdown," Reyes replied. "The heat alone would be enough to vaporize the lander. But that's not the worst of it. We're carrying about twenty thousand liters of liquid hydrogen, and another ten thousand of oxygen. If the reactor melts down, we're looking at an explosion the size of a tactical nuke."

Gabe nodded. He knew the basic principle of how the reactor worked. Supposedly the reactor recreated conditions that occurred naturally only at the edges of a black hole in order to stimulate proton emission. The reactor could be used to bring about nuclear fission for power generation, but it also served another purpose: the lander's relatively small fuel tanks didn't carry enough fuel for it to break free from the gravity of a planet the size of Earth, requiring the lander to literally create its fuel as it went. On a planet like Earth, the lander could simply suck water vapor out of the air and split it into hydrogen and oxygen, but on many planets there wasn't enough water or free hydrogen for that. In such cases, the lander could take in another gas—carbon dioxide or methane, for example—and transmute its atoms into hydrogen and oxygen. After launch, it would skim the top of the atmosphere until its fuel tanks were full and then use the stored fuel to break orbit. Thanks to the proton reactor, the lander could take off from virtually any planet, given at least a trace atmosphere.

"All right," Gabe said. "No reactor. We conserve power. That means no heat. What about the portable transmitter?"

"It works, but we won't have line-of-sight again with *Andrea Luhman* until tomorrow morning. By then, they'll be out of range. And will be for the next six weeks."

"Copy that," Gabe said. He had figured as much. He wondered how much longer Reyes could sustain this delusion that they were still getting off Earth. To Gabe it had been clear since those first railgun shells hit the lander that they were going to be stuck here. But then, he hadn't bought the theory that they had traveled back in time thirteen hundred years either, and here they were.

He hoped Reyes came around soon. The sooner she accepted the fact that they weren't getting off Earth, the sooner they'd be able to get started on the business of survival. Their knowledge of history might not help them much, but their knowledge of science and technology certainly could—to say nothing of their possession of the most valuable artifact on the planet. In raw materials alone, the lander was worth a fortune. The trick was going to be holding onto it—or at least getting something in return for giving it up.

If he knew Reyes, though, she wasn't going to give up anytime soon. She'd most likely be working on getting the lander's systems back online all night, which meant that Gabe was on guard duty for the foreseeable future. Fortunately he had a pocketful of stimulants. Eventually, though, he'd need to sleep, and Slater or Reyes would have to take over.

It was late afternoon when he once again heard the crunching of snow in the distance. He got up and scrambled on top of the lander to get a look. This time it was about a dozen men, arriving on foot. They were coming from the south, as the others had. Gabe slid down the side of the lander and strolled around to greet them.

As they came closer, he saw that they were dressed more plainly than Harald's men, wearing ragged fur coats rather than neatly tailored wool clothing. Several of them were armed with axes and spears, but only the man in the lead had a sword on his belt. They wore leather helmets and had round wooden shields strapped to their backs. The lack of uniform attire gave Gabe hope: perhaps this was a rival faction to Harald's men. If they could play the two groups off each other, they'd have a better chance of getting out of this alive.

The man with the sword, who was burly and had long brown hair flecked with gray, waved as the group approached. Gabe waved with his right hand, still holding the pistol in his left. He stood his ground, wondering how many of them he could take out before he ran out of ammo or was impaled by one of those spears.

The man with the sword stopped a few meters in front of him, and the others remained a few paces back, regarding him curiously. Their eyes flitted back and forth between him, his gun, and the lander.

The man in front said something that Gabe couldn't decipher.

"Sorry, friend," Gabe said. "I don't speak Old Norse. Or New Norse, for that matter. I don't suppose you speak any English?"

"Sprecest þū Englisc?" the man said.

"More or less," Gabe replied. If the Norseman spoke English, it would be what people of Gabe's time called Old English. It was closer to German than the English Gabe spoke. Still, he had managed to communicate rudimentary facts to Gunnar's man—for all the good it did either of them.

The man spoke again in the same language.

"Slow," Gabe said, holding up his hand. He knew a fair amount of German, but even with that advantage it was going to be tough going. He had a pretty good idea what the man was asking, but he might as well establish right now that they were going to have to take it slow. He also wanted the option of pretending he didn't understand what the Norsemen were saying.

The man repeated the question, more slowly.

"My name is Gabe," he said, tapping his chest. He pointed to the lander. "That is my ship. It flies through the sky. The ship had a problem and it fell to the ground."

"Ic beo Sigurd," the man said. "Bist þū wunde?"

Gabe stared at Sigurd, not understanding. Sigurd raised his finger to his cheek.

Puzzled, Gabe did the same. When he pulled his hand away, he saw flecks of blood. He shook his head. "No, it is not my blood. Men attacked me. I killed some of them." He held up his gun to let them know that wasn't averse to killing to protect their ship. Besides, it's not like he could hide the three corpses lying in the snow on the other side of the lander.

The man said something else, only one word of which Gabe understood.

"Did you say Gunnar?"

Sigurd nodded. "Harald."

"Yes, Harald's men. They came from that direction."

Sigurd asked him a question that Gabe didn't understand. Having just gone through this with Harald's men, he took a shot at answering it. "My people are at war. I was looking for a new place for our people to settle. Our enemies found us. There was a fight. My ship was damaged. It fell to the ground." That ought to cover it, Gabe thought.

An older man with a thick auburn-and-gray beard said something to Sigurd in what Gabe assumed was Norse. The man had a tough, weathered look to him. Gabe noted that he was missing the two smaller fingers on his left hand. Sigurd replied to him in a curt but genial tone. The two conversed for some time, and then Sigurd turned back to Gabe. He said something, pointing to the lander. Gabe realized he was asking for permission to approach the ship.

Gabe thought for a moment. If the crew was going to survive more than a few days in this place, they needed allies. This group seemed like a better bet than the last one. "Yes," Gabe he said at last. "Just you."

Sigurd pointed to the older man he'd been speaking to.

"Fine, him too. The rest of them wait here." He held up his hand as if barring the rest of the group.

Sigurd nodded. He turned to the group and spoke briefly to them. The others didn't seem happy with this development, but no one protested. One strapping young man asked Sigurd a tentative question, but Sigurd shook his head. Sigurd then put his hand on the lad's shoulder and gave it a squeeze before turning to face Gabe again. Was this young man Sigurd's son? There was definitely a likeness. Gabe counted fourteen men altogether, including Sigurd and his friend. They wore layered wool clothing and ranged widely in age. Sigurd's son, if that's who he was, appeared to be the youngest. Sigurd's friend, who must have been around sixty, looked to be the oldest.

"After you," Gabe said, motioning for the two Norsemen to lead the way.

Sigurd nodded and walked past him. If he feared the strangely dressed man who had fallen from the sky, he didn't show it. The second man paused briefly before Gabe and patted his chest. "Arnulf," he said.

Gabe nodded. "Arnulf," he repeated. The man smiled and walked after Sigurd. He too showed no fear. So different from Harald's man, Gunnar, whose fear Gabe had sensed immediately. It hadn't surprised him when Gunnar ordered his men to attack, nor when Gunnar "slipped" on the snow, allowing the others to die in his place. Gunnar had the air of a man whose self-regard rested on his position in a social hierarchy. Sigurd and Arnulf seemed like men who took responsibility for their own fates. Whatever authority either of them had over the others seemed to arise from mutual consent.

The three of them rounded the tail of the lander. The two men didn't pause when they saw the three corpses. Sigurd walked to the one called Ivar and kneeling down next to him. He muttered something Gabe didn't catch, but the tone was clear. It echoed his own thoughts: *he was just a kid.*

"I had no choice," Gabe said. "They were trying to take my ship."

Sigurd stood up and faced Gabe. He asked a question, and Gabe readied himself to explain what had happened. But then he saw that Sigurd's eyes were on the gun on his belt. Sigurd wasn't questioning Gabe's motives; he was curious about his methods.

"Yes, I used this," Gabe said, drawing the weapon. "Gun."

"Gun," Sigurd said.

"Figures that would be the first English word you learn," Gabe said. He pointed the pistol at one of the dead men and pantomimed the kickback from firing. Sigurd seemed puzzled.

Gabe was going to take another stab at explaining when he heard a faint noise from inside the lander. Sigurd turned his head. It was clear he'd heard it too. He spoke a brief question.

"Yes," Gabe said, holding up three fingers. "Three more." He supposed there wasn't much point in lying about the number of crew members at this point.

Sigurd asked another question. When Gabe didn't reply, he pointed to his own face and then to Gabe's.

"No," Gabe said. "Not injured. Just hiding." Better for these men to think they were at full strength for now.

Sigurd said something else, motioning toward his mouth.

"No. Thank you. We have food."

A more complicated question followed. After some back and forth, Gabe determined that Sigurd was asking what the crew's plans were.

"We do not intend to stay here. We will repair our ship and continue on our way." As he said it, he realized he was unconsciously making his speech more formal in an attempt to be clear. But this was counterproductive: words like *intend* and *repair* were probably unfamiliar to these people, as they had Latin roots. He tried again. "We will not stay here. We will fix our ship and go away." Gabe knew the odds of them getting the ship airborne were slim, but there was no point in complicating matters.

This time, Sigurd seemed to get the gist of it. He shook his head and spoke in an ominous tone. Gabe caught the name "Gunnar." Sigurd made a motion with both of his hands like groups of men converging on a point.

"I know," Gabe said. "They'll be back. We have to stay to protect our ship."

Sigurd shook his head.

Gabe shrugged. "We have no choice."

CHAPTER FIFTEEN

Sigurd turned to Arnulf. "They are going to stay with their ship," he said.

"Then they are fools," Arnulf replied.

"Fools who killed three of Harald's best men."

Arnulf shrugged. "This is not our fight."

"Weren't you just bemoaning our lack of allies? Harald will want this ship. If Gunnar has gone to him with news of what happened here, Harald will soon send many more men to claim it."

"And we will be home in our beds."

"Don't you see, Arnulf? These people have forced Harald's hand. He will not expect us to help the foreigners, and he will not have time to assemble his full force in any case. If we fight alongside these people now, we could deliver a defeat to Harald such that he will think twice about sending men to Haavaldsrud again."

"We know nothing of these people."

"We know they have weapons capable of doing this." He gestured again to the three men. "Look at this ship. It's like nothing we've ever seen. You've heard the stories of the powerful weapons once used by those in the East. Perhaps that is where these people are from."

"We don't know where they are from. We don't know anything about them. We can't even speak their language!"

"I cannot force you to fight, but I intend to stay and wait for Harald's men."

"I suggest a compromise," Arnulf said after a moment, a mischievous grin playing on his lips. "We kill them and take their ship and weapons."

Sigurd laughed. "Go ahead and try. I'm curious to see how that weapon works."

Arnulf sighed. "Well, if you're going to stay, then I suppose I will have to keep you from getting yourself killed."

Sigurd grinned. He turned back to the man who called himself Gabe and pointed behind the lander. "We need a moment to speak with the others."

Gabe nodded, a slightly puzzled expression on his face.

Sigurd and Arnulf walked back to the group. "What is happening?" Jannik asked as he approached. Jannik seemed annoyed to be left out of the discussion.

"The crew of this ship are explorers. They were fleeing from an enemy. Gunnar and his men must have seen the ship crash. They tried to take the ship, but the foreigners fought back and killed three of Harald's men. Gunnar and one other escaped."

"Harald will send more men soon," said Jannik.

"Yes," Sigurd replied. "And Arnulf and I intend to help the foreigners defeat them."

Several men spoke at once. Some were confused or skeptical; a few seemed game for any chance to kill some of Harald's men.

"We volunteered to investigate the thing that fell from the sky," Jannik said. "Not to start a war with Harald."

"We're at war with Harald whether we like or not," Arnulf said. "I voted against this war, but now that we're in it, I intend to win."

"Arnulf is right," said a tall, young man named Brynjarr. "We knew when we voted that we would have to fight Harald eventually." Brynjarr's brother, Agnar, nodded.

"How is helping these foreigners part of our war?" another man, named Vilmar, asked.

Sigurd made his case again: by allying with the foreigners, they could surprise Harald, striking a blow against him before he was ready. This would at least delay Harald's attempts to take the valley by force, and might dissuade him of the idea altogether. In the end, only four men opted to return home.

"There is no shame in leaving," Sigurd assured them. "As Jannik said, this is not what we came here to do, and we should not leave the valley unprotected for much longer. Yngvi, you'll have to go back."

"But Father, I want to stay and fight!"

"I know, son. But it is important for some able men to return to protect the valley. If some of us don't return soon, the women will start to worry."

"Yes, Father," Yngvi answered glumly.

"Who else is going back?" Sigurd said.

"I've got cows to milk," said Vilmar. Two others, in addition to Jannik, said they would be going back.

"Good," said Sigurd. "That leaves us with a decent fighting force. Go now then. I expect to be able to send word of our victory by tomorrow morning."

"May the gods be with you," Jannik said coldly.

Sigurd grunted thanks and embraced Yngvi. "I will see you soon."

Yngvi nodded and joined the others, who were already making their way back to the woods.

*****

"Did you get any of that, Reyes?" Gabe asked in her ear.

"Some," Reyes said, lying on her back in the cockpit, staring up at a mass of scorched circuitry. Slater sat quietly in the seat nearby. O'Brien was still asleep in the back. "I gather they're not fans of this Harald character."

"I'd say that's a fair assessment."

"Do you trust them?"

"Not sure yet. I think they might be plotting to kill us right now."

"All right," she said, sitting up. "I'm coming out."

"Did you hear what I just said?"

She stood up, grabbing the pistol from the seat where she had left it. "Yeah. Sounds like you could use some help. Besides, I'm going stir crazy in here." She hadn't left the lander since the crash. "Be right back," she said as she walked past Slater. Slater nodded slightly. She looked exhausted, but Reyes had told her to stay awake for a few hours in case she had a concussion. Reyes went to the hatch and cranked the latch. She pushed the door open and climbed out, blinking in the bright light.

"You know how to use that?" Gabe asked, raising his eyebrow at the gun in her hand.

"I'm an engineer, Gabe. Not a baboon."

"I'm just trying to avoid getting shot in the back."

As he said this, Sigurd came around the tail again. He started at the sight of Reyes.

"This is Reyes," Gabe said. "She's actually in charge of this expedition."

"In-charge?" asked Sigurd.

"She's our chief. Our *jarl*," he added, remembering the word from which the English got the title *earl*.

"Sigurd," said Sigurd, patting his chest. He reached out and clasped Reyes's hand.

He said something, patted the hilt of his sword, and then gestured toward the others.

"That didn't seem like a threat," Reyes said.

"No. I think he's offering to help us against Harald's men."

"Why?"

"You may have noticed I don't speak Norse any better than you do."

She scowled at Gabe and turned back to Sigurd. "You are offering to help us?"

Sigurd nodded. "Help."

"Why would you help us?"

"Harald, enemy," said Sigurd, using the word Gabe had used when referring to the Cho-ta'an.

"That may be the most thorough explanation we're going to get," Gabe said.

Reyes nodded and smiled at Sigurd, holding out her hand. "We accept."

"Just like that, huh?" Gabe asked.

"You said it yourself. Holding off a Viking horde with a railgun is not a long-term strategy. We need help."

Sigurd shook her hand and smiled back. He pointed at the lander and asked a question, holding up four fingers.

"Yes, there are two more. They are...injured. Hurt."

Sigurd glanced at Gabe, who met his eyes but did not respond. Sigurd could hardly blame him for lying about crew members being injured.

Sigurd asked another question, pointing again at the lander. When Reyes didn't reply, he took a step forward.

"He wants to take a look inside," Gabe said.

"Yeah, I got that, thanks."

"You're thinking of letting him?"

"If we're going to fight with these people, we're putting our lives in their hands. What's the point of half-measures?"

Gabe nodded, ceding to her judgment.

"Just you," Reyes said to Sigurd. She pointed to his weapon. "Leave your sword here."

Sigurd seemed to understand. He unstrapped the scabbard and lay it on top of one of the insulation panels Harald's man had left on the snow.

"You stay out here, Gabe," Reyes said.

"Yes, ma'am," Gabe replied. He stepped away from the lander, holding his gun in front of him.

Reyes pulled the hatch open. "Slater, you awake?"

Slater mumbled something in response.

"We've got a visitor. He's a, um, Viking."

Slater's response was unintelligible.

"After you," Reyes said to Sigurd.

Sigurd nodded and ducked down to enter the craft. He moved slowly, taking everything in with wonderment in his eyes, dried foam pellets crunching under his feet. Reyes followed closely behind him. She had to stifle a laugh at his reaction to the interior of the lander: he seemed as amazed at the upholstery as any of the twenty-third century technology.

"O'Brien," Reyes said, pointing to the sandy-haired man asleep under a blanket in the rear of the lander. She patted her side with her left hand. "Hurt."

Sigurd nodded.

"Slater," she said, pointing to the chair where Slater sat. "She's the pilot."

"Pilot?" Sigurd asked.

"Driver," Reyes said. "She flies the ship."

Sigurd still didn't seem to understand, so Reyes let it drop. "Hurt," she said, pointing to her head.

Sigurd nodded. He pointed to the gun in her right hand and spoke a question. When she didn't answer, he made a motion like drawing a sword. He pointed at the gun again, and then pointed to O'Brien and Slater.

"Yes," Reyes said. "We have more weapons. Five guns." She held up the fingers of her left hand and then raised the gun in her right. "Five. Guns." In addition to the ones she and Gabe carried, there were three pistols in the arms locker. Exploratory missions weren't exactly well-stocked with weapons by IDL standards, but they'd brought every weapon from *Andrea Luhman* on the lander. The pistols were probably older than the IDL.

"Five guns," Sigurd replied.

Reyes nodded. "Seen enough?" She pointed to the exit.

Sigurd reluctantly left the craft. "O'Brien and Slater," he said. "Magan nāh feohtan." He pointed to Reyes's pistol.

"No, they cannot fight," Reyes said.

"Guns," Sigurd said. He pointed to himself and then gestured in the direction of the others.

Reyes turned to Gabe. "What do you think? Give guns to three men?"

"You want to leave O'Brien and Slater unarmed?"

"They're in no shape to fight. If we're going to trust these guys to help us, we're better off with guns in the hands of people who can use them."

Gabe sighed. "I can't believe we're even talking about this. These men have zero experience with firearms. Even assuming we can trust them, they'd be as likely to shoot one of us as hit one of Harald's men." He turned to Sigurd and pointed to the sun. His finger traced an arc toward the west and then raised the barrel of his gun as if targeting an enemy. "How long?"

Sigurd pointed to the sun as Gabe had, and then traced an arc to the horizon. "Niht," said Sigurd. "Betwix middeneaht and dægrǣd."

"Sounds like he expects them to arrive between midnight and dawn," Gabe said.

"We've got several hours then," Reyes said. "You could train three men to shoot by then, couldn't you?"

"Depends. How much ammo are you willing to waste?"

"If we don't survive the next twenty-four hours, it isn't going to matter how much ammo we have left."

"All right," Gabe said. "I'll see what I can do." He turned to Sigurd. "Three men," he said, holding up three fingers. "Three guns."

"Three men, three guns," Sigurd repeated.

Gabe touched his chest and pointed to the lander. "Guns." He pointed to Sigurd and gestured toward where the group of men still waited. "Men."

Sigurd nodded. He picked up his sword and began to walk away. But then he stopped and turned, pointing to the lander. "O'Brien and Slater. Hurt." He pointed to the southwest and spoke a phrase that meant nothing to them.

Reyes shook her head. "I'm sorry, I don't understand."

Sigurd pointed to the sun. He traced the arc to the west again and then said, "Niht. Cald." He hugged his shoulders and shivered. Then he pointed to the southwest again. A peaceful look came over his face and he let his head fall to the side as if falling asleep.

"He thinks we should take O'Brien and Slater to his village," Gabe said.

"What do you think?"

"I think he's got a point. They can't fight. If we have to run—"

"If we have to run, we're dead. We don't leave the lander, no matter what."

"Still, it's going to be cold. We've got no heat. Can't very well start a fire in the lander. And they're just going to be in the way if you're trying to work on it. Like you said, if we're going to trust these people, there's no point in doing it halfway. Use the resources we have. Get non-essential personnel out of the line of fire."

Reyes thought it over. "All right," she said at last.

"The problem is, I'm not sure we have time." Gabe turned back to Sigurd. "Time," he said, pointing to the sun again. "We need to be here when Harald's men return."

Sigurd nodded. He turned and ran to the tail of the lander. Cupping his hands over his mouth, he shouted something to one of the men. He turned and spoke a few more words they didn't catch. Then he jerked his thumb away from the lander and said, "O'Brien and Slater. Ūt."

"Got it," Gabe said. He turned back to Reyes. "I think he's sending one of his men to go after the group that just left, to get them to take our wounded back to their village. Let's see if we can rig up a stretcher for O'Brien. Maybe one for Slater too."

CHAPTER SIXTEEN

With the help of Sigurd and Arnulf, Gabe and Reyes rigged two stretchers using some of the loose heat shield panels and four poles the Norsemen cut from saplings at the edge of the forest, securing them with some carbon fiber cord from the lander's supplies. Gabe smiled as the Norsemen marveled at the cord, amazed that the foreigners would use it for such a mundane purpose. Slater protested that she didn't need the stretcher, but Reyes insisted. Gabe agreed: the more rest she got, the sooner she'd be back at a hundred percent.

By the time they were done, the men who had started back to the village had returned. Sigurd explained the situation to them, and they agreed to carry the two injured foreigners back to the village. Meanwhile, the men who had chosen to stay and fight were busy with other work. Their first task had been to drag the three corpses into the woods; now they were busy cutting more saplings down with their axes. Two piles of logs had already begun to grow, one at the front of the lander and one near the tail. The man called Arnulf had taken charge of constructing a defensive perimeter around the lander.

"And I don't get any say about being sent to a primitive Viking village?" Slater asked, peering out of the lander. She squinted as if the bright light hurt her eyes.

"None," Reyes said. "Sorry, Slater, you're no good to us in your present condition. Get some rest and we'll regroup after this scuffle is over." Reyes didn't want to say it, but Slater wouldn't be of much use even if she weren't injured. She had no hand-to-hand training and Reyes doubted she'd ever fired a gun.

"Scuffle, huh?" Slater said, eyeing Sigurd and the other Norsemen standing outside the lander. "That sounds optimistic."

"They're bronze age people," Reyes said. "They don't even have forged steel weapons. I'll take my chances on Gabe and twenty-third century tactics. Not to mention the railgun."

"You're gonna make me blush, Reyes," Gabe said. "Okay, Slater, get over here." Sigurd motioned for the two Norsemen standing by to take their positions at the stretcher. Slater complied, stepping lightly though the snow, with Reyes guiding her by the arm. She lay down on the stretcher and the two men hoisted her to waist level. The man in front was Yngvi, the one Gabe had thought looked so much like Sigurd. The other one was called Erland.

While Reyes spread a blanket over Slater, Gabe looked up to see O'Brien outside the hatch, leaning against the side of the ship. Reyes had removed the top of his flight suit and wrapped his ribcage with a thick bandage. A blanket was draped over his shoulders.

"Whoa," Gabe said, moving toward him. "Take it easy, man."

"I... ugh... suppose that other stretcher is for me?" O'Brien asked, his face contorted with pain.

"Latest model," Gabe said. "Come on, I'll help you over." He took O'Brien's arm and helped him walk to the stretcher. O'Brien lay down, wincing and biting his lip.

As Gabe tended to O'Brien, the man Sigurd had called Jannik came around the tail of the lander, looking irritated. He barked a question at Sigurd. Sigurd said something to Jannik in a chiding tone, and Jannik replied tersely. Then Jannik turned and walked away, disappearing around the tail of the lander.

"What's up with that guy?" Gabe asked, looking at Sigurd.

Sigurd seemed to get the gist of the question. He motioned in Jannik's direction, shaking his head and muttered a string of harsh syllables. Gabe didn't understand the words, but the tone was clear. Clearly there was no love lost between Sigurd and Jannik.

The two men assigned to O'Brien lifted their stretcher. The one in front, whose name was Vilmar, nodded his head toward Sigurd and spoke briefly.

Sigurd nodded back and spoke a brief farewell.

"Thank you," Reyes said, putting her hand on the shoulder of the man at O'Brien's feet. She looked at the others. "All of you. Thank you."

Sigurd spoke a brief phrase to the men. They nodded toward Reyes. The man named Vilmar spoke a few words to Reyes, and Reyes smiled back. She touched O'Brien's shoulder.

"Get some rest," Reyes said. "We'll regroup soon."

"Comm range is eighty klicks over flat ground," Gabe said. "Stay in contact. Let us know when you get there."

O'Brien nodded and smiled weakly. Just getting from the lander to the stretcher had taken a lot out of him.

The two men carrying Slater walked away through the snow. The two with O'Brien followed close behind.

"You sure we can trust these guys?" Reyes asked.

"Oh, you are not putting this on me," Gabe replied, watching the group disappear around the tail of the lander.

"It was your idea to get them out of here."

"It was Sigurd's idea. And it was your idea to trust Sigurd."

Sigurd's eyebrow arched as Gabe said his name. Gabe smiled in an attempt to reassure him.

"I'm still blaming you if this goes horribly wrong," Reyes muttered.

"I think we passed 'horribly wrong' when we crash-landed in fucking Norway during the Middle Ages."

Sigurd gave a whistle and began walking toward two men carrying a log to the pile at the rear of the lander. The men looked up and Sigurd waved at them to come over.

"How far do you think it is?" Reyes asked.

"To the village? Gotta be ten klicks at least. Sigurd said they left there around mid-morning."

"Five people are going to carry two of ours ten klicks across rough terrain?" Reyes asked.

"Make it four people," Gabe replied. "That Jannik guy didn't seem very helpful. You saw those guys, though. They're tough. That kid can't be older than seventeen and he looks like he could wrestle a bear."

Reyes nodded. "Let's just hope he doesn't have to wrestle anything for the next few hours."

The two men Sigurd had summoned approached. They were both lean and tall, and looked to be in their twenties. They stopped in front of Sigurd and Sigurd spoke briefly to them. They nodded. Sigurd turned back to Gabe. "Agnar," he said, pointing to the young blond man on Gabe's right. He pointed to the other man. "Brynjarr." Tall and lean, with thin blond hair, the two looked like brothers.

Gabe spoke his own name and patted his chest. Then he gestured toward Reyes. "Reyes. *Jarl.* She's in charge of this catastrophe."

"Kiss my ass, Gabe," Reyes murmured.

For a moment, Gabe stared at the newcomers, wondering why Sigurd had introduced them.

"Guns," Sigurd said, pointing at the gun holstered at Gabe's hip.

"Oh, our gunmen!" Gabe said, realization suddenly dawning on him.

Sigurd smiled and nodded. "Gunmen."

Gabe spoke his own name, pointing to his chest. "Hold on." He held up a hand and ducked into the lander, returning a few moments later with a large plastic box. He set the box on the ground and flipped the lid open. Inside were the other three pistols and several boxes of ammunition. Gabe picked up one of the guns, holding it before him. "Gun," he said. He nodded to the three men.

"Gun," they repeated.

"Barrel," Gabe said, indicating the barrel.

"Barrel."

This went on for a while, with Gabe identifying the trigger, the sight, the grip, magazines, bullets, and other parts of the guns. Reyes stuck around for the training—whether this was to see what he was teaching the Norsemen or to brush up on her own knowledge Gabe couldn't say. When the Norsemen had learned the basics, Gabe made sure the safeties were on and then handed a gun to each of them, showing them how to hold them without putting their fingers on the trigger. When he was reasonably certain they weren't going to kill themselves, he grabbed a belt and holster from the box. He wrapped it around Agnar's waist and demonstrated how to tighten and secure it, naming the various parts as he did so. Then he took the pistol from Agnar and slipped it into the holster. Agnar's eyes lit up as he saw how the gun fit snugly in the holster. He grabbed the gun, pulled it out of the holster and pointed it at Reyes, whose eyes lit up in terror.

"No!" Gabe snapped, grabbing the gun barrel and pointing at the ground. He'd already been over this, but Agnar had forgotten the rule in his excitement. He pantomimed aiming a gun at Agnar and shook his head. "No," he said again. "Nei. Nein. Never."

"Enemy," Sigurd said.

Gabe nodded. "Enemy," he said, pointing his imaginary gun toward the south, where they expected Harald's men to appear. "Only enemy."

Agnar and Brynjarr nodded soberly.

Gabe reached into the box and got a gun belt and holster for Sigurd and Brynjarr as well. He took their guns while they figured out how to put them on, then handed the guns back to them. They slid the guns into their holsters. The looked like prehistoric bank robbers.

"Good God," Gabe said, smiling weakly at them. "What have I done?"

"You're a born teacher," Reyes said. "It's inspiring."

The three Norsemen regarded them curiously.

"Right," Gabe said. "We need some targets." He pointed to Sigurd and said "One." Then he pointed to Agnar and said "Two." He pointed to Brynjarr and said, "Three. Then he held up three fingers. "Three."

Sigurd nodded. "Three," he said.

Gabe pointed to the stack of logs at the front of the lander. "Three," he said. He pointed to three points on the ground a few meters away, counting off as he did so. "One, two, three."

Sigurd nodded, seeming to understand. He said something to the others and began walking toward the pile. Agnar and Brynjarr followed him.

"Good luck," Reyes said to Gabe, as she turned to head back to the lander.

"You going to oversee the defenses while I'm getting these guys up to speed?"

Reyes stopped, watching as Arnulf barked orders to two men near the tail of the lander. "I think they've got this covered." She looked to Gabe. "Unless you have some suggestions?"

Gabe shook his head. "Looks like they've done this before. Given the technological limitations, we're probably best off trusting the Norsemen's expertise. I'm hoping we can scare these guys off with the guns before the fighting really gets started, but if they come at us in big enough numbers, it's going to come down to a melee. I'm going to go out on a limb and figure that our Viking friends can handle themselves in close combat."

"My thoughts as well," Reyes said. "I'm going to keep working on the lander. We're going to need life support working soon. And if we can't get the data cells back online, we'll never get out of here."

Gabe nodded. *We're never getting out of here anyway*, he thought. The data cells were the least of their problems. Still, getting life support and the data cells back online were worthwhile tasks—assuming they lived through Harald's assault. But there really wasn't much else for Reyes to do.

Reyes walked back to the lander as the three Norsemen approached Gabe, each carrying one of the birch poles. Gabe walked twenty paces away from the lander and pointed to the ground. He dragged his heel in the snow, making a mark. "One." He said. He made a right angle turn to his left and walked three more paces. Dragging his heel again, he said, "Two." He walked three more paces and did it again. "Three."

Sigurd spoke briefly to the other men and they nodded, seeming to understand. Each of them walked to one of the marks and set the pole down on the ground. Gabe suspected the ground was too hard to allow hammering the poles into it, but the snow was deep and dense. The Norsemen came to the same conclusion: they hacked into the snow with their axes and then used the axe heads to shovel it aside. Soon they had excavated three holes, about half a meter deep. They placed the poles in the holes and then filled in the impressions with snow, mounding more snow against the base of the poles to give them additional stability. Glancing toward the lander, Gabe saw the other men were doing more-or-less the same thing: Arnulf was having them create a barrier of sharpened spikes pointed outward from the lander. The poles had been cut to about three meters and sharpened at one end with an axe. The bases of the poles were roughly half a meter apart and five meters from the lander, giving the Norsemen room to maneuver behind the barrier. One man dug holes, another gathered and placed the spikes, and a third packed snow around the base. Most of the rest of the men were still busy cutting saplings, stripping them of branches, cutting them to length, sharpening them, and transporting them to the lander.

Gabe regarded the work of the three aspiring gunmen before him. He grabbed one of the poles and tried to shake it. It held firm. He began walking back toward the lander, motioning for the men to follow him. He stopped about twenty meters from the poles. Ideally his gunners would have an effective range of more than twenty meters, but he was going to be happy if these men could put the fear of God into Harald's men and avoid accidentally shooting their own. If they actually hit a few of the enemy, that would be a bonus.

Gabe was pleasantly surprised by the Norsemen's marksmanship. Once they got over the shock of the noise and recoil, they were able to hit their targets close to half the time. They had good eyesight and hand-eye coordination, and no bad habits to unlearn. The two younger men were better shots than Sigurd, but even Sigurd hit his tree three shots out of ten.

"Good," Gabe said, looking at the chewed-up birch poles. "Very good." Each Norseman had fired twenty-four rounds, replacing their magazines twice, and burning through about a quarter of the lander's ammo supply. They now each had a full magazine, and Gabe handed each of them two spares to tuck into their belts. Gabe would have liked to clean the guns before having to rely on them in combat, but he didn't have time to do it himself or to show the Norsemen how to do it. He'd just have to figure the odds were against any of the guns jamming.

He left the men momentarily to retrieve the portable railgun from the rear of the lander. "Portable" was relative—the gun itself was a little bigger than the standard-issue IDL automatic rifle, but the battery pack weighed thirty kilograms and was the size of a large backpack. It had a handle and wheels, but the wheels were worthless in the snow. Gabe slung the rifle across his back and dragged the battery pack toward the Norsemen, who watched with interest.

"Railgun," Gabe said, plugging the gun into the battery pack. He flipped a switch on the pack and it began to hum as the compulsator spun up. The compulsator, a basketball-sized unit that sat on top of the battery, acted like a capacitor, gathering energy from the battery and storing it so that it could be released as a high-power output. A thick, high-amperage cable connected the compulsator to the gun mechanism. After a few seconds, the compulsator beeped, indicating it was ready to power the railgun.

Gabe made sure the gun was set to single fire and then raised it to his shoulder. He aimed it at one of the posts and squeezed the trigger. The gun boomed, and the top meter of the post exploded into splinters. The Norsemen gasped and then cheered. He repeated the experiment several more times, with similar results. He turned to see the Norsemen looking at him with awe. He could only imagine what they were thinking. As members of a militaristic culture, they could certainly appreciate such a weapon, but at the same time he wondered if they would consider it unsportsmanlike to cut one's enemies down in such a way. With a weapon like this, anyone could be a great warrior. The men had taken to the pistols well, but the railgun was several times as powerful as the pistols—and they hadn't seen it on full automatic.

The sun was now nearing the horizon, and he could sense that the men were on edge. Agnar and Brynjarr kept looking to the south, where they expected Harald's men to appear. Sigurd seemed less concerned; he was convinced it would take Gunnar several more hours to get a sizeable force in place for an attack. In any case, it would be difficult for Harald's men to sneak up on them: they could see for over a kilometer in every direction, and Sigurd's men were felling logs in the woods to the east. From what Sigurd had told him, he understood that Harald's men would have to cross a bridge southwest of them to get to the lander, so it was unlikely they'd be able to sneak a large contingent of fighters past Sigurd's men. In the growing dark, though, the threat began to seem more real: he and Reyes were stranded on an alien planet with limited ammo, relying on allies they'd just met to hold off an attack by a force that could number in the hundreds. He could only hope Harald's men didn't have the wherewithal to conduct an extended siege: thanks to the copious snow, water wouldn't be a problem for either side, but the food in the lander wouldn't last more than a week.

Gabe heard footsteps behind him and turned to see Arnulf approaching. Arnulf stopped, shouted something to Sigurd, and then made a beckoning gesture.

Gabe met Sigurd's eyes and nodded. "All right, everybody behind the barrier. Holster your guns."

The men complied, making their way back to the lander. The men who had been working in the woods had returned and had begun to congregate near the hatch. Gabe slung the railgun over his back and dragged the battery pack across the snow and through a gap in the spike barrier. The ring was nearly complete; only one gap of about three meters remained near the lander's tail. Gabe was setting the railgun down next to the lander when Slater's voice crackled in his ear.

"Say again, Slater?" Gabe said, pressing his hand to his ear and walking toward the nose of the lander. Several men shot concerned glances in his direction.

"I said we made it to the village," Slater replied. "Well, it's an exaggeration to call it a village. More like a collection of houses scattered across a valley floor. But it seems safe enough."

"They're treating you okay?"

"Yeah. Better than okay. I tried to walk part of the way, but they wouldn't let me. They carried me and O'Brien the whole way. We're staying in a longhouse with a farmer and his wife. The food is going to take some getting used to, but we're comfortable enough."

Reyes broke in: "How's O'Brien?"

"About the same. Can't get up without a struggle. He's been taking meds to manage the pain."

"Well, at least he's no worse," Reyes said.

"How are things there?" Slater asked.

"Oh, you know," Gabe replied. "Just preparing for the big Viking battle."

"We're good, Slater," Reyes said. "You guys should get some rest. We'll connect again tomorrow morning."

"Copy that. Slater out."

Gabe turned and headed back toward the group near the hatch. About halfway between the spike barrier and the hatch, a lanky man with wispy blond hair and a sparse beard was working on building a fire. A stack of logs rested to one side, and he was striking a piece of metal against a flint rock, scattering sparks toward a pile of shredded birch bark. Gabe walked over to him, pulling a lighter from his pocket. He touched the man on the shoulder. When the man looked up, Gabe tapped a button with his thumb and a flame flickered to life at the top of the lighter. Several of those nearby gasped in awe. "Take it," Gabe said, taking his hand off the button and holding the lighter in his palm.

The man took the lighter and, after turning it over a few times in his hand, gingerly pressed the button as Gabe had. When a flame sprung from it, he was so startled that he dropped it, and those standing around burst into laughter. He cursed at them, picked up the lighter and tried again. This time he slowly moved the flame toward the shreds of bark. The flame caught after a few seconds, and soon the pile of bark was ablaze. The man standing nearby mumbled their approval. The man held the lighter up to Gabe.

"Keep it," Gabe said. "You're our fireman from now on." Gabe had another lighter, and the other spacemen each had one as well.

"Braggi," the man said, getting to his feet and patting his chest.

"Gabe," said Gabe, gesturing to himself. He pointed to Braggi. "Fire man."

Braggi gave him a puzzled look.

Gabe pointed to the fire and said, "Fire." Then he pointed to Braggi. "Man. Fireman."

"Fireman," Braggi said, grinning a mouthful of rotten teeth. He started placing logs on the fire.

CHAPTER SEVENTEEN

I t was evening by the time Gunnar and Leif reached the fortress at Svelvig. The fortress was a massive square building constructed of pine timbers at the top of a steep cliff. Surrounded by a low stone wall that enclosed the plateau at the top of the cliff, it overlooked a fjord that snaked inland from the sea. The fortress had been built as part of Harald's campaign to secure Vestfold and the area north of the fjord mouth, called the Vingulmark. Lately it rarely housed more than thirty fighting men, but now that Vestfold had largely been pacified, Harald had been consolidating his troops there. It was rumored that Harald intended to put down any resistance in the valley to the north before continuing his campaign to conquer Hordaland and Rogaland in the southwest.

Gunnar wasn't privy to the details of Harald's plan, but his own mission gave credence to the notion: his nominal goal was to inform the valley's residents of Harald's claims to their land, but he'd also been tasked with gathering data on the number of fighting men in each community and the disposition of the community leaders toward Harald. The reactions had been decidedly mixed: the valley's denizens were fiercely independent, more so than the people of Hordaland and the other petty kingdoms, who had already accepted the rule of a monarch. But that independent streak would likely be their downfall: they were too scattered and disorganized to mount an effective defense. Gunnar was of the opinion that Harald should strike soon, making an example of Haavaldsrud. Given a strong show of force, the rest of the villages would fold, and Harald would be able to refocus his efforts in the southeast.

Gunnar and Leif were met outside the gate by a sentry, who announced their arrival to those inside. The great wooden gate swung open and they entered the yard. A guard greeted them and escorted them inside the great hall, where a ruddy bald man with a great paunch sat by the fireplace, holding a mug of ale. He beckoned for them to come inside, and the guard returned to his post. Gunnar saw that the fat man's left leg was missing below the knee.

"Welcome, Gunnar Bjornson!" the man cried as they approached. "Forgive me for not getting up." He gestured to his leg. "I am not as spry as I once was."

"No forgiveness needed, Ragnar Ivarsson. Your conquests are known across the lands of the Norsemen. Even Odin himself gave an eye in exchange for wisdom."

"I wish I'd managed such a bargain," Ragnar said. "Please, sit. Alvar, get our guests some ale. Are you hungry?"

"Famished," said Gunnar.

"Get them some meat and bread as well, Alvar. Are there only two of you? I expected a larger party."

"Aye, sir," said Gunnar. "We set out from Trondheim with a party of five men. Leif and I are all that's left."

"You were attacked by men from the valley?"

"They were not from the valley. Did you see the strange craft in the sky this morning?"

"I heard reports of an object in the sky," Ragnar said. "And everyone heard the noise when it passed. You are saying it was a ship?"

"It crashed into the ground not far from here. We detoured to investigate it. I would not believe it if I hadn't seen it myself, but it was a sky ship, made of metal. Leif can confirm this."

Ragnar turned his face to Leif.

"It is as Gunnar says, sir," Leif said. "I spoke to one of the men from the ship. He said he came from a faraway land, pursued by enemies."

"He spoke our language?"

"He spoke something similar to the tongue of the Saxons. I was able to understand some of it. I told him that this was Harald's—"

"He attacked us," Gunnar said. "With a weapon unlike anything I've ever seen. He killed three of our party before we could strike a single blow."

"But you did kill him?"

"If we had pressed our attack, we would have died as well," Gunnar said. "Neither of us fears dying in battle, but if he'd killed us, we'd have been unable to report to you. The ship would likely fall into the hands of the residents of the valley."

Ragnar regarded him dubiously. "What is your concern with this ship?"

"Sir?" Gunnar said.

"You were instructed to gather information about the communities in the valley, were you not? Why did you not stick to your task?"

Gunnar was momentarily speechless. Leif answered, "Sir, we thought the sky ship might be of strategic importance in the valley. The metal alone…"

"You don't need to lecture me on the value of steel, boy," Ragnar snapped. "I'll send men to investigate this sky ship at the first opportunity. But enough of that. What is the disposition of the valley? Will they accept Harald as king?"

Gunnar struggled a moment to reframe his argument. He hadn't expected Ragnar to be so blind to the importance of the foreigner's ship. "They will need some convincing," he said. "Haavaldsrud was hostile; it would make for a good example to the others. But respectfully, sir, our first priority must be seizing that ship."

"I do not understand your obsession with this 'sky ship,' but in any case, our full force has not yet assembled. We are still awaiting sixty men from Sogn. It would be foolish to launch an assault now."

"It is a matter of timing, sir. If the villagers ally themselves with the foreigners…"

"Ally? You said they attacked you, unprovoked. What makes you think they'll make peace with the villagers?"

"I'm only saying we cannot dismiss the possibility. This ship promises unimaginable wealth for the residents of the valley. If they make a united stand with the foreigners against us, we may not be able to defeat them, even with your full force. And that will only embolden the rest of the valley to stand against us. Unless Harald wants to spend the next twenty years suppressing revolts in the valley, we must seize the sky ship now!"

"I am still a young man," Leif said, "but having seen the craft with my own eyes, Gunnar is right. Harald could arm a thousand men with the metal from the sky ship's hull. With that crash, the landscape of the valley has changed."

Ragnar looked from Gunnar to Leif and nodded. "Perhaps I have grown a bit inflexible in my old age. As you say, things have changed, and that requires us to assess our situation anew. How many of these foreigners are there? Given these powerful weapons you spoke of, how many men would we need to defeat them?"

"We saw only one man," Gunnar said. "But he killed three of us as if it was nothing. And I suspect there were more hiding inside the craft."

"How many more? If they all have weapons like the—"

The guard, Alvar, interrupted. "I'm sorry, sir. There is someone else here to see you. A man and his family. He claims to have information for you."

Ragnar scowled. "Who is this man?"

"He calls himself Jannik Ingolfson, sir. He is from Haavaldsrud."

Ragnar glanced at Gunnar, who made no reply.

"Make sure he is unarmed and send him in. We'll see what this Jannik Ingolfson has to say."

*****

Gabe turned to face the men. Arnulf, Sigurd, Agnar and Brynjarr stood nearby, and the other men, having finished their tasks, began to assemble around the fire. There was just one more thing to do. "Wait here," he said to his three gunman. They nodded assent and he went into the lander, rummaging around until he found a pencil and paper. He drew a quick sketch and then went back outside. The sun had dipped below the horizon, but there was enough light for his three gunmen to get a good look at the drawing. Gabe tapped the drawing and then pointed to the top of the lander.

The men looked confused at first, but then Brynjarr seemed to piece it together. He spoke rapidly, tracing his fingers along the lines of the drawing and then pointing at the pile of stripped sapling trunks at the front of the lander. After a moment, the others seemed to get it as well. Sigurd nodded and went to enlist two more men for the task.

"What is it?" Reyes asked, coming out of the hatch.

"A hunting blind," Gabe said. "Well, more accurately, it's a casemate. A place for our guys to shoot from."

"On top of the lander."

"Best visibility. It's only temporary."

Reyes shrugged. "Clearing some twigs from the lander is hardly the biggest barrier to getting it airborne right now. Do what you have to do."

Gabe nodded. He turned to give the men instructions, but they had already started. The design was simple: four low walls of interlocked logs that the men could take cover behind while shooting over (or through). The structure would be rectangular to accommodate the lander's oblong design. It would have no door; they'd have to climb over a wall to get in or out. Insulation panels or shields hung on the outside walls would provide protection from arrows and thrown spears. Gabe debated building a ramp or ladder to make it easier to get to the top of the lander, but ultimately decided against it. Anything they built could be used against them. If it was difficult for their own people to get up and down, it would be even harder for Harald's men to do it under fire.

The gloom of twilight lasted a long time in the high latitude of Norway, but the sky grew dark before the project was completed. Gabe fabricated a torch by dousing a rag in cleaning solvent and wrapping it around the end of one of the birch poles. He stood with it on top of the lander for another hour, shivering with cold as he supervised the completion of the casemate. When the men finally finished, they slid down the side of the lander and Gabe lashed the torch to one of the corners of the casemate. He was sure it could be seen for miles, but that was partly the point: to let Harald's men know they weren't afraid.

Gabe slid down the side of the lander, coming down with a thud on the packed-down snow. Most of the men were standing around the fire. A few sat on logs or storage crates that Reyes had pulled out of the lander. Gabe's stomach growled as he saw that they were eating dried food that they had carried in their packs. Someone had even produced a small keg of beer, and they were passing a horn around, each drinking a full draught in turn. They joked and laughed loudly.

Gabe was about to go into the lander to get his own dinner when Sigurd stepped in front of him, putting his hand on his chest. Gabe stared at him, but Sigurd simply pointed toward the top of the lander. "Fire," he said. Then he pointed toward the darkness beyond the spike barrier.

Gabe sighed and nodded. He'd meant to put a man on this task, but he'd had too much to do to stop and explain it to someone, and then he'd forgotten. He went into the lander and grabbed the container of solvent and a cloth blanket, which he tore into strips. He brought these outside, where he found Sigurd standing next to Braggi, who was holding several birch poles.

"Fire man," Sigurd said, patting Braggi on the back.

Gabe smiled and nodded. He set the container at Braggi's feet and handed him the pile of rags. Sigurd spoke instructions to Braggi, pointing toward the poles that had served as targets earlier. Braggi nodded and then walked off into the darkness. Gabe went into the lander and grabbed a bag of water and two of the prepackaged IDL dinners from their food supply, then joined Sigurd and the rest of the men around the fire. He offered some of his meal to Agnar, who stood on his left, but the young Norseman made a face at the strangely textured vegetable protein wafers. He and the others had been eating bread, nuts and various dried meats from their packs. It didn't look very appetizing, but then, neither did the IDL meals.

In the distance, Braggi was planting torches about twenty meters apart and twenty meters from the spike barrier. He would wrap a rag around one end of the pole, douse it in solvent, light it, and then plant it in the snow. Then he would pace twenty steps and do it again. When he was finished, the torches would illuminate a band roughly forty meters wide just outside the spike barrier.

The men around the fire were now taking turns telling stories. A young hunter named Njáll seemed to be the favorite. He had a pleasant, booming voice with a remarkable range, allowing him to assume the tone and mannerisms of giants, dwarves, witches, gods, and who-knew-what-else. Gabe found himself wishing he could understand the language. The Norsemen were legendary storytellers, but because of their lack of a written language most of their tales were lost to history.

When he'd scarfed down the two meal packets, Gabe sought out Sigurd. Sigurd was listening intently to Njáll's story, which seemed to center around a giant terrorizing a village. Gabe tapped Sigurd on the shoulder and Sigurd stepped away from the fire to face him. Through a series of gestures and generous use of the few English words Sigurd understood, Gabe managed to explain his plan for manning defense points around the lander.

Gabe suggested they post a man at each of the four corners of the lander, just outside the torches. Additionally, one of the five people trained in using guns would need to be stationed in the casemate. Those not on guard duty should try to get some sleep over the next few hours: as many as could would cram into the lander, and the rest would have to sleep outside. As they were expecting Harald's men to arrive some time after midnight, they would try to be close to full force from midnight until dawn. The four men who had taken the first guard duty shift would sleep while the others waited outside, forming a perimeter around the lander. All of the gunners—including Reyes—would then be in the casemate.

Sigurd nodded his head and went to get Arnulf. The two of them spoke briefly and then Arnulf went about selecting the four guards. Gabe found himself fascinated by the way the men cooperated. He'd noticed it already when they were working on their defenses: there was no clear hierarchy, but the Norsemen had no trouble dividing tasks among themselves and working together. Older men were given deference, and Sigurd and Arnulf had almost unquestioned authority—but all the men were clearly acting of their own volition. There were no slaves or enlisted men among the Norsemen. They worked together like brothers.

Gabe's eyes landed on Reyes, who stood across the fire, munching on a food packet and staring at the flames in deep thought. Or maybe she was just tired. Gabe felt like he could sleep for a week. It was hard to believe they'd only been on Earth for a few hours.

Earth. He still couldn't wrap his head around it. They were on Earth. They'd really done it—gone back in time thirteen hundred years to crash land in the womb of humanity. If it weren't for the aching cold in his fingers and the smoke burning his eyes, he might be able to convince himself it was all a dream.

Reyes caught his glance and smiled. Gabe envied her faith, and he wished there was a way he could save it. He wondered if O'Brien and Slater had figured it out yet, that none of them were ever getting off this planet. That humanity was doomed. Twelve hundred and some years from now, a scout ship called *Ubuntu* would come across a Cho-ta'an mining colony, and from that moment on, humanity's doom was sealed. The Cho-ta'an would hunt them to the end of the galaxy.

What a silly, stupid thing to know. The most useless piece of information in the world, and it was indelibly imprinted on Gabe's mind: humanity had just over thirteen hundred years left.

He wondered again if it really was unstoppable. Schumacher had said paradoxes couldn't happen, which meant that humanity couldn't both meet and not meet the Cho-ta'an. Only one of the two could be real, and Gabe knew for a fact it had happened—or would happen. If it hadn't, he wouldn't be here. On the other hand, maybe reality could split. Maybe the lander's crew could set humanity on a different path simply by being here. But how? If they could warn the people of the future somehow… write a message and hide it somewhere it would be discovered in the distant future, a few years before the *Ubuntu* incident. He shook his head. Even if it were theoretically possible, it was a fantasy. They were trapped in a semi-civilized wasteland in northern Europe. It wasn't like he could hide a message in a bottle under a rock. So few artifacts of Norse civilization survived that it had taken until the late twentieth century for archaeologists to piece together the basics of their culture. Hell, they'd left so little mark on North America that nobody had known for sure until the 1960s that the Vikings had been there. No, hiding a note under a rock wasn't going to cut it. If they were going to change the future, they were going to have to go big. Go to Otto I with plans for the steam engine and the Bessemer furnace. Show his advisers the formula for gunpowder and teach them how to make penicillin. Kickstart the industrial revolution seven hundred years early. Then when humanity finally met the Cho-ta'an, they'd be so far ahead technologically that they'd be able to set the terms.

There was, of course, no way to know what sorts of side effects such an action would have on history. Maybe humanity would wipe itself out with nuclear weapons in the fourteenth century. But at least they would have a chance. If they did nothing, humanity had thirteen hundred years left. But first they had to live through the night.

"You should get some sleep," said a voice in his ear. Reyes had crept up on him. "I'll take the first shift in the… what did you call it?"

"Casemate," Gabe said. "We can call it a bunker if you prefer."

"I'll take the first shift in the bunker."

Gabe shook his head. "Those pistols aren't going to be effective at more than thirty meters, and I don't trust any of you with the railgun. I'll be heading up shortly."

"You're going to be up all night?"

"No choice. Try to get some sleep. Come up when you can."

While they spoke, Sigurd was giving instructions to the other men, occasionally pointing to the lander. Gabe had told him how to get the hatch open, and gave him permission to let the men sleep anywhere they could find room.

"Not to stereotype or anything," Reyes said, glancing from the men to the lander, "but…"

"They're Vikings, yeah," Gabe said. "We should probably make sure all the valuables are locked up."

CHAPTER EIGHTEEN

Amazingly, all ten men who weren't on guard duty managed to find a place to sit or lie down inside the lander. Gabe shouldn't have been surprised; he'd seen full-sized replicas of the longboats the Vikings had used to cross the North Sea, and they weren't much bigger than the lander. It wasn't uncommon for groups of settlers headed to Iceland or Greenland to bring *livestock* with them. The lander was crowded and stuffy, but for the Norsemen it was luxuriously warm and comfortable.

Even without livestock, the smell and crowding was too much for Reyes. She'd grabbed as many blankets as she could lay her hands on and climbed up to the bunker to join Gabe. She dozed quietly in a corner while Gabe surveyed the area around the lander. When his eyes began to glaze over, he popped one of the stimulants from his pocket. The ring of torches illuminated enough of the plain to give him a few seconds' warning before an attack, but that advantage would be squandered if he wasn't alert. The four men posted just outside the torch ring might see something before he did and give him a few seconds of warning, but visibility had to be pretty poor outside the light of the torches. Gabe had the best vantage point on top of the lander, but that wasn't saying much. The Moon hadn't come out, and a bank of clouds had moved in to obscure what light there was. Gabe could no longer even see the outline of the mountains against the sky.

He tapped a button on his flight suit, overriding the automatic temperature control, then loosened the seals, letting some cold air in. Better to be a little cold than to fall asleep on the job. Too much was counting on him: he had the one long-range weapon, the only weapon capable of eliminating a significant number of enemies before they reached the spike barrier. A lag of a few seconds in his response time could mean the difference between victory and death for all of them.

Sometime around midnight, Arnulf came out of the lander with several other men. Four of them went to relieve the four guards outside the torch circle, and the guard went inside to get some sleep. Braggi came out and placed some more logs on the fire, and the rest of the men who had been sleeping gathered around it, yawning and speaking softly to each other. Once Agnar and Brynjarr had warmed themselves by the fire, they climbed up wing of the lander to join Gabe and Reyes. Reyes stirred to life as they climbed into the casemate. Gabe greeted them and then checked each of their weapons as best he could in the low light and then assigned them each a side to watch. Sigurd remained down below with the others, which was probably just as well. He could help Arnulf direct the men, and it wouldn't hurt to have one man with a gun near the hatch.

They waited until almost dawn, but the attack didn't come. Gabe wondered if Gunnar's men were waiting for daylight, but it seemed unlikely. A night attack would have given them a better chance at surprise, as well as the ability to hide their numbers. Was he wrong about Harald wanting the ship? No, he had seen the look in Gunnar's eyes. He knew the value of the lander. And Sigurd had known it too—he wouldn't have camped here all night with his men unless he believed there was a threat. Or was this all some elaborate ruse? Had Sigurd made a deal with Gunnar for the ship? If so, what were Sigurd's men waiting for?

No, Gabe was convinced that Sigurd and the others were as puzzled as he was. They had expected an attack before dawn—had been certain of it. Talking with Sigurd, Gabe had determined that it was about a four-hour journey by foot from Harald's fortress to the lander. Sigurd believed Gunnar would have no trouble raising a force of fifty or more men if Gunnar impressed upon him the lander's value. Gunnar had had plenty of time to get to Svelvig, make his case, gather his men, and return to the lander. So what had happened? Had Gunnar been waylaid on the way to Svelvig?

He was still pondering this when Slater's voice crackled in his ear again. She sounded panicked.

"Say again, Slater," said Reyes, standing next to him. "Slow down."

"—Harald's men. Attacking the village. I got away, but everything's on fire. My God, everything's burning!"

A sickening sensation struck Gabe's gut. He'd know what had happened as soon as he'd heard the fear in Slater's voice. He cursed himself for not figuring it out. Sigurd had told him Gunnar had threatened his village, and they'd handed him the perfect opportunity by keeping most of the fighting men at the lander all night. But how the hell had Gunnar known? Had they spied their defenses from a distance and decided not to attack? Judging from Sigurd's map, traveling to the lander from Harald's fortress would take them a good two hours out of their way. Even if Gunnar had managed to raise his force instantaneously, it would have taken them until dawn to get to the village from the lander. No, somehow Gunnar had known where they would be

"Slater, where are you?" Reyes asked. Agnar and Brynjarr stared at her, concerned looks on their faces. They'd grown accustomed to the foreigners speaking with each other over long distances, but it was clear they'd picked up on the edge in Reyes's voice.

"I'm… I don't know. Up in the hills somewhere. Cold as hell. Jesus, Reyes, they're dead. They're all dead!"

"Slater, calm down," Gabe snapped. "I need a coherent status report. What is happening?"

"We were asleep. Me and O'Brien. Something woke me up. It was dark. I heard shouts outside and smelled smoke. The farmer and his wife weren't there. I went outside and saw… I don't know. Chaos. Couldn't see anything but fires in the distance and shadows of people running. Screams. A man approached me with a torch. He had an axe, not one of the men from the village. He stepped over a body to get to me, I think it was the farmer's wife. Torn in half. He shouted something at me, couldn't understand it. I ran. Just kept running until my lungs hurt. When I finally looked back, the man was gone and most of the buildings were on fire. I kept running, don't know where I am. Jesus, Gabe. I don't know what happened to O'Brien. He's not answering his comm. I think he might be dead. I left him. I had to!"

"Are you safe now, Slater?" Reyes asked.

"Yeah, I think so. I must have run two klicks into the woods. Nobody's around. I might freeze to death though. Shit, it's cold."

"Are you wearing your suit?" Gabe asked.

"Yeah, slept in it. Managed to get my boots on before I went outside."

"Okay, then you'll be fine. Make sure your suit is tight. If you get cold before dawn, walk in circles. Don't light a fire. We'll get there as soon as we can."

"Maybe I should go check on O'Brien? It sounds like Harald's men are gone. I think I can find my way—"

"No, don't go back to the village. Stay where you are. We'll find you. Hang on, Slater. I've got to confer with Reyes. I'll get back to you in a minute. If you need anything, we're here."

"All right," Slater said. "Please hurry."

Gabe closed his comm channel and Reyes did the same.

"Shit," Gabe spat. "Fucking Vikings outsmarted us. How did they know?"

"Must be a spy at the village," Reyes said. "Unless one of Sigurd's men slipped away?"

"They'd have had to leave before dark. Somebody would have noticed."

Agnar and Brynjarr continued to stare. Below them, Sigurd shouted a question. They looked to see him glaring up at them, a stern look on his face. He'd deduced something was wrong.

"What do we tell them?" Gabe asked.

"The truth. Their village was attacked."

"And then what?"

"What do you mean?" Reyes asked.

"I mean half our crew is over there. We need to go after them."

"We need to protect the lander."

"The lander is worthless without a crew. Who's going to fly it?"

Sigurd shouted his question again. Agnar and Brynjarr, conferring with each other, were becoming increasingly agitated.

"Sigurd and his crew can handle themselves," Reyes said. "Sounds like Harald's men are gone already. We'll tell Slater to wait a couple hours and then—"

"I'm going," Gabe said.

"No, you're not," Reyes snapped. "I'm in command of this mission."

"I just told Slater I'm going after her," Gabe said. "That's what I'm going to do." He swung his leg over the casemate wall and slid down the side of the lander, landing on the hard-packed snow. Then he approached Sigurd and Arnulf, who were speaking quietly together.

"Enemies," he said to the two Norsemen. "Harald. Feotan. Gunnar and his men attacked the village." He pointed in the direction from which Sigurd's men had come.

The two Norsemen seemed to understand almost instantly. Arnulf turned toward the group of men warming themselves by the fire and shouted something. He was greeted with gasps and angry shouts. A brief, chaotic exchanged followed. Agnar and Brynjarr climbed down the side of the lander to join in, as did the four men on guard duty. Sigurd spoke a few curt words and the men began hurriedly gathering their items. Agnar and Brynjarr tried to give their guns back to Gabe, but he held up his hand. Probably better to let them keep them for now.

"You're not going," Reyes said tersely, coming up behind him.

"I am," Gabe replied. "If you want to stop me, you'll have to shoot me. Guess we'll see how good a shot you are."

"Shut the fuck up, Gabe," Reyes snapped. "You didn't let me finish. I'll go with Sigurd's men and rescue Slater and O'Brien. You stay here with the lander."

Gabe stared at her "Why...?"

"You've got the railgun, smart guy. If Harald's men are done with the village, they might come here next. Keep them away from the lander. I'll be back as soon as I can." She went into the lander and came out with a backpack, which she slung over her shoulders. She walked after the Norsemen, who had begun following Sigurd toward the village.

"Hey, Reyes," Gabe called. She stopped and turned to face him. He tapped his ear. "Stay in touch. Good luck."

Reyes nodded and fell in line behind the others. They disappeared around the tail of the lander, and soon he could no longer hear the sound of their feet crunching on the snow. Gabe was alone.

*****

The Norsemen moved single-file across the snowy plain and back into the woods. At first Reyes had been at the rear, but Agnar, holding a torch, soon dropped behind her. Sigurd, also carrying a torch, was leading the group.

They moved swiftly, their long legs making long strides along the narrow path. Reyes had to jog to keep pace. At one point the man in front of her, a great hairy beast of a man, offered to carry her, but she shook her head. If her crew was going to survive here, the Norsemen needed to be able to take her seriously as a leader. So she pressed on, her side aching and her lungs hurting as she panted in the cold night air. Making things more difficult, the path was strewn with roots and dead branches that she couldn't see thanks to her own shadow from Agnar's torch. Several times she tripped and nearly fell. How the big Norsemen managed to navigate the forest without trouble was a mystery to her.

When they emerged from the forest, Reyes gasped as she saw vast luminescent green swirls sweeping across the sky to her right. Overcome with amazement, she came to a stop, and Agnar nearly ran into her. Ahead of them, the others continued across a narrow bridge over a river, which babbled and glittered beneath them. The hills in the distance were visible only as great sloping masses of black below the greenish haze of the sky. Agnar gave her a light shove and spoke a curt sentence.

She nodded and started walking again, her eyes still transfixed by the glowing green swirls in the sky. She wanted to ask what it was, but she was out of breath and any explanation Agnar gave would be lost in translation anyway. And as he would have only a bronze age man's understanding of the phenomenon in any case, he'd be more likely credit fairies or dragons than to give her anything resembling a scientific explanation. As the luminescent swirls seemed to dominate the northern horizon, her best guess was that they had something to do with cosmic radiation interacting with Earth's magnetic poles. She'd heard of similar phenomena occurring on other planets with strong magnetic fields, but had never seen it herself—nor had she known that it happened on Earth. Whatever it was, it provided enough light to see the path in front of them for a few meters. Sigurd doused his torch, and Agnar then did the same.

Reyes followed the others across the bridge and then half-walked, half-ran behind them along the rocky, snow-packed path for a good hour. The men in front of her seemed to need no rest, and she didn't dare ask them to stop. She massaged the stitch in her side and tried to ignore the burning in her lungs. Like the rest of the crew, she engaged in regular calisthenics to stay fit during *Andrea Luhman*'s voyage, but her regimen clearly hadn't prepared her for this.

She heard fearful and agonized cries ahead, and at first thought they were under attack. She slowed and put her hand on her pistol. But when she rounded a bend in the path, she saw the reason for the uproar: in the distance, the hills and valley floor were dotted with dozens of fires. Reyes didn't know what these represented, but she could guess: homes, barns, workshops, storehouses. These men were not wealthy people. Everything they owned was down there—along with their wives, children, friends and relatives.

Once the men had recovered from the shock of the destruction, they started off again, even faster than before. Reyes despaired of keeping up, and Agnar seemed to know there was no point in pushing her. He took her arm and they walked side-by-side down the path. After some time, they reached a wider road. Up ahead on the right the embers of a large fire glowed.

"Sigurd," said Agnar, pointing to the remnants glowing red in the dark.

"Oh, no," Reyes said, peering into the distance. She thought of young Yngvi, the boy she had thought might be Sigurd's son. Did he have other children as well? A wife? When they reached the track that led to Sigurd's property, she wanted to turn, but she thought better of it. The mission came first. Her own people came first.

She tapped her cuff. "Slater, do you read me? It's Reyes."

"I read you, Reyes. Where are you?"

"Just got to the valley floor. Where are you?"

"In the hills to the south somewhere. Is it safe?"

"I think so. Sigurd's group is up ahead and I don't hear any fighting. Try to make your way back down. I'm going to find O'Brien."

"Copy that."

*****

Sigurd ran down the path to his house, not caring whether any of the others followed. Wisdom counseled him to keep the men together in case Gunnar's force was still here, but he ignored it. Even the house he'd worked so hard to build was of no concern. The only thing that mattered to him now was Yngvi.

There was little left of the house. The roof had collapsed into a pile of rubble and embers; anything inside of value had been destroyed. He approached the wreckage, wanting to reach down with his bare hands and move it aside—hoping and dreading to find some sign of his son.

Something moved to his right, and Sigurd drew his sword. Between the light of the aurora and the glow of the embers, there was enough light that he could make out a figure lying on the ground some twenty paces away. He sheathed his sword and ran to the figure, who lay on his back clutching his belly, his blond hair matted with blood.

"Yngvi!" Sigurd cried, crouching down next to his son.

"Father," Yngvi said weakly. "I tried to stop them, but there were... too many."

"It's all right," Sigurd said. "I know you did what you could. It was my fault. I shouldn't have left you. Can you get up?" It was hard to see how badly Yngvi was wounded in the dim light.

"I... think so," Yngvi said. "Head... hurts a lot."

Sigurd leaned toward Yngvi's face, trying to see where he was hurt. He pressed his fingers to the boy's scalp, probing the area carefully. There was quite a bit of blood, but little swelling, and the skull didn't seem to be fractured. Maybe Gunnar's men hadn't been trying to kill him; they were just trying to burn the buildings to demonstrate Harald's claim on the valley, and Yngvi had gotten in the way.

"Here, boy," Sigurd said, wrapping his left arm around Yngvi's shoulders. "Get up. We've got to get you to Gunhild. She can give you something for your head. We'll have to sleep at the fire pit tonight, but the weather is good and..."

Yngvi cried out weakly as Sigurd lifted him. "No, Father! Stop!" Sigurd felt something warm and wet against his thigh. He set Yngvi down again and pulled away, trying to see in the dim light.

"Move your hand, Yngvi," Sigurd said. "I need to see."

Yngvi groaned and shook his head. Both of his hands were clutched tightly to his belly now.

"Please, son," Sigurd said. "I won't hurt you."

Yngvi slowly moved his hands away. Sigurd tried not to retch as the odor reached him. It was like a mix of blood, bile and vomit. Harald's man had cut deeply. Too deeply.

"Am I going to be all right, Father?" Yngvi asked. He had past puberty some time ago, but now his voice sounded small and weak again, like the little boy he had been years ago.

"Yes, son, of course," Sigurd said, forcing himself to meet Yngvi's gaze. "We just need to get you to Gunhild."

"I don't think I can move."

"It's all right, son. She'll come here." Sigurd managed to keep his voice from breaking.

"I'm cold, Father."

"Hold on." Sigurd stood up and removed the broach from his cape. He pulled the cape off his shoulders and lay it on his son. He pulled off his tunic, rolled it up and put it under Yngvi's head.

"I'm cold, Father," Yngvi said again.

"I'm sorry, son. Shall I start a fire?"

"Yes, Father."

"All right. I'll be right back." Sigurd walked toward the house, finding a fragment of a board at the outskirts of the rubble. He used it to drag several coals across the ground to where his son lay. After shoving the coals together, he gathered some other small pieces of wood and piled them near the coals. He blew on the coals until a flame flickered, and then gradually lay more wood on top. Soon a bright fire illuminated the area. Sigurd was warm even without his cape and tunic. He turned to look at his son.

Yngvi's eyes had closed. Even in the dim light of the fire, Sigurd could see he had gone pale. He leaned over and brushed Yngvi's cheek with his thumb. "How do you feel, son?"

"Tired, Father," Yngvi said, his eyes flickering open. "But my head doesn't hurt anymore. Will Gunhild be here soon?"

"Yes, son. She's on her way now. Why don't you get some sleep."

"Yes, Father."

"You were very brave today, Yngvi. I am proud of you."

"Thank you, Father," Yngvi said with a slight smile. Then his face relaxed as he slipped into unconsciousness.

Sigurd stood. For some time, he watched the shimmering glow of the aurora in the north. Then he cast his eyes back to Earth, where he saw Yngvi's spear lying a few paces away, its head dark with blood. His son had fought bravely, but there had been too many of them. Sigurd walked to the spear, picked it up, and wiped the blood on the snow. Then he returned to his son, kneeling beside him. He lay the spear across Yngvi's chest and placed the boy's hands on it, right over left, as he would have held it while defending their home. He held his son until the boy's breath stopped.

CHAPTER NINETEEN

The sky was beginning to lighten in the east when Reyes saw Slater making her way down the hillside toward the main road. Everywhere Reyes looked, homes and other structures had been reduced to charcoal. Slaughtered goats and pigs littered the landscape; occasionally she spotted a person among them. Sigurd's men had scattered across the valley floor, looking desperately for their loved ones. Anguished wails broke the stillness of morning. The scene reminded her of medieval depictions of hell.

Slater ran toward her, practically weeping with relief at seeing a familiar face. But Reyes's eye were fixed on the horrors around them. Slater stopped a few paces from her, taking in the scene. "My God," she said. "I knew it was bad, but I thought... I thought maybe it was just panic. I thought things would look better in the daylight."

"They don't," Reyes said grimly. The fires she had seen in the distance had looked downright cheery compared to this dismal gray hellscape. And an insistent voice in the back of her head kept telling her: *this is your fault.*

She pushed it away. "Any word from O'Brien?"

Slater shook her head. Reyes had tried to get through to him a few times, but had gotten no response.

"Where were you and O'Brien staying?"

"Um," Slater said, looking around in confusion.

"Seriously?" Reyes said.

"It was nearly dark when we got here. And the buildings were still intact."

Reyes nodded. "Sorry," she said. "It's been a long night. Take your time."

"This way, I think," Slater said. "Come on."

Reyes followed her down the road about half a klick, and then turned left on a narrower path. Soon they came to a long, squat building that looked like it was made of grass and mud.

"What the hell is that?" Reyes asked.

"O'Brien called it a longhouse. They build them from turf. Cheaper than wood, I guess."

Two corpses lay in the snow near the front of the building, a man and a woman. The man had been beheaded; the woman had hewn nearly in two by an axe. Slater ran past them to the longhouse and threw open the door.

"O'Brien!" she called. "Are you all right?"

Reyes came up behind her in time to hear a man's groan from inside. Alive. O'Brien was alive. The damn turf house had saved his life: Gunnar's men hadn't been able to burn it.

They went inside. It took a few seconds for their eyes to adjust to the dim light. They found O'Brien lying on one of the benches that lined both sides of the building. He was struggling to sit up.

"Stay there, O'Brien," Reyes said. "This is probably the safest place in the valley right now. How do you feel?"

"About the same," O'Brien said. "What happened? I woke up and everybody was gone. I heard screaming. Tried to get a hold of Slater, but these damn turf walls make it hard to get a good signal. So I tried to get up, but…"

"You did the right thing. The village was attacked. Gunnar's men tricked us."

"What? How?"

"Not sure yet. Do you need anything?"

"Thirsty," O'Brien said.

"We'll get you something. Slater, can you stay here with O'Brien? I need to see what Sigurd and his men are up to."

"Yeah, we're good. Go."

Reyes went back outside. She tapped her comm. "Hey, Gabe," she said.

After a few seconds, he replied. "Reyes. What's up?"

"Village is destroyed. Slater and O'Brien are alive. What's your situation?"

"Same as two hours ago. Sitting on top of the lander, trying to stay awake. Scanning the horizon for Vikings. That sort of thing."

Reyes smiled at Gabe's confidence, but she could hear an undercurrent of worry in his voice. Now that they'd taken out the village, it was only a matter of time before Gunnar's men attacked the lander. Gabe couldn't fight them off forever.

"I'll get back as soon as I can," Reyes said. "Things are pretty grim here, but we're safe for now."

"Copy that," Gabe said. "I'll let you know if I see any guys with horns on their hats."

"That's a myth, you know."

"No fucking way."

"Talk to you later, Gabe."

*****

Dawn had arrived by the time the survivors gathered at the meeting place. Men and women sobbed and screamed at the heavens. The voices of children were conspicuously absent: none had survived the attack. Only thirty-six of the valley's inhabitants remained alive, and several of them were wounded. Sigurd had been one of the lucky ones: he had gotten to say goodbye to his son. He had held the boy's lifeless body, weeping silently over him, until sunrise.

Several people, including some children, were still missing. Some of these may have escaped by running to the hills, as the foreign woman had done, but Sigurd scanned the hillsides with no success. The foreigner named Reyes was walking up the road toward them from Magni's house. One of his men had reported that Magni and his wife Dagrun had been found dead in front of their house.

The destruction was almost too much to comprehend. Sigurd had seen several raids—and had participated in them when he was younger—but raiding was for gathering wealth. Raiding among one's own people was questionable enough, but this sort of wanton destruction was unforgiveable. Harald's men had raided not for silver or cattle, but simply to crush the spirit of the valley dwellers.

This was not the time for mourning, though. That would come. Now was the time for vengeance.

"Last night our enemy attacked us in our homes," Sigurd said, addressing the group. "That snake Gunnar and his band of hired cowards attacked while most of our fighting men were away. They fought not bravely, as warriors, but as brigands and assassins, with no end other than destruction of our families, our homes and our community. I have warned you in the past of Harald's ambitions, and I cannot express how saddened I am to have been proven right."

"Harald!" shouted a tall, dour woman named Ulla. "This is not Harald's doing. This is your fault!"

A few murmurs of agreement went up from the group.

"Please, Ulla," Sigurd said. "You are aggrieved over your husband's death, as I am by my son's. But let us not waste our anger quarreling amongst ourselves. Our enemy is Harald. We must take this fight to him."

"What kind of father are you, Sigurd?" Ulla shrieked. "You speak of such things while your son lies dead in your own yard!"

It was true. Yngvi still lay on the cold ground, covered by a wool blanket. It had not yet been decided what to do with the dead. Some were agitating for an immediate burial, but as it was unclear whether the community would survive, others suggested holding off on burials until they knew where they would settle. Sigurd gritted his teeth, not responding to Ulla's deprecations. He feared that if he lashed out at this woman, he might find himself unable to control his rage.

"Take the fight to Harald!" another woman, named Birjitta, shrieked. She had lost two of her four sons in the attack. "We can't even defend our own home. You should have been here, Sigurd! You and your men! We could have fought them off, but you were off... doing what? Finding foreigners to bring into our valley?"

Sigurd took a deep breath, steadying himself. "We believed, with good reason, that Harald would attack the foreigners' ship," Sigurd said. "We thought fighting with the foreigners was our best chance at defeating them." He knew in his head that he was right, but his heart was not in it. Part of him wanted to tell Ulla that she was right. It was his job to protect them, and he had let them down. If only it had been he who had been gutted by Gunnar's men, instead of Yngvi.... He put the thought out of his head. *Not yet. Now is not the time.*

"It saddens me to say it," Arnulf said, "but Ulla is right. We were misled. I was willing to go along with the will of the majority, but it is clear now that standing up to Harald was a mistake." Arnulf's own wife had been killed in the attack.

"Then we must surrender," said Brynjarr. "Send a messenger to Harald and tell him we accept his terms."

"Why would he accept now?" said Gunhild. "He will never trust us."

"Then we will give him something he wants," said Ulla, glancing at the dark-haired foreign woman who had just joined them. The woman looked back at her, suspicious.

"What makes you think Harald wants these people?" Arnulf said.

"Not them," said Ulla. "Their ship. You said Harald wants it."

"We don't have their ship," Arnulf said. "One of the foreigners is guarding it."

"Only one man?" Birjitta asked.

"He has a very powerful weapon," Arnulf said. "Like the one Sigurd carries, but bigger. With it, he is a match for twenty or more men. We could not take the ship if we tried."

"Gods, you men are dense," said Ulla. "We don't have to take the ship. We trade this man the ship for his three people. This woman and the two others staying in Magni's house."

"These people are our guests, Ulla," Sigurd said sternly.

"I didn't invite them," Ulla snapped. "And I'm not feeling very hospitable now that my own house has been burned down."

Reyes glanced to Sigurd, a concerned look on her face. It was clear she could sense something was wrong.

Arnulf shook his head. "I can't go along with that, Ulla. The gods will punish us for treating guests in this way."

"Then you are fools," Ulla spat. "Do you think it's a coincidence these people showed up just as Harald moved in?"

"What are you saying, woman?" Arnulf asked. "You think the foreigners are in league with Harald? I've seen no reason to believe—"

"Where is Jannik?" Sigurd said. He'd been trying to determine which men had been lost, and he realized that Jannik was missing. But he hadn't been reported among the dead. When no one answered, he spoke again. "Has no one seen him?"

"Not since we returned last night," said Erland. He was the only one of the five returnees present. A blood-soaked bandage covered his right eye and much of his head. The bodies of Vilmar and Sten had been found, bloody and broken, on the roadside.

"Their house is empty," Agnar said. "I checked it myself."

"Dead?" Arnulf asked.

Agnar shook his head. "Not that I saw."

"Are we certain he returned to the village?" Sigurd asked.

"We were carrying the foreigners," Erland said. "Jannik went on ahead."

"So he may have strayed off the path and let you pass," Sigurd said. "Did anyone see him in the village last night?"

No one spoke.

Arnulf turned to Sigurd, anger sweeping over his face. "Jannik betrayed us."

Sigurd nodded slowly. It was hard to come to any other conclusion. He cursed himself again. How had he not seen it? He'd pretended to return to the village but had gone to Svelvig instead. How long had he been planning his betrayal? Jannik had voted to stand up to Harald, but that may have been a ruse.

"It changes nothing," Ulla said. "We cannot stand against Harald. We must submit to his authority."

Arnulf no longer seemed so sure. "If Jannik betrayed us, he must pay."

Sigurd nodded. "Jannik betrayed us, and Gunnar betrayed us before that. Or have you all forgotten that Gunnar was once one of our own? Our mistake wasn't standing up; it was not killing that rat when we had a chance."

"What would you have us do, then?" Ulla asked. "You failed once to defend this valley. You think you can do it now, with half our men dead?"

Sigurd gritted his teeth to keep from shouting at Ulla. "We must take the fight to Gunnar. Fight alongside the foreigners."

"Have you learned nothing?" Ulla snapped. "Even a child learns not to stick his hand in the fire twice."

"Look around," Sigurd said. "What do you see?"

"What do I see? I see burned houses and dead children!"

"Exactly," Sigurd replied, barely controlling his fury. "They killed indiscriminately. Didn't bother to take the women or the children as slaves. Why not?"

"Because Harald was making a point," said Njáll. "He doesn't need our people. He only wants control over our land."

"Have you ever known Harald to give up easily-acquired plunder?"

No one spoke.

"Harald demands tribute from all his dominions," Sigurd growled. "Those who resist fare even worse. You heard about old Kjetil, who led a rebellion of some of the estates to the west. Harald had him executed and took both of his daughters and all of his goats. Not only that, but Harald left half his force in place until autumn, to ensure that he would have no more trouble in the area. Where are Harald's men? Why did they leave so quickly?"

"They knew we would return," Arnulf said.

"Maybe," Sigurd replied. His rage had subsided a bit. "But seeing what they did here, I would guess they had a force of at least fifty. If they'd wanted to waylay ten men coming down from the hills, they had the opportunity. In fact, the only way they could have avoided us is by passing the bridge, crossing the river farther west and doubling back."

"That would take them right past the foreigners' ship," Arnulf said.

Sigurd nodded. "That's what Gunnar is after. We were right to try to ally with the foreigners. Taking the ship was Gunnar's intention all along. Jannik provided them an opportunity to raze our homes as well. They probably waited in the hills, watching for us to return. And now that we're here, they've headed back to the ship."

"So Gunnar played us for fools," Ulla asked. "We defend one place and he attacks another. How many times do you have to be burned to stop playing his game? What if Gunnar returns while you are gone?"

"And does what?" Arnulf asked. "Brings our cattle back to life? There's nothing left here for him to take. I don't like it, but Sigurd is right. Gunnar is going to attack the foreigner's ship."

"And what is that to us?" Birjitta asked. "Let them have it!"

"This is our only chance," Sigurd said, trying to remain patient. "My men and I are exhausted. When we got here, our houses were on fire and our families were dead. I just held my son while he died in my arms. I want nothing more right now than to open my wrists and allow the life to flow out of my body. To be free of this sorrow and pain. But we have no choice. If we are ever going to get our vengeance against Gunnar, against Harald, we must strike now! The foreigners have weapons that will—"

"Enough about the foreigners!" Ulla cried. "It is because of them that my husband is dead. If you are still men, kill the three of them and put their heads on a stake!"

"We're getting nowhere," Arnulf said. "Ulla, shame on you. Whatever events have transpired since they arrived, the foreigners are our guests. Anyone who wishes to harm them will have to go through me." He picked up his axe from where it rested at his side. "Come on, then. Let's get this over with." He moved to stand in front of Reyes, who watched the proceedings with a baffled look on her face.

No one volunteered to take up Ulla's cause. Her face turned a deep crimson. Sigurd saw Reyes moving away from the group, and at first thought she was afraid for her life, but then he noticed she was pressing her hand to her ear, the way the foreigners sometimes did when they were communicating over long distances with each other.

"Good," Arnulf said, setting down his axe. "Now, the next question. Sigurd is right. We are all tired and grieving, but if we are ever going to strike back against Gunnar, now is the time. Who wishes to fight?"

"Hold on," Sigurd said. "If we are going to have a chance, we need all the fighting men. We must vote, as we did before. All heads of households. If we vote to fight, all able-bodied men go to the lander. If not, we surrender." As Sigurd said it, he realized he had no intention to surrender, no matter how the vote came out.

"We don't need to surrender," Ulla said. "We can stay and rebuild."

Arnulf shook his head. "You said it yourself. We no longer have enough men to defend the village. If we rebuild, we're simply inviting Gunnar to attack again. There are only two choices: attack now or submit to Harald's rule."

"We can't stay here either way," said Gunhild, who had listened quietly up to this point. "Most of our animals are dead and our food stores are smoke and ash. Even if we were safe from another attack, we don't have the resources to rebuild."

"What do you suggest, Gunhild?" Arnulf said.

"We go east. Many of us have kin around Uslu. They will take us in, at least temporarily. We will bury our dead there and take time to grieve. Those of us who can find work may wish to stay there. Those who wish to return here will do so."

"Don't be coy, woman," Birjitta snapped. "You know full well that if we bury our dead in Uslu, we will never return to this valley."

Gunhild nodded slowly. "It is as you say, Birjitta. I mean only to say that no one will be barred from returning. But yes, we need to be realistic. We do not have the numbers to sustain a community anymore. Sigmund the blacksmith and Odd the baker are both dead. Even if we all wished to return, we would be hard-pressed to survive the winter."

"We could go north," Njáll said. "We may be able to convince the people of the valley to make a united stand against Harald," Njáll said. "Now that Harald has made his intentions clear, we should have no trouble rallying men to defend the valley."

There was little enthusiasm for this idea. Many had kin in Uslu, but the people to the north were mostly strangers. They would not bury their dead in the north.

"Go north, go east, stay, fight, surrender," Arnulf muttered, shaking his head. "Too much to decide in too little time, with no sleep."

Several men nodded wearily. Sigurd looked around at the people and saw defeat. There was no way this group was going to vote to take the offensive against Gunnar. Not after what they had just been through. But Sigurd knew he could not let his son's death go unavenged. He would take the fight to Harald if he had to do it alone.

"Arnulf is right," Sigurd said. "It is too much to ask you to decide your future right now. I do not know myself what I am going to do tomorrow. But I do know one thing: I must avenge my son's death."

"It is well that you should do so," Arnulf said. "But must we first not at least bury our dead?"

Gunhild spoke again. "Those of us who make the journey to Uslu will take the dead with us. We can salvage some carts from the debris, and may yet recover some mules or oxen. Sad as it is to say, we have little else to carry."

Sigurd nodded. "I am very much obliged, Gunhild."

"Don't thank me," Gunhild said. "I don't intend to carry anything but my own weary bones—if that."

Several in the group chuckled. Even Sigurd managed a smile.

"Who then will go with Sigurd?" Arnulf asked. "It is a brave and important thing he is doing, but there is no shame in going to Uslu. The dead must be laid to rest, and the living must live on."

Four hands went up: Braggi, Brynjarr, Njáll and Agnar. Sigurd was disappointed at the number of volunteers, but heartened that both of his gunmen were among them.

"All right," Arnulf said. "Then the rest of us will go to Uslu, myself included. I let my Edda down once, and I cannot do so again. I will carry her to Uslu in my arms and bury her with my bare hands if I have to."

"What of those of us who don't wish to travel to Uslu?" Ulla snapped.

"Then you'll stay here and rot with your boys," Arnulf growled. "We're a community. We live or die together." He reached out to take Sigurd's hand. "May Odin himself be with you," he said.

"Thank you, old friend," Sigurd said. "I will see you in Uslu soon."

CHAPTER TWENTY

Gabe spotted the first of Gunnar's men shortly after dawn. They were coming straight across the plain from the forest to the south, iron helmets gleaming in the ruddy light, making no effort to conceal themselves. His eyes were glazing over from exhaustion, but he counted somewhere between fifty and sixty of them. They made a wide arc around the lander, fanning out across the plain until they formed a semicircle about a hundred meters out from the lander, a few meters separating each man. Many of them had bows slung over their shoulders. For now, they seemed content to wait. Gabe popped two more of the stimulants and tapped his cuff.

"You copy, Reyes?"

For several seconds, Gabe heard only muffled scratches. Then Reyes's voice, barely above a whisper: "I'm here, Gabe. What's up?"

"Found my Vikings," he said. "You were right. Not a horned helmet in sight."

"How many of them?"

"Fifty-five, give or take. They're about a hundred meters out. I think I spotted Gunnar. They came from the south."

"Must be the same group that sacked the village," Reyes said. "I think they left shortly before we got here. You know how I suggested there was a spy among Sigurd's people?"

"Jannik, right?"

"How the hell did you know that? I just figured it out myself. Sigurd's men were talking about him."

"I've had a lot of time to think. Should have known as soon as I laid eyes on that asshole."

"What are Gunnar's men doing?"

"Nothing, yet. Just watching the lander."

"Any idea why they're not attacking?"

"I've got a guess. They've got me surrounded to keep me from running, but they left a gap at the south end of their formation. They're waiting for reinforcements."

Reyes didn't speak for a moment. "They've got you outnumbered fifty to one and *they're* waiting for reinforcements?"

"I guess Gunnar was pretty impressed with my gun. What's your status?"

"It's grim here. I was listening in on a meeting of the village's survivors when you commed. Can't follow much of it, of course, but I think they're blaming us for the attack."

"Understandable," Gabe said. "What are they going to do about it?"

"One woman in particular seems to have it in for us. I think Sigurd and the others managed to talk some sense into her."

"Any chance I'll be getting some reinforcements?"

"I'll try, but frankly I'm going to be happy if we get out of here alive. You're going to have to hold them off for a few hours on your own, at the very least. I'm sorry, Gabe."

"Copy that," Gabe said. He surveyed the line of men arcing around across the plain, regarding him stonily. Most wore helmets of leather or metal and carried round wooden shields. Spears and axes were the most common weapons; Gunnar and a few of his lieutenants carried swords. Toward the middle of the line, Gunnar was conferring with several of these men.

They had to be waiting for more men. That was the only explanation. If this was their complete force, they would have encircled the lander and launched their attack without delay. Whatever Gunnar had told Harald, he'd definitely impressed upon him the danger of these foreigners—as well as the value of the lander. Gunnar had probably left to sack the village before the full force was assembled, with the plan to meet the rest at the lander.

That was good and bad news. Good because it gave Gabe a bit of a reprieve—as well as a chance that Reyes would return with reinforcements before the assault began. Bad because even with Reyes and the other gunmen, they couldn't defeat a hundred Vikings. He didn't have much confidence in the Norsemen's ability to use a gun under fire, and they would be cut off from the lander and easily surrounded. The railgun had a maximum rate of fire of ten rounds per second, but he'd have a hard time hitting much of anything at that rate. He had plenty of ammo for the railgun, but it required a lot of power and he only had one battery. Generally a fully-charged battery was good for about a hundred rounds.

His best bet, then, was to force Gunnar to act. Get him to attack before his full force had assembled. That should be easy enough to do: just start picking them off at a distance. Gabe was familiar enough with Viking culture to know that running away from battle was frowned upon; they'd have little choice but to attack en masse. He hoped.

Gabe picked up his helmet from the floor of the casemate and put it on, sliding the visor down. The helmet had a shell made from a lightweight carbon fiber that would provide good protection against the Norsemen's weapons. The flight suit wasn't quite as tough, but it had a layer of nanofiber armor that would suffice to deflect arrows and thrown weapons. Gabe unslung the gun from his shoulder and checked the battery connection for the twentieth time. The battery light was green; the readout on the battery read eighty-four percent.

He took several deep breaths to steady himself, then got into a crouch, resting the gun on the top of the casemate. He lined up the sights, zeroing in on one of Gunnar's lieutenants. He'd have gone for Gunnar himself, but he wasn't completely certain the men wouldn't rout if Gunnar was killed. If they ran, they might return later, after the rest of the force had arrived. Better to piss them off by taking out a few of the henchmen.

"I've got to be out of my fucking mind," he said aloud, as he took aim at a big blond man's chest. The Norsemen gave no indication that they thought Gabe was a threat. Even given what Gunnar had told them about their weapons, it probably never occurred to them that he could attack from this distance. He almost felt bad for them.

Gabe clicked a switch on the side of the railgun, setting rate of fire to one round per second. It could fire much faster, but at a cost of diminished accuracy, greater recoil, and much faster battery drain. Because the railgun used an electrical charge rather than a chemical explosive to move the projectiles, its muzzle velocity and rate of acceleration were variable. At a lower rate of fire, the gun could control the projectile's acceleration rate to minimize kickback. Between the controlled acceleration and the action of the gun's built-in inertial compensators, the recoil was negligible. The gun would still kick upwards slightly with each shot, but it was weighted so that if you held it correctly, it was self-leveling. That meant if he was careful and focused, he could take out a Viking every second.

He tapped his cuff. "Hey, Reyes."

"I'm here, Gabe. What's happening?"

"I'm about to make history," Gabe said. He shifted his aim as the man took a half-step to his left.

"Don't do anything crazy. I'll be there as soon as I can. Sigurd is trying to get a group together."

"Sorry, Reyes, can't wait. If I don't make it through this, well… good luck. You're going to need it."

"Gabe, stop! What are you—"

Gabe tapped his cuff again, switching off the comm. He inhaled and exhaled deeply three times and then squeezed the trigger.

There was a crack as the bullet left the gun moving at over a thousand meters per second. The noise was from the bullet breaking the sound barrier; the gun itself was virtually silent. The gun was capable of propelling projectiles at speeds of up to two thousand kilometers per second, but that seemed like overkill when dealing with guys carrying wooden shields. Besides, the higher the velocity, the faster his battery would drain. He thought he had enough of juice to dispatch all of Gunnar's force, but there was no point in pushing it.

His first shot hit the unlucky Viking dead center in his chest. Gabe moved the gun half a degree to the right and the gun fired again. This shot was a little low, penetrating the second man's abdomen. The third man managed to get his shield up, but it made no difference. Splinters flew as the shield cracked in half. The first man hadn't even hit the ground.

None of the Norsemen tried using their bows, confident in their ability to overwhelm him in a melee. To their credit, fleeing never seemed to occur to them. Gabe heard someone—probably Gunnar—shouting an order, but it seemed perfunctory. The Vikings rushed toward the lander as one.

Gabe forced himself to breathe slowly, willing his body not to be overcome with adrenaline. The Vikings could use their rage to their advantage, but Gabe had to fight his instincts. If he was going to get through this, he needed to remain cool-headed and in absolute control.

Another loud crack and a fifth man fell. Sloppy. Gabe had hit him just above the knee. He was still overcompensating for kickback. He raised the gun and pivoted slightly to the right. Amazingly, the man in his sights seemed to anticipate the shot, dodging right at the last moment. It had taken these guys less than six seconds to adapt to his tactics. Time to mix things up a little.

He let his finger off the trigger for a moment, refocused on the closest man to the lander, and squeezed the trigger again. The man jerked left and fell backwards as the bullet ripped through his shoulder. Gabe pivoted left as the gun fired again, penetrating another's shield. The man fell. The Norsemen were almost to the spike barrier, and he'd barely put a dent in the numbers. He swung right and dropped two more before stopping to bump the fire rate up to ten rounds per second. The battery would drain a lot faster at this rate of fire, but Gunnar's men were now close enough that he could probably hit several with a burst.

One man had raised his axe to knock down one of the spiked poles; Gabe sprayed him and the two behind him with bullets. Before the three men hit the ground, several more were already hacking at the barrier. Gabe took aim and fired again, dropping two more of them. They were too spread out for him to hit them all, though. He saw out of the corners of his eyes that some of them were running around to the other side of the lander. Soon he'd be surrounded. About half of the men had dropped their shields, having deduced that they were worthless against the railgun. These guys were smart.

Norsemen were now streaming through half a dozen gaps in the barrier, running toward the lander with spears and axes. Gabe dropped three more of them and then ducked as a spear shot over his head. Somewhere among these men was Gunnar, but Gabe had lost him in the chaos. He fired several more quick bursts, dropping another dozen attackers.

With the final burst, the rate of fire had dropped back to one round per second. Glancing at the battery pack on the floor of the casemate, Gabe saw a warning light glowing red: he was nearly out of juice. A group of men had reached the wing in front of him, and were scrambling to get on top of it. Gabe allowed himself a split second of satisfaction: shortly after Reyes had left, he had rigged a hose to the lander's water supply and sprayed down the wings and sides of the lander. The water had frozen quickly in the cold air, giving the lander a slippery coat of ice that was nearly impossible to climb.

That's what Gabe had thought, anyway. Even though he'd been firing ten rounds a second at close range, two of the men managed to get on top of the right wing before he could cut them down. And now others were climbing on top of the dead and wounded, clawing desperately to reach the casemate. Gabe let loose three more shots and then dropped the railgun. It was firing too slowly to keep up with the Norsemen's advance. He drew his pistol. As he did so, something hit him hard in the left shoulder, knocking him forward and almost causing him to fall over the side of the casemate. To his left, a spear clattered against the top of the lander and fell to the ground. Cold air hit his skin where the spear had torn his flight suit: the built-in layer of nanofiber armor had probably saved his life.

He spun around, bracing himself against the casemate wall, firing three shots at a man on the wing holding an axe. Only one shot hit the man, just above his left knee, but it was enough. The man yelped, lost his footing, and fell. His head clanged against the wing and he slipped to the ground. Three more men, armed with spears, took his place. Gabe steadied himself and fired three shots, hitting all three in the chest. They fell and slipped off the wing to join the others on the ground.

Gabe had just enough time to spin around again and drop two more men with axes who were coming up the other side. The pistol slide locked and he ducked as a third man hurled a spear at him. Gabe fell to the floor of the casemate, popping the magazine from his pistol as he did so. He grabbed a replacement from his belt, slammed it into place, and raised the gun again as the man came over the casemate wall, holding a knife in his right hand. Gabe fired three times, and the man screamed and crumpled to the floor next to him. Shaking and exhausted, Gabe got to his feet. The men were still coming.

He emptied his second magazine as well, dropping four more men, then grabbed his last remaining magazine. He slapped it in place, barely able to get it aimed before a man with a spear lunged at him. He fell to his left as he fired, and the man's body landed with a crash next to him. The top half of its head was missing. Gabe tried to get up, but his legs wouldn't move. His hands shook and his heart raced.

He blinked hard and shook his head, forcing himself to take deep breaths. Becoming aware of a burning sensation on his thigh, he looked down, puzzled. He was sitting with his legs bent unnaturally underneath him, the pistol resting on his leg. The red-hot barrel was burning a hole in the fabric of the flight suit. He jerked it away just as another man vaulted over the casemate, landing hard right in front of him. The man brought his axe back but Gabe managed to get the gun aimed in more-or-less the right direction before he could bring it down. The man's jaw exploded and he stumbled backward, falling out of the casemate. He slid with a scream down the side of the lander.

Gabe pulled himself to his feet in time to get the pistol aimed at three more men who had gotten onto the wing. They were literally standing on the corpses of their fallen comrades. They stood for a moment, brandishing their spears at him as he did his best to keep the gun pointed toward them. His hands were shaking so badly that even at a range of less than five meters, his odds of hitting any of them were probably fifty-fifty—and he was nearly out of bullets.

After some time, the man in front dropped his spear. He turned and climbed down from the wing. The other two glanced at each other and then did the same. They made their way over the pile of dead and dying men and walked away. They threaded their way through the spike barrier and continued across the plain, in the direction they had come.

Looking around, Gabe realized he was the last man standing. He had done it. He was still alive and the lander was safe.

CHAPTER TWENTY-ONE

G abe's reprieve lasted only a few seconds. Many of the men he'd hit were merely wounded, not dead, and one of them might still try to take the lander. He pulled himself to his feet and surveyed the area. A few of the men on the ground had gotten to their feet, but none seemed particularly eager to continue the fight. One man lay on his back on the wing, moaning, his tunic soaked with blood. Gabe took a seat on the casemate wall. He grabbed a box of bullets from the crate on the floor of the casemate, reloaded one of the magazines, popped the empty one out, and shoved the refilled magazine into place. When it was clear that none of the survivors was up for more, he holstered the pistol. After resting a moment, he reached down and grabbed the spear that had belonged to the man whose head he'd shot off. Then he climbed over the casemate wall and approached the wounded men. He lifted the spear over his head, and shouted, "If you can walk, go! Anyone who remains behind will be killed." To punctuate his point, he drove the spear into the man's heart. The man's body jerked wildly for a moment and then he lay still.

The other survivors seemed to get the message. Those with minor injuries helped some of the more severely wounded men to their feet. Those with non-life-threatening wounds were bandaged up; those who were beyond saving were put out of their misery. All in all, eighteen men limped away from the battlefield. Gabe thought one of them was Gunnar, but he couldn't be sure. When they'd cleared the spike barrier, Gabe climbed down from the lander and looked for other survivors. He found two more men who were barely holding on. One had apparently been hit in the head with an axe—a friendly fire incident. He was babbling incoherently and drifting in and out of consciousness. Gabe stabbed him through the neck. He gave the same treatment to another man with a massive chest wound who was lying on his back, gasping for breath. And then, at last, there was silence.

Gabe fell to his knees and vomited into the snow. For some time he crouched there, trembling, aware of nothing. Then he rolled onto his back and lay in the snow, staring up at the sky. The sun was still just above the horizon; the entire battle had taken only a few minutes. It had seemed like hours.

He closed his eyes only to be met with a barrage of images of men being torn apart. The faces of the men were a blur—all except the last two, whom he'd killed in cold blood. He told himself he'd had no choice, that the men were going to die anyway. He didn't have the time, expertise or facilities to save their lives. It was better to kill them quickly than to let them suffer. But it didn't matter what he told himself. He'd cut the lives of two healthy young men short, because it was inconvenient to allow them to go on living.

When the cold began to seep into his skin, he sat up and then slowly got to his feet. He stood for some time regarding the carnage. *What a waste,* he thought. He'd had nothing against these men; they were probably just farmers and fishermen who'd been forced into Harald's service or bought off with a promise of security for their families. They had fought bravely, and well—as well as any men Gabe had ever seen or heard of. They fought for their lives, for their families, the same as he did. He knew all too well he was no better than these men; he just happened to be the one with the railgun.

He could tell himself he was fighting for the future of the human race, but that was bullshit. He doubted even Reyes still thought they were getting off this planet. And if they did, then what? Travel across the galaxy to deliver a bomb to an organization that wouldn't even exist for twelve hundred years? The plan had been absurd from the beginning. No, Gabe was fighting for survival, pure and simple—his own and that of his crew. And protecting the lander was vital to their survival. He had no illusions about holding onto it for good, but the longer they could hold it, the more power they had. At some point the lander was going to be taken, either by Harald's men or some other group, and probably torn apart to be made into weapons and other tools, and Gabe wanted to have as much control over that process as possible. The lander could be traded for food, shelter, land, weapons, security—anything they'd need to survive this unforgiving land. Establishing an alliance with Sigurd's people was good as far as it went, but to survive, they needed to hold the lander.

*****

Gunnar slowly sat up, gritting his teeth as pain shot through his shoulder. Dead men lay all around him. The only sounds were muffled groans from the few men still alive. Looking up, he saw that the foreigner still stood inside the makeshift fortification on top of the sky ship. Three men with spears stood on the wing, facing him. The foreigner held his small weapon pointed at them. Even from this distance, Gunnar could see the man's hand was shaking. Gunnar watched for a moment as the Norsemen regarded the foreigner, assessing their chances. *Attack!* thought Gunnar. *He can't beat all of you!*

But after a moment, the man in front dropped his spear. He turned and climbed down from the wing. The other two did the same. They made their way over the pile of dead and dying men and walked away. One of them saw Gunnar struggling to his feet and went to help him, but Gunnar waved the man off. "Coward," Gunnar muttered under his breath. The man shrugged and went to help another man, whose leg had been blown off below the knee. Gunnar struggled to his feet and appraised his shoulder.

He'd been within ten paces of the ship when the foreigner's terrible weapon hit him just above the armpit, knocking him to the ground. In the few seconds it had taken for him to get his bearings and sit up, the battle had ended. The foreigner had fought fifty men—and won. Gunnar was torn between anger at the foreigner's unfair tactics and envy of his weapon. A man with such a weapon could conquer all of Norway, and probably Denmark as well.

The weapon seemed to have torn a hole clear through Gunnar's shoulder. It hurt and made it near-impossible to use his left arm, but if he could get the wound clean in time, it probably wouldn't fester. In a few months, it might heal completely.

He turned and staggered after the others. Behind him, the foreigner was yelling something. Gunnar glanced back to see the man stab a wounded man through the chest. Gunnar and the others got the point: they could walk away or they could meet the same fate.

A group of maybe a dozen and a half men staggered and limped away from the scene. The less seriously wounded helped those who couldn't walk on their own. They moved slowly across the plain, without speaking. For most of them, surviving a battle in this way was worse than dying. Death in battle was a guarantee of a seat at Odin's table in Valhalla. Limping away meant only scorn and humiliation. Their only chance at redemption was to rejoin the fight when the reinforcements arrived.

They met the rest of Harald's men not far from bridge. By this time, two more men had died of their injuries. The newcomers stared at the survivors in horror.

"Is this all that is left of your force?" asked the leader, a man named Geir. The survivors were a desperate-looking bunch. Upon sighting the reinforcements coming over the bridge, many of them had sat or lay down, unwilling or unable to go any farther. The others stood, many leaning upon each other, dripping blood onto the snow.

"The foreigners have weapons unlike anything we've seen," replied one of the survivors, a young man whose right hand had been shot off. A strip of cloth had been tied around his forearm to keep him from bleeding to death.

"You were supposed to wait for us," Geir said.

Gunnar, who had been lingering toward the rear of the group, took a step forward. "They attacked," he said, following the other man's lead in using the plural to refer to their enemy. It was simply too humiliating to admit they'd been defeated by a single man. "Their weapons are deadly even at great range. If we had waited, we'd have been cut down without ever striking a blow."

Geir nodded, taking this in. "Then the others... they are all dead?"

"Every one," said the man who had spoken before.

"How many of the enemy are left?" Geir asked.

For a moment no one spoke. "It is difficult to be certain," Gunnar said at last. "They hide behind a fortification on top of their ship, and strike at a distance."

There were murmurs of agreement.

Behind Geir, men grumbled angrily. They had come to fight, and they weren't going to let a little thing like the slaughter of the first wave of attackers deter them. But Geir's confidence had clearly been shaken by the sight of the bloodied men before him.

"Then," he began cautiously, "do you counsel sending for still more men?"

Several of the survivors murmured vague approval of this sentiment, but it was Gunnar who spoke the loudest. "No," he said. "They are only men. We came very close to overcoming them. I myself was within a few paces of the sky ship when I was hit. By the time I got to my feet, the rest of our force had surrendered."

When no one contradicted his claim, Gunnar was emboldened to continue. "They are tired, and we are strong. If we attack suddenly, without warning, we can overcome them. Here." He knelt down, smoothing out an area of snow with his right hand and then placing a piece of bark in the middle of it. "This is the sky ship. They have a barrier of spikes about here. We will be approaching from this direction. There is no cover in the area, so when you reach the edge of the forest, charge at full speed toward the barrier. Men with axes should lead the way, to make gaps in the barrier. Drop anything that will slow you down. Arrows will not penetrate their armor, and wooden shields are useless against their weapons. Our only option is to overwhelm them with speed and sheer numbers."

"Good," said Geir, somewhat encouraged by Gunnar's confidence. "We will need all the men we can spare, so if you can walk, you fight."

Murmurs of assent went up from the survivors.

"Just don't get in the way," said Gunnar. "If you can't keep up, stay toward the back. Use your bows if you can't get close."

"All right," said Geir. "You heard Gunnar. Let's go! Men with axes, up front. Wounded to the rear. Leave your shields at the bridge."

Gunnar watched approvingly as the men dumped their shields and packs at the bridge and then assembled themselves as he'd suggested, following Geir down the path through the woods. Only three men, too hurt to fight, were left behind. Gunnar spent a moment tending to these men before following the rest down the path.

Geir led the men through the woods and across the plain. When he spotted the ship, he barked an order to attack, and ran toward it. The men followed, axemen first, the wounded last. No one noticed that Gunnar had stayed behind in the woods.

*****

Gabe made a slow circuit of the lander to make sure there were no other survivors, keeping an eye on the horizon to watch for Harald's reinforcements. He saw no sign of movement except a flock of geese flying overhead. Gabe went back to the front of the lander and sat down on the crate he'd left by the hatch. He tapped his cuff.

"Reyes," he said.

"Gabe! You're alive!" Reyes was clearly out of breath.

"Yeah, barely."

"Are you hurt?"

Gabe reached over to feel his shoulder. It was bruised but the skin wasn't broken. "No," he said. "Just a little shook up. There are... a lot of dead Vikings here."

"But you're okay? The lander is safe?"

"Yeah. Still expecting reinforcements though. Could be here any minute."

"We're about an hour out," Reyes gasped. "Moving as fast... as we can. Six of us. Including... our three gunmen."

"What about the rest of them?"

"Heading east to another village. Uslu or something."

"O'Brien and Slater too?"

"No, they stayed behind."

"Is that safe?"

"As safe as sending them along with a bunch of people who think we're to blame for the murders of their families, yeah. Anyway, O'Brien can barely move."

"Copy that," Gabe said. "I'll try to hold out until you get here. Gabe out."

He wearily got to his feet. How many more men would Harald send? Fifty? A hundred? Physical exhaustion aside, the lander's defenses had been damaged and he was running low on ammo. He still had plenty of rounds for the railgun, but the battery was dead and he had maybe two and a half magazines of ammo left for the pistol.

He got to his feet. *Okay*, he thought. *First things first. Recharge the railgun.*

He went into the lander and rummaged around until he found a twenty-meter power cord. He pulled the female end out the hatch, climbed up to the casemate, and plugged it into the railgun's battery pack. After scanning the horizon for Harald's men, he slid back down the lander, went inside and plugged the male end into a power jack at the rear of the cabin. The display on the jack read twelve percent.

"Fuck," Gabe said. He tapped his comm. "Reyes, we've got a problem."

"What... is it?" Reyes said after a moment.

"Lander batteries are at twelve percent. And the railgun is dead."

"What?" Reyes gasped. "What have you... been doing?"

"Besides killing Vikings? Not a damn thing. We must have a short, draining power. How much is twelve percent?"

Reyes didn't speak for a moment. "Maybe... ten shots with the railgun."

Gabe cursed to himself. Reyes's answer jibed with his own educated guess. Even if he could get all the power from the lander's batteries to the railgun, it wouldn't be nearly enough. "I'm going to have to fire up the reactor."

"Can't do it," Reyes said. "Shutdown. Ten minutes. Maybe five... more shots."

Gabe had anticipated this answer as well. Because the reactor's control systems were offline, the safety override would shut the reactor down after ten minutes. He'd get a little more power, but not enough. And then the reactor would be hard down for six hours. "Can I disable the override?"

"No!"

"The vehemence of your reply indicates I can."

"No, Gabe. Not safe."

"I know. Meltdown. Big explosion. We covered this earlier. How long would I have?"

"Another five minutes. Maybe ten. Not worth it."

"Even if it means losing the lander? Because if I can't get forty shots out of the railgun, I might as well start running."

For some time, there was no response.

"Reyes?" Gabe said. "Gonna need an answer here. I'm out of options."

"You can wire around the override," Reyes said at last. "It's like a fuse. Open panel. Little green box. Pull it, connect contacts... with copper wire."

"Copy that," Gabe said.

"You'll get... fifteen minutes total. Shut down or... we're screwed."

"Understood," Gabe said. "Gabe out."

Gabe checked the jack readout: it was down to ten percent. At the rate the railgun's battery pack was charging, the lander's batteries would be drained in less than ten minutes. That would give him about ten shots. This was the downside of the railgun: as deadly as it was, it took a hell of a lot of power to get those bullets traveling at over a thousand meters a second. He might get another ten if he pushed the limit on the reactor. It wasn't going to be enough. Might as well wire the override and then run. Destroy the lander and, with any luck, take out Harald's men at the same time. Twenty thousand liters of hydrogen would make a hell of an explosion. If there was anything left of the lander, it would be scattered over many kilometers. The fireball would probably be a couple hundred meters in diameter. With the proton reactor melting down, radiation was another concern. He'd want to avoid being downwind for a few days. At this point, it was starting to seem like the best option.

But was there any reason the muzzle velocity needed to be that high? Gabe had been trained to fight against Cho-ta'an, who used carbon-fiber body armor. These guys were wearing chain mail and leather. At a thousand meters a second, the bullets had torn through their wooden shields like paper. Hell, the pistols topped out at four hundred meters per second, and they were plenty deadly. So: crank down the muzzle velocity to five hundred meters per second. The railgun wasn't very efficient; about half the energy was lost with every shot. But halving the velocity should increase his capacity by close to fifty percent. If he pushed the reactor to the limit, that was about thirty shots. Between that and the pistol, it might be enough.

The first step was to wire around the override. That was easy enough: he grabbed the electrician's kit found a length of copper wire, located the green box Reyes had mentioned, yanked it out, and wired the two contacts together. For good measure, he used a battery-powered soldering gun to make sure the connections were good. On a whim, he grabbed several rolls of solder and shoved them into the pockets inside his suit. Then he held his breath as he threw the switch to fire up the reactor. A series of lights flashed, and a warning appeared telling him that a problem had been detected with the fusion regulation system. He tapped a PROCEED button, and was prompted for a root access code. He entered the code and the reactor hummed to life. Then he set his comm to give him a warning at ten minutes, and again at fifteen. Hopefully he'd be done before Harald's men showed up, because otherwise he was going to have to climb down into the lander in the middle of the fight to keep the reactor from going critical.

That raised another question: if the Vikings showed up while he was still charging, they might be smart enough to cut the cable. They had no understanding of electricity, of course, but every time he'd made the mistake of thinking of them as primitive people, they'd surprised him with their canniness. All it would take was one stray swing of an axe and he'd be screwed. The solution was brutal but elegant: lacking any heavy-duty power tools, he cranked the muzzle rate of the railgun back up to a thousand meters per second and fired a round right through ceiling. The hole was just big enough to thread a cable through. After assessing his options, he decided to move the battery back and compulsator inside the lander, where they would be less vulnerable to attack. He threaded the thick cable from the compulsator through the hole in the ceiling to the gun.

While the battery charged surveyed the horizon from the casemate. Still no sign of Harald's men. Had he been wrong? Or had the survivors met the reinforcements and warned them against attacking? There was no way to know, and nothing to do but prepare for the worst. He could only hope Reyes and the others arrived before Harald's men did.

Gabe spent the next ten minutes shoring up the spike barrier as best he could, resetting the poles that had been knocked over and replacing some that had been hacked in pieces. Another key element of his defense was in the process of disappearing: the ice on the lander was melting in the warm sun. All he could do is drag the bodies off the wings and away from the lander so as not to give the attackers any additional advantage.

He was finishing this task when he spotted a group of men advancing across the plain from the south. They were moving fast. He checked the railgun's battery before climbing into the casemate. It read thirty-one percent. At five hundred meters per second, that would give him maybe twenty shots. If he kept the reactor running—and stayed alive—for another five minutes, he might get ten more. The group moving across the plain toward him looked to be at least sixty strong.

The Norsemen were bunched together, so Gabe set the rate of fire to two per second. That gave him just enough time to shift his aim from one man to the next without spending more than one bullet per man. When they were a hundred meters out, he started firing.

CHAPTER TWENTY-TWO

Gabe managed to drop about twenty of them before they reached the spike barrier. Most of these were only wounded; at the lower velocity, the bullets didn't tear through armor and flesh the way they had with the last bunch. The compulsator was having a hard time keeping up the rate of fire, indicating the battery was getting low. There was nothing for it but to keep shooting. Twenty or so men with bows held back, firing arrows at him from about fifty meters. Gabe ignored them; arrows that went over the casemate wall bounced harmlessly off his helmet or made superficial tears in the flight suit. The worst they could do was bruise him; the velocity of the arrows wasn't great enough to penetrate the nanofiber armor. Gabe focused on the men trying to get past the spikes, taking out four more before the gun quit. He dropped it and drew his pistol, hitting three more men as they hacked at the spikes.

Before those three even hit the ground, a dozen more were at the barrier, swinging axes or shoving the poles out of the way with their hands. The others swarmed around the other side of the barrier to come at him from all sides. Gabe hit as many as he could as they came through, but there were just too many. They swarmed through gaps in the barrier and climbed over their fallen countrymen and onto the wings. On the left side, which was still in shadow, the men had to tread carefully to avoid slipping on the ice, but those approaching from the east had little trouble. Gabe emptied his magazine into the three men nearest the casemate, paused to reload, and then emptied another magazine at the next bunch. The eastern wing was now clear, but five men remained on the ground on the east side, and the ones on the left wing were almost on him. He climbed on top of the eastern wall of the casemate and jumped, popping out the empty magazine as he did so.

Gabe landed hard on the snow about ten paces from the lander and rolled, grabbing another magazine from his belt. He slapped the magazine in place and turned to face the lander, putting two bullets in a man approaching with a spear. There were two more men right behind him; Gabe managed to put them down with one bullet each. He had exactly three bullets left, and one chance to save the lander.

Men were now swarming all over the wings and fuselage, but the closest able-bodied man on the ground was a good ten meters away, toward the nose of the lander. Gabe got to his feet and sprinted toward the hatch. The man near the nose, brandishing an axe, tried to intercept him, but Gabe shot him between the eyes. Gabe slammed into the hatch, tapped the code and yanked on the latch. As the hatch slid open, Gabe turned to his left and shot another man, who had jumped down from the wing. There were three more behind him. Gabe stepped into the lander, slamming the hatch shut behind him. He collapsed onto a seat and exhaled in relief.

Outside, Vikings swarmed over the lander. It didn't take them more than a few seconds to start with the axes, trying to chop their way through the craft's metal exterior. The lander was pretty tough, but it had been badly damaged in the crash. If the Vikings were smart—and there was every indication they were—they'd have no trouble locating the weak points. They learned quickly that the ballistic polycarbonate used for the windshield and portholes was stronger than the rest of the exterior and that the reinforced steel of the hatch made it an unattractive target. They set about banging on any crack or seam they could find; any man who didn't have an axe grabbed one from one of the fallen. The sides of the lander crashed and shuddered around him. He figured it would take them fifteen minutes, max, to get inside.

Gabe's comm chimed with an alarm, indicating that the reactor had been running for five minutes beyond the automatic shutdown point. Reyes had said he had at most another five minutes before the reactor exploded. He began to get up to hit the shutoff but then changed his mind and sat down again.

He tapped his comm. "Hey, Reyes, you there?"

"Here," Reyes said. "What the hell's that noise?"

"That would be the angry Vikings trying to chop their way into the lander with axes," he said, yelling to be heard over the racket.

"You're... inside the lander?"

"Didn't have any choice. I think I may have to let the reactor blow."

"What?" Reyes asked. "No! We're thirty minutes out. If you can—"

"In thirty minutes, the lander is going to be in pieces. I'm sorry, Reyes. I did my best. Doesn't look like we're getting off Earth."

"Even if…" Reyes started. She gasped for breath. "Still need lander."

Gabe sighed. It sounded like Reyes was starting to accept the reality of their situation. That was good. But he had more bad news for her. "I've been thinking about that," Gabe said. "The lander is valuable, but it's also a magnet for trouble. I think we have to accept that Harald wants it more than we do. These guys aren't going to stop."

"Half an hour," Reyes said. "We have guns…"

"I'm sorry, Reyes. I'm not going to hold out that long. Save your ammo and keep your distance. The explosion will take out the rest of Harald's men. If we destroy the lander, maybe he won't send more right away. At the very least, it'll give you time to get away before more come."

"Gabe, God damn it—"

"It's been an honor working with you, Chief," he said. "Gabe out." He cut the comm.

Reyes would hate him for this, but that was okay. He knew he was right, and he didn't have time to explain it to her. He had been wrong about the lander. All it had done was make them a target of every spear-toting asshole in Norway. If they'd been smart, they'd have taken anything valuable that they could move out of the lander and left the lander itself for Harald. Because of their insistence on holding onto the lander, they were going to lose everything. Sure, he could shut down the lander and wait for Reyes and Sigurd to arrive, but he knew how that would go: even armed with pistols, Reyes and the others wouldn't be able to defeat thirty men—particularly once the Norsemen had control of the lander. And if by some miracle they did take the lander back, it was only a matter of time before Harald sent more men. When he did, they'd be out of ammo. They might be able to grab the portable transmitter and a few other items, but it wasn't worth the risk. Better to conserve ammo, eliminate as many of Harald's men as they could, and deny him the prize of the lander.

As the banging outside continued, Gabe shook his head. So this is how it was going to end—hacked to death by Vikings. It would be funny if it weren't so horrific. Would they kill him quickly or make him suffer? He had read once about the Viking method of execution called the "blood eagle," in which the ribs were severed from the spine and the lungs pulled through the opening to create a pair of "wings." The odds were that they were all going to die in a fireball pretty soon, but he had no doubt Harald's men could cause him a great deal of pain during the few minutes he had left. He drew his pistol. It still had two bullets left. One would do.

As the Norsemen stomped all over the lander, looking for weak points to exploit with their axes, it occurred to Gabe that he'd left the railgun battery charging. He wouldn't put it past these guys to figure out how to use the railgun. He'd come to terms with the fact that he wasn't getting out of this, but he didn't particularly want to die slowly of a bullet to the spine or abdomen. He walked to the battery pack and yanked the cord from the compulsator. As tempting as it would be to leave the cable in place and hope one of the Vikings would hack through it and electrocute himself, he couldn't risk it. Besides, they'd be as likely to electrocute him as themselves.

The idea stuck in his head. Those bastards were crawling all over the lander's exterior, which was made of a steel alloy. It was also wet, and the Harald's men were wearing boots made of cloth or leather. A high-voltage electrical charge running through the lander might incapacitate enough of them long enough for him to escape. The heat shield panels on the bottom of the lander would probably provide enough resistance to keep the charge from running directly to ground. He wouldn't be able to save the lander, but he might be able to get away.

A glance at the railgun's battery indicator indicated it was at seven percent. That should be enough to charge up the compulsator one more time. If he could channel that power through the lander's hull rather than sending it to the railgun, it would create a hell of a shock. It might not kill the Norsemen, but it would definitely stun them for a few seconds.

He pulled as much of the cable through the hole in the ceiling as he could, chopped the end off, and stripped the leads. He tied one to a cargo hook near the stern. Holding onto the insulation of the other lead with his gloved hand, he plugged the cable back in and turned on the compulsator. While he worked on this, one of the Norsemen manage to break through the ceiling with an axe a couple meters behind him. Sunlight was already streaming through another gap in the paneling toward the cockpit. Somebody had shoved one of the spiked poles through it and was trying to get enough leverage to pry the panels apart. They'd be inside any minute now. Between them and the impending explosion of the reactor, he didn't have much time.

The compulsator beeped, indicating it was fully charged. Gabe took a deep breath, drew his gun, and crouched down on the padding that lined the floor of the lander. Without the rifle's trigger mechanism acting as a switch, the compulsator's charge would drain as soon as the circuit was completed. After making a final check to make sure he wasn't touching any metal, he reached toward the door with the lead. Electricity arced from the lead to the door, followed by a loud pop as the wire contacted the metal.

Several men yelped in pain or fear. The axes stopped their banging and for a moment Gabe heard nothing but men falling and sliding off the lander. He drew his gun and pulled the hatch open.

Two men stood immediately in front of them. He put a bullet in each of them, slid his gun into the holster and ran out of the hatch. A dozen men lay near the lander on both sides of the hatch, groaning and looking around in confusion. Several more, who hadn't been touching the lander when the compulsator went off, stood in front of Gabe. They stared at him, clearly amazed by whatever magic had just struck down their comrades. Gabe turned to his left, drew his knife and ran.

A man who had been standing clear of the lander came at him with a spear. Gabe stabbed him in the belly with the knife. He caught a glimpse of the man's face as he fell—he was just a kid, no older than sixteen. Gabe pulled the knife back, put the kid's face out of his mind and ran. Two more came at him from his right, but the one nearest him was still dazed from the shock. Gabe sliced at the man's neck and he dodged clumsily, stumbling into the other man. The two of them fell to the snow. Gabe ran.

Some others noticed him as he neared the nose, and one of them shouted and pointed. Soon a dozen men were chasing him. A spear whizzed past his left ear, sticking in the snow some twenty paces ahead. He kept running without looking back. He had no clear goal in mind— only to get as far away from the lander as possible. The prevailing wind was blowing north, and he was heading east, so he'd probably be safe from fallout—assuming he survived the initial blast.

The alarm chimed again in his ear. Ten minutes past the failsafe point. According to Reyes, the reactor could blow at any moment. How long would it take for the heat from the meltdown to reach the fuel tanks? He had no way to know, but he suspected it wouldn't be long. Even running at top speed, he'd be hard-pressed to get out of the blast range in time. He ran.

He heard men yelling not far behind him. Something hard struck his lower back, nearly knocking him off his feet. Probably a spear. The nanofiber shielding had saved him again. His legs were getting tired and his lungs burned. The forest was now less than fifty meters off. If he could make it there, at least he'd have some cover. Gabe had been the fastest runner in his class at the academy, but he'd been cooped up in a spaceship for way too long. The odds were pretty good that at least one of these strapping Norsemen was faster than he.

He reached the woods just as an axe slammed into a birch tree a meter to his left. He kept running, keeping as best as he could to a straight line while putting some trees between him and his pursuers. The crunching on dead twigs behind him told him that the nearest man was now only about ten meters back. They were gaining on him.

He couldn't keep up this pace much longer, and the forest presented new challenges. The trees were far enough apart here that he could still run at a near-sprint, but the ground was littered with leaves, twigs and roots that were mostly covered by the snow. One wrong step and he'd go sprawling to the ground. The men behind him continued to gain, and he didn't dare slow down. He lungs were on fire and his legs felt like rubber, but he kept running.

And fell. His left foot hooked under a root and a half-second later he was prone, sliding on his belly across the rough, snowy forest floor. The first man was on him by the time he managed to turn around. Gabe got his left arm up just in time to block the spear thrust. The spear slid across the outside of his forearm, tearing his sleeve open and slicing a gash in his skin. The spearhead missed his ribcage by the width of a finger, embedding itself into the snow and earth. Gabe gripped the shaft with his right hand as the man tried to pull it away, giving him a hard kick in his sternum. The man huffed and stumbled backwards, letting go of his weapon.

Another man, this one armed with an axe, shoved the spearman aside as several others approached from both sides. Gabe scrambled away, but there was nowhere to go. He was surrounded.

"Hvaðan ertu?" the man with the axe barked.

"The ship is yours," Gabe gasped. "Take it."

"Hvað heitir þú?" the man demanded.

"I'm Gabe. Gabe Zuehlsdorf."

"Harald es jarl minn. Kom aptr með oss til hans."

"I'm sorry, I don't understand."

"Statt upp," the man said, gesturing upward with his hand.

Gabe stared at him, pretending not to understand.

"Statt upp!" the man barked again, kicking Gabe's shin.

Gabe shook his head. The man with the axe barked something to the others. Two of the men crouched down to grab Gabe by his arms. As they did so, the sky behind the man with the axe lit up with a blinding flash. Gabe had just enough time to shut his eyes, clamp his hands over his ears and roll into a ball, turning his back to the blast. He dug his face into the cold snow.

The shockwave was like being hit with a two-by-four over every inch of his body. The Earth shifted beneath him. A deafening boom sounded a second later, followed by a blast of scorching wind. The man with the axe fell on top of him, inadvertently shielding him from the worst of the fireball. Even so, the exposed parts of Gabe's skin felt like they'd been pressed against a griddle. The hot wind continued for several seconds and then faded, replaced by a cold counter-draft sucking air back into the vacuum left by the blast. Gabe became aware of a droning hum that he realized after a moment was the man on top of him screaming. The wind settled to a strong breeze.

Gabe opened his eyes and crawled out from under the man. All around him, trees were on fire. The snow had melted as far as he could see; steam was hissing up from the hot ground. Closer to the lander, nearly half of the trees had been knocked down, and flaming limbs were falling all around. As the breeze faded, the air became so hot that it stung his eyes and made it hard to breathe. Some of the men lying nearby began to stir. Their clothes—and in some cases, their hair—were on fire. Muted screams filled the air.

The skin on the backs of his hands was already beginning to blister, and the pain on the back of his neck was nearly unbearable. He scooped up a handful of muddy snow from where he had been lying and slapped it on his neck. Cold water ran down his back underneath the flight suit. He struggled to his feet.

A vast mushroom cloud towered over the plain. The lander and anything within a hundred yards of it had been vaporized. His view of the cloud grew fuzzy as the steam and smoke mingled around him, obscuring his vision. Gabe turned away from the explosion and stumbled forward, coughing in the smoke and doing his best to shield his face from the heat of the fires all around him. Soon he could barely see his feet in front of him, and the melting snow was turning the ground to muck, but he trudged on, doing his best to avoid burning limbs and fallen logs.

After a few minutes, the smoke began to thin and he saw fewer and fewer trees burning. In the distance, there were still patches of snow on the ground. The nape of his neck felt like it was on fire again, so he pressed on toward one of the patches. When he reached it, he fell to his knees, gasping for breath. Sparing a glance behind him, he saw that he was alone. The Norsemen chasing him were either dead or too badly burned to continue pursuing him. Allowing himself a moment to rest, he scooped up some more snow and pressed it against his neck. When his lungs had stopped burning, he struggled to his feet.

He heard the footsteps too late, his hearing dulled by the blast. He'd just gotten the pistol out of its holster when something hard struck him alongside his temple. He fell sideways into the snow, dazed. Some seconds passed, and when he reached again for the gun, it was gone. Looking up, he saw a large man standing over him. The man held a sword in his right hand, and Gabe's gun in his left. He had a forked, braided beard and a jagged scar running from his left cheek to his chin. His tunic was stained with blood. The man grinned at Gabe. "Stattu upp," he said.

It was Gunnar.

CHAPTER TWENTY-THREE

Reyes, Sigurd and the others were still about three klicks out when she saw the flash. She spun around and yelled, "Down!", and then dropped prone with her hands over her head. She could only hope the others had understood the warning. If they weren't following suit, they'd understand what she was doing soon enough.

A split-second after she hit the ground, the shockwave hit, followed closely by a deafening boom. Wind rushed over her; even at this distance, she could feel the heat. She kept her eye clamped shut for another ten seconds as debris clattered to the ground around them. Hearing awed murmurs and gasps, she opened her eyes and got to her feet.

Sigurd and Njáll stood just behind her, staring at the mushroom cloud rising above the trees. The others—Agnar, Brynnjar and Braggi—sat on the ground, dazed. None of them looked seriously injured.

"Hvat es þetta?" asked Sigurd at last.

"The lander," Reyes said. "Our ship." She sighed. She hadn't allowed herself to believe that Gabe would really do it. She knew he must have felt he had no choice, but she had actually believed Gabe would find some way to save the lander. Now they were stuck here. Gabe was dead, and the human race was doomed.

They stood for some time watching the cloud billow and slowly dissipate. Sigurd's face held only grim horror; the others were literally gaping open-mouthed. These men had never even seen a firecracker.

Reyes had never seen an explosion of such magnitude up close either, but she'd been inured to this sort of destruction. Humanity had been at war with the Cho-ta'an since before she was born. In a strange way, the explosion of the lander marked the end of that war. Humanity had been defeated.

She tried to make the words mean something, but she felt nothing but numb. Getting the bomb to the IDL had always seemed like a long shot, and in some ways it was good to have the matter settled. She—and the rest of humanity—had been clinging to shreds of hope for far too long.

Pressing more heavily on her was the fate of Haavaldsrud. More than fifty people had been slaughtered, including Sigurd's own son. Sigurd's rage was the only thing keeping him going now; he was determined to kill the men responsible for his son's death. She suspected he would take little comfort in the knowledge Harald's men had died in the explosion. Judging by the look on his face, he had already figured it out. There was nothing for them to do but go back for Slater and O'Brien, who were waiting in the longhouse. The rest of the villagers had traveled south.

Sigurd took a step forward, as if he planned to get a better look at the destruction. Reyes put a hand on his chest and shook her head.

"No. That explosion… Dangerous." How the hell was she going to explain radiation to pre-industrial people who didn't even speak English? The amount of fissile material in the proton reactor was relatively small; she doubted there was much danger at this distance, but she wouldn't want to get any closer—at least not until the debris settled. Fortunately the wind was blowing almost due north, away from Haavaldsrud.

Sigurd took her hand and gently moved it aside. He strode forward, and the others followed him. Reyes continued to protest, but it was no use. They were determined to get a closer look. Reyes debated whether she should go with them or return to her crew. How much longer did she really expect to live in this environment anyway? She'd probably be impaled by a spear or eaten by a bear before she succumbed to radiation poisoning. But at last caution won out. She tapped the open channel icon on her cuff to let O'Brien and Slater know she was on her way back. Her heart jumped as she saw the green dot next to Gabe's name. That meant his comm was still functioning. If he'd died in the explosion, the comm would have gone with him.

She tapped his name. "Gabe," she said. "Gabe, come in. It's Reyes."

There was no reply. She waited several seconds and tried again. Still no reply. Sigurd and the others had disappeared around a bend in the path. She had been resigned to let them go without her, but now things had changed. She needed to find Gabe. But how? She could estimate distance based on signal strength, but triangulating his location would be impossible without another receiver. She could go get Slater, but if Gabe was being held captive, he could be a hundred klicks away before they pinpointed his location.

She ran after the Norsemen, stopping on the trail just behind Agnar, who was bringing up the rear.

"Wait!" she cried. "Stop!"

Sigurd halted and the others did the same. "Hvat es málit?" asked Sigurd.

"Gabe," Reyes said, tapping her ear. "Alive."

*****

Gunnar couldn't help chuckling to himself as he followed the foreigner through the woods. This had worked out far better than he had imagined. Having seen what the foreigners' weapons could do, he'd never believed Harald's men could take the lander. In fact, he suspected the only reason they had come so close was that something had gone wrong with Gabe's weapon. He had either run out of the projectiles it fired or something had broken down within the mechanism itself. Gunnar assumed that Geir's men would be defeated; his plan was to wait for the foreigner to get tired and then sneak up on the ship, hiding among the dead and waiting for an opportunity to disarm the foreigner. If the opportunity didn't come, he could still walk back to the fortress at Svelvig. He doubted anyone would question his valor: he'd been seriously wounded in the first attack, and he could certainly make up an explanation for how he was able to escape again. Besides, Ragnar would be too interested in hearing about the foreigners' weapons to worry much about Gunnar's curious penchant for survival.

But this! This was too much to ask for. The foreigner had practically run right to him! When the foreigner had fallen, Gunnar had thought he'd missed his chance, but then the ship had burst into flame, incapacitating the other Norsemen. Gunnar had nearly been killed himself; it had only been instinct that had caused him to dive behind a large oak stump a moment after the flash. Even so, his hair had been scorched in the blast and his ears were still ringing.

"Left!" he shouted to the foreigner, who was trudging along some five paces in front of him. Gunnar had tied his hands behind him with a strip of a dead man's cloak.

The foreigner veered right, and Gunnar yelled, "Left, you fool!" This time the foreigner went the correct way.

Gunnar was tempted to try to fire a warning shot with the weapon he'd taken off the foreigner, but he feared he would do it wrong and the thing would explode in his hand. It wasn't necessary anyway: the wound in Gunnar's shoulder made running difficult, but the foreigner wouldn't get very far with his hands tied behind his back. The foreigner didn't know this land, and he had no friends here. His only hope was to do as Gunnar instructed and hope he would be allowed to live.

Not wanting to risk meeting enemies coming across the bridge, Gunnar had opted for a different route. They would move southeast through the woods until they hit the river. They would then follow the river to the next village, where they could take a boat down the river to the fortress at Svelvig. It was a more treacherous and time-consuming route, but he couldn't risk the chance of someone waiting for him at the bridge.

Gunnar panicked for a moment as he heard a voice, then realized it was the foreigner talking to himself. Or was he speaking with someone else? Did the foreigners have some way of speaking to each other over great distances?

Gunnar drew his sword and took several quick steps forward. He brought the sword back and cracked the foreigner on the top of his head with the flat of the blade. "Quiet!" he shouted. The foreigner stumbled, reeling into a tree. Steadying himself, he started walking again, without making a sound.

*****

Sigurd approached Reyes, a curious look on his face. "Á lífi? Hvar?"

Reyes held up her hand. "Gabe, come in," she repeated. "This is Reyes. We're near the lander. Where are you?"

"East of the lander site," Gabe's voice said quietly. "Maybe three hundred meters, heading southeast. I can't—" His voice cut off abruptly.

"Gabe," Reyes said. "Gabe, are you there?" The channel was still open, but there was no sound.

"Hvar?" Sigurd asked again.

"I don't know," Reyes said. "I think he's been taken captive."

Sigurd stared at her.

"Captured." She gripped her left wrist with her right hand, pantomiming someone being taken against their will. "Enemy. Hvar?"

Sigurd nodded, seeming to understand. "Brú," he said, pointing back the way they had come.

Reyes hesitated. She knew what he was saying: the road south to Svelvig was on the other side of the river. To get there, you had to cross the bridge. But Gabe had said he was east of the lander, heading southeast. Assuming he was being taken to Svelvig, that meant that either there was another way south, or there was another way across the river.

She crouched and drew a wavy line in the snow. "River," she said. She placed a twig across the wavy line. "Brú." Then she placed a pebble a few centimeters down the wavy line. "Us," she said, pointing at the pebble and then at herself. She placed another pebble where she guessed Gabe was, relative to them. "Gabe." She put a piece of bark farther down the river and said, "Svelvig." Then she picked up the twig. "Nei brú," she said. "How does Gabe get to Svelvig without crossing the bridge?"

Sigurd nodded. He turned and discussed the matter with the other men for a moment. Then he knelt down and drew a line on along the eastern side of the river. At the end of the line, he placed a piece of a leaf, then set the pebble representing Gabe on top of it. "Bátr." He dragged the leaf across the river to piece of bark.

"Bátr," Reyes repeated. "Boat. They'd follow the river south and then take a boat across to Svelvig."

Sigurd nodded again. He got to his feet and barked orders to the others. After a brief exchange, Agnar, Brynjarr and Njáll set off running— Brynjarr to the south, Agnar and Njáll to the southeast. Reyes had understood enough to know that he had sent Brynjarr to watch the bridge and the others to the riverbank to the south. With any luck, one of them would spot Gabe. She hoped that Sigurd had instructed them to return to them if he did; she wasn't anxious to see just how good the Norsemen were with their pistols.

"Gabe, it's Reyes. Cough if you can hear me."

After a moment, she heard Gabe cough.

"We think they're going to take you south along the river and then take a boat across to Svelvig. If you've reached the river, cough."

There was no response.

"Agnar and Njáll are headed toward you. Brynjarr is watching the bridge. They're going to try to get to the river before you. Move as slowly as you can."

Gabe coughed once more.

While Reyes was talking to Gabe, Sigurd and Braggi had started walking to the northeast.

"Wait," Reyes said. Sigurd turned, frowning at her. "Shouldn't we return to the bridge?" She pointed in the direction Agnar and Njáll had gone.

Sigurd shook his head and said something she didn't understand. He pointed to a hill about half a klick away. Reyes understood: if Gabe was still in the area, they might be able to see him from atop the hill. But their path was going to take them uncomfortably close to the lander site. Reyes moved in front of them, holding up her hands. She shook her head. "No. Nei. Danger. Poison."

Braggi looked ready to brush past her, but Sigurd put a hand on his shoulder.

Reyes made a sweeping motion, indicating they should make a wide arc around the lander site. Sigurd nodded, and she led the way. The wind was steady from the south, so the risk from fallout was minimal. By this time, the plume had mostly dissipated; the only sign of the explosion was a roughly circular area of brown, muddy ground, about three hundred meters in diameter. In the middle of it, barely visible at this distance, was a crater that appeared to be about fifty meters wide. The only remnants of the lander were small bits of metal and other debris that lay scattered across the field. Out of the corner of her eye she saw Braggi reaching down to pick up a shiny fragment of steel.

"No!" Reyes shouted, running toward him. Startled, Braggi backed away. "Do not touch," Reyes said, shaking her head. It was impossible to know without a Geiger counter how badly contaminated the metal was, but it probably was not safe to touch. Cleaning the metal would remove the radioactive particles on the surface, but radiation from the explosion would have made the metal itself radioactive to some degree. It was probably inevitable that these chunks of metal would eventually make it into weapons and other tools, but the longer they waited, the better.

"This way," she said, continuing her march across the plain. If she kept them moving, they might be less likely to investigate the debris. Reyes scanned the plain in both directions as they walked, but saw no sign of Gabe or anyone else. Reyes led them up the hill where they could overlook the blast site. Her comm chirped as she neared the top. It was Slater.

"Reyes, you there?"

"This is Reyes."

"What's happening? We heard something like an explosion."

"Yeah, that was the lander. Gabe triggered a meltdown."

"What? Why?"

"No choice. I'll explain later."

"Is Gabe alive?"

"Yes. Trying to find him now. How's O'Brien?"

"About the same. Resting."

"Okay. I'll comm you again when I know more."

"Copy that. Slater out."

Reyes continued up the hill, joining the others who were already looking over the plain. The extent of the destruction was stunning. There was nothing left of the lander but a smoking hole in the ground. The crater was almost perfectly round, at least ten meters deep. The ground was scorched and barren for a good eighty meters out from the crater, and the snow had vanished from a vast ring around the scorched area. The bare area was devoid even of fragments of the lander; the nearest pieces lay in the snow at least two hundred meters away. Other than the corpses of dead Norsemen, there was no sign of anyone else in the area.

A faint voice came over her comm.

"Gabe?" she asked. "Is that you?"

The voice spoke again. It sounded familiar, but it wasn't Gabe. The man was shouting in the Norsemen's language. Two gunshots sounded a few seconds later. Then the channel went dead. She tapped her cuff. "Gabe," she said. "Gabe, come in." There was no response.

Reyes turned to Sigurd. "Agnar and Njáll," she said. "They found Gabe." She pointed southeast.

Sigurd asked her a question, which she didn't understand.

She held up her hands. "I don't know any more than that. I heard gunshots." She pantomimed shooting a pistol and tapped her ear.

Sigurd regarded her for a moment and then spoke briefly to Braggi. They set off down the hill, toward the southeast. Reyes followed. They traveled for nearly an hour, with Reyes trying every few minutes to contact Gabe. She still got no answer. Sigurd slowed, holding up his hand, and Reyes drew her pistol. Two men approached: Agnar and Njáll. She put the gun away.

The five Norsemen conferred briefly together. Sigurd turned to her. "Gabe alive. Mit Gunnar."

"He's with Gunnar? How the hell...?"

Sigurd shrugged. "Bátr. Svelvig."

"Gunnar's taking Gabe south on a boat. To Svelvig."

Sigurd nodded.

So Agnar and Njáll had caught up to Gunnar and tried to stop him, but Gunnar had gotten away, taking Gabe downriver in a boat.

"We should follow?" Reyes said, pointing to the southeast.

Sigurd shook his head. "Engin Bátr. Brú." He pointed the direction they had just come.

It took Reyes a moment to understand: they had no boat, so they'd be unable to get across the river to Svelvig. They would have to backtrack to the bridge. Reyes cursed under her breath. That was why Sigurd had waited to go after Agnar and Njáll. He suspected this might happen.

Reyes nodded and gestured to indicate that Sigurd should lead the way. She was exhausted; they all were. It was now afternoon and she'd had three hours of sleep over the past two days. The Norsemen had been up almost as long, and they didn't have the benefit of chemical stimulants. If they could keep going, she would as well. She popped another of the pills and went after Sigurd.

It took over an hour to reach the bridge, which was a narrow but sturdy construct of pine logs surfaced with planks. They crossed the bridge and continued south for another hour. She continued to occasionally try to raise Gabe on the comm, without success. By the time they finally stopped, Reyes was barely aware enough of her surroundings to put one foot in front of the other. By some miracle, she managed to avoid tripping and falling on her face. If she had, she doubted she'd be able to get up again.

Sigurd directed them off the trail toward a hidden vale near a frozen creek bed. Reyes stumbled toward a rotting log covered with snow and sat down. She closed her eyes, resting her head on her arms.

Some minutes later, she awoke with a start as someone put a hand on her shoulder. After a moment of panic, she realized it was Sigurd. He was pointing to a bedroll near a fire that Braggi was tending. She nodded and Sigurd wordlessly guided her to the bedroll. Agnar and Brynjarr were already lying on their own bedrolls, snoring peacefully, while the others tended to the camp. She lay down and fell asleep.

Reyes was awoken by snowflakes falling on her cheek. It was dark, and the others were still sleeping. One man—she realized after a moment that it was Brynjarr—was standing guard, facing the trail. She got up and walked toward him. The air was cold on her skin, but the flight suit kept her warm.

"Brynjarr?" she said, and he turned to face her. He was leaning on the shaft of a spear, but the pistol was still in the holster on his belt. Reyes patted her own pistol. "I can take watch." She pointed to herself and then to where Brynjarr was standing.

Brynjarr shook his head. He pointed to his mouth and then toward the fire. Reyes's stomach growled at the thought of food. How long had it been since she had eaten?

She went back to the fire, found her pack, and opened one of the meal packets. While she was eating, Sigurd cried out in his sleep. His eyes opened and he looked around in confusion for a moment. When he realized where he was, he sighed heavily and stared at the heavens for some time. Big flakes of snow continued to drift slowly down, obscuring the sky. Reyes looked away, focusing on the fire.

Sigurd said something to her, and she saw he was pointing at the keg of ale Njáll had been carrying. She shook her head. Apparently these people drank beer all day and night, but it was a little early for her. She would have killed for a cup of coffee, but she would have to settle for sucking on clumps of snow.

Sigurd sat up and stared into the fire for some time. The look of determination had left his face; Sigurd now looked sad and lost. He looked much older than he did when she'd met him—only yesterday! But as she watched, the mask came back over him. He stood up and barked an order to the others. His tone was firm, not angry, but Reyes could see now the deep sadness that drove him. She wondered if he would get his vengeance, and if he did, whether it would help.

The men began to stir in response to Sigurd's order. Once they had woken up and relieved themselves, they set about packing up for the day's travels. Braggi kicked the logs apart, letting the fire die. The men's faces showed little but tiredness. They had lost people too, she knew. Brothers, sisters, parents, friends. Probably none of them had really come to terms with their losses yet. They merely plodded along, trusting Sigurd to lead them out of this somehow.

Did they blame her? She wondered. She hadn't sensed any hostility from the men, but to some degree they must hold her and her crew responsible. Whatever quarrel they'd had with Harald, it had been the crash of the lander that had brought them into direct conflict. And as many of Harald's men as Gabe had killed—a hundred? More?—she doubted it evened the scales in their minds. Maybe they just hadn't had time to process everything yet, but at some point they would. If she wanted to survive the next few days, she was going to have to remember that despite the Norsemen's cooperation, their motivations were not her own.

They set out again on the trail before dawn, Sigurd leading them in the near-darkness. When the sky began to lighten, Reyes found that they were now on a path overlooking the river, to their left. The snowfall had abated, but she figured the crash site must have gotten two centimeters of snow. That was good news for any living things in the region: the snowfall would help settle any radioactive material in the air and cover any irradiated materials scattered across the plain. In a few weeks, the debris might be safe to handle. The wind continued to blow from the south, carrying any remaining fallout away from the more densely inhabited areas.

An hour or so after dawn, Sigurd veered off the trail, leading them up a rocky embankment. Reyes didn't protest; if Sigurd had wanted to explain what they were doing, he would have—and she would be unlikely to understand him in any case. She focused on keeping her footing on the slippery rocks, following a few paces behind Sigurd. The others followed single-file behind her.

They climbed for perhaps twenty minutes, eventually coming out on a small, rocky plateau. Snow had begun to fall again, limiting visibility, but it was clear why Sigurd had selected this vantage point: on the other side of the plateau was a high hill overlooking the river. At its summit was a formidable wooden building surrounded by a spiked palisade. It had to be Harald's fortress.

"Holy shit," Reyes said, gazing at the massive structure in the distance. "That's where they're holding Gabe?" It looked impenetrable. Even with a hundred men, they wouldn't be able to get Gabe out of there.

Sigurd nodded. "Nótt," he said, and then made a gesture like something going over a barrier. "Niht." He'd used the latter word before, when talking to Gabe.

Reyes stared at him. He couldn't be serious. "You want to wait for nightfall and then climb over the fence? That's... suicidal." She was saying it more as a sanity check than to communicate with Sigurd.

"Men dead," Sigurd said, pointing in the direction of the blast crater.

"Yeah, okay," Reyes said. "They're short on men. But if there are even a dozen inside that thing...." She was no expert on combat, but she felt fairly certain that if Gabe were able to talk, he'd tell her this was a terrible idea. They had superior weaponry, yes, but the pistols were loud. Any advantage they gained from stealth would be eliminated the first time one of them took a shot.

Sigurd spoke an instruction to Agnar, who spoke a few words back, nodding his head, and then took a couple steps toward the precipice. The discussion apparently over, Sigurd led the rest of them back down the rocks. He found them a flat area sheltered from the wind and instructed Braggi to get a fire going. He sent Njáll and Brynjarr off on some task, presumably to gather firewood. The others set up camp and then sat around the small fire Braggi had started with the kindling he'd been carrying. Njáll and Brynjarr returned not much later, carrying an impressive amount of wood. Soon they had a pleasant fire going. The men ate and joked and told stories, and Reyes did her best to follow along.

Around noon, she heard Agnar shouting down from the plateau. He was beckoning toward them. Sigurd got to his feet, spoke a few words to the others, and then started up the embankment. No one else got up. After a moment, Reyes went after him.

When she reached the top, Agnar and Sigurd were standing at the edge, looking down toward the valley floor. Coming up beside them, she saw the focus of their attention. Several people were on the road that wended alongside the river, heading north, leading two pairs of oxen pulling carts. Reyes saw now that the road snaked back and forth along the hillside across from them, terminating at the entrance to the palisade. Whoever these people were, they were headed to the fortress.

Sigurd and Agnar had another brief exchange, after which Sigurd hurriedly climbed back down the embankment. Reyes followed him. When they reached the camp, he stopped and turned, holding up his hand. His meaning was clear: wherever he was going, Reyes was not to follow. She wanted to argue, but lacked both the words and the energy. She sighed and returned to the fire as Sigurd walked away.

He was gone for almost an hour. When he returned, Reyes saw renewed determination on his face. He approached the fire and spoke for some time with the other. Reyes understood none of it except the name "Harald." When they had finished talking, Sigurd turned to her. He paused for a moment, as if trying to come up with the right words. He pointed toward the road and then put his index fingers next to his forehead, indicating horns.

"Oxen on the road," Reyes said. "Got it."

"Oxas," Sigurd said, nodding. "Oxen." He pointed to his mouth.

"Eat the oxen?" Reyes asked, confused.

Sigurd frowned at her, not understanding. He stood up and walked slowly away from her, hunched down with his hands clutched at his shoulder, like a man dragging something. "Vagn," he said.

"Wagon," Reyes said. "Like a cart. Oxen pulling a cart. There's food on the carts?"

"Food on the carts," Sigurd repeated. Then he spread his arms wide.

"Lots of food," Reyes said. "Much food."

"Much food," Sigurd said. He walked toward her again, his legs splayed apart and his chin thrust out, holding his hands to indicate a large belly. "Harald." Several of the other men laughed and clapped at the impression.

Reyes stared for a moment, trying to understand. "Much food… for Harald? A feast? Harald is coming here?" She pointed in the direction of the fortress. Sigurd nodded. As he did so, Brynjarr walked past, carrying a bundle of dead twigs toward the fire. Sigurd slipped behind him, wrapped his left arm around his neck and held his right thumb under Brynjarr's jaw. Brynjarr yelped and dropped the firewood.

The meaning of Sigurd's presentation was beginning to sink in. "Oh, God," she said. "Oh my God. You want to kidnap the King of Norway."

CHAPTER TWENTY-FOUR

G abe awoke in a dimly lit room, lying on a hard wooden bench. The air was cold, and wind whistled through timbers around him. He sat up and looked around. The floor seemed to be hard-packed dirt; the walls were pine logs. The only light came from small cracks in the ceiling. His gun, sword, and wrist cuff were missing, along with the three rolls of solder he'd stuffed into the flight suit.

As he got to his feet, pain surged into his head. Where was he? How had he gotten here? Putting his fingers on his cheek, he found dry blood. Memories began to return.

Gunnar had marched him south to the river, where he'd had stolen a rowboat from some poor fisherman. Gunnar had held his sword to Gabe's back, forcing Gabe to row the boat. They'd just pushed off shore when Njáll and Agnar emerged from the woods, pointing their pistols at Gunnar and yelling at him to stop. One of them had fired and Gabe had tried to duck out of the way. The next thing he knew, something had struck him hard on the temple. A massive bruise had already formed, making his skin feel hot and tight. How long had he been unconscious? An hour? Longer? Was this Svelvig?

While he was straining at the locked door, he heard voices approaching outside. He stepped away as the door opened. A man with a short sword at his side strode in. Behind him was Gunnar, his left arm in a sling. The first man barked an order at Gabe. When Gabe hesitated, he drew his sword and motioned for Gabe to get up. Gabe got to his feet.

Gunnar followed as the guard escorted Gabe down a hallway lit by torches in wood sconces to a much larger room. A fire burned in a large stone fireplace at one end. Standing in front of it, staring into the flames, was a fat, bald man whose left leg ended in a wooden peg. The guard escorted Gabe to him. Gunnar came to stand beside him, while the guard waited behind Gabe, with his sword drawn.

Gunnar spoke to the fat man, and the man turned his face toward them. Gabe saw now that he was much older than his bearing indicated. His balding head was shorn to stubble and deep creases in his face suggested he was in his seventies. He held something in his hand. A gun. Gabe's gun. Gabe's momentary fear dissipated as he remembered the gun was unloaded and there wouldn't be any place to get ammo for it for a thousand years.

"Hvat es þetta?" asked the man.

"Gun," Gabe said.

"Gun," the man repeated. He pointed it at Gabe and pulled the trigger. As the action clicked, Gabe winced involuntarily. Gunnar chuckled.

"Not loaded," Gabe said. "No bullets."

"Bullets?"

Gabe held out his hand. The man regarded him skeptically for a moment and then handed him the gun. He felt the point of a sword in his back. The fat man held up his hand.

Gabe carefully ejected the magazine and handed it to the fat man. "Empty," he said. "No bullets."

The man nodded, seeming to understand. He took the gun back from Gabe and slide the magazine back into place. He grinned and shook his head as it made a satisfying click. "Hvar bullets?" he asked.

Gabe shook his head and spread his hands.

Gunnar spoke briefly to the fat man. The fat man nodded and turned back to Gabe. "Ek em Ragnar Ivarsson," the man said, holding out his hand.

Gabe stepped forward and clasped the man's hand, trying to hide his excitement. Was it possible this man was the legendary Ragnar Loðbrók? There were certainly plenty of Ragnars in the region, but given the man's obvious importance, it seemed like a definite possibility. A warrior named Ragnar figured prominently in Nordic sagas and poetry, but historians had never settled the matter of whether Ragnar was a real historical figure. This man was about the right age; According to this traditional literature, Ragnar distinguished himself by many raids against Francia and Anglo-Saxon England during the ninth century. Perhaps this man had conducted these raids under the authority of Harald and then returned to Norway, whereupon he was given a cushy job overseeing this fort as a reward for his service.

"I'm Gabe. Gabe Zuelsdorf."

Ragnar nodded. "Hvaðan ertu, Gabe?"

"I come from another land," Gabe said. "Far away." He still wasn't sure how to answer this question. Even if he spoke Ragnar's language, any answer he gave would be incomplete and misleading. Did the Norsemen even have a word for "planet"? In their mythos, Earth was "Midgard," the place between Asgard and Hel. He wondered what reaction he would get from Ragnar if he told him he hailed from Asgard, the home of the gods. It was probably as accurate an answer as he could give, but he thought it better to play it safe for now.

Ragnar asked him a question he didn't understand. When Gabe didn't respond, Ragnar repeated a word, pantomiming something falling from the sky and hitting the ground. Obviously Ragnar had been briefed on the crash—maybe had even witnessed it himself.

Gabe nodded, seeing no point in lying. "Ship," he said, imitating Ragnar's gesture. "Crash."

Ragnar held out his palm again, as he'd done a moment ago to indicate the land into which the ship had crashed. "Land mitt," said the man. "Skip mitt."

Gabe said nothing. Ragnar's meaning was clear enough: the land where the ship crashed belonged to him, so the ship belonged to him too. And Gabe had destroyed it. In Ragnar's mind, Gabe had stolen from him— which was apparently a bigger concern than the hundred-something men Gabe had killed.

"Gun. Bullets. Silfr. Skip," Ragnar said. "Mitt."

Gabe spread his hands helplessly. "Gone," he said. "There is only one ship."

Ragnar nodded thoughtfully. He spoke to the guard, who handed him something: one of the rolls of solder Gabe had saved from the lander. As Gabe watched, Ragnar unrolled several centimeters of the solder. "Silfr," he said.

Gabe nodded. "Silver." He wasn't actually sure of the composition of the solder. He knew it was at least fifty percent silver. The rest was probably zinc, tin, or some other inexpensive metal. Still, it would be very valuable to the Norsemen, even if they couldn't separate out the other metals—which was why he'd salvaged it. "Yours," he added.

"Meira silfr?" Ragnar said.

Gabe shook his head. "That's all there is. There may be more metal scattered across the plain." He did his best to pantomime the explosion and pieces falling to the ground.

Ragnar seemed displeased with this. He asked another question.

"I'm sorry," Gabe said. "I don't understand."

Ragnar asked the question again: "Hversu margir?" He pointed to Gabe, then gestured as if counting on his fingers.

Gabe swallowed hard. He knew now what Ragnar was asking. How much did Ragnar actually know? Was this a test? Gunnar must have briefed him already, but Gunnar had never seen anyone but Gabe. And the rest of the crew was gone when the attack began. He shook his head and held up one finger, then pointed to himself. "Me. Alone."

Ragnar glanced at Gunnar, who shook his head. Ragnar gestured. Before Gabe knew what was happening, his legs had been kicked out from beneath him. The guard's sword was at his throat.

Ragnar knelt down in front of him, placing his finger under Gabe's chin to make Gabe look at him. He asked the question again, counting off on his fingers. "Hversu margir?" Einn? Tveir? Þrír?"

Gabe shook his head again. "Just me," he said. "Alone."

Ragnar sighed. Gunnar laughed.

A boot struck the side of Gabe's head.

*****

Harald Fairhair sat astride his horse, deep in thought as his procession advanced up the snow-covered road. There were six men on horseback in front of him and another six behind—brave and sturdy men all, wearing the finest chain mail and carrying swords at their sides. They had been traveling since dawn, visiting towns and fortifications all along the coast, and hoped to reach the fortress before nightfall. Harald had much to do, but if there was any truth to what the messenger had said, this would be time well spent. The only thing that mattered was the task he had set out for himself.

Harald couldn't help but smile at the thought. There had been a time when those around him would have laughed at the idea of a unified Norway, if he'd dared speak it aloud. Now that possibility seemed within his grasp—and if what the messenger had said was true, it might come even sooner than he had imagined.

A metal ship, falling from the sky. He'd never heard anything like it, even in the stories of old. His mind boggled with questions: where had it come from? Where was it going? Who were its crew? Gods? Men? Dwarves? Giants? Some other race entirely? Could they be made to see things Harald's way? If not, could they be killed?

But dreamer though he was, Harald remained above all a practical man. Putting aside whatever wonders might be aboard the ship, imagine employing such a craft in battle! The mere sight of it, soaring across the sky like a giant metal dragon, would cause brave men to quake and run. He supposed that such a craft would take skill to pilot; perhaps he would need to keep the crew and press them into service. But the messenger had said the ship was badly damaged; it might well be beyond repair. Even so, its value was incalculable. If it really was made from steel, how many swords could be forged from it? A thousand? Ten thousand? Harald pictured his bodyguards wearing plates of steel, as some Frankish knights did. Norsemen in such armor would be unstoppable! And that was to say nothing of the weapons the messenger had said the foreigner wielded. Three of Gunnar Bjornson's men killed before they could even raise their spears! The messenger, a young man named Leif, claimed to have seen it with his own eyes. Leif remained imprisoned at a fortress in Vestfold, where Harald's party had spent the prior night. He would be tortured and executed if he'd been found to be lying or even exaggerating, but his account had remained remarkably consistent under interrogation, and by all accounts he was a trustworthy young man, devoid of treacherous motives.

It was now late afternoon and they were nearly in sight of the fortress, which served these days mainly as a garrison for Harald's troops. Since he'd consolidated his holdings in the north, silver had been flowing consistently into his treasury, and he'd found it advisable to keep several hundred men on retainer, to be dispatched to the more troublesome areas as he or his jarls saw fit. The strategy had borne fruit over the past several years: he would dispatch emissaries—often men with local ties, like Gunnar—to sell the villagers on the wisdom of a shared defense, using the threat of violence as an additional incentive. Many of the communities on the coast remained stubbornly independent, but their independence could be used against them: their failure to create strong alliances with neighboring villages made it easy to isolate and crush them.

The fortress could house as many as two hundred men in a pinch, but generally fewer than a hundred were stationed there at any given time.

According to Leif, some seventy men had been there when the ship crashed, and another sixty were due to return shortly from a campaign in Vestfold. He assumed by now that his forces had taken control of the ship, but it was odd that he'd received no news since Leif's initial report. Surely the force Gunnar had led to the ship had been sufficient to take it and subdue the crew? Leif had seen only one man, but he'd been clear that the ship was big enough to hold several more. If there had been a dozen or more armed with the sort of weapon Leif had seen, it was not inconceivable that they could have defeated the entirety of Gunnar's force. That would explain why no more news had been forthcoming: all of Gunnar's men were dead or captive. The thought was unsettling. Harald had become used to the idea of being able to overwhelm his enemies with superior numbers. In his haste to investigate, he'd dismissed a troubling possibility: perhaps no number of Norsemen were a match for the foreigners.

If that were true, then Harald himself was in danger. He considered for a moment the possibility of turning around and returning to his well-guarded lodge to the southeast. But this would mean only a temporary reprieve. If Leif's words were true, then his fate lay with the foreigners, one way or another. Cowardice would not fulfill his ends. He would seize their ship or die in the attempt.

It was not long after he made this decision that the man in the lead of the expedition, Fritjoff, stopped his horse and held up his hand. He turned to bark an order at the others: there was a man ahead on the trail, blocking their way. Fritjoff and the second man, Gustav, would investigate while the others protected Harald.

Fritjoff and Gustav rode their horses slowly around the bend. Harald heard voices, but could not make out what was said. Two loud cracks, like thunderclaps, followed. Harald's horse reared up onto its hind legs, whinnying in alarm. Several of the other horses followed suit. Harald managed to get his horse under control, but a new wave of panic swept over them as the horses Fritjoff and Gustav had been riding galloped madly around the corner toward them. There was not enough room for them to pass, and for a moment all was chaos as horses reared and whinnied, throwing several of Harald's men to the ground. Harald kept control of his own mount for several seconds, but he saw that it was a lost cause. Once they got turned around, the horses were going to bolt, and he was not about to flee from whatever lurked around that corner.

Harald leaped clear of his horse, landing hard on the packed snow and rolling aside. The horses, several of them still carrying their riders, were now galloping away from the fortress. Harald got to his feet. Only three of his men stood with him. They moved toward him, drawing their swords and turning to face the trail ahead. Two men stood in front of him and one behind. Harald drew his own sword.

A man walked slowly and deliberately around the corner. He was burly, with thick brown hair that was beginning to turn gray. A sword hung from his belt, and in his hand he carried something made of dull gray metal. He pointed the object at Harald.

"I am here for the man who calls himself King," the man said. "The rest of you are free to go."

None of the men moved. Nor would they—these were Harald's personal bodyguard, loyal unto death.

"Kill him," Harald said, more as an answer to an unasked question than an order.

The two guards in front advanced toward the stranger. The stranger pointed the object first at one, and then at the other, releasing two more thunderclaps. One man fell to the ground, gasping and clutching his chest. The other staggered backwards, holding his left shoulder. Blood ran down his arm, dripping on the snow-packed path.

Who was this man? Harald wondered. He looked and spoke like one of the villagers from the southeast, but he wielded a weapon like the one Leif had described. Harald's anger bubbled up inside of him. What gave this man the right to interfere with Harald's destiny? Harald ran toward him, raising his sword over his head.

The burly man pointed his weapon at Harald, but Harald did not falter. If he was his fate to be cut down by this man, then so be it. He did not recognize this man's right to possess this weapon—much less to threaten him with it. He had not become the ruler of most of Norway by allowing such insolence to go unanswered.

Harald was nearly on the burly man when another person—a woman!—darted out from behind the rocks toward the man, shouting something at him in a strange language. She didn't reach the stranger in time to keep him from using the weapon, but she distracted the man long enough for Harald to take a step to his right. The weapon boomed again, tearing into the sleeve of Harald's tunic.

Harald brought his sword down, but the woman was in the way. His blade came down between her neck and her shoulder, knocking her to the ground. He was amazed to see that the sword had not penetrated her odd, tight-fitting clothing. If she wore armor, it was exceedingly thin and well-hidden.

The burly man was momentarily stunned by the woman's fall, and Harald used the pause to press the attack, swinging downward toward the man's forearm. The stranger pulled his arm back, but not quite in time: the blade struck the strange weapon, knocking it out of his hand.

Harald stepped over the woman, who lay motionless on the ground. Four more men ran toward him. Two of them carried spears, but two held the same gray metal weapons their leader wielded. If they intended to kill him, this fight would not last much longer. He brought his blade back and swung again at the stranger. To his left, one of the weapons boomed, and he heard a grunt from behind him. That would be Njord, the last of his guards. The burly man ducked under Harald's blade and dived toward him while he was still off-balance, knocking him off his feet. Before he knew what was happening, the man was on top of him, one knee on Harald's chest and the other on his bicep, pinning his sword arm to the ground. Something sharp cut into the Harald's neck: a knife.

Somewhere behind him, the woman gasped a desperate plea at the man. Harald had met Saxons, Danes, Friesians, Franks, Rus, and many other peoples, but he was certain he'd never heard this language. He had the feeling, though, that she was interceding for his life. Why?

"This man is responsible for the death of my son," the stranger said, in words that were perfectly clear to Harald. The other men standing nearby showed no sign of wanting to interfere. If this man intended to kill him, he could do so. And yet he hesitated. The woman, who had gotten to her feet, pleaded with him again. She was holding her right hand to her left shoulder, where he'd struck her, but there was no blood.

The blade cut into Harald's skin. He winced but didn't cry out. He would not give these people the satisfaction. "Finish it, then!" he growled at the man.

But the pressure eased. The man got up and walked away.

Harald permitted himself a smile. So the stranger hadn't had the courage to kill a king after all. Harald sat up, still gripping his sword. The two men pointed their strange weapons at him, as if daring him to use it. He got to his feet and handed the sword to the man on his left, pommel first. The man took it and tucked it into his belt.

"Tie his hands," the burly man said.

Harald did not resist. He looked from one man to the next, memorizing their features. At some point in the not-very-distant future, these people were all going to die.

CHAPTER TWENTY-FIVE

G abe awoke again on the wooden bench, feeling even worse than the last time. Ragnar's man had beaten him for some time; he had bruises all over his face and body. He was fairly certain he hadn't said anything about Reyes or the others, but he couldn't be certain. His memories after the first few blows were hazy. He regretted not asking the old man if he was Ragnar Lothbrok. Being interrogated by a legendary Viking warrior would make a good story, assuming Gabe got out of here alive. Killing a hundred Vikings with a railgun wasn't a bad story either, but he felt a little bad about that one. It seemed like cheating.

He wondered if Ragnar Lothbrok—assuming that's who he was— knew he was a legend. Did he even know that name, "Lothbrok"? He'd called himself Ragnar Ivarsson, but then Ragnar Lothbrok may never have gone by that name either. Lothbrok was a nickname. As Gabe recalled, it meant something like "shaggy breeches." He hadn't noticed anything out of the ordinary about Ragnar's clothing. He would make a point to ask next time, if he got the chance. Ragnar would probably punch him for it, but Gabe was pretty sure he was getting punched anyway.

He lay there for several hours, grateful for both the cold that kept the aching in his head to a tolerable level and for the flight suit that kept the cold from creeping into his bones. The flight suits were made to be worn for long periods at a time; they were lined with nano-enhanced fabrics that wicked sweat away from the body and broke down stray organic matter. Even so, Gabe would have killed for a hot shower.

Finally the door to his cell opened again, and the guard who'd beaten him earlier entered. The man barked an order at him. He seemed agitated; something was not going according to plan.

Gabe got to his feet and didn't resist as the man directed into the hall. He was escorted down the hall back to the large room with the fireplace. He steeled himself for round two.

But when they emerged into the room, it was empty. They continued across the room to a massive wooden door. The guard sheathed his sword and pulled the door open. Gray light streamed inside the room.

Outside, snow fell gently on small courtyard that was ringed by a low stone wall. Just beyond the wall, the land seemed to fall away in a steep cliff; the hills across the river were barely visible through the snow.

Ragnar stood just outside the door, facing outward. He glanced back as the door opened. Some ten paces in front of him stood Reyes, Sigurd and several of Sigurd's compatriots. Sigurd was at the head of the group, with his sword against the throat of a heavyset man wearing finely tailored wool clothing. The man's ruddy face was framed by a dense beard and thick locks of strawberry blond hair. Reyes stood just to his left, her pistol in her hand. The others—including the two gunmen—faced outward, their weapons at the ready. Another thirty or so men—Ragnar's, no doubt—stood around the perimeter of the courtyard, spears ready. Ragnar and Sigurd regarded each other coldly.

The two guards escorted Gabe outside, so they stood next to Ragnar.

"Reyes?" Gabe said as he saw her. "What the hell are you doing?"

"Rescuing you," Reyes said. "Are you okay?"

"Banged up, but I'll live." He glanced at the fat man in the fine clothes. "Is that who I think it is?"

"Harald Fairhair," Reyes said, with a nod. The fat man shot a glare at her.

"You kidnapped the King of Norway."

"Seemed like a good idea at the time. I think Sigurd has convinced them to trade you for him."

Gabe nodded slowly.

Sigurd and Ragnar had a brief exchange in Norse, which Gabe couldn't follow. If he had to guess, he'd say Ragnar was balking at Sigurd's demands. But a word from Harald seemed to settle the matter.

"Við höfum samning," Sigurd said to Reyes. Reyes looked to Gabe, who shrugged.

Sigurd pointed to Gabe, and spoke again to Ragnar. He gestured for Gabe to approach.

Ragnar hesitated, but then nodded. He spoke an order to the guards, who reluctantly released Gabe's arms. "Ganga þá," one of them muttered. When Gabe didn't respond, the guard kicked him in the lower back. "Ganga!" he barked. Gabe stumbled forward.

Ragnar growled something to Sigurd, but Sigurd kept his sword tight against Harald's neck.

Gabe stopped. He'd expected Sigurd to release his hold on Harald. "Reyes, what's going on?"

"I don't know," Reyes said. "Outside, he… I thought he was going to kill you-know-who."

"If he does, we're all dead. Even if our gunmen can actually hit something, they don't have enough ammo to—"

"I know, Gabe. Just be ready."

Gabe nodded and swallowed hard. He couldn't blame Sigurd for wanting revenge on Harald. Gabe had never had a family, so he could only imagine the rage Sigurd was holding in right now.

Gabe took another step, and Ragnar yelled something. Sigurd shook his head. Harald gasped as the blade dug into his throat.

"Sigurd, please," Reyes pleaded. "You have every right to do this, but you can't. Please."

You can't, Gabe thought. Interesting choice of words. Not *you shouldn't*, but *you can't*. He wondered if it was true, what Schumacher had said. Paradoxes don't exist. Harald Fairhair had lived well into the tenth century, dying only after he'd united all of Norway. Did that mean Sigurd couldn't kill him? What would happen if he did?

Sigurd yelled something to Ragnar. Ragnar looked displeased, but he muttered an order to one of the men near him. The man bowed, and then he and several others disappeared around the side of the fort. Sigurd said something to Reyes, but she shook her head, not understanding. Gabe remained standing, halfway between Ragnar and Harald, not daring to move while they waited. Gabe recognized one word Sigurd had said— *hestar*—so he had an idea what Sigurd was asking for.

He was proved correct shortly thereafter: the men who had gone away returned, leading horses—seven of them altogether, enough for Gabe, Reyes, Sigurd and his men. Smart. If they were going to get out of this, they needed to be able to make a quick getaway. He saw Reyes breathe a sigh of relief as she realized Sigurd didn't intend to kill Harald after all. Not yet, anyway.

Emboldened by Sigurd's demand, Gabe spoke up. "Gun," he said, looking at Ragnar. "And silfr."

Ragnar growled a curse but he pulled the pistol from his belt and then grabbed the rolls of solder from somewhere in his cloak. Gabe walked toward them and took them with a bow. He holstered the gun and slid the solder rolls into a pocket. He was about to walk to Reyes when Sigurd said something else. Ragnar cursed again, more vehemently, shaking his head.

"What does he want *now*?" Gabe asked. He wondered if he should have let the gun and solder go. If Sigurd kept thinking up more demands, Ragnar was going to lose his patience.

"I don't have a clue," Reyes replied.

Sigurd made his demand again. "Nei!" Ragnar snapped.

Sigurd pressed his sword against Harald's neck, and Harald growled something at Ragnar. This time, Gabe made out a name: *Jannik.*

Ragnar at last agreed, dispatching two men to get Jannik. The man went into the building and returned a couple minutes later, prodding Jannik at the point of his spear. Jannik's face was dour but ashen. Sigurd smiled as Jannik approached. He pulled his sword away from Harald's throat.

Harald breathed a sigh of relief and took a step forward, but Sigurd reached out and put his hand on the king's shoulder, speaking a quiet command. Harald froze. Sigurd turned to Reyes and said, "Gun." He looked at the gun and then at Harald, who scowled at him.

Reyes nodded. She raised her gun to the king's head. Gabe watched in silence. He hoped Reyes knew what she was doing.

Sigurd strode toward Jannik, sword drawn. He said something to the spearmen, and they grabbed Jannik by the arms, pulling him toward the wall. One of them spoke an order, and Jannik reluctantly climbed onto the wall. The men pointed their spears at him as Sigurd approached Jannik, speaking to him in a slow, even voice. Jannik shook his head desperately, mouthing the words: "Ekki! Nei!"

Sigurd spoke to the guards and they stepped away. Jannik's eyes darted left and right, but before he could make a move, Sigurd swung his sword, slicing a long, deep gash in Jannik's belly. Jannik cried out, clutching at his gut to keep his entrails from spilling out. Gabe spoke another sentence and then pressed the point of his sword into Jannik's sternum. Jannik whimpered, took a step backward, and fell into the ravine.

Turning away from Jannik, Sigurd wiped his sword on the snow and sheathed it. He strode toward Reyes, giving her a nod. Harald glanced at Reyes and she nodded, lowering her gun slightly. Harald strode across the courtyard toward Ragnar. Gabe hurried toward Reyes.

Sigurd barked an order at his men, and they began to mount the horses. Reyes kept her gun trained on Harald. Sigurd asked Gabe a question, pointing at the horses. Gabe nodded. "We can ride," he said.

"Speak for yourself," Reyes said. She'd ridden a pony once when she was sixteen.

"The horse knows what to do," Gabe said. "Just hold on." Fortunately these horses actually had leather saddles and stirrups; Norsemen were known to ride on saddles made of turf, with no stirrups. "Watch," he said, pointing to one of the men mounting his horse. "Climb up from the left side, just like they're doing. Here, give me your gun."

Reyes handed him the pistol and he held it on Harald, who remained standing next to Ragnar, just outside the door of the fort. The two men looked angry but resigned. Gabe had no doubt they were plotting their own vengeance, but they would not seek it today. Once Reyes and the others were in their saddles, Gabe handed the gun back to Reyes and got on the last horse. Sigurd was already directing his steed toward the road down the mountain. The others followed single-file, the two gunners still holding their pistols at the ready. Gabe brought up the rear.

They left the courtyard and began to make their way down the hill.

CHAPTER TWENTY-SIX

Thea Jane Slater dipped the wooden ladle into the soapstone pot, extracting a sample of the bubbling brown liquid. She blew on it to cool it and then took a cautious taste.

It was bad, but not terrible. Half an hour earlier the soup had tasted like boiled cardboard with chunks of rabbit meat. Scrounging around the ruins of several of the houses in the area, she had managed to come up with three sprigs of thyme and a small wooden container of salt. Now it tasted like boiled cardboard with chunks of rabbit meat, hints of thyme and too much salt. Still, at least it was hot and offered some variety from the porridge and dried fish she and O'Brien had been eating.

"Smells fantastic," O'Brien said from behind her. He hadn't moved since the Norsemen had laid him on the bench the previous evening. He'd fallen asleep almost immediately and continued to doze on-and-off throughout the day. When he wasn't sleeping, he was chattering semi-coherently about his childhood on the stormy world of Tarchon. How much of this was due to boredom and how much was due to the pain meds was hard to say.

"It smells better than it tastes," Slater said with a sigh. "I was a pretty good cook once, but the selection of ingredients here is decidedly limited." The valley denizens who had fled to the east had been kind enough to leave them an ample supply of food, but it was comprised almost entirely of oats, barley and various types of dried meat and fish. They wouldn't starve, but even the dried IDL meals were beginning to seem attractive in comparison. The main ingredients of the soup were turnips, onions, barley and rabbit.

She heard O'Brien grunting in pain and turned to see him attempting to sit up.

"Easy," said Slater.

"I'm starving," O'Brien said. "Can't eat lying down."

"Then let me help you." She gathered up several of the skins and wool blankets from the other benches and brought them to O'Brien. She put her hand under his back, helping him lean forward, and then stuffed the skins and blankets behind him. O'Brien lay against them, breathing a sigh of relief. Even such minimal movement clearly caused him a great deal of pain. The good news was that there was no sign of serious internal bleeding or organ damage. With a few weeks of rest, he'd heal completely. Unfortunately, they were going to have to move him again soon.

Reyes had contacted her about an hour earlier to let them know that she, Gabe, Sigurd and the others were on their way back. Reyes had been sparse with details, but she'd made it pretty clear they wouldn't be safe in the valley for long.

She wondered once again if she and O'Brien should have gone east to Uslu with the other denizens of the valley. Reyes had left it up to her, but Reyes had indicated that several of the Norsemen blamed them for provoking Harald's attack. But where else could they go? The people of this valley were the closest thing they had to allies.

She ladled some of the soup into a wooden bowl and brought it to O'Brien. "I can't find any spoons, so you'll just have to drink it," she said, handing him the bowl.

O'Brien nodded, inhaling deeply from the steaming bowl. He took a sip from the edge. "Delicious," he announced, with such enthusiasm that Slater nearly believed him. She ladled a bowl for herself and sat down next to him.

"What a clusterfuck, eh?" O'Brien said.

"The soup?" Slater said. "Or...?" She gestured vaguely around her.

"I was talking about our mission going... well, off the rails."

Slater shook her head. "Off the rails doesn't even begin to describe it. Things have gone so wrong that it's almost like we're coming back around to right."

O'Brien took another sip of the soup. "You're still thinking this is a chance to rewrite history? To somehow prepare humanity for the Cho-ta'an?"

"No. At this point in history, the Cho-ta'an are such a distant threat, they're not even worth worrying about. I just mean that… well, you have to admit that even with all our advanced technology and wealth, things in the twenty-third century are pretty screwed up. And not just because of the Cho-ta'an, although that's a big part of it."

"I don't know," said O'Brien. "I'm a geologist. Two hundred years ago, I'd have been lucky to get a grant to visit the Grand Canyon. Thanks to the IDL, I've visited eight planets."

"Is it really because of the IDL, though? What could humanity do with those resources if all our energy wasn't devoted to fighting the Cho-ta'an? And how much time did you really get to work on any of those planets? The IDL has no use for academics; they want iron and uranium."

O'Brien shrugged. "You can't think like that. I'm thankful for the opportunities I get."

"You're married, aren't you, O'Brien?"

O'Brien hesitated. "Yeah. Eight years."

"Kids?"

"Two. A boy and a girl."

"You like being away from them for months at a time?"

"Drop it, Slater."

"I didn't mean to be insensitive. All I'm saying is—"

"I know what you're saying. You're trying to put a nice spin on things, convince yourself that traveling back in time to medieval Scandinavia was just what you needed. Well, it's not what I need. What I need is to go home and see my wife and kids again. But that's not going to happen, because they won't be born for thirteen hundred years. In answer to your question, I didn't like being away from my family for that long, but I sure as hell didn't sign up to vanish without even a chance to say goodbye. So maybe spare me the rationalizations."

Slater nodded, and they finished their soup in silence. O'Brien was wrong, though: she wasn't trying to convince herself of anything. She had never wanted to be in the IDL. She'd never even wanted to be a pilot. She would have been happy to spend her life tromping through the wetlands of Antheia, studying the millions of species of plant life native to her home world. But she was the third youngest of a family of eleven, and her parents didn't have the money to send her to an academy to study biology. So instead she enlisted in an IDL flight-training program, which promised to pay for her schooling if she served three years of active duty.

She spent two years in training and another year flying IDL supply missions in the asteroid belts of the Procyon system. She left the IDL to pursue an advanced degree in xenobiology, but by the time she finished her degree, funding for research positions had dried up. The only people who were hiring were the IDL, so she went back, and spent another three years hopping from planet to planet, mostly writing summaries of other peoples' research. She was convinced that no one ever read the reports, but somebody must have, because she got short-listed for the one of the first missions conducted by the IDL's new Exploratory Division. Ten weeks later she was training for the mission to the Finlan Cluster. That's where she had first met O'Brien and the others. None of them had met before; the Exploratory Division had only existed for six months at that point, and was made up entirely of service members drawn from other branches of the IDL.

Slater had never been much for socializing, but she had gotten to know O'Brien and the others fairly well. Of all of them, she thought she had the most in common with O'Brien, but she saw now that she was wrong. O'Brien didn't resent the IDL, despite the fact that it had kept him separated from his family for weeks or months at a time. In contrast, O'Brien's naturally cheerful personality couldn't hide his disdain for this strange new world in which they found themselves. Slater had no illusions about the challenges they faced here, but to her this place represented opportunity. They were in danger, yes, but they were free to face that danger how they saw fit. Reyes was technically in charge, but at this point only habit was reinforcing that authority. Their ship was gone and the IDL wouldn't exist for twelve hundred years. For all practical purposes, the military command hierarchy had vanished, along with their mission an all the petty regulations and protocols that went with it. For once, Slater felt like she was living life unscripted.

They sat there in silence for some time. The longhouse had no windows; the only sources of light were a small smoke hole in the ceiling and the dim red glow of the coals. Outside it grew dark and Slater was drifting to sleep on the bench when she heard a sound outside. Instantly awake, she got to her feet. The wooden bowl fell from her lap and clattered on the hard-packed earth floor. Grabbing an iron cooking knife, she faced the door. A burly man opened it and stepped inside. After a moment of terror, Slater recognized him as Sigurd. She put the knife down.

Reyes and Gabe came in behind him, along with three other Norsemen who had accompanied Sigurd. Slater breathed a sigh of relief and put down the knife. Slater ran to hug Gabe. "You're alive!" she cried. "I didn't think we were ever going to see you again!"

Gabe groaned, wincing at the embrace. Slater backed off, examining his face in the dim light.

"My God, what happened to you?"

"It looks worse than it feels," Gabe said.

"Jesus, I hope so," Slater said. "Sit down. Reyes, are you okay?"

"Gabe got the worst of it," Reyes said. "It's really good to see you two."

"God, that smells amazing," Gabe said, approaching the soapstone pot.

"Don't get your hopes up," Slater replied. "I did the best I could with the materials on hand." She picked up her bowl from the floor and began ladling some of the soup into it.

Gabe sat on one of the benches, resting the bowl in his lap. Sigurd took a seat to his right, and the other three men found places to sit as well. Slater found some more bowls and began serving the rest of them. She was handing a bowl to Sigurd when she heard a horse neighing outside.

"She's being modest," O'Brien said, opening his eyes to see the newcomers.

"Was that...?" Slater asked. Despite her travels, she'd never seen a horse before.

Gabe nodded. "Horses. Njáll is tending to them."

"Where did you get horses?"

"Stole them from Harald. Had to make a fast getaway after Reyes kidnapped him."

"Making friends all over Norway, I see," O'Brien said.

"Holy shit, so you weren't joking," Slater said. "You really did kidnap the King of Norway."

"Had to," Reyes said. "Gabe got himself captured by Harald's men."

"You left out the part where I fought off a hundred of them single-handedly."

"And nuked our ship, I hear," O'Brien added.

Gabe shrugged. "I was sick of that thing anyway."

"Is someone going to explain why you kidnapped Harald?" Slater asked.

Reyes answered. "We traded him for Gabe. And seven horses."

"And three rolls of solder," Gabe added, pulling the rolls of silvery wire from his flight suit and setting them down next to him.

"I'm not even going to ask," Slater said.

"It was actually Sigurd's idea," Reyes said. "Not the solder. The kidnapping."

Sigurd had thus far remained silent, but his eyes lit up at the mention of his name. Reyes turned to him, pantomiming a sword being held to her throat. "Harald," she said, and pointed her finger at him.

Sigurd nodded but said nothing. He finished his soup, said a thank-you to Slater, and got up, setting the bowl down on the bench. He walked quietly to the door and went outside. The other three Norsemen continued to stare into the coals, saying nothing.

"Is he going to be all right?" Slater asked.

"Harald's men killed his son," Reyes said. "These people see a lot of death. They're used to it, but..."

"But they killed his son," O'Brien said. "I know cultures vary, but that's not something you just get over."

"It was horrible," Slater said. "They murdered half the village and burned most of the buildings. I thought we were all going to die."

"I was pretty sure I was a goner too," Gabe said. "It's a miracle we all survived."

"No more splitting up," Reyes said. "From now on, we stick together."

"Agreed," O'Brien said.

"These people are going to want vengeance," Reyes said.

Gabe nodded. "The Vikings were big—are big—on vengeance. Sigurd can't even begin to mourn his son's death until his murderers are killed."

"I thought the men who killed him were part of the first wave that attacked the lander," Slater said.

"They were," Gabe replied. "Most of them, anyway. A dozen or so limped away."

"But that's not enough."

"No. Revenge is personal with these people. Sigurd wanted to do it himself."

"You'd think his bloodlust would have been sated after what he did to Jannik," Reyes murmured.

Slater glanced at Gabe. Gabe shook his head. "You don't want to know."

The door opened and Njáll entered. They greeted him and Slater got him a bowl of soup. He and the other Norsemen seemed very happy to have a hot meal; if they found the soup disagreeable, they didn't show it. When he'd downed his first bowl, Njáll explained through a series of gestures that Sigurd had agreed to take the first watch, and that Njáll had volunteered to be second.

"God, he must be exhausted," Slater said. "Maybe I should…"

"Forget it, Slater," Reyes said. "Let Sigurd do his thing."

"We don't actually expect them to attack tonight?" Slater asked.

"Not likely," Gabe said. "Harald doesn't know how much ammo we have, and he's lost over a hundred men already. I think he's going to err on the side of caution. In any case, time is on his side."

"How is that?" Reyes asked.

"Harald Fairhair united all of Norway. It's a historical fact. If we run to Uslu with these people, all we've done is decide where Harald is going to attack next."

"You think we're that important to him?"

"He's seen our ship and our weapons. Yeah, I think we're that important."

"But our ship was destroyed and we're almost out of ammo."

"He's not after the objects themselves, Reyes," Gabe said. "I mean, yeah, he'd have loved to get his hands on the lander, but these people understand the concept of technology. What he's really after is what's in our heads. He thinks we know where he can get more guns, or how to make them. And he's right. Any one of us has enough knowledge in our heads to reshape Europe."

"I'm a biologist," Slater said. "How do you figure I'm going to reshape Europe?"

Gabe ticked off items on his fingers. "Crop rotation. Germ theory. Evolution."

Slater was dubious. "If Vikings torture me for my knowledge of the twenty-third century and I start talking about crop rotation and natural selection, they're going to cut my head off just to make me stop talking."

"Point is," Gabe said, "Harald is right, although maybe not in exactly the way he thinks. O'Brien could teach them how to refine iron into steel. Reyes could teach them about electromagnetism. I could teach them field medicine. Any one of those discoveries, introduced at the right place at the right time, could change the world."

"So what do we do?" O'Brien said. "If Uslu isn't safe, then where?"

"Uslu isn't safe, but it's probably the safest option for now," Gabe said. "There's no way we can survive on our own at this point. We don't speak the language, we don't know the terrain or the people, we don't have much in the way of supplies."

"But if we go with them," Reyes said, "we'll be putting them in danger."

"Yes," Gabe replied. "But we can also hold our own in a fight. My suggestion would be to stick with Sigurd's people as long as they will have us."

"And then?" Slater asked.

"I don't know, Slater. I'm tired and sore. I don't think I have it in me to plan more than a day in advance at this point."

"We're all tired," Reyes said. "We need to sleep." The three Norsemen had already lain down. Brynjarr was snoring loudly.

"Agreed," Slater said. "We can talk more tomorrow."

CHAPTER TWENTY-SEVEN

I t took them until after sunset the following day to get to Uslu. They got a late start, as Reyes and Gabe spent the morning rigging a stretcher that could be carried between two horses lengthwise. They strapped a pair of long poles to the saddles of the horses and then hung the insulation-panel-stretcher from the poles with pieces of cattle sinew Sigurd had found in the ruins. It would still be a bumpy ride for O'Brien, but the sinew would absorb at least some of the shock.

Sigurd led the way on foot, followed by Njáll and Brynjarr. The seven horses came next. Reyes rode the first one; behind her were the two horses carrying O'Brien's stretcher. Gabe and Slater followed on the two horses after that. The last two horses carried only food and other supplies. Reyes had suggested that they take turns on the horses, but Sigurd insisted that the Norseman walk. Gabe was recovering from his injuries, and Sigurd was convinced that Reyes and Slater would only slow them down. Reyes felt guilty about it, but she couldn't deny being relieved that she wouldn't have to try to keep pace with the Norsemen. Her calves still ached from running after Sigurd to the lander two days earlier. Being stuck on a spaceship for six weeks was poor preparation for traveling forty klicks cross country over rough terrain.

Having nothing to occupy her other than staying atop her horse, Reyes had plenty of time to think. Gabe was right about Harald: he would never stop looking for them. They'd counted on twenty-third century technology to give them an advantage, but in the end it turned out to be a liability. They'd have been better off rigging the lander to self-destruct immediately, getting as far away as they could and doing their best to blend in. Now they were a target for the most powerful man in Norway and all of his sycophants. From what little she could understand of what Sigurd had told them, the current jarl of this area, Ari Birgirson, was no friend of Harald's, but Ari had to know his territory's days as an independent jarldom were numbered. Harald had been consolidating his power in Norway for twenty years; besides Ari's jarldom, only three petty kingdoms in the southwest and a few communities in the valley remained independent. Would Ari trade them to Harald for a guarantee of continued independence? Reyes found it hard to believe Sigurd would knowingly lead them into such a trap. Whatever the others thought of the spacemen, Sigurd seemed to have accepted them as true allies. Even Sigurd could make mistakes, though— he'd already made a big one by assuming Harald's men would attack the lander rather than the valley. On the other hand, Ari would be a fool to trust Harald. According to Gabe, Harald had eventually conquered all of Norway. Assuming they couldn't undo settled history, Ari was doomed to either die or accept Harald's dominion.

Uslu was a village of a few dozen buildings clustered north of a fjord that led ultimately to the sea. The travelers were warmly welcomed by Ari Birgirson and his wife, Astrid, who had been advised of their impending arrival by Arnulf and the others. Reyes gathered that arrangements had been made for them to stay with some of the locals that night. Reyes, as the leader of the spacemen, was invited to stay at Ari's house. Gabe and Slater stayed with the local butcher's family, a few houses down, and O'Brien was put under the care of an elderly woman and her daughter, who spent their days weaving wool cloth. Unable to communicate in more than the most rudimentary manner, Reyes enjoyed a quiet meal of boiled chicken and bread with Ari and Astrid, after which the family retired for the evening. Reyes slept in the main room with their three young children.

The next day was devoted to funeral services for those killed in the attack. After breakfast, the survivors, along with the spacemen and several dozen residents of Uslu, including Ari and Astrid, met in a field at the edge of town, where they buried the dead in a mass grave. Each of the fallen was respectfully laid to rest, one by one. Some of the more badly mutilated corpses had been cleaned up, but for the most part they were buried as they had fallen. Most of the men were buried with spears or axes, and sometimes shields. The blacksmith was buried with his hammer. All of these things had been carried from the village specifically for this purpose. It seemed like a tremendous waste to Reyes, given the immense value of these items and the poverty of the survivors, but it was not her place to complain. In any case, there was enough animosity toward the spacemen among these people without her making things worse. Fortunately, it seemed that most of the villagers had come around to the idea that the spacemen's arrival was more a convenient excuse for Harald than the cause of the attack. Only a few of the survivors—notably the one woman, Hella, whom Sigurd had warned them about, shot them hateful glances. The rest were neutral at worst, and most seemed to appreciate the foreigner's presence at the ceremony. After the burials, the assembled spent several hours listening to stories about the fallen. Reyes could understand little more than the names, but such was the skill of the various storytellers that several times she broke into laughter and many more times was reduced nearly to tears.

A feast commemorating the dead followed, held in a large hall in the center of town. It was the first meal Reyes truly enjoyed since their arrival. There were several types of meat, from rabbit to pork loins, as well as bread, a variety of fish, hazelnuts and the ever-present porridge. For drinking, there was buttermilk, beer, ale, and even a little red wine. Reyes and her crew ate and drank their fill, pausing only to thank their hosts profusely for their hospitality. Reyes made sure that some food was brought to O'Brien, who remained mostly bed-ridden.

She didn't know how long it would last, but she was determined to enjoy it while she could. Ari—a ruddy-faced, stout little man without a hair on his head—stood during the middle of the feast to give an eloquent and heart-felt toast to the fallen. Reyes couldn't understand a word, but again found herself strangely moved by the poetry of the Norse words.

At some point, Ari and Sigurd left the table to retreat to a back room, and Reyes felt a twinge of concern as she realized important decisions were going to be made without her. In the end, though, there was only so much she could control. For now, they were dependent on Ari's hospitality and Sigurd's friendship. Glancing across the table, she caught a moment of worry on Gabe's face as well. Neither of them liked having to rely on allies they knew little about, but there was nothing to do now but hope for the best. They couldn't afford any more enemies in Norway.

*****

Sigurd sat down in the heavy wooden chair across from Ari Birgirson.

"For Yngvi Sigurdson," Ari said, raising his cup. "May he have smooth sailing to Valhalla."

Sigurd raised his own cup and downed the wine. A pleasant heat filled his chest.

"Frankish wine," Ari said, when he had emptied his own cup. "Ten bottles cost me twenty yards of homespun."

"Too pricey for me," Sigurd said. "But you are a wealthy man. And I appreciate you dipping into your stores for the sake of my son and the others we have lost."

"The gods gave us wine for such times as this," Ari said. "He was a brave and strong boy, and he died protecting your home from Harald's thugs. I am sure he drinks in Valhalla even now, probably of a much finer vintage than this!"

"As we may, in the near future," Sigurd said.

Ari shook his head. "I am too old to die in battle. I'll leave such glories to younger men."

"Then you will not stand with us against Harald's men?"

Ari frowned. "Is that why you came here? To convince me to make a stand against Harald?"

"I came to bury my son. But I do not intend to flee from my enemy. I have dealt with the traitors who betrayed my people, but I will not stop fighting as long as Harald remains alive."

"You intend to go to war with the king?"

"Norway has no king," Sigurd said. "Harald is a pretender whose ambitions outstrip both his wisdom and his grasp. The foreigners have forced his hand and weakened him. They claim to have killed more than a hundred of his men."

"And you believe them?"

"I've seen their weapons. They are like nothing else on Earth. Men armed with such weapons could bring down giants."

"But the foreigners are not interested in a war with Harald."

"They are in a war, whether it interests them or not."

Ari sighed. "Sigurd, my hospitality has no limits as far as you and your people are concerned. But you have made an enemy of Harald. And these foreigners...."

"The foreigners are our allies. And our guests."

"And by extension, my allies and my guests, is that it? No, I'm sorry, Sigurd. You and the foreigners can stay for a few days, but then you must move on. I am not inclined to submit to Harald's rule, but I will not volunteer my people to be slaughtered in service of your futile attempts at vengeance. You must take your war elsewhere."

Sigurd leaned forward. "You call my quest to avenge my son futile?"

"I call it what it is," Ari said, meeting his glare. "Bold. Necessary, perhaps. But futile. Even with these foreigners' help, you'll never get close to the king."

Ari's remark struck him like a blow. If only Ari knew how close he had gotten! A flick of his wrist, and Harald would be dead. But he'd given up his chance. Why? To spare a man he'd only met two days earlier? No, he'd spared Harald because the woman, Reyes, had begged him. Sigurd thought of his failure and felt shame. There was a reason he'd left the kidnapping out of his story when he'd told it the night before.

"Perhaps you are right," Sigurd said. "Perhaps I will fail in my effort to kill Harald. If so, I will die trying."

"Ah," said Ari. "And that's what you're really after, isn't it? You seek penance, not vengeance. You hope to be forgiven for your failure by dying in your attempt to kill Harald."

"I seek to kill him. Whether I die is of no great importance."

"Then I suggest you put aside your self-pity and do what it takes to get your revenge."

"Meaning what?"

"You have told me how powerful these foreigners' weapons are. You have told me of their metal ship, which soared through the air. It is clear that wherever they are from, they have knowledge of weapons and crafts far beyond anything we have imagined. What if these people are the key to your vengeance against Harald?"

"I have told you I will not ask them to fight for me."

"Your anger has clouded your mind. I'm not speaking of launching an assault on Harald tomorrow. I'm asking you to think to the days ahead. What do you think these foreigners are up to?"

Sigurd frowned. "Their ship crashed. They are just trying to survive."

"For now, yes. But they are unable to return to their home. With your help—yours and your men's—there is no reason they cannot survive, and even thrive. At some point, they will stop running. And when they do, they will be a force to be reckoned with."

"That may be, but there is no place in Norway for us to go. Even my friends and kin reject me now."

"Then leave Norway."

"You would have Harald chase us from our home."

"He has already done so. If you truly seek vengeance, there is no place for you here. Go with the foreigners somewhere you can bide your time and build a force to oppose him."

Sigurd shook his head. "That could take years."

"And if it does? You prefer to die without plucking so much as a hair from Harald's beard?"

"Where then shall we go? Shall we take our horses across the sea to Anglia?"

"Surely your mind is not so clouded that you have forgotten the seasons."

Sigurd leaned back in his chair, regarding Ari. "You suggest we join the raiders going south."

"I suggest nothing, but merely speak the truth. If you wish to survive long enough to have your vengeance on Harald, you must leave Norway—and soon."

"You know of an expedition that is leaving from Uslu?"

"I do indeed. The boats have already arrived. Men are coming from all over the south of Norway. Four ships, with forty men on each. They leave in a week, weather permitting. I believe they plan to spend the summer raiding in West Francia."

"You seem well-informed of this expedition, Ari. Am I correct to assume you have an interest in it?"

Ari smiled. "Little happens in this area without my involvement," he replied. "However, in this case my concern is only that you escape Norway in one piece."

"And avoid dragging you into a war with Harald."

"A war is unavoidable. However, I'd prefer to delay it until the odds favor our side."

"When will that be?"

"When you return to Norway with a fleet of ships."

Sigurd laughed, but Ari was not smiling. "You really believe that will happen?"

"It's the only chance we have," Ari said. "I have to believe it."

Sigurd stared at the old man for some time. "This expedition," he said at last. "Do they have room for nine more?"

"They were trying to fill four ships. I suspect able-bodied fighting men would still be welcomed."

"And the less able-bodied?"

Ari shrugged. "You should be prepared to make sacrifices."

"You mean leave some of the foreigners behind. But you will not allow them to stay in Uslu."

"I am sorry, Sigurd. If Harald's men come for them, I will have no choice. Speak to the organizer of the expedition. His name is Dag Erikson; you will find his house on a promontory near the water. Perhaps he can make room for you."

CHAPTER TWENTY-EIGHT

G abe sat atop a boulder near the side of the main road leading into Uslu. It was nearly noon, and the air was cold but still. Over his shoulder, the sun shone brightly in an azure sky.

Having little else to offer the townspeople in exchange for their hospitality, he had volunteered for sentry duty, watching the road for signs of Harald's men. Since the foreigners' arrival, Ari had doubled the number of sentries, but this was probably an abundance of caution. Sigurd and Ari were in agreement that it was unlikely Harald would attack anytime soon. Even if he had somehow found out where the foreigners had gone, it would take time to assemble a force capable of taking Uslu. Given his recent losses, Harald would undoubtedly have to pull men from several southern garrisons.

It was a dull assignment; Gabe had been here since dawn and so far had seen only an ox-cart bearing oats coming into town and three fur-clad hunters leaving. His wounds still ached, but he was too restless to spend the day in bed. Now another figure was approaching from the town. Her small size and strange clothing made it easy to identify her at half a klick away.

"Hey, Chief," Gabe said as Reyes approached.

"How goes guard duty?"

"Can't complain. I've seen three rabbits, and eagle and an elk. What brings you up here? Is Ari kicking us out?"

"He wants us gone by tomorrow morning," Reyes said. "But I just talked to Sigurd. He's got a proposal for us."

"Really."

"An expedition is leaving for mainland Europe from a village on the coast in a week. Sigurd thinks we should try to get on board."

"What about Sigurd and his men?"

"They'll be coming as well. Sigurd, Braggi, Njáll, Agnar and Brynjarr."

"The warriors," Gabe said. "When you say expedition…"

"I gather that it's a raiding party, yeah."

Gabe grinned and shook his head. "An actual Viking raid. Unbelievable."

"At least pretend you have some qualms about this."

"Do we have any other options?"

"Not that I can think of. Seems like we're going to have to trust Sigurd."

"He's certainly given us no reason to distrust him. He and his men could easily have taken the lander from us if they'd wanted to. They were ready to fight and die alongside us to defend it from Harald. And unlike some of the others, Sigurd doesn't seem to blame us for the attack."

Reyes nodded. "And you didn't see him with Harald on the road. Gabe, he wanted to kill him. Would have killed him, if I hadn't begged him not to. He gave up his one chance at vengeance to save you."

"I suspect he did it more for you than for me," Gabe said with a smile. "But we're in agreement. We can't possibly go it alone at this point. We need allies. If we can't trust Sigurd, we're as good as dead."

"Then you think we should go?"

"How's O'Brien?"

"A little better, I think. I'm not sure a sea voyage on a Viking longboat is what he needs right now, but he'll survive."

Gabe nodded. "All right, then. Njáll is relieving me at noon. Then we can go tell O'Brien and Slater."

Njáll arrived shortly before the sun reached its zenith. Gabe and Reyes returned to the village, finding Slater tending to O'Brien. Slater was dubious.

"What is the purpose of this expedition?" she asked.

"It's a raiding party," Gabe answered.

"You mean they're going to kill people and steal things," O'Brien said.

"I would expect so," Gabe replied. "They're Vikings. It's part of their culture."

"That doesn't make it right," Slater replied.

"No, it doesn't," Reyes replied. "Fortunately, we're not here to rectify the inequities in Norse culture. As Gabe said, these people are Vikings. This is what they do."

O'Brien spoke up. "These people are angry that Harald destroyed their homes, and now they're going to do the same to a bunch of strangers?"

"To the Norsemen, theft and murder are different from raiding," Gabe explained. "They were betrayed by one of their own and then attacked by their own countrymen, who killed women and children indiscriminately."

"I can't believe you're rationalizing Viking raids," Slater said.

"I'm not rationalizing anything," Gabe replied. "I'm saying that for Sigurd's people, there's a clear difference between murder and raiding. Whether *you* see the difference is not a big concern of theirs. In any case, this is all academic. History happened. We're not going to convince Vikings not to raid."

"No, but we don't have to aid and abet them."

"We're hitching a ride on a boat, Slater," Reyes snapped. "Nobody is asking you to bludgeon any peasants to death."

"We're being hunted," Gabe said. "No place in Norway is safe for us, and this is our one chance to escape. If you want to take your chances here, feel free."

"No," Reyes said. "We stick together. If any of us falls into enemy hands, he or she is a danger to the others. We're leaving with those ships."

"I'm fine with that," O'Brien said, "but is there going to be room for me? I'm going to be useless on a ship. I'd be worried I'd be in the way."

"We'll figure something out," Reyes said. "We stick together, no matter what."

"So Sigurd and his men are coming too?" Slater asked.

"That's right."

"They're going to join in the raiding?"

Gabe sighed. "Slater, we've been through this…"

"No, listen," Slater said. "What I'm asking is this: what is Sigurd's motivation in going with us? Why doesn't he stay here with the rest of the refugees from the valley?"

O'Brien nodded. "It's a good question."

"The honest answer," Reyes said, glancing at Gabe, "is that we're not sure. The others are young men without attachments. They'll follow Sigurd wherever he goes. Sigurd may just be looking for a new start."

"You think Sigurd is running from Harald?" O'Brien asked. "He doesn't seem like the running type."

"No," Gabe said. "I think he's still intent on vengeance. Accompanying us to Europe may be a strategic choice on his part."

"You think he's going to enlist us in his war against Harald," Slater said.

"He hasn't asked us for anything," Reyes said.

"Tell me you're not that naïve," Slater said.

"No, you're right, Slater," Gabe said, "My guess is that at some point Sigurd is going to want something from us. So what? Again, we have no other options. Sigurd is a friend. I trust him. Without friends on this planet, we're as good as dead."

"He's not going to ask us for *something*," Slater replied. "He's going to ask us to do the impossible. Literally, the impossible. He wants to kill a guy we know for a fact dies of old age decades from now. When did you say Harald dies, Gabe?"

"I don't remember the exact date, but it was well into the tenth century."

"Is somebody going to tell this to Sigurd at some point?" Slater asked.

"It took an hour for me to understand what he was saying about the ships," Reyes said. "If you think you can explain to him that his quest for vengeance is doomed because you come from the future and you know for a fact that Harald Fairhair dies of old age, please give it a shot. And make sure you're prepared for the follow-up questions about where you're from and what Earth is like in your time."

"We can't tell him anything," Gabe said. "It would be pointless, even if we could communicate it. If and when Sigurd asks for something from us, we evaluate the request within our current mission parameters."

O'Brien laughed and then groaned in pain. "Mission parameters? What might those be under the circumstances? I assumed our mission died the moment Gabe nuked the lander."

"Our mission at this point," Reyes said, "is to stay alive, stay together, and reestablish contact with *Andrea Luhman* as soon as possible."

"Why?" Slater said.

"Which part?"

"I mean, I understand all those are good things, but what's our actual mission? Are we really still thinking we might get off Earth?"

"We don't have enough information to make that decision. That's why we need to reestablish contact with *Andrea Luhman*."

"There is no conceivable information that is going to get us off this planet."

"Perhaps not. But at this point we still work for the IDL. That means we need to get in touch with the captain and brief him on our status."

"*Andrea Luhman* is still almost six weeks out," Slater said. "And we have no transmitter capable of reaching them."

"We can build a transmitter," Reyes said. "For now our mission is to stay alive."

No one else spoke. There was nothing to say. Reyes was right; for now, all they could do is try to stay alive.

Reyes and Gabe left shortly thereafter to find Sigurd. They went with him to meet Dag Erikson, the organizer of the raiding expedition. Dag was a stout, white-haired man whose intense eyes darted back and forth under a shaggy white brow. He seemed displeased to have his plans disrupted, but a mention of Ari's name mollified him somewhat. The four of them sat drinking ale in Dag's house in sight of the fjord. The four longboats were visible in the distance, anchored just offshore. Dag had agreed to accept the able-bodied men—including Gabe—but balked at the women and O'Brien. The issue seemed to be one of physical strength and endurance more than anything else: all the travelers were expected to be able to row for long periods when the wind was not amenable to sailing. Dag didn't believe the women had the strength to pull the oars, and O'Brien could barely move. Dag was still short of men, but it was clear he wasn't going to accept dead weight to get Sigurd and his men on board.

Clearly frustrated, Sigurd turned to Reyes and held up his hands. Sigurd had made it clear he and his men weren't going on the expedition without all four spacemen, so they were at an impasse.

At last, Gabe pulled one of the rolls of solder from his flight suit, setting it on the table in front of Dag. Dag's eyes went wide. He picked up the roll and began to pull on the end of the wire, bending it straight to inspect it. He spent some time bending the wire into various shapes and straightening it again. He smiled and looked at Gabe. "Silfr?" he asked.

Gabe nodded. "That's right. I give you that, you let our people on your ship."

Sigurd and Dag had a brief exchange, after which Sigurd turned to Reyes and Gabe again. "Einn silfrstrangi, einn maðr." He held up a finger.

"This is bullshit," Reyes said. "Kilo-for-kilo, Slater and I are as strong as any of these Vikings."

"Easy, Reyes," Gabe said. "We're also not partaking in the looting and pillaging. I assume he makes his money by taking a cut of the spoils, so he's not going to make anything on us. He's right; we're not pulling our weight."

"We literally will be pulling our weight," Reyes replied.

"It's an expression, Reyes. If he's willing to take the three of us for three rolls of solder, I say we do it."

"I can't believe I'm buying my life with a roll of electrical solder."

Gabe held up three fingers. "Three rolls of silver, three people."

Dag nodded, and Gabe pulled the other two rolls of solder from his pocket and set them on the table. Dag smiled. "Týsdagr," he said, holding up seven fingers. "Sjau dagar."

Gabe nodded. "Seven days. We'll be here."

*****

It was three days later that Gunnar Bjornson came to the village. Ari stood outside his house, having been apprised by the sentries that Gunnar was on his way. Sigurd, Gabe and Reyes, who had been meeting with Ari, waited inside.

"Welcome, Gunnar," Ari said, as Gunnar slid off his horse. "You're a bit stiff getting out of the saddle. Are you hurt?"

"Nothing to concern yourself with, old man," Gunnar said with a smile. "Although if you're worried about my comfort, perhaps you might invite me inside."

"I'd be glad to," Ari replied, "but my elderly aunt was recently forced to flee her village, so she'll be staying us for some time. She took ill on the journey east, and she just got to sleep. It wouldn't do to disturb her."

"I see," said Gunnar with a nod. "Would your aunt happen to be a raven-haired young beauty who recently masterminded a plot to kidnap King Harald?"

Ari didn't crack a smile. "My aunt is certainly a handsome woman, but I don't believe she's masterminded any kidnappings lately. I'll be sure to ask when she wakes up."

"Yes, do that. The woman I'm searching for is one of four foreigners who is wanted for destruction of the king's property, kidnapping and theft of several horses. In fact, it's the horse tracks that led me to your village."

"We have only a few workhorses in this village."

"Is that so? Then if I were to look in that barn, I'd find only workhorses, and not seven priceless Frisians?" He pointed to the large wood plank barn some fifty yards down the road.

"I don't know anything about Frisians, but I wouldn't recommend sniffing around old Aghi's barn, though, unless you want a pitchfork in your ribs."

"That's unfortunate," Gunnar said. "The king is offering a reward for the horses, as well as for the thieves themselves."

"I'm afraid I can't help you, Gunnar. But you should know that even if I could, I would not. If I were hiding foreigners here, they would be my guests. You would need to kill me to get to them. Speaking of which, you do seem to be favoring your shoulder. Are you certain you're not hurt?"

"I'm bored of these games, Ari. Are you refusing to give these thieves up to Harald?"

"I don't know what you're talking about, Gunnar. Please be on your way, as I need to tend to my aunt."

"Fine, Ari. Keep playing at your silly ruse. But understand this: Harald will not rest until the foreigners are in his hands. Already he has sent for as many men as can be spared from the garrisons along the western coast. A fleet of ships will arrive within two days. If the foreigners are still here when those men arrive, no one in the village will be spared."

CHAPTER TWENTY-NINE

Ari came back inside, looking agitated. Reyes hadn't been able to follow much of the conversation, but the tone was clear. By employing gestures and the few words they had in common, Sigurd managed to fill in the gaps: many men were on their way from the coast, specifically to capture Sigurd and the spacemen.

Once the spacemen were up to speed, Ari and Sigurd continued to discuss the matter in their own language.

"Do you think he's bluffing?" Reyes asked Gabe. The two of them sat together on one of the benches in Ari's house. Ari and Sigurd sat across from them.

Gabe shrugged. "I'm sure Harald understands the strategic importance of capturing us. Whether he can produce an army in a few days, we have no way of knowing. All I know is that Ari and Sigurd are taking the threat seriously."

Indeed, the discussion between the two Norsemen was becoming more heated. Sigurd was growling demands at Ari, but Ari simply shook his head, saying, "Nei, nei, ég get það ekki!"

Ari abruptly got up and walked outside. Sigurd sighed and turned to Reyes and Gabe. "Skip koma fljótlega."

"Ships come," Reyes said. She couldn't make sense of the third word.

"Fljótlega," Sigurd said. "Einn dagr. Tveir dagar. Eigi fjórir dagar."

"One or two days," Gabe said. "Not four days. He's saying we don't have time."

Sigurd nodded. "Engi tíð. Ari lætr oss eigi bíða." He pointed to the door.

"Ari is going to kick us out before the ships leave," Reyes said. "Got it. But where can we go? Hvar?"

Sigurd shook his head. "Þú verðr at tala við Dag Erikson. Meira silfr?"

"He thinks we might be able to talk Dag into leaving sooner," Gabe said. He turned back to Sigurd. "No. Nei meira silfr."

Sigurd thought for a moment. "Hestar," he said after a moment.

They recognized that word. "Yes," Reyes said. "It's worth a try. We can try to trade him the horses."

*****

Dag Erikson was not pleased with their request. After Sigurd had explained the situation, he erupted into a string of incomprehensible words peppered with instances of "Ekki!" That was a word they'd been hearing a lot lately. *No.*

"Big boats," Sigurd said, turning to face the spacemen. "Much men." His English was progressing faster than their Norse.

Reyes nodded, understanding the gist of what Sigurd was saying: the boats required a large crew, and some of the men wouldn't arrive for a few days. Still, she had to assume it was possible to go to sea with less than a full crew. Otherwise, how did they get back after they'd lost men in raids? Leaving without a full crew presented risks, but there were ways to compensate for increased risk.

"Did you ask him about the horses? Hestar?" Reyes asked. She didn't have a clue what horses sold for, but their rarity in this area suggested they were extremely valuable. The only other horses she'd seen since they'd landed were a few scraggly, stout beasts used as pack animals or plow horses. Gabe had said Harald would have had to ship the Frisians across the sea from mainland Europe.

Sigurd nodded and turned back to Dag. Another terse exchange followed. Dag seemed interested, but one name kept coming up in his responses: *Harald.*

Sigurd sighed, turning back to Reyes. "Hestar Haralds," he said, holding up his palms.

"Everybody knows they're Harald's horses," Gabe said. "He'd be taking a big risk by accepting them."

"He could sell them," Reyes said. "They shipped them across the ocean once, and if we leave early we'll be short on crew anyway. If there's room on the ships…."

"You want to share a Viking longboat with seven horses?" Gabe asked.

"They got them here somehow."

"Probably on a knarr. A cargo ship. And he'd have to find a buyer, somebody who's not averse to acquiring horses stolen from the King of Norway. I don't think it's going to happen. Not in time for us to escape Harald, anyway."

While Reyes and Gabe spoked, Sigurd and Dag continued their negotiations. After some time, they seemed to make progress.

At last, Sigurd nodded. He turned to Reyes and Gabe. "Yes. Vér forum á morgun." He held up a finger.

"We leave tomorrow," Reyes said, breathing a sigh of relief. But there was a look of concern on Sigurd's face. It seemed there was a catch. "All of us?" Reyes asked. "O'Brien and Slater?"

Sigurd nodded, holding up seven fingers. "Sjau hestar." He bit his lip, seeming unsure how to make himself clear. At last he said, "Hestar. Dauðir."

"Dauðir?" Reyes asked.

"Dêaðwêrig," Sigurd said, looking at Gabe.

"What is he saying?" Reyes asked.

"I'm not sure," Gabe said. "It sounds like… *dead*. Dead horses?"

Sigurd nodded. "Dead horses," he repeated.

"No," Reyes replied. "The horses aren't dead."

"Hestar Haralds," Sigurd said, holding up his palms. "Kjöt. Engar hestar."

Reyes frowned. "Gabe, what in hell is he saying?"

Sigurd stood up, patting the knife at his belt and then drawing a finger across his throat.

"Oh, God," Reyes said. "Please, Gabe. Tell me he's not saying what I think he's saying."

Sigurd pointed to his mouth. "Kjöt. Matur."

They knew the second word: *Matur* was food.

"I think he's saying what you think he's saying," Gabe said. "The Norsemen ate horsemeat."

Reyes stared at him in horror. "But they can't! Gabe, those horses are beautiful! They can't murder them for food!"

Sigurd seemed puzzled at Reyes's vehemence. "Ertu kristinn?" he asked.

"I don't understand," Reyes replied.

"He's asking if you're a Christian," Gabe said. "Christians had a taboo against eating horses. The Scandinavians only stopped eating horse after the Christians outlawed it."

Reyes hesitated, unsure how to answer. She'd been raised Catholic, but hadn't thought much about her faith since joining the IDL. In any case, she was a long way removed from any historical taboo Christians had about eating horses. Most colonists ate synthesized protein, and a movement had arisen to make consuming animal meat illegal across all systems, but it had stalled in the face of the war effort. On many worlds, such as Geneva, hunting was necessary to keep animal populations in check. Reyes had eaten venison and rabbit, as well as farmed chicken, turkey and salmon. But horses were kept only for recreational riding and show purposes. Eating one of these huge, magnificent animals just seemed *wrong*.

"Nei," she said. "Hestar nei matur."

Dag turned to Sigurd, an exasperated expression on his face.

"Reyes, they're animals," Gabe said. "I don't want to see them killed any more than you do, but it's the only way we can—"

"It's not the only way!" Reyes snapped. "It's stupid and pointless. These are smart, beautiful, elegant animals, and they're the only reason we managed to get away from Harald in one piece. They've done everything we asked of them, and this is how we repay them? It's wrong, Gabe. It's just wrong. These horses didn't ask to get in the middle of this stupid war."

"None of us asked for this, Reyes. If you want to cry, cry over the hundred Norsemen I slaughtered at the lander. You think those guys had a choice? You think they woke up that morning and said, 'I think I'll throw myself at a fucking railgun today?' They did what they had to do—what they thought they needed to do to survive. I mowed them down. And for what? For nothing. I had to blow up the lander anyway. This is all fucking pointless, Reyes. The question is whether we're going to keep going anyway. If you want to stay here in Uslu until Ari throws us out or Harald attacks, I won't argue. Just tell me what the plan is."

Reyes was silent for a moment, taken aback by Gabe's outburst. Sigurd and Dag were staring at her, waiting for her to make a decision. She wondered if they should ask O'Brien and Slater for their input. After all, they were in this together. Slater had been particularly taken with the horses. Would she go along with selling them to Dag, knowing they'd be butchered for meat? And if she didn't, then what? Gabe was right: if they turned down this deal, they would have to beg Ari to let them stay in Uslu, provoking Harald to attack. And how many people would die in that assault?

No, Reyes had accepted command of this mission, and she had pledged to keep their party alive and together. Their best chance—their only chance—was to go south with the raiders.

"All right," she said, turning to Dag. "Take the horses."

*****

They made their way to the shore at dawn the next morning. The temperature had dropped overnight, and a steady wind continued to blow from the south. A dozen or so men were already milling about, loading supplies from carts and checking oars, sails and riggings. Dozens more people—mostly women but a few children and older men—huddled together in the gray light, saying their goodbyes to the departing men. Each man stood next to a heavy sea chest that contained everything he would be taking on the journey. The only Norsemen Reyes recognized were those that had gone with her to rescue Gabe: Sigurd, Njáll, Agnar, Brynjarr and Braggi.

Reyes and the other spacemen stood apart, shivering in the cold and trying to stay out of the way. They'd each been supplied with a fully stocked chest as part of the deal they had made with Dag. O'Brien and Slater hadn't been told what they'd had to do to get Dag to agree to an early departure; they knew only that they'd traded the horses. Reyes and Gabe had agreed there was nothing to gain in telling them more. This voyage was going to be enough of a challenge for them without the added weight of the deaths of innocent animals on their consciences.

The four boats—called *Bylgjasverð*, *Hreindýr*, *Sjóhestr* and *Ísbátr*—rested in a line on the shore a few paces apart, water lapping at their bows. These were medium-sized longboats, called *snekkja* by the Norsemen. Similar in size and appearance, each was roughly seventeen meters long and two-and-a-half meters wide, with twenty sets of oars. Two men would man each oar, for a total of forty oarsmen. An additional man—the coxswain—would sit at the rear of the boat, controlling the steering oar and shouting orders to the oarsmen. A sail of woven wool cloth hung from a halyard secured to a heavy wood mast that was nearly as tall as the ship was long. The sails were currently furled to the halyard and would remain so until the boats were well offshore. Just below the sail, over the heads of the men on the ship, was a wooden rack supported by two vertical poles. On top of the rack, parallel to the strakes of the boat, lay the oars. All four snekkjas were adorned with intricately carved dragon figureheads.

The boats had decks made of removable planks, below which were storage holds for food and other supplies. Dag Erikson stood a few paces down the beach, shouting orders at the men loading provisions into the holds. The mood was tense. Many of the men had been up late drinking the previous night; they'd been roused early in the morning and informed the expedition would be leaving four days early. Even with the newcomers, the expedition was sixteen men short, which meant that each boat was down four crew members. That wouldn't be a problem as long as they were under sail, but rowing would be that much harder. Reaching the coast of Europe was expected to take three or four days, depending on the wind. They hoped to make a brief stop on the Frisian coast before continuing west.

"So the plan is to travel to Normandy?" Slater asked, shouting to be heard over the wind blowing in their faces.

"Ultimately, yes," said Reyes. "I understand we'll be sailing south to Denmark first. They don't have any instruments to speak of, so they have to navigate by the sun and stars. If they can keep the coastline in sight, it makes it a lot easier."

"Forgive my ignorance," Slater said, "but you said 'sailing.' Isn't Denmark south of here?"

"Yes, why?"

"Because the wind is coming from the south," Slater said. "Looks to me like we're going to be doing a lot of rowing."

"Not necessarily," said O'Brien, standing next to her. He was still in some pain from his cracked ribs, but was able to stand for short periods of time. As the only one among them with sailing experience, he was particularly interested in seeing the Norsemen prepare for their voyage. "The Vikings figured out how to tack against the wind. Basically, you turn your sail at an angle to the wind, letting it push you sideways. Some of that force gets channeled into forward motion, so you end up traveling at an angle, moving toward your destination at the same time as you're being pushed to the side. Then you come about, letting the wind push you the other way for a while. You keep zig-zagging like that until you get to your destination."

"If you say so," Slater replied. "It sounds impossible. And I say that as someone who flies giant metal sky ships for a living."

"It's not easy, that's for sure," O'Brien said. "Even with a modern sailboat with a triangular sail, it takes some skill, and you've got to have some speed to make it work at all. With the shallow draft of these boats and the short keel, it would be even harder. I sure wouldn't want to try it."

Slater raised an eyebrow at him. "You're not reassuring me, O'Brien."

O'Brien shrugged, and then winced. "The Vikings were the greatest sailors of their day. If anybody can do it, these guys can. And they've got a strong, steady headwind, which should make it easier."

Dag approached them, pointing Sigurd and his men to *Ísbátr* and the spacemen to *Sjóhestr*. Sigurd protested, shaking his head. Reyes couldn't follow much of their exchange, but it was clear that Sigurd was not going to be separated from either his own men or the spacemen. Dag, now red-faced with frustration, finally relented. The nine of them were assigned to the front of the last boat. Gabe and Sigurd climbed in first. Agnar and Brynjarr then lifted O'Brien on his stretcher to them. Once O'Brien was safely aboard, the others climbed in. Reyes and Slater arranged a bed on the second row for O'Brien while the others hoisted the chests aboard. They arranged the chests in lines, just behind the oar holes in the gunwale. The sturdy wooden chests, of a roughly uniform shape and size, would serve as benches for the duration of the journey. Sigurd and Gabe sat on the outside of the first row, with Reyes and Slater between them. Njáll, Brynjarr, Agnar and Braggi sat behind them. The next several rows were men who had volunteered for the expedition. About half of them were from Uslu or nearby settlements; the rest had traveled from the valley, Vestfold or even farther west to take part in the raiding. The last few rows were empty; a dozen or so men remained on shore, waiting to push the boat into the water.

Sigurd and his men introduced themselves to the other Norsemen, exchanging pleasantries and wishes of goodwill for the voyage. Each boat had a coxswain who had been personally selected by Dag. The coxswain of *Ísbátr* was a jovial, red-haired man named Skeggi. As he joked and laughed with the crew, Reyes could feel the tension draining from the air. She gathered that some of the men had been grumbling that leaving early—and leaving behind those who were still on their way to Uslu—was a bad omen for the voyage. But Skeggi put them at ease, and a spirit of hopefulness and adventure seemed to come over the men.

At long last, the first boat, *Bylgjasverð*, pushed out into the fjord. Cheers went up from the men on the boats and on shore as the long, graceful figure of *Bylgjasverð* slid into the water. As the stern came free from the beach, the men running behind leaped and pulled themselves into the boat. *Hreindýr* came next, and *Sjóhestr* after that. When *Sjóhestr* had launched, the men behind *Ísbátr* leaned into the stern, grunting and heaving forward. It picked up momentum and finally slid free of the shore. The men clambered into the boat, splashing and hooting in the cold water. Those still on the shore waved and shouted goodbyes.

Skeggi shouted, "Ára!" and Reyes turned to see a pair of men a few rows behind her stand up and take down one of the oars from the rack overhead. They handed the oar down to the men next to them. While these men passed the oar forward, the pair removed another oar from the rack. Sigurd reached over to open a small shutter that covered the opening for the oar and motioned for Gabe to do the same on his side. Behind them, the others sitting closest to the gunwales opened the other shutters. The first oar was passed to Sigurd, who turned it perpendicular to the gunwale and threaded it through the slotted opening, stopping when the butt end of the oar was in front of Reyes. She took hold of it, mimicking his grip, and he nodded. Gabe did the same with the oar that was handed to him, and he and Slater held it while the other oars were put into place. Glancing back, Reyes was amazed at the speed and precision with which the men worked. Less than two minutes after Skeggi shouted his order, the oars were ready.

Skeggi emitted a monosyllabic shout, and the men leaned forward, pushing their oars with them. With the exception of the first row, which lagged a bit, the men moved as one. The oars hit the water. Skeggi gave another shout and the men pulled and leaned back. This time the first row moved in sync, but the oar pulled by Gabe and Slater skipped along the surface of the water, smacking into the oar behind it. Gabe murmured an apology to Braggi, in front of him, but Braggi just laughed. On the next push, they made sure to submerge the flat of the oar. After a few more tries, they were moving in time with the rest of the men.

As they sank into a rhythm, Skeggi's gruff chant turned into a baritone song. Many of the other men joined in. In the distance, they could hear the rowers on the other ships singing a different song, but to the same rhythm.

"What happened to sailing?" Slater shouted. She had already worked up a sweat from the exertion.

"They'll want to be on the open sea, where the wind is consistent," O'Brien said from behind her. He was standing with his hand on the gunwale, too excited to lie down. "Tacking requires a lot of open space and room for error. We don't want to be blown back into the shore."

They rowed until mid-afternoon, when Skeggi at last gave the order to pull in the oars. Reyes had never felt such relief. Her arms continued to burn long after they stopped rowing. Skeggi gave another series of orders, and four men seated near the center of the boat began to work on unfurling the sails. In the distance, Reyes saw that the other crews were doing the same. *Bylgjasverð*'s sail, already unfurled, was barely visible on the horizon. The boats had maintained a roughly constant distance from each other, with the first ship just visible to the last, traveling in a straight line. Now, though, the other ships were well off to starboard and heading farther west. Whether they had passed some landmark that signaled it was time to unfurl the sails or Skeggi was just following the lead of the other ships, Reyes couldn't say. She saw now that the sails were constructed of vertical panels of woven wool cloth that had been stitched together. The panels alternated in color, with a neutral beige or tawny color accented by panels that had been died blue or red. The stripes on *Ísbátr*'s sail were a deep blue.

Once *Ísbátr*'s sail was unfurled and its riggings were secured, Skeggi brought the boat about, using the steering oar and the boat's forward momentum to bring it in line with the others. The boat's sails were trimmed close, nearly parallel with the ship's keel. The wind caught the sail and Reyes's heart leaped in her chest as the boat began leaning to port. But the keel and the *Ísbátr*'s momentum kept the ship upright, and soon *Ísbátr* was skimming across the water again, heading southeast. The crew erupted into cheers. For some time, at least, they'd get a respite from rowing.

The boats were now heading southwest along the rocky coast of southern Norway, which was visible over the starboard gunwale. The coast seemed to extend in a southwesterly direction as far as they could see; if the wind held steady, they'd be able to stay on this heading for some time. They were on their way.

CHAPTER THIRTY

D an O'Brien was dozing in the bow of the ship when he heard the alarm. Men shouting, but not merely to be heard above the surf: there was an edge in their voices, something that portended danger.

Pulling himself slowly into a sitting position, he saw several men pointing at something over the starboard bow. No, not something. Several somethings. A fleet of ships.

There were at least six of them, and more might be hidden over the horizon. They were larger than the snekkjas of the raiding expedition, and they were getting closer. The ships were tacking southeast, on course to intersect the snekkjas' course at near right angles. There was no question of the fleet's intentions, given its course. Someone had gotten word of their departure to Harald or one of his lieutenants, who had redirected the fleet to intercept them. Skeggi stood at *Ísbátr*'s stern, waiting for a signal from the other boats. The crew sat in silence, waiting for instructions from Skeggi.

As the fleet got closer, O'Brien counted eight ships. The first two, it seemed, would miss the snekkjas if they remained on their current course, passing a hundred meters or so in front of *Bylgjasverð*. Harald's ships could change course, but that would be a delicate maneuver that could result in the fleets ships colliding with each other or missing the raiders entirely. Most likely the fleet would maintain its current course, hoping to get close enough to attack with their bows or even ram the snekkjas. The question was whether *Bylgjasverð* would stay its course, trying to slip past Harald's fleet. If she did, the fleet would never catch her, but she would be leading the other snekkjas right into the thick of Harald's ships.

O'Brien watched as *Bylgjasverð* turned into the wind, its sail going slack. A moment later, *Skeggi* shouted an order. He pulled hard on the steering board, turning *Ísbátr* to match the course of the other ships. Soon their sail was filled with wind from the opposite side, and *Ísbátr* was following *Bylgjasverð* and the other boats on a southeasterly heading. The king's ships, staying their course, trailed them on their starboard side. The lead ship, its red-and-yellow sail taut in the wind, was less than a hundred meters from *Ísbátr*'s stern. With an infinite sea and a constant wind, Harald's fleet would never catch them. Unfortunately, they were now heading the wrong direction: the Frisian coast was southwest of them, and Normandy was still farther west.

"What's happening, O'Brien?" Reyes asked. She could see the other boats as well as he, but couldn't interpret their movements. "Are those Harald's ships?"

"That would be a good guess," O'Brien said. "We tacked to avoid them. Problem is, we can't maintain this heading forever. Eventually we're going to hit land."

Gabe nodded. "Denmark," he said. "If this wind keeps up, I'd guess that we've got maybe three hours."

"And then what?" asked Reyes.

"Then we have to tack again," O'Brien said. "Or head farther east."

"What's to the east?"

"Sweden," Gabe said. "We could skirt the Swedish coast, but we'd have to tack southwest again, and we'd end up trapped in the strait between Sweden and Denmark. We'll never outmaneuver them there."

"So assume we tack southwest before we reach Denmark," Reyes said. "Then what happens?"

"If the wind holds, we'll be on an intercept course with Harald's fleet," O'Brien said. "We might slip past them, in which case we'll have a straight shot to the Frisian coast. But it will be close."

"How close are we talking?" Gabe asked. "Bow range?"

"Probably," O'Brien said. "For a minute, maybe longer."

"We've got weapons too," Reyes said.

"We're outnumbered," Gabe said. "Those ships look like they hold close to eighty men each, and there are at least eight of them. If we get between two of those ships and they concentrate their fire on us…"

"They don't know which ship we're on," Slater said.

O'Brien nodded. They were wearing cloaks over their flight suits; there was no way for Harald's men to tell from this distance that *Ísbátr* held the people they were looking for.

"It may not matter," Gabe replied. "We have to assume they're prepared to kill as many men as they have to. Harald only needs one of us alive."

As he spoke, *Ísbátr*'s sail fluttered above them. O'Brien had his eye on Skeggi, who was watching the clouds. "Hang on," O'Brien said. "I think we're about to tack again."

He was right. The wind had backed southeast, making their current heading unsustainable. They would either have to tack south toward Denmark or try coming about to port and head west. Skeggi shouted an order as the ship turned to port. The riggers adjusted the sail, and soon it was taut again. They were heading due west, on a collision course with Harald's fleet, which had tacked south. Over the port gunwale, O'Brien saw that the other snekkjas had done the same. The raider's boats and Harald's fleet were coming together like teeth on a zipper.

"Bows!" Skeggi cried as Harald's ships drew closer. Everyone on *Ísbátr* except for the spacemen had bows and quivers with them. Many had them slung over their shoulders or hung on their back; the others kept them at their feet. The men stood, readying their bows, but didn't move from their positions. Until the ships got closer, it was hard to know which side would be better to fire from, if they got the chance at all. Intercepting another ship on the open sea was far from an exact science.

It soon became clear that the enemy would be unable to catch *Bylgjasverð*; the lead snekkja was simply too far ahead. As it slipped out of view behind one of Harald's ships, cheers went up from the men on *Ísbátr*. If the wind stayed favorable, *Bylgjasverð* had a straight shot to the Frisian coast.

The cheers rapidly dissipated. The second snekkja, *Hreindýr*, was cutting it much closer. The crews of *Ísbátr* and *Sjóhestr* watched breathlessly as *Hreindýr* converged with one of Harald's vessels, a great beast of a ship with a carving of a wolf head on its prow. When it was clear the two ships would come within bow range of each other, the men of each ship oriented themselves—the men on *Hreindýr* aiming to starboard, those on Harald's ship aiming to port. The archers formed two rows, one kneeling behind the row of shields hung on the gunwale, another standing behind them.

As if responding to some secret signal, the men on both ships let loose a volley of arrows. O'Brien heard a few distant cries as men were hit, but most of the arrows struck nothing but wood or water. A few more men dropped in the next volley. There wasn't time for a third. The two ships were going to collide.

Men on both sides dropped their bows and braced for impact. The prow of Harald's ship struck the starboard side of the *Hreindýr* a few meters from the prow. *Hreindýr's* hull held, but the snekkja was pushed off its heading by the heavier ship. *Hreindýr's* sail went limp and its stern swung around so that it was almost touching the bigger ship's hull. The deck of the larger ship was nearly a meter higher than that of the snekkja, and Harald's men had no trouble leaping the gap. Men with axes and spears swarmed onto *Hreindýr's* deck while archers lined up along the gunwale to fire at the men below.

The men aboard *Ísbátr* and *Sjóhestr* didn't have time to concern themselves with the fate of those aboard *Hreindýr*, as they were approaching their own moments of reckoning. *Sjóhestr* slipped neatly between two of Harald's ships, but paid a heavy price. Archers on both sides had enough time to direct three full volleys at them, hitting at least a dozen of the crew. Those aboard *Sjóhestr* got off a few shots as well, but had little success against the men on the higher ships.

Ísbátr fared slightly better, passing through a larger gap. The ship to their port side was too distant to worry about, so they focused their fire to starboard, where one of Harald's ships passed within fifty meters. Only a few of their arrows hit their targets, but their adversaries had even worse luck, as they were firing into the wind. A few arrows clattered against the far gunwale or whizzed overhead; most of the rest bounced off *Ísbátr's* hull or landed in the water, well short of their target. Only one man onboard *Ísbátr* was hit: a skinny young blond man who took an arrow through his bicep.

Reyes had ordered her crew to hunker down and not engage, as the risk of revealing their location was greater than that posed by the archers. Several of the Norsemen glared at them as they crouched beneath the gunwale, but Gabe assured her it was the right decision. If they fired their guns now, they'd only waste ammo and direct more attention to *Ísbátr*.

In any case, the *Ísbátr's* engagement with the enemy didn't last long. Moving past each other at close to eight knots, the two ships were out of range again within a minute. Glancing to port, O'Brien saw *Sjóhestr* about two hundred meters away, moving parallel with *Ísbátr*. *Bylgjasverð* and

Hreindýr were nowhere to be seen. They could only hope that *Bylgjasverð* was still speeding toward the southwest; *Hreindýr* was undoubtedly lost.

Behind them, three of the enemy ships were coming about, preparing to continue their pursuit of the two snekkjas. Three other ships remained visible farther to the southeast, but O'Brien couldn't tell from this distance where they were headed. For now, they only had three ships to worry about, and Harald's men would have to divide their attention between *Sjóhestr* and *Ísbátr*. Not using their guns had been the right call.

Skeggi shouted something to be heard over the din of the men chattering on the deck. O'Brien couldn't make out any of his words except *Sigurd* and *Reyes*. Sigurd touched Reyes on the shoulder and pointed to the stern, where Skeggi stood watching the enemy boats in pursuit. Reyes nodded and said something to Sigurd. The two made their way along the port gunwale toward Skeggi. An animated discussion followed. O'Brien couldn't make out the words, but he got the gist of it: Skeggi was demanding to know why the hell his ship was being attacked by Harald's fleet. O'Brien wondered how much Dag had told him and the other coxswains. Did Skeggi have any idea of the importance of the people he was carrying? For a moment, his mind went to the story of Jonah, who had been thrown overboard to appease God. If the Norsemen had any idea of the spacemen's history with Harald, they might well do the same. Several of the Norsemen joined in the discussion, but Skeggi silenced them with a word. For once, O'Brien was glad to be left out of the discussion.

Sjóhestr continued to sail alongside them while Harald's three ships trailed the snekkjas of about three hundred meters. They were all riding the same wind, but the snekkjas seemed to be slightly faster. By the time Sigurd, Gabe and Reyes returned to the bow, the snekkjas had crept a small, but noticeable, distance ahead.

"Are they going to throw us overboard?" Slater asked, echoing O'Brien's own thoughts.

"I wouldn't put it past them if they thought it would help," Reyes said. "I get the impression Dag didn't tell him we were wanted by Harald."

"Well, he knows now."

"How much *does* he know?" O'Brien asked.

"Sigurd told him about the horses. I think that's all. Skeggi thinks Harald wants us dead."

"The good news," O'Brien said, "is that we're outrunning them. If this wind holds for a while, we're home free."

The skies had remained clear most of the day, making it easy to determine their heading. O'Brien knew the Vikings had ways of navigating under cloudy skies, but these were imprecise. Prior to the invention of the astrolabe and compass, it hadn't been uncommon for sailors to be lost at sea for weeks at a time.

The wind held until late afternoon, when it slowly died to a barely noticeable breeze. The enemy ships were hidden over the horizon. Skeggi ordered the sail taken in and the men switched again to rowing. To port, they saw the crew of *Sjóhestr* doing the same. The two ships had closed the gap between them, so they were now only a stone's throw away from each other.

They rowed at a moderate pace for the next hour, until Skeggi spotted one of the enemy ships on the horizon. They were gaining on the snekkjas, taking advantage of their greater rowing power relative to the mass of their ships. Skeggi switched to a song with a quicker tempo, and the men responded by rowing faster. But still the enemy ships gained.

More worrying, *Sjóhestr* was having trouble keeping up with *Ísbátr*. It looked to O'Brien that at least three of their crew had been killed by arrows and another half dozen were too badly wounded to row. Already undermanned, the boat didn't have a chance to outrun a fully crewed ship. Unless the wind picked up again, their only chance was to evade Harald's ships until nightfall, when they might lose them in the dark.

It soon became clear that this wasn't going to happen. *Sjóhestr* would be caught for certain, and it was looking increasingly unlikely that *Ísbátr* would escape. All three enemy ships were now visible in the distance, the nearest one less than three hundred meters behind *Sjóhestr*. The men of both snekkjas rowed with all their strength into the setting sun, but still the enemy gained.

At last, Skeggi called to *Sjóhestr*, now at least two boat-lengths behind, and after a moment the coxswain answered him. Skeggi called again, his voice holding a pleading, desperate tone. The man guiding *Sjóhestr* called back with a resigned answer. Skeggi switched to a slower song, and *Ísbátr*'s pace slackened. O'Brien soon realized what the discussion had been about: the two snekkjas were gradually converging.

Within two minutes, the two boats were so close that their oars were in danger of colliding. Skeggi barked an order, which was echoed by the coxswain on *Sjóhestr*, whose name was Birgir. The men ceased rowing and began pulling their oars in.

"What is happening?" Reyes gasped, as she and Sigurd passed their oar forward.

"Reallocation of resources," Gabe said, putting his hand on his gun. "Stay alert. This could get ugly."

Someone held an oar out toward *Sjóhestr* and one of the men on that boat grabbed hold of it. Men on both boats grabbed onto the oar and pulled, bringing the two boats within an arm-span of each other. Ropes were thrown over and tied to hooks, securing the boats together. Birgir, a short, stocky man with closely cropped blond hair, climbed onto the gunwale of his boat and leaped over to the deck of *Ísbátr*. He made his way to Skeggi, and the two conferred quietly for a moment. Meanwhile, Harald's ships continued to gain, closing to within two hundred meters.

After a moment, Skeggi and Birgir seemed to come to an agreement. Skeggi shouted an order, which was greeted with murmurs and shouts of anger. Birgir growled something at them, pointing to the enemy ship approaching from behind. There were a few more murmurs, and then silence. Several men began looking in the direction of the spacemen.

Sigurd turned to Reyes. "Wounded and... konur," he said, and pointed to *Sjóhestr*.

"Konur?" O'Brien asked.

Sigurd pointed to Slater and then Reyes.

"Women," Reyes said. "They're going to try to unload the weaker crew members to *Sjóhestr*. Sacrifice her so *Ísbátr* can get away."

O'Brien swallowed hard. He knew where he was going to end up.

"Fuck that," Gabe said. But already the young man who had been hit with an arrow was being helped onto the other boat, and Birgir was directing several of the stronger men from *Sjóhestr* to *Ísbátr*. Many of the Norsemen toward *Ísbátr*'s bow were now facing the newcomers. Sigurd spoke an order to his men, who stood between the spacemen and the rest of the crew. They brandished their weapons.

"Maybe we should just go," O'Brien said. He'd felt like a drag on the crew ever since the lander crashed, and he was tired of people putting themselves in danger for his sake. He hated to admit it, but Skeggi and Birgir were doing the right thing: this was the only way any of them were getting out of here.

CHAPTER THIRTY-ONE

"**S**hut up, O'Brien," Gabe said. "We're not leaving you."

"I'm dead weight, Gabe," O'Brien said. "If I go willingly, maybe they'll let Reyes and Slater stay. They're not going to kill me. Harald needs at least one of us alive."

"No," Reyes said. "We stay together. No matter what."

O'Brien sighed. The matter was out of his hands. The crewmen stood regarding Sigurd's men, trying to decide if they had the numbers to overwhelm them and seize O'Brien and the women. Skeggi was making his way toward the spacemen, his face contorted with rage. And behind them, the enemy ships continued to get closer.

Skeggi shouted an outburst at Sigurd, who shot back with his own. Skeggi pushed aside two of the crewmen and approached Sigurd, a spear in his hand. Sigurd didn't move except to pull his pistol from its holster and point it at Skeggi's forehead. A look of confusion came over Skeggi's face. A split second later, the back of his head exploded. He fell limp to the deck.

Sigurd pointed the pistol at another man, who dropped his spear and took a step backward. Sigurd issued a challenge, but no one seemed willing to take him up on it. He barked orders and men began to move. Two men grabbed Skeggi's body and hefted it over to the crew of *Sjóhestr*. Three of the men who had just come over from *Sjóhestr* reluctantly returned to their ship. Two more men grabbed oars and pushed *Ísbátr* away from the other boat. The oars were distributed once again. Sigurd shouted something to Reyes and Slater, who stood perplexed until two of the men who had come over from *Sjóhestr* took their seats.

"What the hell?" Slater said.

Sigurd repeated his order, pointing to the bow of the boat.

"Move," Reyes said. "We're being replaced."

O'Brien picked up his bedding and moved aside as Reyes and Slater joined him in the bow. There was just enough room for the three of them to sit in front of the first row of benches.

"This is humiliating," Slater said.

"Welcome to my world," O'Brien replied.

As he spoke, an arrow shot past his head, bouncing off the bow. Several more whizzed past on the port side. Somewhere toward the stern, a man cried out. Glancing toward the stern before hunkering down in the bow, O'Brien saw that the enemy ship had closed within a stone's throw.

Birgir, who had been selected by Sigurd to replace Skeggi, shouted the order to row, and the oars hit the water. He shouted again, and the men pulled. Birgir began to sing. His voice broke at first, but he kept going, gaining in volume and confidence. The men joined in, and *Ísbátr* began to creep away from the enemy ship. A few more arrows cracked against the hull, but no more hit their targets. Soon their pursuers had to put their bows away and take up their oars again. Two enemy ships broke off to board *Sjóhestr*. The last one stayed on *Ísbátr*'s tail. The chase had resumed.

They rowed at full speed until well after sunset, the enemy ship tailing them at less than eighty meters. *Ísbátr* lost her pursuer for some time in the dark, but the near-full-Moon rising in the east revealed that the ship remained on the snekkja's tail. Eventually Birgir had to let the men take breaks in turns to eat, but even that decrease in manpower allowed the pursuers to gain some distance, the ship closing nearly within bow range. Reyes offered to relieve the men near her, but was rebuffed. None of the Norsemen was going to be the one to give his seat to a woman.

Some time around midnight, when the men could barely keep rowing, clouds came over the moon and the pursuers were once again lost in the night. Birgir gave the order to cease rowing. It was a risky tactic, but it made sense: if the cloud cover held, Harald's men might slip past them in the dark. In any case, they had little choice: the men simply had no strength left. They stopped to eat and drink, Birgir hissing at them to be quiet whenever one of them made any noise. When the somber meal was finished, the crew lay down to get some sleep while they could. Reyes volunteered to take the first watch, and Sigurd reluctantly agreed. He put another man on watch at the stern and then lay down to sleep.

"Let me know when you get tired," O'Brien whispered to Reyes.

"You should rest," Reyes replied. "Slater is up next."

O'Brien sighed and leaned back against the gunwale. Being worthless was beginning to wear on him. His side still ached, but he'd been weaning himself off the pain meds and he felt much better than he had a few days earlier. The motion of the boat made him a little queasy, but it was manageable. You couldn't qualify for a position as a crew member of an IDL ship if you had any propensity for motion sickness.

He spent the next two hours staring up at the sky, hoping to catch a glimpse of a star or the Moon, but there was nothing but endless gray. Somewhere, trillions of kilometers beyond that blanket of gray, was a world called Tarchon, populated at this point only by plants and primitive animal life. Twelve hundred years from now, a probe would land on that planet and send a signal back to its owners that Tarchon could support human life. Thirteen hundred years from now, the planet would be teeming with people, one of whom was a geology student and amateur sailor named Dan O'Brien. O'Brien would marry a woman named Cara Miller and they would have two children together. Unable to find academic employment, O'Brien would join the Interstellar Defense League and be assigned to an elite exploratory mission aboard a ship called *Andrea Luhman*. After sending a message to IDL command that they had acquired an object of strategic importance, *Andrea Luhman* would vanish, never to be heard from again. And thus would die the last hope of the human race.

Or would it? That part of history hadn't been written yet. Maybe by some miracle, *Andrea Luhman* might still get back to Geneva, with or without O'Brien and the others. It was hard to imagine how that might happen, though; he might as well hope that another group of dissident Cho-ta'an were hiding another planet-killer somewhere. If he was going to count on a *deus ex machina*, one was as good as another.

He wondered if Mallick, Carpenter and the others aboard *Andrea Luhman* had any idea how horribly wrong things had gone down on Earth. *Andrea Luhman* had been out of radio range by the time the lander's crew regained consciousness, but at the very least Carpenter knew they had had a very rough landing. He had to know it was unlikely they'd ever get off Earth. Given that knowledge, what would they do? Try to limp back to an IDL outpost on aux thrusters? That would probably be pointless, but no more pointless than returning to Earth in the hopes of getting a new ionization manifold.

No, the captain would return *Andrea Luhman* to orbit around Earth as scheduled. That would be about five weeks from now. The question was what he would do when it got here. If the landing party was unable to rig up a transmitter by then, what would the *Andrea Luhman*'s crew be able to determine from orbit? They'd have no trouble spotting the blast crater where the lander had been, certainly. Beyond that, they'd be hard-pressed to gather any information about the landing party's status. They'd probably assume the entire party was dead. How long they'd wait for a sign the party had survived was anybody's guess.

He tried telling himself that it didn't matter, that he had just as much of a chance to live a happy life in ninth century Europe as he did as an IDL geologist in the twenty-third century, but it was no use. It wasn't just that he was never going to see his wife and kids again, although that pained him terribly. It was the fact that no matter what he did here in this time, he would be living life under a pall, like the endless gray sky that seemed to swallow *Ísbátr*. He and his crew had glimpsed the end of humanity, what the Norsemen snoring on the deck in front of him would call Ragnarok. Fenris the wolf would swallow the sun, and everything humankind had created would be wiped out. He wondered not for the first time why the crew was even bothering to fight for their survival. What was the point?

Schumacher had told them paradoxes didn't exist, which seemed to imply that the crew's appearance would have minimal effect on civilization. Harald wanted them for their knowledge of future technology, but if history had been changed by a group of time travelers in 883 AD, they'd have heard about it. Similarly, if they made it to Normandy and used their technical knowhow to build steam engines and electric generators, history would have turned out entirely different. The fact that the industrial revolution hadn't started until the eighteenth century proved that the lander's crew hadn't lived to spread their knowledge. Even if they somehow survived this voyage, they were doomed to live inconsequential lives. Their lives would be, in the words of a political philosopher who wouldn't be born for nearly seven hundred years, "solitary, poor, nasty, brutish, and short."

Eventually he drifted off to sleep. When he awoke, Slater had taken Reyes's place on the bow. He greeted her with a nod, and then they sat silently in the darkness for some time. O'Brien tried to sleep some more, but his body wouldn't cooperate. At last he gave up, content to stare into the inky sky and contemplate his fate. When Slater's shift was over, she got up to wake Gabe.

"I'll do it," O'Brien whispered.

"You need to rest," Slater replied.

"I've done nothing but sleep since we got here. I can't do much, but I have a pair of eyes. I'm going to be awake anyway." He got slowly to his feet.

Slater nodded. "Wake Gabe if you get tired." She lay down and closed her eyes.

O'Brien peered into the blackness, shaking his head. Keeping watch seemed even more pointless than their struggle to stay alive. The sky was still cloudy; there was barely enough light to see water below. There could be a ship a stone's throw away and he'd never see it. But he'd told Slater he'd do it, and it wasn't like he had anything better to do.

While he occupied himself with thoughts of his home on Tarchon, a thick fog began to roll in, and with it an uneasy sensation. He had been assuming he and the others would die a quick, violent death: if they somehow managed to evade Harald's fleet, they would die at the hands of Frisians or Franks defending their territory. But the fog presented another possibility: they would be lost at sea indefinitely. If they couldn't see the sun or stars, navigation would be difficult. He had seen Skeggi holding a piece of translucent crystal stone—presumably one of the mythical "sun stones" that the Vikings had used to determine the location of the sun by using the stone's ability to polarize sunlight. This method was imprecise, though, and gave only a general idea of the direction they were heading. If you got far enough off course, knowing where the sun wasn't much help. And he had no idea if Birgir had one of the stones; Skeggi's was presumably with his body on *Sjóhestr*. The Vikings could catch fish if they got hungry, but they'd run out of water—and ale—in less than two weeks.

As a boy, O'Brien had once been lost on the Aleron Sea on Tarchon for a few hours, thanks to a broken compass. He'd been able to call for help, but the experience was frightening enough that he'd sworn he'd never be in that position again—and now here he was, adrift in the middle of the North Sea, with no charts, no compass, no instruments at all.

Eventually the sky began to lighten, but it was impossible to tell where the sun was. The entire sky seemed a uniform shade of gray. Visibility was still poor; he could barely see the water meters from the hull. Across the ship, he could just make out the form of the Norsemen standing watch, leaning heavily on a spear. As he turned his gaze back across the bow, a slight breeze pushed the veil of fog away momentarily, and he caught sight of a curved line in the distance. O'Brien's heart began to pound in his chest. He blinked his eyes, but it was gone. Had it been a ship? Was it just his imagination? The blanket of fog remained stubbornly in place.

O'Brien moved to wake Gabe but then hesitated. What if he was wrong? Worse, what if he was right, and waking the crew only drew attention to *Ísbátr*? They might be better off keeping quiet and waiting for the ship to drift away.

But that wasn't O'Brien's call. At the very least, he needed to wake Gabe, who could give a tactical assessment of the situation. He stepped over Reyes, who was sleeping nearby, and shook Gabe lightly by the shoulder. Gabe jerked awake with a startled gasp, and O'Brien put a finger to his own lips. For a moment they listened, but there was only the sound of men snoring.

"I think I saw a ship," O'Brien whispered.

"Where?" Gabe asked, sitting up.

O'Brien pointed into the gray haze. "About twenty degrees to port. Maybe a hundred meters away."

Gabe nodded, taking a moment to assess the situation. "Wake the gunmen," he said. "Tell them to watch the bow."

O'Brien nodded and then did as instructed. While he woke Sigurd, Agnar and Brynjarr, Gabe briefed Reyes and Slater. Reyes joined Agnar and Brynjarr at the bow, guns ready, while Sigurd conferred with Gabe. O'Brien, standing behind Reyes, still saw no sign of the ship, and he was becoming more and more convinced he'd imagined it. Even if he hadn't, there was no telling where the ship was now, or if there were any others nearby. Sigurd walked away from Gabe, disappearing into the fog. Moments later, figures began to move about on the deck. O'Brien thought he heard oars hitting the water.

Gabe approached them. "Sigurd is going to bring the boat around to port."

"Port?" Reyes asked. "We're not going to try to evade them?"

"Evidently not," Gabe said, as the boat began to move. "Ready your guns. Stay alert. Don't fire until I give the order."

Gabe disappeared again into the fog, and the others kept watching over the bow. The air against O'Brien's face told him they were creeping forward. They were planning to attack. O'Brien was torn between fear that he'd imagined the ship and fear that he hadn't.

Agnar, to his right, gave his shoulder a tap. O'Brien turned to see Agnar pointing into the fog. At first, O'Brien saw nothing, but then his eyes focused on the shape of a dragon looming in the fog. He tapped Reyes's shoulder and she nodded. The others had seen it as well. Within a few seconds, the bow came into view to the left. Standing just behind the dragon carving was a man with a bow, staring obliviously in the opposite direction. Somewhere behind O'Brien, an oar clacked against the deck. The man on the bow spun around and for a moment shock came over his face. He opened his mouth to issue a warning, but before he could make a sound an arrow pierced his throat. The man stumbled backwards with a gasp. Another arrow hit him in the shoulder and he tumbled backwards into the water. Glancing back, O'Brien saw Sigurd set down his bow and draw his pistol. Braggi was rousing the rest of the men.

Ísbátr was now less than twenty meters from the enemy ship, its bow aimed at the starboard gunwale a few meters behind the dragon figurehead. Men on the other ship began to stir in response to the noise. Several of them spotted *Ísbátr* at once and began to shout warnings. The crew scrambled for their bows.

"Fire!" Gabe shouted.

A series of gunshots rang out across the water and three men on the enemy ship fell to the deck. Four more fell in second round of shots. Arrows fired by men standing on the sea chests or leaning over the gunwales felled three more. Harald's men were falling almost as fast as they could get to their feet.

"Gunners, move aside!" Gabe shouted. Those with pistols moved along the gunwales toward the stern as men from behind them poured toward the bow. The men braced themselves for a moment and then, when *Ísbátr*'s bow struck the hull of the enemy ship, they leaped forward, spears and axes in hand, landing on the deck of the other ship. The enemy ship's deck was higher, but their angled approach allowed them to jump directly from *Ísbátr*'s bow to the enemy deck.

*****

Sigurd led the charge. It was a slaughter.

A few men on the enemy ship managed to fire arrows before the melee began, but half of the enemy were still asleep, and the others barely had time to switch from bows to spears before being cut down by Sigurd or one of the others advancing from *Ísbátr*. The gunners, along with several archers, lined up along *Ísbátr*'s port gunwale and continued to fire, taking out any man who dared stand. After a third of the enemy ship's crew had been killed, wounded, or thrown overboard, the men began to throw down their weapons. The surprise attack, along with the shock of the foreigners' weapons, was too much for them. Harald's men surrendered.

"Throw your bows overboard," Sigurd barked, and the prisoners did as instructed. Sigurd saw that among them was a large man with a forked, braided beard and a jagged scar that ran from his brow across his left cheek and down to his chin.

"Gunnar," Sigurd said, grinning as he stepped toward the prisoners. Gunnar had been attempting to hide at the rear of the group, but now that he'd been spotted, he thrust his chin forward defiantly, making his way to the front. His left shoulder was still in a sling.

"Before you do anything," Gunnar said, "I suggest you remember that I'm a representative of King Harald himself."

Sigurd guffawed. "Gunnar, you've always had a gift for words, but your gift has failed you today. I had little sympathy for you before you opened your mouth, and I have none now." He turned to Agnar and Brynjarr, who stood beside him. "Tie his hands and feet."

The men did as they were asked. There was no complaint from anyone on board the enemy ship but Gunnar himself, who yelped in pain as Brynjarr jerked his hands behind his back. When Agnar and Brynjarr had finished, Sigurd grabbed Gunnar by his arm, pulling him toward the gunwale. His feet tied, Gunnar was forced to hop to keep from falling over. He stared into the fog, terror in his eyes.

"Please, Sigurd," Gunnar begged. "What are you doing?"

"Fishing," Sigurd said, and shoved Gunnar overboard.

CHAPTER THIRTY-TWO

O'Brien moved aside as the attackers returned to *Ísbátr*.

"Keep an eye out for the other ships," Gabe said. "Anybody within twenty klicks must have heard those shots."

O'Brien nodded, and began peering into the fog again. But he was distracted by a hand gripping his left leg. Glancing down, he saw Slater looking sitting on the deck, leaning against the gunwale. She looked at him with a strange, pleading expression on her face. O'Brien saw now that an arrow was sticking out of her chest.

"Gabe!" he shouted, dropping to his knees. "Slater's been hit!"

Gabe approached, kneeling down next to Slater. Her flight suit was open to halfway down her chest; the arrow had just missed the zipper, striking her below her left collarbone. Blood pooled on her chest and ran down her neck. Slater moaned with pain. Even in the dim morning light, O'Brien could see her face had gone pale.

"Reyes, give me some light," Gabe said.

Reyes tapped her cuff, turning on the LED flashlight. Slater's wound looked bad.

"What can I do?" O'Brien asked.

"Keep watch," Gabe said. "Let me know what's going on."

"Copy that." O'Brien stood and surveyed the situation. The attackers had begun going through the supplies on the enemy ship. Barrels of water and ale were being handed over *Ísbátr*'s bow to be carried to the hold. Others were collecting arrows, while a small group continued to guard the prisoners herded into the stern. Sigurd was barking orders, trying to get the men to hurry up. Scanning the fog around *Ísbátr*, O'Brien saw no sign of the other ships, but they would undoubtedly be here soon.

"Everything looks to be under control," O'Brien said. "No sign of other ships. Looks like we'll be underway shortly."

"Good," Gabe said. "Do we have anything we could use as an antiseptic?"

"Ale," Reyes said. "There might be some wine in the hold."

O'Brien nodded. "I'll look around."

Making his way toward the hold, O'Brien ran into Sigurd. "Slater," O'Brien said, tapping his chest where Slater had been hit. "Do you have wine? Vin?"

Sigurd glanced over O'Brien's shoulder to see the Reyes and Gabe huddled over Slater. He frowned and brushed past O'Brien. O'Brien watched as Sigurd knelt beside Reyes and dipped his fingers in the pool of blood collecting in the hollow of her throat. He brought his fingers to his nose and then tasted the blood. He shook his head. "Dauðir," he pronounced.

Gabe and Reyes exchanged glances.

"No," O'Brien said. "She's not dead." Slater had lost consciousness, but her heart was clearly still beating.

Sigurd shrugged and walked away.

"We need help, you preliterate thug," O'Brien snapped. "Antiseptic. Vin."

Sigurd ignored him, going back to shouting orders at the men. The attackers had all returned from the enemy ship, having thrown the enemy's weapons and half their oars overboard. Sigurd was doing his best to get the men back into rowing positions.

O'Brien drew his knife and took a step toward Sigurd. Reyes came up behind him, grabbing his arm. "No, O'Brien. Sigurd's one of us."

Sigurd glanced at O'Brien, saw the knife in his hand, shrugged, and went back to barking orders.

O'Brien let the knife fall to his side. "Fine, then help me find some wine."

"Forget it," Gabe said.

They turned to look at him.

"Sigurd's right. The arrow pierced her carotid artery. If I remove it, she dies. There's no way I can operate on her in these conditions."

"And if you leave the arrow in?"

"She still dies. A little slower."

"There's got to be something we can do," O'Brien said.

"I've got basic combat medic training, O'Brien. "I don't think I could stitch together an artery even if we had an operating room. And even if I could, she'd need a transfusion. She's lost at least two liters of blood already. You got any ideas how to hook up an IV under these conditions?"

O'Brien said nothing.

The Norsemen had returned to their seats and taken up their oars. Birgir gave the order to begin rowing, and *Ísbátr* began to creep away from the other ship. There was still no sign of any of Harald's other ships. Shouted insults from the enemy ship faded in the distance as the ship disappeared in the fog.

Reyes and Gabe did what they could to make Slater comfortable. She slipped in and out of consciousness for several minutes, and then finally succumbed. Her breathing stopped and her heartbeat faded to a faint flutter and then stopped completely.

Two other crew members of *Ísbátr* had died in the fight; men had dragged their bodies to the bow, leaving them lying on the deck next to Slater. When Sigurd saw that she had passed, he found a tarp of oil-soaked wool cloth and covered the three bodies. He spoke briefly to the three of them what they assumed were words of comfort. O'Brien nodded, accepting the words numbly. Sigurd returned to his chest and resumed rowing. Not knowing what else to do, the three spacemen did the same. Gloom hung to *Ísbátr* like the fog.

They rowed until mid-morning. Gradually the fog cleared, but there was no wind and the sky remained cloudy. Several times O'Brien caught Birgir consulting a piece of crystal stone similar to the one Skeggi had carried. Anxious for a distraction from his thoughts, O'Brien asked Birgir if he could see it. To his surprise, Birgir was more than happy to give a demonstration.

The sun stone was a roughly square, nearly transparent crystal, small enough to fit in the palm of Birgir's hand. O'Brien recognized it as crystallized calcium carbonate, once known as Iceland spar. First, Birgir pointed to a black mark that had been made on the top of the crystal. Then he held it up to the sky, looking at the mark from below. There now appeared to be two marks, less than a centimeter apart. This effect, O'Brien knew, was the result of the crystal polarizing the light. Birgir rotated the crystal until the two dots lined up, then pointed with his finger in the direction the stone's top was facing. "Sól," he said. O'Brien nodded. The sun rose east-southeast, which made it a simple matter to estimate the south-southwesterly course they would need to take to reach the Frisian coast.

A little before noon, Birgir ordered half the men off the oars. For the rest of the day, they rowed in shifts of about an hour. O'Brien gathered that Sigurd and Birgir were fairly certain they'd lost Harald's ships, so they'd shifted to a more sustainable pace. It simply wasn't possible for a man to row all day at full speed.

Their progress was slow. It was hard to tell without any landmarks, but O'Brien estimated they were traveling at about four knots. At that rate, it would take days to reach the mainland. There was no wind to speak of, so rowing was their only option. While the others took turns rowing, O'Brien stood at the bow, watching *Ísbátr* cut through the water and trying not to think about the dead woman lying next to two Vikings at his feet.

He couldn't help feeling responsible for Slater's death. If he hadn't said anything, the enemy ship may well have drifted away without anyone else knowing it was there. But he had to open his stupid mouth, and then the idiot Vikings had to attack rather than do the prudent thing and just row quietly away—not that there was any reason to think these people would act prudently. *Viking* was basically synonymous with *impetuous and violent*. It was little consolation that the attack had been a great success, tactically speaking. Slater was dead, and it was largely his fault.

They rowed until just after sunset, when the sun stone could no longer guide them. The men ate their evening meal and then went to sleep. Not long after, the air pressure dropped and a breeze picked up. The men who didn't already have their tents out rooted through their chests to get them. The tents were not glamorous affairs; essentially they were oil-soaked cloth or leather tarps that were propped up by a simple stick frame.

O'Brien and the other spacemen had found their own tents in the chests Dag had provided, and had crawled into them to get out of the rain. The others quickly fell asleep, but O'Brien remained awake. It wasn't just the pain in his ribs and the guilt about Slater's death keeping him awake. Something else was bothering him: a steady wind was blowing now, but they were letting it go to waste. By tomorrow morning it might die down again, and the crew would be stuck rowing all day.

He crawled slowly out of his tent and found Reyes. He shook her by the shoulder.

"O'Brien? What the hell?"

"The motor that runs the climate control system in the flight suits," O'Brien said. "It has a magnet in it, right?"

"Uh, I suppose so. A small one."

"Do you think you could take it out without wrecking the suit?"

"Sure. But why...?"

O'Brien's eyes fell on one of the furs that Reyes was using as a blanket. "Never mind," he said. "Can I borrow this?"

"Will you let me go back to sleep?"

"Yep."

Reyes waved at him. O'Brien grabbed the fur and wrapped it around his neck.

Finding a wooden cup and water to fill it was easy enough, but he spent the better part of two hours trying to locate a needle. His first thought had been to use a pin from one of the Norsemen's broaches, but found out after a few tense and confusing exchanges that the broaches were made almost entirely of bronze. Finally Birgir intervened, and O'Brien was able, with some effort, to make him understand that he was looking for a small piece of iron. When Birgir produced an iron needle from a chest near the stern, O'Brien nearly kissed him. Along with the needle, Birgir had spools of thread and folded pieces of wool cloth: it was Skeggi's sail repair kit.

O'Brien sat on the gunwale and brushed the fur against the needle rhythmically for a minute. He stuck the needle through a tiny fragment of rotted wood he'd pulled from the deck, so that half of the needle stuck out of either end. Then he gently placed the needle and wood in the wood cup, which he'd half-filled with water. He held the cup in his hand, shining the light from his cuff into it. After a moment, the needle began to move, but it was hard to tell whether it was magnetism of the movement of the boat. The needle moved to the side of the cup and stuck there, adhered by surface tension. He dislodged it and tried again, with the same results. What he really needed was some kind of gimble to hold the cup steady. Barring that, a larger cup might do. He went on another scavenger hunt, eventually finding a good-sized wooden bowl. He filled this with water and placed the needle and wood fragment in it. Standing and holding his hands away from his body so as to absorb as much of the motion of the boat as he could, he watched as the needle gradually oriented itself approximately perpendicular to Ísbátr's keel. After waiting a few seconds to be sure the needle had settled, O'Brien gave it a push with his finger, causing it to spin about ninety degrees to the left. The needle slowly stopped and then reversed its spin, orienting itself as it had before. O'Brien stifled a cry of excitement.

The question now was whether the needle pointed north or south. He could make a pretty good guess based on the orientation of the boat, as it was unlikely they'd drifted a hundred and eighty degrees, but a mistake would be costly. He had brushed the fur away from the point of the needle, which—he was fairly certain—would make the needle's head the magnet's north pole. He'd learned while studying Earth's geology that its poles were named backwards: Earth's "North Pole" was actually its magnetic south. That meant the head of the needle would be pulled to face north; the sharp end of the needle would point south. Currently the needle was pointing toward the port side of the boat, which was roughly where O'Brien expected it to be, given their last known heading. Without knowing the location of the north pole in advance, O'Brien knew of no way to be more certain which way the needle was pointing.

He returned to Reyes's tent and woke her again.

"Damn it, O'Brien," Reyes growled, blinking at him in the dim light. "Now what?"

"I made a compass," O'Brien replied.

"And?"

"And… I know which direction north is."

"Go to sleep, O'Brien."

"Listen to me, Reyes. We've got a steady wind of about ten knots from the southeast right now. If we unfurl the sail, we could cover close to a hundred klicks before dawn."

"Or we could wait until morning."

"We have no idea how long this wind will last." When Reyes still looked skeptical, he added, "That's a hundred klicks you don't have to row."

Reyes groaned but nodded and began to climb out of her tent. Pulling her cloak around her, she said, "Let's go talk to Sigurd."

Sigurd was unexpectedly receptive to the idea. Once O'Brien demonstrated to Sigurd's satisfaction that the needle would always orient itself in the same direction, he agreed that it would be prudent to use the wind while they could. He seemed to be concerned that Harald's other ships might still find them. If they could travel a hundred klicks while the enemy ships drifted aimlessly at sea, that would be one less thing to worry about.

Birgir was less enthusiastic, but Sigurd insisted. Birgir woke his riggers and they unfurled the sail, setting it at an angle that would propel them toward the southwest—assuming O'Brien's educated guess about the compass' orientation was correct.

Once *Ísbátr* was underway, O'Brien lay down and tried to get back to sleep. He had already been second-guessing himself about getting Slater killed, and now he worried that he may have sent *Ísbátr* on a course back toward Norway. He finally fell asleep just before dawn.

When he awoke, the rain had stopped but the sky was still cloudy. The sun was hidden, but judging by the light, it was mid-morning. He sat up and watched the rest of the crew as they lounged about the deck, eating, drinking, gambling with dice, or simply staring out to sea. After some time, he saw Birgir checking the position of the sun with his crystal. Seeming satisfied, he slipped it back into his pocket. O'Brien let out a sigh of relief. Apparently he'd made the right call; the sun stone had confirmed their heading. They were on their way toward the Frisian coast.

The wind held for most of the day and into the night. O'Brien spotted land off the port bow on the afternoon of the fourth day. Cheers went up from the men. By the time they reached shore, it was too late to scout the area to make sure it was safe to make camp, so they spent the night on the boat. The next morning, they rowed some distance down the coast to the west, until they located a sandy beach where *Ísbátr* could be brought ashore. As they approached the shore, twenty or so men near the bow put away their oars and jumped into the water. They ran alongside *Ísbátr*'s stern, pushing her toward the shore. When she stopped, only the tip of her stern remained in the water. The rest of the crew got out, some of them pulling ropes, and hauled *Ísbátr* firmly onto the beach.

Sigurd picked ten men to scout the area, leaving Birgir in charge of the rest to make camp at the shore. The men seemed to have accepted Sigurd as their leader, but O'Brien noticed that he left Brynjarr and Braggi behind, probably to make sure there was no talk of mutiny while he was gone. Sigurd informed the spacemen of his plans but didn't ask if they wanted to come along on the scouting expedition. In O'Brien's opinion, it was just as well. He was still too hurt to travel, and Reyes wouldn't go for splitting up their party anyway.

Those on the beach set up tents, built a fire, and dug graves for the three dead. The scouting party returned late in the afternoon. From what he was able to understand of Sigurd's report, they hadn't found much of interest: only a small farming community some distance inland. The

Norsemen weren't averse to stealing from farmers, but O'Brien gathered that these people didn't have enough wealth to be worth the trouble. The good news was that they had a pretty good idea where they were: the villagers had told them the river Rotte was just to the west, which meant they were in Frisia, about three days travel by sea to Normandy. It was unclear to O'Brien why they had to travel all the way to Normandy, but he suspected that the Vikings had already picked over this area of Europe pretty well. They were hoping to find unspoiled cities farther to the west.

At dusk, they had a quiet ceremony to honor their dead. After the Vikings had said their part about the two fallen men, the spacemen were invited to speak about Slater. Reyes couldn't bring herself to deliver a eulogy, so she deferred to Gabe, who stood and gave a short but heartfelt speech about their fallen comrade and friend. The two Vikings were buried with their spears; the spacemen buried Slater with only her flight suit. They debated burying one of the pistols with her, but in the end decided it was a meaningless gesture. Slater wouldn't want it, anyway. She was a scientist and pilot, not a warrior. They removed her cuff and earpiece, but left her flight suit. They filled the graves with sand and then sat around the fire with the Norsemen, eating and drinking until late in the evening.

CHAPTER THIRTY-THREE

Sigurd arose at dawn the next morning. Except for the man who was keeping watch, the rest of the crew was still asleep. Sigurd let them be, taking some time to warm himself by the fire. The crew had worked hard, and there was no hurry now that they'd escaped Harald's fleet. They'd been up late celebrating the lives of the fallen, and they could use the rest.

Around mid-morning, after they'd eaten breakfast, the crew packed up camp, and pushed *Ísbátr* back into the water. A breeze was once again blowing out of the southeast, and they rode it along the coast for the next two days. The morning of the third day, *Ísbátr* passed through the strait between England and Francia. The sight of the chalk-white Cliffs of Dover to the north excited the crew; it was a sign that they were less than a day's travel from their goal, the mouth of the River Seine.

The wind finally gave out later that morning, and the crew had to row hard to reach the Seine by dark. They slept on the boat, anchored in the cove just offshore. The next morning, they rowed up the Seine, where they hoped to make contact with some of the other Norsemen who had settled here. Expeditions from Denmark and the other Nordic lands had been raiding along this coast for nearly a century now, and settlements near the water had been pretty well picked over or demolished. The cathedrals, which had provided so much easy gold and silver in the early days, had mostly been abandoned or burned down. Those that remained had been fortified so much as to make unattractive targets. Most of the natives had fled to the cities inland, and they'd gradually been supplanted by settlements of Norsemen. Lately, the Vikings had begun moving farther inland themselves, particularly in the highly desirable region of the Seine

Valley. Raiding was no longer the free-for-all it had been in the days of Sigurd's grandfather; raiders coming to the area now had to deal with the established Norse chieftains in addition to the native powers. A hierarchy had been established, and woe to the adventurer who didn't give the vanguard their due.

The nexus of Norse power in Europe was in the Seine Valley, where several men from Denmark and Norway had set themselves up as petty chieftains. The amount of territory nominally under their control was small relative to the Frankish empire, but they owned much of the coast and had made it virtually impossible for ships to travel down the Seine to Rouen or Paris without paying a toll. From their bases in the valley, they also projected power by raiding throughout the countryside, as far away as Nantes in the southwest. The Frankish kings had done what they could to defend their territory, but they were scattered and disorganized. By the time they knew the Norsemen were on their way to a village or cathedral, it was too late.

Much opportunity still remained on the continent for determined raiders, but a party the size of Sigurd's simply didn't have the manpower to go it alone. If they set up camp anywhere within a hundred miles of the mouth of the Seine, they'd be under constant threat of attack from one of the competing chieftains. Even if all four of their boats had made it, they wouldn't have had the numbers to resist such an attack. If they were able to get the backing of one of the local chieftains, though, they'd be relatively safe: the other chieftains would be unlikely to risk a war by attacking them.

Its rolling hills blanketed with snow, the Seine valley was a breathtaking sight. This was a more gentle and fertile land than Norway, and it was not difficult to see why so many of his countrymen had come here in search of wealth and opportunity. Rich farmland broken by lush groves of maples and oaks gave way gradually to pine-covered hills. Already buds were forming on the trees; in a few weeks the entire regions would be awash with green and accented with pink and white blossoms of fruit trees.

A few miles up the Seine, *Ísbátr* was hailed by a sentry on a tower on the south bank of the river. Looking up, Sigurd saw a dozen or so archers, their bows at the ready. Sigurd looked to Birgir, who gave him a nod and steered the boat toward a dock that extended out from the base of the tower twenty yards or so into the river. Birgir docked the boat and Sigurd leapt onto the dock, greeting the sentry, a young man named Alaric, who hailed from a village not far north of Sigurd's. Sigurd explained their intentions, noting that he hoped to come to an understanding with one of the local chieftains.

As it turned out, there was really only one chieftain they needed to concern themselves with. It had been several years since Sigurd or any of *Ísbátr*'s crew had ventured this far west, and since then an alliance had united most of the Norsemen in the valley under a Norwegian chieftain called Hrólfr. Sigurd was familiar with Hrólfr; he was a kinsman of Harald's.

"This Hrólfr," Sigurd said. "He is allied with the King of Norway?"

The man shrugged. "I don't know of any such alliance. As far as I know, Hrólfr left Norway to make a name for himself away from Harald."

Sigurd nodded, somewhat relieved. If Harald and Hrólfr were close, it wouldn't matter that Sigurd's enemies were across the sea. "Very good, Alaric," Sigurd said, clasping the man's hand. The man nodded, shaking his hand, and then made his way back up the ladder to the tower. Sigurd got back in the boat and they pushed away to continue upstream. As Sigurd approached the bow, Gabe asked him a question.

"We have to talk to Hrólfr," Sigurd said. "He's the local chieftain. The jarl."

"Rolf?" Gabe said, mangling the pronunciation. He said something that Sigurd didn't understand, ending his sentence with something that sounded like *Rollo*.

Sigurd frowned. "Göngu-Hrólfr," he said, using the appellation by which Hrólfr was sometimes known.

Gabe nodded excitedly. He held his arms out at his sides, as if mimicking a very large man.

Sigurd's brow furrowed. Did the foreigners somehow know of Hrólfr? Had they been to this area before? He nodded. "He's a very big man. They call him Göngu—walker—because he's too big for his horse."

Gabe nodded and spoke briefly with the others, Reyes and O'Brien. Whatever Gabe told them, they didn't seem to share his enthusiasm. This wasn't the first time Sigurd had noticed Gabe getting excited over some detail about Norse politics that was of little interest to the others. It was as if he had visited this area once as a child, and was excited to find that some things were still as he remembered. But that couldn't be it; Hrólfr had only ascended to his current position as ruler of the Seine Valley in the past few years.

Gabe turned to him again and asked him another question. He pointed to the land beyond the riverbanks. Sigurd understood he was asking where they would be setting up camp.

"We need a permanent base," Sigurd said. "Someplace to build a fort."

Gabe nodded, recognizing the word. He turned to explain the situation to the others.

*****

Reyes considered what Gabe had said. "It sounds like Sigurd is planning to stay here beyond the summer," she said. In halting conversations with some of the other Norsemen, it had become clear that most of the crew intended to raid during the summer and then return to Norway before the weather got cold.

"That's good, right?" asked O'Brien. "You think he's rethinking his plan for vengeance on Harald?"

"Not a chance," Gabe replied. "He's playing a long game, counting on his alliance with us to give him his vengeance."

"And when he finds out that's impossible?" O'Brien asked.

"Let's not borrow trouble," Reyes. "Sigurd and his men wanting to settle here is good news. We're going to need them if we're going to survive. Harald's not going to stop coming after us, and we can't fight him alone. Not yet, anyway. We need time to plan and work on our defenses."

"I'd suggest not speaking that name," Gabe said. "The less said about our run-ins with you-know-who, the better."

"You think they'd turn us away if they knew about that?" Reyes asked.

Gabe shrugged. "We're not the first political refugees to flee an overbearing ruler," he said. "Iceland was settled by people trying to get away from you-know-who and his like. I'm thinking it's a don't-ask-don't-tell kind of situation."

"Why stop here, then?" O'Brien asked. "Why not keep going? Travel east to Constantinople, or Byzantium, or whatever it's called right now? Go somewhere outside of Har—you-know-who's area of influence? Try to blend in, wait for him to forget about us."

Reyes shook her head. "We have no money, no friends… and we don't speak the language. And blending in doesn't seem to be our strong suit. No, I think we have to stick with Sigurd and his crew for now."

Gabe nodded in agreement. "We've got knowledge we could theoretically trade for money, but that goes against the idea of keeping a low profile. It would be easy enough to mass produce compasses and sell them to sailors, but how long do you think it would take for you-know-who to hear about it?"

"So then what's the plan?" O'Brien asked. "We set up shop here, build houses, start raising goats, what?"

"We follow Sigurd's lead," Reyes said. "The first step is to find a defensible piece of land. We don't know how long it will be before you-know-who comes for us, and we need to be ready."

Finding a piece of defensible land was going to be more difficult in the Seine Valley than in the mountains of Norway. With the exception of some low, tree-covered ridges a few klicks from the river, the land was low and flat.

They spent the next hour rowing and watching the snow-covered valley roll past. Occasionally they would see some signs of human habitation—a cattle fence or a small house with smoke pouring out the chimney, but they saw very few people. Those she saw were mostly men. This land had only recently been seized by the Vikings, and the people here were still the first wave of settlers. The men here were either unmarried or had left their families home until it was safe to bring them.

Reyes's thoughts went to Slater, the only other woman who had come along on the voyage. Maybe it was for the best she'd died before reaching Normandy; Slater wasn't cut out to be a Viking. It wasn't her fault she'd been killed, though. That arrow could have hit any of them. It was a wonder that the rest of them had survived this long. Shaw's death had hit the team hard, but Reyes didn't have the luxury of blaming herself. She was still in charge of this mission, and O'Brien and Gabe were counting on her to keep it together. Gabe played the tough guy pretty well, but even he had his limits—and he tended to be overprotective. If he got the sense Reyes was breaking down, he'd try to fill the void, and his own responsibilities would suffer. So Reyes kept her head up and focused on what needed to be done.

At present, her main task was finding a place they could settle where Harald couldn't get to them. The only natural barrier in the area was the river, which snaked back and forth across the valley floor, and it wouldn't be much of a barrier for the seafaring Vikings. What they needed was a hill overlooking the river, with a hundred meters or more of open ground in between. Scanning the river banks, it took over an hour for Reyes to spot a potential candidate. She almost pointed it out to Gabe, and then realized there was already a large, squat building perched atop the hill: they had reached Rollo's fortress.

"This is amazing," Gabe said, staring up at the fortress. "We're going to see Rollo!"

"Should that mean something to me?" O'Brien asked.

"He's the first Duke of Normandy!" Gabe exclaimed. "I mean, he's not yet, but he will be. Rollo is responsible for uniting the Viking settlements in France into a single country, which becomes Normandy. They call him Hrólfr. Without him, there's no William the Conqueror. Without William the Conqueror, there's no Norman invasion of England. And if the Normans never invade England—"

"Yeah, we get it," Reyes said. "So this is our hypothetical test case come to life. We could kill Rollo and alter all of history."

"Please don't threaten to kill the Duke of Normandy," O'Brien said. "We're in enough trouble on this planet."

"We're not going to kill him," Gabe said. "We need him. You can't settle around here without his okay."

"I didn't realize Vikings were so big on rules," Reyes said.

"Think of it like this," Gabe replied. "The Vikings in Europe are basically an extra-legal entity, like criminal gangs, or the mafia. They don't technically own much territory, but they have a lot of influence. They control the traffic down the Seine, and they demand tribute from the local Frankish rulers."

"Like protection money," O'Brien said.

"Exactly like protection money."

"That doesn't seem like a very well-thought-out strategy, from the European's perspective," Reyes said.

"It's not," Gabe said. "It's just a delaying tactic. The longer it goes on, the more powerful the Vikings become. Later on, it actually becomes encoded in Frankish and English law. There's a tax called the danegild—literally Danish tax—that is levied specifically to pay off the Vikings to keep them from attacking. At this point it's a little more informal. The kings know it's going on, but it's bribery under the table."

"So the actual raiding," Reyes said, "that's basically done by this point?" She sounded hopeful.

"Oh, no," Gabe replied. "There's still plenty of raiding going on. It takes a long time for this to all settle out, politically, and there's a lot of land that's still in dispute. But before these guys do any raiding, they're going to have to get permission from Rollo. Hrólfr, I mean."

Birgir and the crew guided *Ísbátr* to a grassy bank. As she approached, several men jumped out and helped her up onto the shore.

Sigurd spoke briefly with Birgir and then returned to the bow. "Hrólfr talk," he said.

"You go, Reyes," Gabe said.

"We should all go."

"I'm not making that hike," O'Brien said, looking at the winding path leading up to the fortress.

"I'll stay with O'Brien," Gabe said.

"No, I need you, Gabe."

"I'm not an infant," O'Brien said. "I'll be fine. These guys aren't going to hurt me."

Reyes nodded. "All right. Make sure your comm is on."

"As always. Go."

"All right," Reyes said, turning to Sigurd. "We're ready."

They trudged through the thin grass and made their way to a rocky path that wended past several buildings and up the hill. As they walked, they caught occasional glimpses of men tending to livestock or engaging in other menial tasks. The men glanced suspiciously in their direction, but didn't seem terribly interested in the visitors.

As they neared the gate of the fortress, a man emerged from a copse of trees to their left. The man was huge, with broad shoulders and midsection like a barrel. A great bow hung over his left shoulder; his right hand gripped the rear hooves of a deer, the rest of which dragged on the ground behind him. Birgir and Sigurd stopped at the sight of the man, unsure how to react. The man walked up to them, letting the deer fall to the ground behind him, and held out a massive, blood-streaked hand. Sigurd shook it and the man bellowed a greeting. The only word Reyes recognized was a name, but there wasn't much doubt who this man was, given Gabe's description. So this was the first Duke of Normandy, she thought. He was certainly more impressive than Harald Fairhair.

Sigurd introduced the others and Hrólfr led them inside the fortress. If he was at all concerned for his safety, he didn't show it. Gabe, just a couple paces behind the deer Hrólfr was dragging, could easily have put a bullet in the back of his head, and that would be that. No Normandy, no England, no United States of America, at least not as it existed in the history books. What would happen if Gabe tried to kill him? Would the gods themselves come down from heaven and stop the bullet? It was a question that she wouldn't get an answer to, at least not today. History books or not, they needed Hrólfr alive.

*****

"Is this your entire party?" Hrólfr asked. He sat across from Sigurd and the foreigners in the great room of his lodge. A wooden tray of meats and cheeses lay before them, and a beautiful Frankish slave girl kept their cups full of ale.

"We left Uslu with four ships," Sigurd said. "Two were lost at sea. We were separated from the fourth, but they may yet arrive."

Hrólfr raised an eyebrow. "The sea has been calm for a week," he said.

"We chose an unlucky course," Sigurd replied. If Hrólfr wished to press him on the matter, he was going to have to be explicit. But Hrólfr simply smiled. "Well, it is good that you made it. I hope your comrades arrive in good health. But what of these strangers?" He didn't break eye contact with Sigurd, but Sigurd understood he meant the foreigners.

"They come from a land very far away, called Eidejel. Their boat capsized not far from my home, and my people took them in. They have been good friends to me."

"Are there more of them?"

"Just one. He is injured and could not make the walk here." Sigurd had debated whether he should bring the foreigners along to speak with Hrólfr, but decided to err on the side of transparency, at least in this matter. Hrólfr was going to find out about the foreigners eventually, and he didn't want Hrólfr to think he was hiding anything from him. Besides, their presence gave him some cover for their intention to settle in the valley.

"Where were these people traveling to when their boat capsized?"

"I'm not certain they had a definite destination. They were fleeing from enemies."

"And what of these enemies? Who are they?"

"A belligerent power threatening to overthrow Eidejel," Sigurd replied.

"Their kingdom is at war, and they flee here?"

"They are not warriors," Sigurd said. "Except for this man, who is charged with protecting the others. My understanding is that they were on a diplomatic mission, seeking allies to help defend Eidejel. They were intercepted by an enemy ship and forced to flee westward. The enemy ship sank, but these foreigners made it to our land."

Hrólfr glanced at the foreigners and then back at Sigurd. He was clearly dubious of Sigurd's story; the question was how hard he would press for the truth. If he asked a direct question and Sigurd lied to him, it would render any agreement with him null and void.

"You intend to set up camp in the valley to raid for the summer?"

"To begin with," Sigurd replied. "Most will return to Norway in the fall, but some intend to stay longer."

"The foreigners," Hrólfr said.

"Yes, along with me and some of my friends."

"The foreigners do not intend to return to their land?"

"They hope to, but lack the means at present. They will likely stay here for some years."

"And if their enemies find them?"

"They were pursued only by one ship, which sank. None of the crew survived, and no one else knows of their mission. Their enemies will not find them here."

Hrólfr nodded, rubbing his beard and regarding Reyes and Gabe. "If they do, you will not be able to count on my protection. Whatever enemies you have, they are yours. Not mine. Do you understand?"

"I do, Hrólfr," Sigurd said. "Thank you." Hrólfr's meaning was only too clear. Hrólfr was too shrewd to ask him directly about Harald, but he'd now made it plain that he wouldn't intercede in any conflicts between Sigurd and his enemies.

"How many men do you expect to stay through the winter?" Hrólfr asked.

"I would guess at least ten, perhaps as many as twenty. More if the other ship from our expedition arrives."

"If you intend to stay more than a year, you will want some land for grazing and crops."

Sigurd nodded. This was going to be tricky. He was going to have to negotiate for a parcel of land they could defend if Harald's men attacked, while maintaining the fiction that he was unconcerned about foreign enemies. "We will be occupied mostly with raiding at first," Sigurd said. "Our main concern is setting up camp in a place where we can safely keep our spoils."

"You'll have no trouble from the other Norsemen in this area," Hrólfr said. "Everyone in this valley recognizes my authority. If we come to an arrangement, you are guaranteed protection. For a small fee, of course. Ordinarily I charge one tenth of the spoils."

"I have no doubt you are more than capable of dealing with thieves," Sigurd replied, "but all the same, I do not like depending on others for my security."

"You will pay the tenth regardless," Hrólfr said.

"Understood," Sigurd said. "Consider it an expression of goodwill."

Hrólfr smiled. "Then it is settled. I cannot house your entire crew, but you and the foreigners may sleep here tonight. Tomorrow you can survey the area to find a parcel to your liking."

*****

After a brief discussion, Reyes and Gabe accepted the offer to stay in the lodge overnight. Gabe was concerned that staying in the lodge would stoke the simmering resentment the Norsemen already felt for the spacemen, but in the end their concern for O'Brien was the deciding factor. He needed a good night's sleep in something that could pass for an actual bed. Whatever improvement they'd seen in his condition since the crash was being rapidly undone by having to sleep on the deck of a Viking ship. Since Slater's death, Reyes was more determined than ever to keep the crew together as much as possible, so she decided they'd all be sleeping in the lodge.

They returned to *Ísbátr* and Sigurd briefed Birgir and the rest of the crew. Reyes and Gabe helped O'Brien out of the boat and up the path to the lodge while Sigurd stayed behind. He and his men would sleep on the boat to make sure the crew wasn't getting any ideas about replacing him as their leader.

The next day, Reyes and Gabe left O'Brien in the lodge and returned to *Ísbátr*. Hrólfr had had a servant draw them a rough map on a scrap of parchment the afternoon before, indicating some of the better parcels in the valley. The servant had scribbled names in some places, indicating territories that had been claimed by sub-chieftains, but most of the valley was wide open. At one point, Reyes assumed, all this land had been owned by the Franks, but they had mostly fled further upriver. It was one gigantic Viking campground now.

They spent the day cruising up and down the river, occasionally pulling *Ísbátr* onto the bank to explore the territory further. By the end of the day, they had marked three potential areas on Hrólfr's map. They returned to the lodge that evening to speak again with Hrólfr. When he saw the areas they'd marked, he laughed. He spoke to Sigurd, who shrugged, a smile playing at his lips. Reyes shot a quizzical glance at Gabe, who shook his head. Whatever was going on between Hrólfr and Sigurd, it was probably best to play dumb.

Reyes and Gabe sat and drank their ale while Hrólfr and Sigurd negotiated. At last Sigurd turned to them with a sigh and said, "Much silfr."

"He wants us to pay for the land?" Reyes asked. "I thought he was getting one tenth of the spoils from raiding?" Sigurd had summarized the content of their previous meeting.

"Tenth, yes," Sigurd said. "And much silfr."

"How much?" Gabe asked.

Sigurd frowned, then held up ten fingers. He made fists and then made ten fingers again.

"A hundred?" Reyes said.

Sigurd shook his head, then made ten fingers again. "Hundred."

"Ten hundreds?" Reyes gasped. "He wants a thousand pieces of silver?"

"Thousand silfr," Sigurd repeated, nodding his head. Then he held up a finger. "One Moon."

"A thousand silver pieces in one month," Gabe said. "I'm not an expert on Viking economics by any means, but that sounds like a hell of a lot."

"He knows we're up to something," Reyes said.

Gabe nodded. "He knows we've got enemies, and he's going to make us pay."

"Will he accept payment in kind?"

"I would imagine so. We may be at his mercy in terms of prices, but clothing, cookware, farm animals... I'm sure he'd take them. Worse case scenario, we sell them to someone else in the valley."

Sigurd pointed to one of the other areas they'd marked on the map— their second choice—and then held up seven fingers.

"Seven hundred," Reyes said.

Sigurd nodded.

"Hell," Reyes said. "If we're going to promise seven hundred, we might as well go all out and get our first choice. We're probably screwed either way."

"I don't think we want to be in debt to the future Duke of Normandy for a thousand silver pieces we can't pay back. We could probably sack ten villages and not find a thousand pieces of silver. You saw the way Dag's eyes lit up when he saw those rolls of solder. Those things are the equivalent of what, twenty-five silver coins each? These people don't see sums like that often."

"Can we haggle him down?"

Sigurd seemed to understand the question. He turned to Hrólfr and spoke again. Another curt exchanged followed, after which Sigurd turned back to Hrólfr. He held up two fingers.

"Two hundred?" Reyes asked hopefully.

"Two Moon," Sigurd said.

"He's going to give us two months to pay it," Gabe said.

"What do you think?"

"I think if we had twice as many men, we might be able to do it. But with this crew?" He shook his head.

Reyes turned back to Sigurd. "Should we take it?" she asked, hoping her tone was clear.

Sigurd sighed. He picked up the map from the table and pointed at a wide open space. Reyes remembered the area. It was just a wide open field dotted with copses of birch. They'd never be able to hold it if Harald attacked. Sigurd moved his finger to their preferred site. "Two Moon," he said.

"Take the one site now and save up for the other," Reyes said. "Hope that our friend doesn't decide to visit in the meantime."

"I don't like it," Gabe said.

"Do you like it more or less than owing a money we can't possibly come up with to a guy who will kill us if we don't pay?"

Gabe sighed. "Take the wide open parcel. We'll get used to sleeping with our eyes open, I guess."

"All right," Reyes said. She tapped the parcel Sigurd had indicted. "Take it."

Sigurd nodded. He turned to Hrólfr and began to speak, but as he did so the door to the room opened. A sentry entered and announced, "Skip!" Reyes knew that word: *ship*.

Hrólfr marched outside and the others followed him. A snekkja, roughly the size of *Ísbátr*, was being pushed onto the muddy bank. *Bylgjasverð* had arrived, and all thirty-seven Norsemen appeared to be on board. Gabe grinned at Reyes. She smiled at him and turned back to Sigurd. "Tell him we'll take the parcel on the hill."

CHAPTER THIRTY-FOUR

The Norsemen spent most of the next week felling trees. The land at the top of the hill had to be cleared before it was usable, and they were going to need the lumber. Most of the trees in this area were maples and other short-trunked trees, not suitable for building walls or fences, but there were uses for this sort of wood as well. Closer to the river were stands of birch and beech, and scattered firs. While the area was being cleared, they slept on the boats. There were open areas that would have sufficed as a campsite, but the nights were cold and the Norsemen preferred to sleep in close quarters. Reyes suspected they also didn't completely trust Hrólfr's assurances of safety. On the boats, anchored a stone's throw off the bank, they felt safe.

Once the trees at the summit of the hill had been cut down, the Norsemen dug around the stumps until the roots were exposed nearly a meter down. They hacked away as much of the stumps as they could, and burned the rest. It was slow work, as they were using shovels with wooden blades that had been hacked out of maple trunks. After they'd filled the holes, they raked the area smooth and tamped it flat. Next, a trench was dug at the perimeter, which was partially filled with gravel brought up from the riverbed. Poles hewn from beech or fir were placed vertically in the trench, and then the trench was filled the rest of the way with more gravel. The poles were carefully selected and hewed so that they fit together snugly, with no gaps, and secured together with thin leather straps. The leather came from deer and other animals in the area; a small contingent of men had been tasked with keeping the settlement supplied with meat. The end result was an impenetrable wall nearly three meters high, topped with spikes.

Several men grumbled about the time being spent on defenses. These were mostly the short-timers, those who were planning on returning to Norway in the fall. The short-timers were already upset about the thousand silver owed to Hrólfr, which came to twelve silver pieces per man. Reyes and Sigurd had mitigated the problem somewhat by getting Hrólfr to extend the deadline by another month and prorating the amount owed per man: each man would pay four silver per month, due at the end of the month. Those who planned to stay through the winter would owe another six silver at the end of the third month. Whether this solved the problem or merely distributed the discontent more evenly was hard to say. Additionally, they ran the risk of a majority of men opting to depart in the fall, leaving those who remained with an outsized balance they couldn't pay. There was nothing for it, though; they would just hope the summer's raiding was successful enough to cover their debts and tempt a sizeable contingent to stay.

Hrólfr had also agreed not to begin extracting his tenth of the spoils until after the three month deadline. That meant that any spoils they garnered before midsummer could be applied directly to their debt. Before the raiding could even start, though, they needed a place to secure their treasure. That was the story Sigurd had given the men, anyway. The real purpose of the wall was to stave off an attack by Harald. A week after their arrival, no news had come of an impending attack, nor any news of the situation in Norway at all. Reyes kept expecting Hrólfr to show up one day in a rage, demanding to know why they hadn't told him Harald wanted their heads on a plate, but so far everything was quiet.

Once the fence was complete and a gate had been constructed, the tents and the rest of the men's belongings from the ship were brought inside. More permanent lodgings would need to be constructed before winter, but for now, the tents would do. Soon, the weather would warm and the close quarters of the ships would be uncomfortable for sleeping.

As the fortifications neared completion, Sigurd took Birgir and twenty-nine other men aboard *Ísbátr* for a reconnaissance expedition. They returned five days later with a report on optimal targets for raiding. From what she could understand of Sigurd's report, Reyes deduced that the Seine Valley didn't offer much in the way of prospects. Earlier arrivals had looted the towns and cathedrals; only the well-fortified city of Rouen remained relatively untouched. Hrólfr undoubtedly had plans for that city, but such a prize was out of reach for a small band like Sigurd's.

More tempting were the towns along the Orne and the Douve, farther to the west. Sigurd announced his intention to launch a raiding expedition with both ships in three days. The men spent most of that time whittling spears and arrows and mending armor and shields. Gabe insisted that the pistols be left at the fort. They couldn't spare the ammo, and using them would draw undue attention. The Norsemen would have to earn their spoils the old-fashioned way.

Gabe was tempted to go along with the raiders, but relented to Reyes's demands that he stay behind. O'Brien was healing well, but he was in no shape to go on a raiding expedition, and some men needed to remain behind to guard the fort in any case. Sigurd and the others departed, leaving the spacemen behind with seven Norsemen.

Reyes had begrudgingly accepted that raiding would be necessary to pay their debt to Hrólfr. She didn't like it, but there was no way around it. If they didn't come up with the silver, Hrólfr would evict them from Normandy, and they had nowhere else to go. For once, she was glad Slater wasn't with them: she'd never have gone along with the raiding. Slater had been too soft-hearted for this life.

She was also thankful for once that she didn't speak the Norsemen's language: she suspected she didn't want to hear what sorts of exploits they were planning, to say nothing of their bragging after the fact. She did make one demand of Sigurd: the men were not to bring any captives back to the fort. Sigurd agreed, but she suspected this was more out of his own practical concerns than deference to her scruples: at this point, slaves would just be more mouths to feed.

While the raiding party was gone, Gabe and the other Norsemen began planning for building a small watchtower inside the perimeter fence, from which they would be able to see boats coming up the river. The tower would be supported by four long poles cut from the trunks of firs that had been hauled up the hill a few days earlier. The floor of the building would have to be at least ten meters above ground level for the men to see over the treetops. The building itself would be small, allowing for a maximum of four archers. The primary purpose was not defense, but simply to provide warning in time for men to get inside the fort and secure the gate.

Reyes, meanwhile, sketched out plans for a radio transmitter. She would need to build a receiver as well, but the main thing was to be able to transmit a signal capable of reaching *Andrea Luhman* when she attained orbit in a little over a month—even if that signal was only Morse code for "We're still alive." Without some kind of indication the landing party survived, there was a risk that Mallick would decide the mission had failed and begin the long, probably futile, journey back to IDL space. Reyes guessed they would wait a couple weeks at least, but she didn't want to take any chances. Mallick might still decide to scrap the mission even if they successfully made contact, but at least it would be an informed decision.

The suit radios would suffice for a receiver; all she needed was an antenna capable of picking up signal from space. An iron rod attached to the roof of the guard tower would work fine. Rigging a transmitter was a tougher problem: there was no simple way to amplify the signal from the suit transmitters. Doing so would require vacuum tubes or transistorized diodes, neither of which were in ready supply in ninth century France.

So she would have to build a transmitter from scratch. The main thing she needed was a large quantity of conductive metal, preferably copper. She intended to build what was known as a "spark gap transmitter," which used an arcing electrical current to generate a radio wave. Spark gap transmitters were inefficient and imprecise, but it would work for her purposes. If she could run sufficient voltage through such a device, it would theoretically be capable of transmitting a simple signal several hundred kilometers into space. If *Andrea Luhman* scanned the surface near the crash site for radio signals, it would most likely pick up the broadcast. Transmitting a decipherable audio signal would be beyond the capabilities of such a transmitter, but transmitting in Morse would be no problem. Reyes had given Sigurd specific instructions to get her some copper if at all possible.

Sigurd and the others returned a week later, triumphant from their raiding. None of the men had been killed; three had minor injuries. They brought little in the way of coins, but they were laden down with candlesticks, jewelry, silks, furs, various tools and—most importantly from Reyes's perspective—several pieces of copper cookware. The spoils were brought to a central meeting area inside the fence. When Reyes had taken the items she needed—including a hammer, tongs, and several of the higher-quality copper items—Sigurd ordered the rest of it brought to Hrólfr. He and his men returned from Hrólfr's several hours later with bad news: all the spoils they'd delivered were worth less than a tenth of what they owed. Hrólfr gave them the option of trying to sell the goods for silver, but he assured them they would not do much better anywhere in Normandy, and Sigurd believed him. At this rate, they'd have to raid almost constantly to cover the balance by the deadline, which was now less than six weeks away.

Hrólfr had indicated he might be willing to push the deadline back another month if they made significant progress paying down the balance over the next few weeks, but that required remaining on good terms with him. Any day news of their fugitive status might arrive from Norway, and from that point on they wouldn't be able to count on any favors from Hrólfr. If they were going to renegotiate the terms of their deal, they needed to do it soon. And that meant they needed to show Hrólfr they were serious. So it didn't surprise her when Gabe suggested the three spacemen meet to discuss how they were going to come up with the money. They went for a walk along the riverbank one afternoon.

"We're going to have to get more personally involved in the raiding," Gabe said.

"How will that help?" Reyes said. "You have a way of making raids more lucrative?"

"I have some thoughts. We need to hit higher value targets. Forget these little towns."

"That's going to require different tactics," Reyes said.

"We do have more powerful weapons we could be using," O'Brien said.

Reyes shook her head. "We need to save the guns for emergencies. We have limited ammo and they draw too much attention."

"Guns won't help much anyway," Gabe said. "We can't use them to threaten force, because nobody knows what they are. All guns do is help us kill more efficiently. They won't change the fact that the people we're killing don't have anything worth killing them over."

"Jesus, Gabe," Reyes said. "How many more people are you planning to kill anyway?"

"None, if I can help it. What do you know about making bombs?"

"From scratch? Not much."

"I could make a bomb," O'Brien said.

They turned to him.

"I got a master's degree in chemistry before I switched to geology. What kind of bomb do you want?"

"Something to knock a hole in the wall around Rouen."

Reyes frowned. "Did you miss the part about not wanting to draw attention?"

"We're going to have to risk it, Reyes. If we don't come up with that money, we're dead."

Reyes sighed. "What kind of bomb are we talking about, O'Brien?"

"Black powder would be easiest to fabricate," O'Brien said. "We just need charcoal, sulfur and potassium nitrate. Charcoal is easy. We could find raw sulfur around a volcanic vent or hot spring, if there are any around."

"And potassium nitrate?" Reyes asked.

"That's easy too. Unpleasant, but easy. You can get it from manure. We'll need a lot of all three. Black powder isn't particularly powerful. Figure we need a barrel full to be sure."

"How long would a bomb like that take to fabricate?" Reyes asked.

O'Brien shrugged. "We can make enough charcoal in a few hours. Just need to get a fire going and then starve it of oxygen. Throw some green pine branches or something on top. Saltpeter is a matter of manpower. Basically we need to send men around to every barn or latrine in the area. Anywhere there's a pile of shit that's been sitting a while. Saltpeter is the white crystals that form on top. With the number of big Norsemen and domesticated animals in this valley, there's got to be plenty of it around. Figure twenty men could collect all we need in a day. The sulfur will be a little trickier. Any idea what the Norse word for 'hot spring' is?"

"Let's find out," Gabe said.

*****

They found Sigurd sitting by the fire, sharpening his sword with a piece of flint. Gabe did his best to explain to him what they were attempting to do. Sigurd had picked up a fair amount of English, but he seemed perplexed by the idea of building a bomb to get into Rouen.

"Like a gun," Gabe said. "But bigger." He spread his arms apart. "Big boom. Make a hole in the wall." He pointed at the perimeter fence.

"Big boom," Sigurd repeated.

Gabe turned to Sigurd. "We are looking for a place where there is hot water."

"Hot?" Sigurd asked.

Gabe pointed to the fire. "Nei kalt."

"Heitt vatn?" Sigurd asked.

Gabe nodded. "That's right. Heitt vatn."

Sigurd's brow furrowed. He pointed to the fire.

"No," Gabe said. "Heitt vatn... in the ground. Like river, but hot. Heitt áin."

Sigurd nodded, seeming to understand. "Hver," he said.

"If you say so," Gabe replied. "Hvar? Hvar hver?"

Sigurd shrugged. He called to Agnar, who stood a few paces away. Agnar answered. They had a brief exchange, after which Agnar nodded and walked away. "Ask other men," Sigurd said.

"Good," Gabe said. "Ask the neighbors."

"Wait!" O'Brien called. Agnar stopped to look quizzically at O'Brien. "We're looking for springs that smell like sulfur. Like rotten eggs."

"Egg?" Sigurd said, knowing the word. He pinched his nose with his fingers.

"Yes!" O'Brien said. "It smells like bad eggs."

Sigurd shouted further instructions to Agnar, who nodded again and walked away.

"We could get by without the sulfur in a pinch, but the bomb won't be nearly as powerful."

"Silfr?" Sigurd asked.

O'Brien shook his head. "Not silver. Sulfur. The bad egg stuff."

"Bad egg stuff for big boom?" Sigurd asked, and the spacemen erupted into laughter. Sigurd glared at them crossly.

"We're sorry, Sigurd," Reyes said, choking back her laughter. "Yes. We need the bad egg stuff for the big boom."

*****

Such was Sigurd's faith in the foreigners that when told they needed twenty men to scour the latrines of the valley for white crystals, he ordered them to do so without a second thought. The men muttered to each other as they set off down the hill, but they did as they were told. Two more men were set to work building a fire with the express purpose of generating as much charcoal as possible. The men seemed to understand the concept; they may have needed to create charcoal at some point for cooking or powering a forge.

The charcoal creation was well underway when Agnar returned with the news that there was indeed a hot spring about a day's travel south of Caen, which could be reached with a few hours' sail to the west. The problem was that the snekkjas each required a crew of at least twenty, which would put a severe dent in their labor force for the duration of the trip. The bomb-making project was occupying half their men and one of their ships. No raiding—and little other work—would go on for the next few days. In the end, though, Reyes decided they had no choice.

"This had better work," she said to O'Brien as he got ready to join the rest of the crew that had been selected for *Ísbátr*. O'Brien's ribs were still tender and he tired easily, but he didn't trust anyone else to identify sulfur deposits. "We're putting all our rotten eggs in one basket."

"It'll work, chief," O'Brien said. "It's just chemistry."

"It's not the chemistry part that worries me," Reyes said.

"It'll work. Just make sure everything else is ready when I get back."

Reyes nodded. "Go. Good luck."

She wasn't worried about the other tasks that needed to be done for the project. Making charcoal was simple and several men had already returned with handfuls of potassium nitrate crystals. The other major task was building a boat, and she had no doubt the Vikings were up to that task.

The snekkjas were too large to sneak up the river unseen, even on a moonless night. What they needed was a rowboat, something big enough for the bomb and a few people to carry it, but small enough to avoid detection by sentries. Reyes explained their requirements to Sigurd, who picked several men from the group who had experience in ship-building. There was plenty of lumber at hand; they just needed to split it into boards, which would be shaped and fitted together to form the hull of the boat. The boards overlapped, clinker fashion, and were caulked with animal hair and secured with metal nails, a supply of which had been brought over on the ships.

When O'Brien returned three days later, the boat had been finished, and adequate supplies of both charcoal and potassium nitrate had been manufactured. Unfortunately, O'Brien came bearing bad news.

Reyes met him as he was coming up the hill. He was accompanied by a score of Norsemen who were carrying what appeared to be piles of rocks bundled in their cloaks.

"What the hell?" Reyes asked. "That... doesn't look like sulfur."

"Couldn't find any sulfur deposits, per se," O'Brien said. "The source of the spring was inaccessible, and I didn't smell any sulfur in the area. So I had to go with plan B: pyrite."

"You sent the Vikings on a quest for fool's gold."

"Correct," O'Brien said. "I figure we've got enough for one barrel-sized bomb."

"O'Brien, there's got to be half a ton of rocks here."

O'Brien smiled. "It's just chemistry."

*****

Performing basic chemistry turned out to be fairly challenging under the circumstances. To extract the sulfur from the pyrite, the rocks had to be heated to nearly five hundred degrees Celsius. At that temperature the sulfur would boil, at which point it needed to be collected and re-condensed. Fortunately Reyes had already secured a substantial supply of copper for her transmitter, so this was repurposed for the task. Three copper pots were torn apart and flattened into sheets, which were heated and hammered together until they comprised one long, narrow sheet. This was rolled into a tube, which was then coiled several times. The tube was welded onto a funnel, which was placed over a ceramic pot. The other end of the tube drained into another pot.

To free up as much sulfur as possible, several Norsemen were tasked with pulverizing the pyrite with rocks and hammers. The pot was filled with dust and rubble and set over a fire, which O'Brien had suggested be built downwind, outside the perimeter fence. "The fumes are toxic," O'Brien cheerfully explained.

It took nearly two full days to extract enough sulfur for a bomb. In the meantime, they had to solve another problem: how to mix the ingredients without accidentally triggering a spark and killing everybody in the vicinity. The obvious solution was to saturate the ingredients with water before mixing them, but that meant they would have to wait for the powder to dry before it would be usable. For that, they would need a large, flat surface where they could spread the powder thinly to allow the water to evaporate. They debated using tents for some time before O'Brien suggested the obvious: using the snekkjas' sails.

The sails were taken down and carried inside the perimeter fence. Reyes couldn't tell how much the Norsemen understood of what they were doing. Only Sigurd's men had seen the explosion of the lander, and only those aboard *Ísbátr* had seen a gun fired. It was doubtful any of the others had seen an explosion of any kind. She didn't even know if Sigurd had explained they were going to try to breach Rouen's walls. Probably not; they'd agreed to handle the project on a need-to-know basis. So far, the men seemed willing to trust Sigurd's judgment, but if this plan went sideways, he'd likely face a mutiny. They'd probably lynch the spacemen too, which was just as well: if they didn't make their payment to Hrólfr, they were as good as dead anyway.

It took another three days for the mixture to dry. They had spread it about a centimeter thick across one of the sails; they set the other sail up as a lean-to to protect the powder from rain and dew. Even when it wasn't raining, there was too much moisture in the air for the powder to dry rapidly. O'Brien brainstormed several ways of channeling dry air over the mix, but in the end it was decided they were all too risky: the only way they had of generating heat was fire, and fire meant sparks.

At last the powder dried enough to be usable. O'Brien scooped the powder up by hand, standing barefoot on the ground to minimize the possibility of static sparks. There was more than enough powder to fill one of the water barrels the Vikings had brought. When it was full, O'Brien carefully set the lid in place. A hole had been bored in the top for a fuse that had been made by soaking a piece of twine in a potassium nitrate solution. They had built a bomb.

*****

Gabe sat in the stern of the small boat as Braggi rowed. In between them sat the barrel full of black powder. It seemed only fair that Braggi, the designated fireman of the group, would get to light the bomb. Braggi took his responsibilities as fireman very seriously, carrying the lighter Gabe had given him everywhere he went. The gift had afforded him a certain status among the other Norsemen that he cherished.

When the walls of Rouen came into view, Gabe directed Braggi to put in to port. They would ground the boat and then carry the barrel along the wall to a point their intelligence had indicated would be minimally protected. The bulk of Rouen's defenses were focused on the section of the wall that ran along the river.

The sky was cloudy, giving the saboteurs good cover. Visibility extended only as far as the light of the torches on the guard towers. Along the riverfront, the towers were only about fifty meters apart, but they were spaced more widely on the other sides. Gabe and Braggi had little trouble carrying the bomb to the designated spot on the wall. Braggi pulled the lighter from his pocket, but Gabe held up his hand. He tapped his cuff. "Reyes, you there?"

"I'm here, Gabe. Go ahead."

"We're in position. No trouble so far. You can give Sigurd the okay."

"Copy that," Reyes said. She was aboard *Ísbátr*, which had been waiting, along with *Bylgjasverð*, just around the bend for Gabe's signal. Every man in their group was aboard one of the two snekkjas. Gabe and Braggi waited in silence for the ships to approach.

"I can see the wall," Reyes said in his ear. "Gabe, are you ready?"

"We're ready," Gabe said. "On your signal."

"Okay," Reyes replied. "Light her up."

Gabe nodded to Braggi, who lit the half-meter-long fuse hanging from the barrel. Once it was lit, they made their way quickly but carefully back toward the riverbank. Their tests indicated they had about twenty seconds to get to a safe distance—however far away that was. Gabe began to count in his head.

As they picked their way through the brush along the bank, they saw scores of sparks arcing across the sky toward the city from downriver. This, the second part of the plan, had been Gabe's idea: camouflage the point of attack by creating confusion throughout the city. Attached to each arrow was a small charge made from black powder—not enough to do any real damage, but enough to make a hell of a lot of noise. Hopefully by the time the defenders realized where the real attack was happening, it would be too late for them to do anything about it.

When Gabe's count reached fifteen, he tapped Braggi on the shoulder and then got down on his knees and clamped his hands over his ears. Braggi did the same. In the distance, they heard the muffled sounds of the their improvised firecrackers, followed by shouts and screams. Then a deafening blast erupted behind them, showering them with shredded bits of wood and gravel. A cloud of dust billowed around them, and Gabe pulled his cloak over his mouth and got to his feet.

When the smoke cleared, Gabe saw the shadowy form of *Bylgjasverð* slipping past on the river below. Half of the men were at the oars, propelling the ship forward; the other half continued to fire explosive arrows over the wall into the city. If the city watchmen hadn't already determined the source of the fiery arrows, they would soon. Then, if the attackers' luck held, the defenders would direct all their fire toward *Bylgjasverð*. Meanwhile, *Ísbátr* had come ashore not far from the rowboat, and its men would follow Gabe and Braggi into the city.

Already Braggi had gone to check the blast site and returned, giving Gabe a grin and a thumbs up. He held his hands apart, indicating the size of the gap in the wall.

"We're good to go here," Gabe said. "The wall's been breached."

"On our way," Reyes said.

"Well, hurry up," Gabe said. "Somebody's going to notice this gaping hole pretty—okay, I've got you." He had spotted Sigurd heading up the bank, trailed by Reyes and the rest of the Norsemen from *Ísbátr*. As Sigurd approached, Gabe turned and led the way along the wall to the gap, where Braggi waited with his spear at the ready. So far there had been no sign of anyone investigating the explosion.

Gabe and Braggi led the way through the gap. Gabe had his gun drawn. He hoped he wouldn't have to shoot anybody, but he wanted to be able to put down any resistance quickly. With any luck, the sound of the gunshots wouldn't draw much attention, given the exploding arrows raining down on the city.

No one met them on the other side of the wall. Gabe heard people shouting in the distance, but this part of the city was quiet. As men poured through the gap, Sigurd directed them toward different targets in the city. His men had gotten a pretty good idea of the layout of the city from querying people in the valley, but the main thing was to keep the men moving and prevent them from all heading for the same targets. They would spread out across the city, working like ants: those who found treasure would return with news, and those who came up empty-handed would help to ferry the treasures to the boat. It was slow, hit-and-miss work in the dark, but they'd agreed that torches would only draw attention. In the dark, the Norsemen were indistinguishable from townspeople fleeing from an attack.

"This way," Reyes said to Gabe, pointing toward a tall building in the distance. They were the only two spacemen in the city; O'Brien had stayed behind on *Ísbátr* to supervise the lighting of the arrows. Sigurd gave them a nod, and Reyes and Gabe set off into the dark.

It soon became clear where Reyes was headed: the tall building was a church. Several of the Norsemen were already headed that direction. They made their way through the dark streets and alleys toward the distant spire as explosions continued to sound in the distance. The archers aboard *Bylgjasverð* would soon run out of arrows, and then she'd turn around and head at full speed back down river. By now, the city guard would be returning fire from the towers and along the top of the wall, but they'd have a hard time hitting anyone on board *Bylgjasverð* in the dark. *Bylgjasverð* faced serious danger only from ships docked at the harbor that might try to chase after it. The real danger, though, was the possibility that the city guard would figure out that *Bylgjasverð's* attack was a feint. If the commanders realized the wall had been breached, it wouldn't take them long to dispatch a contingent of men to the gap. The city guard vastly outnumbered the attackers; the guards would bar the breach and the attackers would be stuck inside the city walls with no way out.

When Gabe and Reyes reached the church, the doors had already been thrown open. Dim light flickered within. Passing through the foyer, they entered the sanctuary, where several men were already pulling tapestries off the walls. Hundreds of candles burned at an altar at the front of the sanctuary. Before the alter, an elderly priest in a cassock knelt on the floor. One of the Norsemen had a knife at the man's throat.

"Hey!" Reyes yelled, her voice echoing off the high stone walls. The Norseman didn't even look at her.

"Drop the knife!" Gabe shouted, moving down the aisle toward the men. He was pointing his gun at the Norseman, which struck Reyes as funny. She didn't recognize the man in the dim light, and she had no idea whether he was one of the men who had seen Sigurd shoot Skeggi. He certainly didn't have a clue what Gabe was saying.

Still, something in Gabe's voice got his attention. He turned to look at them, still holding his knife at the priest's neck. The priest hadn't moved; his eyes were closed and Reyes saw now that his lips were moving. He was ready to die.

"Put it down," Gabe said. He was now only a few paces from the Norseman, his gun trained on the man's chest. "He's no threat to you."

The Norseman growled something at Gabe, holding up his other hand. Gabe stopped walking. The priest cried out as the knife bit into his neck.

"Gabe!" Reyes shouted. But Gabe, still pointing his gun at the Norseman, didn't move. They remained that way for some time.

At last the Norseman pulled the knife away from the priest's neck. He sheathed the knife, spat on the ground toward Gabe, and gave the priest a kick in the ribs. The priest groaned and fell to the ground. The Norseman stomped past Gabe and began to help the others with the tapestries. Gabe holstered his gun and Reyes breathed a sigh of relief.

The priest looked up at him, confusion on his face. "Wer bist du?" he asked.

"We're Vikings," Gabe said, picking up a silver chalice. He turned to Reyes. "Get those candlesticks and let's get the hell out of here."

CHAPTER THIRTY-FIVE

Harald waited nearly a week for news of the fleet's effort to intercept the foreigners. When the news finally came, it was not good. The foreigners had escaped and many of Harald's men, including Gunnar, had been killed. Harald was discussing his options with Ragnar, several days later, when a Danish merchant arrived, claiming to have information about a group of fugitives from Norway who had settled in Normandy. The merchant, a one-eyed old man named Korr, seemed nervous as Ragnar's guards showed him into the great room. When the guards released him, he fell to the ground, bowing deeply before Harald.

"Stand, friend," Harald said. "If you have news for me, out with it."

"Yes, my lord," Korr said, getting to his feet. "I do, my lord. I've got six brothers, my lord, all businessmen like myself. My brother Bertram sells pottery down the Seine, towards Rouen. I haven't seen him in three years, but he talks regularly with Adelbert, the youngest. I met Adelbert six days ago at Hedeby. You see, Adelbert and I both have an interest in a parcel of land north of—"

"Korr," Ragnar intoned. "I don't believe you came here to give the king a detailed accounting of your family tree or your business holdings."

Harald gave Korr an appreciative nod.

"No, not at all, my lord. Sorry, my lord. What I mean to say is that Adelbert told me that Bertram... that is to say, a group of Norsemen has moved into the Seine Valley. Now you shouldn't get the idea that Bertram tells us about every group of Norsemen that arrive on the Seine. But this group, they're different. They're a small group, less than a hundred strong, but they paid a king's ransom—that is, they paid a great deal of money to Hrólfr to let them settle on one of the best pieces of property along the river, and they've set about building a fort, like they're expecting the Roman legions to return. Mighty strange, wouldn't you say?"

"You sailed across from Denmark to tell us a group of Norsemen are building a fort along the Seine?" Harald asked, dubious.

"It could well be our fugitives," Ragnar said, turning to Harald.

"It could be any group of adventurers," Harald said. As determined as he was to find the foreigners and learn the secrets of their sky ships and weapons, he was wary of attempts to take advantage of his intentions. "I hope you're not expecting a reward for this, Korr?"

"Well," Korr said. "No. That is, I wasn't going to tell you at all. Thought it was strange, is all. But then I was at the inn at Hedeby, talking it over with some of my business associates. You know, the way you talk, sometimes, with business associates, and this man at the next table, he keeps leaning over, like he's listening in. Big tall fellow, wearing the hood of his cloak pulled over his head indoors, like maybe he's one of them lepers in the Bible. I don't think much of it, but when I leave, this fellow follows me outside. Tells me he's interested in my story, says he'll give me a silver if I tell him everything I know. So I tell him. Mind you, this fellow is strange. Raspy voice, barely speaks a word of Frankish. I know a little of every language anybody speaks in this region, and this fellow didn't know any of them. Twenty words of Frankish, maybe. But he makes it clear he wants to know about these people in Normandy."

"Who was this man?" Harald asked.

"I don't know. Didn't get his name. Never saw his face. Anyway, I tell him what I know. I mean, who wouldn't, for a silver? And then do you know what he tells me? He tells me I should come tell you. Says King Harald would be very interested to know about these people. Offers me twenty more silver to make the trip. I had a knarr leaving for Uslu in the morning, so I hitched a ride. And here I am."

Harald learned forward. This man's story had piqued his interest. "This stranger paid you to deliver this information?" he asked. "Why?"

"Well, my lord, I suppose you would have to ask him. I'm sorry, he asked me to speak with you first, as he's not much of a talker. He's waiting outside."

CHAPTER THIRTY-SIX

The raid on Rouen netted them easily ten times the spoils they'd amassed so far. In addition to nearly two hundred silver coins, they acquired candlesticks, tapestries, furs, jewelry and a great number of other items. It was enough to pay off their debt to Hrólfr and then some. They didn't give it to Hrólfr right away, though, as Sigurd didn't think it wise to let on that it was they who had executed the raid. Gabe and Reyes agreed: if Hrólfr got the idea that the newcomers possessed weapons capable of breaching stone walls, they might find themselves pressed into service for him. Hrólfr seemed to be a more honorable man than Harald, but there was no point in tempting him.

Bylgjasverð had been chased downriver by ships from Rouen, finally losing them in the dark some distance out to sea. Once she'd lost her pursuers, she turned around and headed west, raiding along the coast for the next two days. She returned with a modest haul, which was added to the spoils from Rouen. Then a payment was made to Hrólfr, under the pretense that the spoils had been acquired by *Bylgjasverð*. Most of the loot was held in abeyance, and anything that could easily be traced to Rouen was hidden or—in the case of the chalice and candlesticks taken from the cathedral—melted down. The balance of their debt was paid off in several installments over the next few weeks.

The raid on Rouen had been so lucrative that many of the men who had intended to return to Norway in the fall agreed to pay to stay through the winter, presumably in the expectation of more such raids. Sigurd did what he could to temper their hopes, but they had seen what the foreigners could do, and were convinced that great wealth would soon be theirs. Raiding continued through the summer, but the Norsemen relied on conventional methods to avoid attracting unwanted attention. Hrólfr made it clear that he suspected the foreigners had been involved in the raid on Rouen, but he didn't ask and they didn't tell.

The spacemen were, in any case, too busy with other tasks to manufacture explosives. Gabe and O'Brien were working with a crew of Norsemen on the guard tower while Reyes spent her time trying to reestablish contact with *Andrea Luhman*. She now had less than two weeks until *Andrea Luhman* would be in range again, and she wanted to be ready.

She soon realized that building the transmitter was going to be the easy part. The real challenge was powering it. That required first building a battery or, at the very least, a capacitor and some sort of generator. She had most of the raw materials, but fabricating the components under the current conditions was daunting. At the very least, she was going to need a forge of some kind, and some metalworking tools. Experimentation told her it would take two weeks just to build the batteries, and she was dubious she'd be able to stack enough cells to generate the sort of voltage she'd need to power an arc gap transmitter, which meant she'd also need to build a transformer or boost converter.

If she had a general idea where *Andrea Luhman* would be, she could build a directional antenna that would use far less power. But that was the problem in a nutshell: the range of the suit radios was so limited precisely because they sent waves out in all directions. She could probably rig something up to channel the suit radio's transmission in a particular direction, but it still wouldn't be powerful enough to cut through the noise of the atmosphere. If *Andrea Luhman* knew where to look, it could point its antennas toward the signal and pick up enough for them to communicate, but the lander's crew were several hundred kilometers southwest of the crash site. It would be a miracle if *Andrea Luhman* found them.

No, it was time to rethink the problem. Twenty-third century solutions weren't going to cut it. Forget converting an electrical current to radio waves. She needed something simpler. She didn't need to communicate a lot of data; she'd assumed the arc gap transmitter was only going to be good for Morse code anyway. Really all she need to communicate their location: a beacon indicating that the crew was still alive. Once *Andrea Luhman*'s crew had that information, they could work out a better method of communication.

The obvious answer was a signal fire. But it would have to be a hell of a fire, and even then it wouldn't attract the attention of anyone on *Andrea Luhman* unless she had some way of modulating the intensity to make it flash or flicker. A heliograph—mirrors angled to reflect sunlight—was another possibility, but again they would need to have a general idea where *Andrea Luhman* was in the sky. If its orbit was low enough, they might be able to spot it at night—but that wouldn't help with a heliograph.

She came back to the idea of a fire, bright enough to be seen from space, but small enough to cover temporarily with a shutter of some sort. A magnesium fire would do it. She walked from her makeshift work area to where O'Brien and Gabe were placing posts for the watchtower. O'Brien, still not up to performing heavy labor, spent most of his time offering advice and making bad jokes.

"O'Brien," she said, "if I wanted a large supply of magnesium, where would I find it?"

"Pure magnesium?" O'Brien said, looking up from the post Gabe was placing. "Not going to happen. But it's relatively easy to extract from salt water. What do you want magnesium for? I thought you were building a transmitter."

"I am," Reyes said. "I've just moved down the wavelength spectrum a bit."

It took O'Brien a few seconds, but then he smiled. "You're transmitting light."

"That's the idea. A magnesium fire should be visible from space, right?"

"Not exactly my area of expertise, but I'd think so. A big enough one, anyway."

"How big? A meter in diameter?"

"Les than that, I would think. If you knew the exact luminosity, you could figure the dispersal with the inverse square rule, but even then you'd have to take into account the atmosphere and a lot of other factors. Like I said, not my area of expertise. But unless they happened to be looking in the right place at the right time, they'd still never see it."

"I'm thinking some kind of shutter system, to make the light flash."

O'Brien nodded, rubbing his chin. "Or, instead of one fire, a bunch of fires in sequence."

"What do you mean?"

"Dig craters in the ground, a meter wide. Join them with a fuse, like the one we used for our black powder bomb. Put enough magnesium in each of them to burn for a few seconds. One fire goes out, the next one lights up. From a distance, it would look like a single light flashing."

"O'Brien, you're a genius!"

"Well, yes, but the odds are still against them seeing it. And it's not a very efficient means of communication."

"All I need is for them to pinpoint our location. Once they do that, I think we can establish two-way radio contact. So how do we get magnesium from sea water?"

The process of getting magnesium from sea water was, as O'Brien promised, fairly simple. It was also time-consuming and labor-intensive. O'Brien estimated that the proportion of magnesium was about one in one thousand, which meant they'd need to process a lot of salt water to get the amount of magnesium they needed. The "signal fire team" consisted of O'Brien, Reyes, Sigurd, Braggi, and a half dozen other men. As far as Reyes knew, none of the Norsemen truly understood the purpose of this endeavor, but by this time they had seen enough of the foreigners' magic to accept tasks on faith. Most likely they assumed they were building another bomb.

The first problem was finding a source of limestone. Asking around, Sigurd had determined that there was a limestone pit about half a klick to the west. With Sigurd's help, O'Brien and Reyes built a small wooden cart that could be pulled through the woods by a pair of men. Sigurd tasked Brynjarr and Agnar with transporting powdered limestone to the riverbank. From there, it was loaded into the rowboat and transported downriver to the beach just west of the mouth of the Rouen, where O'Brien and Reyes had decided to set up shop. The site was a three-hour trip from their fort by boat, so they would need to camp there for the duration of the project.

Silicon was the other key resource. To refine pure silicon from sand, they built a simple charcoal-powered clay furnace with a built-in bellows to keep the temperature high. The sand was mixed with heated with carbon (charcoal dust), which reacted with the oxygen in the sand to form carbon dioxide, leaving the silicon behind.

The next challenge was finding enough containers in which to process the seawater. While the limestone was being gathered, Sigurd sent several more men out with silver and furs to trade for barrels and buckets. They came up with eighteen barrels and many more buckets. The barrels were cut in half, and then a finger-sized hole was bored in the side of each, a few centimeters from the bottom. A cork stopper was placed in each of these holes. The barrels were stacked on the rowboat along with the buckets, and rowed to the processing site.

A pot full of limestone was heated to drive off the carbon dioxide, leaving calcium oxide, also known as lime. When a supply of lime was ready, Reyes instructed the men to line up the half-barrels along the beach, just above the high tide line, and then fill the buckets with sea water. As the buckets were filled, O'Brien used a wooden cup to scoop lime from the supply, emptying a cup into each of the barrels. Braggi used a wooden pole to stir the limestone into the water, and after a few minutes a salty white precipitate began to form at the bottom of each barrel. After the water had settled, O'Brien pulled out the stoppers, draining most of the water from the barrels. When all that remained in the barrels was a thin layer of precipitate and a few centimeters of water, he plugged the holes with the stoppers and the process started over.

After they had run through this process a few times, the layer of precipitate at the bottom of the barrels had nearly reached the level of the drainage holes. Following O'Brien's instructions, the men scooped the salty slurry with their hands and deposited it into a cast iron pot. When the liquid had boiled off, the precipitate was mixed with the silicon and heated in the clay oven to reduce and vaporize the magnesium. The vapor was caught by the copper pipe contraption they had used to refine sulfur. The vapor condensed into liquid and finally hardened into a powder in a clay pot at the other end of the copper still.

"So that's it?" Reyes asked.

"That's it," O'Brien said. "The lime pulls the magnesium out of the salt water solution, giving us magnesium hydroxide. Further heating converts it to magnesium oxide. Mixing that with silicon and heating it reduces and vaporizes the magnesium, which is collected by the still."

"How pure is it?"

"Pure enough, I would think. Not much but metallic magnesium is going to make it through the still. We can refine the process if the first test batch doesn't give us the results we want, but I think we're in the ball park."

*****

Reyes and O'Brien tested the product for the first time on the second day of their manufacturing operation. The results were more than satisfactory: the magnesium burned steadily and so brightly they had to throw sand on the fire to keep the gawking Norsemen from burning their retinas. O'Brien tweaked the process a bit to get the proportions correct and reduce waste, but the concept was solid.

How much magnesium they needed was the other big question. O'Brien estimated that they could generate about a kilogram of magnesium per hour at their current rate. Further testing indicated that as little as ten grams of their mixture would create a flash that was visible from three klicks away, even in full sunlight—not that they intended to try to signal *Andrea Luhman* during the day. Their best chance to be spotted would be on a cloudless night.

Reyes still hoped to establish one-way radio contact with *Andrea Luhman* prior to sending any signals. Any radio transmission from *Andrea Luhman* would indicate that she was in range and within line-of-sight. If for whatever reason they didn't receive any transmissions by the time *Andrea Luhman* was supposed to be in orbit, they would start sending signals every night. They deemed that a series of quick flashes would be more likely to be noticed than a single, longer burn. Reyes wanted to err well on the safe side in terms of brightness, so she suggested using a hundred grams of magnesium for each flash—ten times as much as they had used in their tests. After some discussion, they settled on five flashes, with a delay of three seconds between each flash. That way, if someone noticed the first flash, they'd have a chance to establish that it was definitely a signal that repeated with regular frequency. If no one saw the signal by the fifth flash, they probably weren't looking.

Ideally they'd repeat the series at regular intervals, perhaps an hour apart. They were at a fairly high latitude and the nights had been getting shorter, leaving them with about nine hours of darkness. If they sent the first signal just after twilight, that was ten signals a night. Ten signals a night, with five flashes per signal, and a hundred grams per flash, meant they would be using five kilograms of magnesium a day. They'd produced that much in their first day of operation, and *Andrea Luhman* wouldn't even be in range for another week.

Reyes kept the operation going for three more days, running from sunup to sundown, with a total output of nearly forty kilograms. They kept the product in buckets, making sure to dampen it occasionally to reduce the risk of accidental fires. In the evening of the third day, they packed up their supplies and ferried everyone back to the fort.

While they were gone, Gabe and Sigurd had completed the watchtower, with the assistance of several of the Norsemen. Others had begun working on additional buildings, including a storage shed, a latrine and a central building that would serve as a barracks and meeting hall. Another group had begun clearing more land in between the fort and the river, with an eye toward planting crops and raising animals. Wood that was suitable for building purposes was brought inside the fort, while the rest was chopped into firewood. Saplings were made into spear shafts, arrows, or handles for tools. Some of the higher quality hardwood was set aside for building furniture over the winter.

Since *Andrea Luhman* was still not in range, Reyes occupied herself by setting up an antenna on the watchtower and testing its ability to receive signals over long distance. She decreased the transmission power of O'Brien's comm by ninety percent and then sent him eight klicks downriver. With her own comm connected to the watchtower's antenna with copper wire, she was able to receive transmissions from him with minimal static. If *Andrea Luhman* broadcast a signal from anywhere in orbit on this side of the planet, she'd have no trouble picking it up.

Unfortunately, she didn't know exactly when *Andrea Luhman* would return, and she couldn't spend all day wired to the watchtower. The only copper wire she had was a two-meter-long piece that had probably been intended for a jeweler. It was just long enough to allow her to stand directly below the antenna. She didn't want to think what might happen if she tried to listen to the radio during a thunderstorm.

As the six week deadline approached, Reyes spent more and more time in the watchtower, hoping to hear from someone on board *Andrea Luhman*. It turned out, though, that the antenna had been overkill. One night while lying in her tent she was awakened by the sound of Michael Carpenter's voice in her ear.

"—of the IDL exploratory ship *Andrea Luhman*," Carpenter was saying. "I'm trying to reach the crew of the lander. If you guys are down there somewhere, let me know."

CHAPTER THIRTY-SEVEN

Reyes wanted to shout, "We're here!" but she knew it was pointless. Her comm would transmit at most a hundred klicks. If *Andrea Luhman* were in orbit, she'd be at least two thousand kilometers away. Still, she had to tell someone. She crawled out of her tent and walked to Gabe's. In her ear, Carpenter continued, "Reyes? Gabe? Anybody there?" There was a long pause. Reyes reached into Gabe's tent and shook him awake.

"Reyes?" he asked blearily. "What the—"

He stopped when he heard Carpenter's voice. Reyes had switched to her external speaker.

"We spotted the lander," Carpenter was saying. "Well, what's left of it. Jesus, what did you guys do? I saw the lander before we lost contact. It looked fine. I was convinced you guys were going to walk away from it. Couldn't raise you on the comm, but… Okay, well, look. Mallick thinks you're dead. He thinks the tanks must have leaked and a short ignited the fuel. My thinking is that if the tanks had ruptured, the lander would have blown up a lot sooner. So my guess is you got away. Some of you, anyway. But, even if you did, without the lander, your mission is DOA. I have an idea for how you might still be able to get off planet, but, well, the captain thinks it's crazy. He thinks we should cut our losses and head back to IDL space, although I'm not sure what good it'll do. Temporal dilation will slow down the aging a bit, but there's no way we'll survive the journey. We're just going to have to program *Andrea Luhman* to show up two hundred years after the war ends and hope someone is still around to use the bomb."

Reyes raised an eyebrow at Gabe. There was another long pause before Carpenter continued.

"Anyway, we're going to stick around for a few days. I'm guessing your transmitter was destroyed with the lander, which is why you're not answering. Or you're dead. But if you're dead, there's no point in me talking to you, so let's forget that possibility. Yeah, so, it looks like we're going to hang around for a few days to see if we can make contact with you. If there's any chance of... I don't know. Your suit transmitters probably won't work. Maybe a signal fire? We're scanning all of Norway and Denmark, so if you make a big enough fire, we'll see it. We're in low Earth orbit, just passing over the Atlantic on the way toward you now. I mean, assuming you're still somewhere in Europe. Orbital period is one hundred nineteen minutes, so we'll be directly over Norway soon. I'll transmit again shortly."

"We've got to send the signal," Reyes said.

"All right," Gabe replied, getting out of his tent. "Let's go."

They woke O'Brien and went to the partially constructed shed where they'd stored the magnesium powder and the other supplies they needed.

"Should we warn them?" O'Brien asked, motioning toward the tents on the ground around them.

"Nah," Gabe said. "If they wake up, they wake up."

"Hopefully they don't panic and impale us with spears," O'Brien said.

Most of the Norsemen were currently gone on a raiding expedition, and those who remained had seen Reyes and O'Brien conducting tests with the magnesium powder. What they would think of the spacemen setting off fireworks in the middle of the night was anyone's guess, but the Norsemen were used to the foreigners doing things that seemed to make no sense.

Improving on O'Brien's idea of connected patches of magnesium, Reyes had built an ingenious contraption for consistently producing flashes of maximum luminosity at regular intervals. It was essentially a tripod with a wooden box on top. Connected to one side of the box was a bellows constructed of two wood panels and deer leather. On the other side of the box was an opening with a door on a spring. Compressing the bellows moved air through the box, forcing the door open and dispersing the magnesium in a cloud of dust. As the hinged door opened, a piece of flint struck against steel, creating a spark and igniting the cloud. The result was an incredibly bright flash that lasted less than a second. You could control the size of the flash by using gradations marked on the inside of the box. Reyes's favorite feature, though, was the catch that held the spring-hinged door closed if you opened the lid on the top of the box, making it impossible to accidentally ignite the powder while filling the box. She added this after a close call that singed her eyebrows. The air was still tonight, so they didn't need to worry about blowback.

"Ready when you are," Gabe said.

"Should I wait until the next transmission?" Reyes asked. "He said they'd be passing over Norway shortly."

"With a period of a hundred and twenty minutes, they could be overhead right now," O'Brien said.

They scanned the northern sky, but saw no sign of the ship.

"We've got plenty of magnesium," Gabe said. "I say go for it. We can try again later."

"Okay," Reyes said. "You ready, O'Brien?"

"Ready," O'Brien said. "Five flashes at three second intervals. Load 'er up."

Reyes reached into the bucket and scooped out a cupful of white powder. She filled the box to the one hundred gram line. "On your mark," she said. "Watch your eyes." Looking at the flash probably wouldn't cause any permanent retinal damage, but it would certainly make you see spots for a few minutes.

"Go," O'Brien said.

Reyes closed her eyes and compressed the bellows. There was a momentary roar, accompanied by a blast of heat on her face. She could see the flash with her eyes closed.

As soon as the flash had dissipated, she got another scoop of the powder and filled the box to the one hundred gram line again. She looked to O'Brien.

"Go," O'Brien said again.

Reyes shut her eyes and squeezed the bellows once more.

They repeated this procedure three more times and then waited in silence for several minutes. At last, Carpenter's voice came over her comm again.

"Passing over southern Norway now," Carpenter said. "Oh, this is Michael Carpenter of the IDL exploratory ship *Andrea Luhman*, calling the... well, if you can hear me, you know who I'm calling. Nobody else is going to have a radio for a thousand years."

As Carpenter babbled on, the three spacemen exchanged glances.

"He didn't see it," O'Brien said.

"How is that possible?" Reyes asked. "Is he even looking?"

"He's looking in Norway," Gabe said. "They've got no idea we traveled seven hundred klicks southwest on a Viking ship."

"When they don't find us in Norway, they'll expand their search parameters," Reyes said.

"So should we wait to try again?"

"No," Gabe said. "We've got clear skies now. Try it once more and then wait for them to come around again."

They sent another series of five flashes, with no response from Carpenter. He sent them one more message before *Andrea Luhman* lost radio contact, but made no mention of the signal.

"Well, that's that," Reyes said. "We should get some sleep. I'll wake you when I hear from Carpenter again."

Another transmission from Carpenter came through a little over an hour later, repeating everything he had told them before. When Reyes exited her tent and looked up, though, she saw no stars. A bank of clouds had moved in. She woke O'Brien.

"You think it's worth trying?" she asked.

O'Brien crawled out of his tent and surveyed the sky. After a moment, he shook his head. "We'd be wasting magnesium. There's no way they'll see it through those clouds. You want me to check again in half an hour?"

Reyes shook her head. "I'll do it. I'll wake you if the clouds clear. Go back to sleep."

She stayed up the rest of the night, through two more of *Andrea Luhman*'s orbital cycles, but the clouds never cleared. They showed some sign of clearing after dawn, but by then it was too late: if Carpenter couldn't see the signal at night, he'd never spot it when the area was bathed in sunlight.

The clouds eventually cleared in the afternoon, but returned before sunset and persisted throughout the next night. Carpenter continued to broadcast roughly every hour—once when *Andrea Luhman* rose above the horizon, once when it was directly over Norway, and once before it disappeared below the horizon in the east. Sometimes the beginning or ending of his transmissions would be cut off, as he was timing them relative to the location of the lander crash. Early the next morning, he switched to a recorded message, which repeated every ten minutes.

Reyes and the others tried to busy themselves with other tasks, but the blanket of clouds hanging overhead were an all-too-obvious metaphor. As long as the sky remained gray, they had little hope of communicating with *Andrea Luhman*. Occasionally Carpenter would break in with a live message, detailing *Andrea Luhman*'s current status. He didn't mention anything about cloud cover, which told Reyes that the sky over Norway was probably clear. That was bad news: if the crew of *Andrea Luhman* assumed the landing party was still in Norway, they'd conclude that Reyes and the others were unable to get a signal to them—and the simplest explanation for that fact was that they were dead.

The clouds remained for two more days. The Norsemen returned from raiding, and work continued on the buildings. It was now nearly summer, and other than the occasional rain, the weather was pleasant to work in. But the spacemen grew more and more anxious, waiting for the clouds to pass. O'Brien suggested taking their signaling apparatus out to sea in search of clear skies, but Reyes nixed the idea. They had no way of knowing where or when the weather might clear, and if they signaled *Andrea Luhman* while a hundred klicks out to sea, it might just confuse matters further. So they waited.

On the fourth evening after Carpenter's first signal, he transmitted an uncharacteristically somber message:

"Hey, guys, It's Carpenter again. I don't know if you're down there. At this point, I kind of hope you're not. Dying in that crash may have been the best outcome. But in case you are... Okay, look. Mallick wants to pull the plug. Shit, that's a bad metaphor. The captain thinks we need to cut our losses. Do our best to try to get to IDL space on aux power. I don't see the point, but then I guess there's not much point in staying in orbit around Earth either. Even if you guys can hear me, there's not much we can do for you. My idea... well, I was thinking we could locate the crashed Cho-ta'an ship and dredge it up from the sea. Repair it and take it back to one of the IDL gates. It's stupid, I guess. It would take years, and by then the seawater would probably... anyway, there aren't a lot of good options. The upshot is, we're breaking orbit in... just over six hours. If you're still down there, and alive... I'm sorry, guys. And good luck."

Reyes broke the news to Gabe and O'Brien, who'd muted the increasingly unwelcome messages from Carpenter. They were sitting around the evening fire, eating porridge and smoked venison. The sun had just gone down, and not a star could be seen in the sky.

"So that's it then," O'Brien said. "We're on our own."

"We could still make contact," Gabe replied. "But yeah, we should prepare for the possibility that we're not going to get any help from Carpenter or the others."

Reyes wasn't sure what sort of help to expect in any case. At the very least, she was hoping to get an update on the status of Harald's forces in Norway. If *Andrea Luhman*'s crew knew where to look, they could provide some detailed surveillance—assuming the skies were clear. "What do you think of the idea of dredging up the Cho-ta'an ship?" she asked.

"Sounds nuts to me," O'Brien replied. "The North Sea has got to be two thousand meters deep. What are we going to do, build a gigantic barge and haul it up with ropes? And how are they even going to find it? They can't see a ten thousand-lumen flash on the top of a hill in the middle of the night."

"They might be able to identify the radiation signature of the reactor, if they have a general idea where it went down," Reyes said. "But yeah, overall the idea sounds pretty crazy."

"So what's the plan?" O'Brien asked. "We hunker down here and wait for Harald to attack? Do we go on the offensive at some point, or do we keep playing defense forever?"

"Let's not get ahead of ourselves," Reyes said. "As long as there's a chance we can get through to *Andrea Luhman*, we have to keep trying. We've got six hours left." She got to her feet. The last gray light of day faded in the distance.

"You're going to keep signaling?" O'Brien asked. "They'll never see it through these clouds."

"I'm an optimist," Reyes said, without breaking a smile. "And I've got a goddamned barrel full of powdered magnesium to use up."

Reyes spent the next two hours loading the signaling apparatus and squeezing the bellows, at intervals of about five seconds. After a few minutes she could do it with her eyes closed, which was a good thing, because even the occasional indirect glimpse of the flashes was enough to temporarily blind her. After two hours, still half-blind and smelling of charred wool, she took a break to get some sleep while O'Brien relieved her. They no longer bothered to pause between signal sequences; they were in no danger of running out of magnesium, and the more flashes they made, the better their chances of being seen. After another two hours, Reyes relieved O'Brien again. Gabe had volunteered to take a shift, but Reyes wanted to be the one manning the apparatus when *Andrea Luhman* dipped below the horizon for the last time. This whole thing was her idea; if it failed, she would take responsibility.

Carpenter's last status report came just before dawn. *Andrea Luhman* would drop below the horizon shortly, and then break orbit to head back into deep space, where it would limp along for the next two thousand years. As the sky began to lighten in the east, Reyes stopped in the middle of refilling the signaling apparatus, realizing it was over. She'd gambled on a visual signaling system and had been foiled by lousy weather. Those were the breaks. Next time around, she thought ruefully, she'd stick with the spark transmitter.

And then something twinkled on the horizon, just above the dull gray haze of morning.

A star!

And then another. And another. The clouds had cleared, at least partially. With a little luck—

She slapped the lid of the apparatus closed and squeezed the bellows, then opened it again, dumped another cupful of powder in and did it again. And again, and again, as fast as she could.

Look, Carpenter, she silently begged. *God damn you, look!*

Still there was no sound from her comm. She fired the apparatus again and again.

Then Carpenters's voice sounded in her ear. "All right, guys. This is it. We're passing below the..."

For a moment, her comm went silent.

"Well," he said, his voice crackling with static. "That's weird. Reyes, is that you? I'm seeing a light, something flashing. Looks like... somewhere in northern France?"

Reyes trembled with excitement. She forced herself to stop loading the apparatus and counted to ten. Then she fired two quick flashes, waited five seconds, fired a long flash by squeezing the bellows more slowly, fired two more quick flashes, paused for another fire seconds, then fired a quick flash, a long flash, and two more quick flashes.

"I... D... L..." she heard Carpenter's voice say. "Holy shit, you guys! You're alive! You have no idea how close you came being—" The transmission abruptly cut off.

Reyes collapsed on the ground, tears running down her face.

She had done it.

CHAPTER THIRTY-EIGHT

When *Andrea Luhman* came around again, Carpenter transmitted another message and Reyes sent several more flashes so he could get a fix on their location. He directed their antenna to their location and within ten minutes of his transmission they'd established two-way contact with their comms. Reyes spent the next hour updating them on their situation. Carpenter was left nearly speechless, which was a first.

"I'm sorry to hear about Slater," he said at last.

"Thanks," Reyes said. "So were we. I didn't foresee having to bury a crewmember on a beach off the Frisian coast. Although to be honest, the remarkable thing is that three of us are still alive."

"I'm still trying to wrap my head around the fact that you kidnapped the King of Norway."

"In our defense," Gabe said, "he was kind of an asshole."

"I thought you'd be more impressed with the gunpowder bomb," O'Brien said.

"I'm amazed by all of it," Carpenter replied. "You're making my idea of recovering the Cho-ta'an ship seem less crazy."

"No, it's still pretty crazy," Reyes said. "Just building a ship capable of hoisting that amount of weight... it would take years."

Mallick's voice broke in. "You have something better to do, Reyes?"

"No, sir," Reyes said. "If you want to try dredging up a twenty-thousand-ton alien spaceship from the North Sea, we're game." If she were honest, she'd admit that their chances of success were around one in a million, but she was willing to go along with the plan if it meant *Andrea*

Luhman would be sticking around for a while. After all, it wasn't like *they* had anything better to do either.

"Good," Mallick said. "And I'm very happy to hear the three of you are still alive."

"Thank you, sir," Reyes replied. "We're happy to hear you're still here."

"Now that we've found you," Carpenter said, "I can redirect our efforts toward searching for the Cho-ta'an ship. I've got video of the crash, so I can pinpoint where she went down within about three hundred meters. We might find her if I sweep the area with sensors."

"Copy that," Reyes said. "We've got a somewhat more pressing issue we were hoping to get your help on, though."

"Go ahead, Reyes," Mallick said.

"We're expecting Harald to launch an attack on us. If he hasn't figured out where we are yet, he will soon. News travels slow here, but it does travel. And we haven't exactly been keeping a low profile."

"You want a status report on Harald's forces?" Carpenter asked.

"That's it," Reyes replied. "I don't expect exact troop counts, but you should be able to give us some warning if a fleet is headed our way, right?"

"I think we can do better than that," Carpenter said. "Give me a few days and I'll see what I can come up with."

*****

While Carpenter used twenty-third century technology to spy on King Harald, work continued on several other fronts. Some men worked on finishing the main hall and barracks, and others had begun digging a defensive trench a few meters on the outside of the perimeter fence. The dirt from the trench was piled up to make a rampart a little farther down the hill. While Sigurd and Gabe supervised the construction of defenses, Reyes and O'Brien began to work on another engineering problem: manufacturing guns.

When Harald attacked, his forces would likely outnumber them by ten to one or more. The defenses would slow them down, but to beat the attackers back, the defenders would need some serious weaponry. They briefly discussed trying to manufacture ammunition for their pistols, but decided it was unfeasible. They just didn't have the tools to engineer bullets with that sort of precision. In any case, only five of them had pistols: Reyes,

Gabe, Gunnar, Agnar and Brynjarr. O'Brien had never bothered to get his gun back from Brynjarr, as the latter was a much better shot.

Building simple guns from scratch was a better bet, especially since they'd already perfected the process of making black powder. Thanks to the recent Viking raids, they had plenty of metalworking tools and scrap iron. What they lacked was a forge.

O'Brien and Reyes enlisted several strong men to transport heavy stones from the riverbed. They stacked these to form an oven with an opening above it where the heat would be channeled. Charcoal would have to suffice for a fuel source, as there was no source of coal in the area. By using the bellows from the signaling apparatus, they were able to get the forge up to fifteen hundred degrees Celsius—the melting point of iron. They tested the forge by fabricating a knife blade and several spearheads, which were hardened by reheating and then submerging them in cold water. These turned out well enough, but the Norsemen disapproved of the end result. A man with some blacksmithing experience, named Arvid, showed them how to make the blades tougher through a process of pattern-welding: the blade was made by forge-welding several layers of iron together and then twisting and manipulating them to form a pattern.

Once they'd gotten the process down, they hoped to increase their rate of production. Unfortunately, they found that the narrow base of the forge didn't allow for enough charcoal to keep the temperature above fifteen hundred for more than a few minutes, and it couldn't be loaded with more charcoal without interrupting whatever work was being done on the forge. Reyes was ready to tear it apart and start over, but O'Brien suggested starting from scratch with a better design and adapting the old forge into an oven for baking bread. They had no trouble purchasing large quantities of wheat from farmers farther upriver, and some of the men had already rigged up a crude millstone. So far, though, they had been eating the wheat ground up into porridge, as they had no oven. Shortly after they began construction on the new forge, Carpenter transmitted his report on the status of Harald's forces.

The good news was that Harald was busy suppressing a rebellion in the south of the country, and that it would probably take him at least until fall to get things under control. The bad news was that when he'd secured control of the southern part of the country, Harald would have unquestioned dominion over all of Norway—and a sizable military force that could then be directed toward other ends. The Norsemen avoided sailing in winter, for good reason, but when spring came Harald would probably have little difficulty dispatching twenty or more ships to deal with the spacemen.

It was vital, then, that the fort had not only good defenses, but weapons capable of turning back such an attack. The new forge was plenty hot, and could be refueled from the rear, so work would not be interrupted by refueling. O'Brien's ribs were nearly healed; these days he could swing a hammer almost as well as Reyes.

Their first attempt at forming a gun barrel took them nearly a week. They began by melting down scraps of iron and then flattening the semi-liquid iron blob into an oblong rectangular sheet. They rolled the sheet into a pipe and forge-welded it along the seam, with a metal rod down the middle to prevent the pipe from collapsing on itself. Finally, the inside of the barrel was bored out. The end result was a barrel suitable for a musket or breech-loaded rifle. They had briefly considered trying to build a cannon, but ultimately rejected the idea. A cannon would require a lot more iron and labor, and would probably be overkill: what they needed were a lot of guns that could be fired quickly.

They settled on a simple breach-loaded design: one end of the barrel was closed off by a metal stopper on a hinge, so ammunition could be loaded without dropping bullets down the barrel. To reduce reload times, they'd also have to manufacture self-contained cartridges containing lead bullets and a black powder charge. A trigger mechanism would be added to detonate the charge, and a wooden stock could be added later to make the gun easier to hold. Rather than attempting to rifle the barrel to improve accuracy, they decided to make long, flechette-like bullets that would be self-stabilizing. Accuracy wasn't a big concern in any case; they expected to be fighting at relatively close range for the most part, and there would likely be so many attackers that it would be hard to miss them.

It took them until October to develop a working prototype. It was loud, unreliable, inaccurate and dangerous. Several Norsemen beat each other bloody vying to be the first one to use it.

Meanwhile, Carpenter had had no luck in locating the Cho-ta'an vessel. Either it had been broken into pieces by the sea, it was too far down to register on *Andrea Luhman*'s sensors, or Carpenter was looking in the wrong place. He had already widened his search parameters several times, with no luck. It was beginning to look like recovering the Cho-ta'an ship was not going to happen. The good news, though, was that Mallick had agreed to keep *Andrea Luhman* in orbit until spring, to continue gathering intelligence on Harald's forces. The captain had evidently decided that if they were going to miss the end of the war by two hundred years anyway, a few more months probably wouldn't make a difference. When Harald's attack finally came, they would have plenty of warning.

In between the various projects, raiding continued throughout the summer, providing both luxury items the Norsemen could sell and items that Reyes or O'Brien had requested for their tasks. The raids garnered more than material goods, though. In the spring, when it wasn't clear they were going to be able to pay their debt to Hrólfr, Reyes had had to promise to relax her "no women" rule for the men who promised to stay through the winter. Sigurd had been pressuring her on this, telling her it was unrealistic to expect the men to go for months with no female companionship. If nothing else, he said, she should do it for her own safety. She thanked him for his concern and patted the pistol on her hip.

Finally, though, she had to relent. She still insisted that no women be brought to the fort against their will, but she had no illusions about how difficult it was going to be to enforce that rule. In the last raid, several men brought young women—some as young as sixteen—back with them, but it was impossible to determine how willing they were. They were certainly scared, but no more so than any girl who had traveled far from her home for the first time. They spoke only a dialect of Frankish, which none of the spacemen could understand. Some of the Norsemen knew a few words, but they weren't eager to interpret. In any case, Reyes had limited options for dealing with the situation. She couldn't very well send the girls home. In the end, she had Gabe take each of the girls aside and explain as best he could they could come to him if they felt like they were in danger. None of them ever did.

Reyes also had Sigurd explain to the men that the women were to be considered full members of the community, not property. Surprisingly, there were few objections to this. She had noticed at Haavaldsrud that the Norsemen treated their women well and didn't seem to keep slaves. That may simply have been because the economics of life in the valley didn't favor slavery, but the fact was that they seemed to be used to treating each other—including women—as equals.

One woman in particular, named Inga, seemed determined to make the most of her situation. She took over cooking duties from the young Norseman who had been performing them thus far with middling results. Reyes had shown Inga how to use the oven, and she immediately delegated the task of bread-making to two younger girls, who were soon producing so much fresh bread that men had to be sent upriver to buy more grain. The settlement was already consuming a considerable amount for the beer-making operation that the men had just begun.

Inga put two other girls in charge of making jams and preserves from the plums, redcurrants, cranberries, gooseberries, cherries, and various other berries men had bought from farmers or picked from bushes in the surrounding countryside. As a result of the efforts of Inga and the other girls, the quality of the food—and thereby the morale—in the camp improved immensely. No one complained when the women were given their own private quarters in the newly constructed lodge, ostensibly as a reward for their hard work. In reality, Reyes wanted to make sure the women had a place to go where men were not allowed. Several of them had been claimed by particular men and others made a habit of switching tents with some frequency. Whether money changed hands in any of these transaction Reyes couldn't say, and she didn't ask. Nor did she plan to intervene if one of them got pregnant. These people would just have to deal with that eventuality however they ordinarily did under such circumstances.

Disease was a bigger concern, but it turned out not to be the venereal sort that posed the greatest threat: in mid-December, a flu-like illness swept through the camp, affecting nearly every Norseman to one extent or other. The only ones unaffected were the spacemen, probably thanks to the adaptive antibiotic nanobots they'd been injected with prior to boarding the lander. The plague took nearly three weeks to pass, leaving three men dead.

Raiding had ceased in the fall, and the men occupied themselves with shoring up the fort's defenses, including building a couple of casemates overlooking the river, and making weapons. They made several dozen spears and hundreds of arrows, using the forge when Reyes and O'Brien didn't need it. If the spacemen failed at making guns, at least they wouldn't run out of arrows.

Over the next several weeks, however, they perfected their gun-making process. By February, they had twenty completed rifles, including triggers, grips and stocks, and four hundred bullets. O'Brien trained Agnar and Brynjarr in the use of the weapons, and later the two selected twenty men to form their rifle corps. They trained far to the west of the fort, where the gunshots wouldn't be heard.

The raiding had gone so well that nearly all the men opted to stay for the winter. Both *Ísbátr* and *Bylgjasverð* remained in Normandy for the winter, although a few men did return to Norway on other ships embarking from the area. They took with them a sizable share of the spoils, most of which was owed to Dag for the use of his ships. Most of the rest was distributed to the families of the men who remained in Normandy.

By the end of February, Harald had suppressed the rebellions in the south, and Carpenter reported that warships were amassing near Harald's palace at Avaldsnes. Hrólfr had visited in the fall to let them know that he had been informed of their history with Harald. He didn't seem angry, but he informed them in no uncertain terms that he would not sacrifice his own men to protect them from Harald. Reyes ended up sending a cartload of furs and silver to him to ensure his neutrality.

On March 28, a little over a year after the lander crashed, Carpenter reported that a fleet of twenty-eight ships had set out across the North Sea. They were headed for Normandy.

CHAPTER THIRTY-NINE

The ships arrived at the mouth of the Rouen on the tenth of April. A sentry posted on a ridge overlooking the beach spotted them in the morning and ran back to tell the others. By the time he arrived, *Andrea Luhman* had come over the horizon and Carpenter had already reported that the fleet was heading up the river.

There was plenty of room along the riverbank for twenty-eight ships, but there was only one path through the woods to the fort, which meant that if Harald's men didn't want to hack through the underbrush with their axes, they had to congregate on the bank and then advance single-file up the hill. That made them easy targets for the archers manning the two casemates a hundred meters or so from the river. The casemates were only large enough for three men each, but they managed to take out twelve of Harald's men before they even reached the path.

The casemates were difficult to access from the shore; a tunnel connected them to the fort. There were heavy iron portcullises at both ends that could be slammed shut with the pull of a chain, making an assault from the tunnel virtually impossible. When the men on the shore began hacking through the woods toward the casemates, the archers fled through the tunnels, slamming the portcullises behind them.

Gabe watched from the watchtower as Harald's men surged up the trail. Carpenter had estimated the total number at just over a thousand. The fort's occupants, including the women, currently numbered seventy-five. They were outnumbered fifteen to one.

That proportion dropped slightly as the lead man stumbled across a tripwire, triggering a black powder charge hidden in the bushes that showered the column of men with iron fragments. Another dozen men fell to the ground, dead or wounded. The corpses and wounded men were dragged out of the way and the assault continued. Undaunted, Harald's men poured out of the woods and began moving in both directions around the fort to encircle it. Archers standing on scaffolds inside the perimeter fence rained arrows down on them, to little effect. Occasionally a man would fall, but the attackers' shields absorbed most of the arrows. Gabe didn't worry until he began to see men carrying wooden ladders up the trail. The ladders appeared to be about five meters long: just long enough to span a forty-five degree angle to the top of the perimeter fence. Someone had definitely been feeding intelligence to Harald.

"You there, Carpenter?" Gabe said into his comm. *Andrea Luhman* was about to slip below the horizon again.

"I'm here, Gabe."

"Would have been nice to know about the ladders."

"Is that what those are? They must have blended in with the decks of the ships."

"Some mystical sky god you are," Gabe said. "See if we sacrifice any more goats to you."

"Sorry, Gabe, you're breaking up. Something about goats?"

"Forget it, Carpenter. See you on the flip side."

"How many ladders?" asked O'Brien, who was waiting below with the rifle corps. Not wanting to risk losing any of the riflemen, Gabe had instructed them to stay out of sight until he had a better understanding of the threat. Reyes was with Gabe in the tower, watching the enemy assemble. All three spacemen were wearing their flight suits; these days they generally wore more conventional clothing, saving the flight suits for times when they needed added protection, either from cold or from potential enemy attack.

"Looks like about twenty," Gabe said.

"Any other surprises?"

Peering at a group of men near the trail that seemed to be coordinating the attack, Gabe realized he recognized one of them. A chill ran down his spine. It didn't bode well for the defenders that the man leading the attack on them was literally invincible. Gabe glanced at Reyes. She had seen him too. But Reyes had given Slater's comm to Sigurd, so if he said anything about Harald on the open channel, Sigurd would hear it. That could only lead to trouble, as Sigurd might take unnecessary risks to get to Harald.

"No more surprises," Gabe said. "Our priority at this point is keeping those ladders down. If they start getting men over the fence, we're dead. We don't have the numbers to fight a pitched battle."

"Understood."

"I've got seven ladders to the east, four to the west, six to the north and three to the south. Position the gunmen accordingly." Narrow scaffolds lined the inside of the perimeter fence, about a meter and a half from the spikes at the top, allowing gunners and archers to fire outside without exposing much of themselves to the enemy.

"Copy that."

Gabe watched as O'Brien ordered the gunmen to their various positions. The spacemen had become reasonably conversant in the Norsemen's language over the winter, and Gabe had made certain that they could communicate basic tactical information without any trouble.

The attack began in earnest before the riflemen had even taken their positions. A volley of arrows rained down on the defenders while small teams of men advanced with the ladders, climbing the rampart. Few of the attackers' arrows hit their target, and the defending archers riddled the ladder men with arrows. The men fell, leaving their ladders where they had fallen. Most of the ladder men hadn't even reached the top of the rampart.

But the attackers regrouped, and as another volley of arrows rained down, more men advanced, running to the ladders. They held their shields up as they ran, making it difficult to hit them until they reached the ladders and had to put their shield aside to heft the ladder. These men too fell, riddled with arrows. The cycle repeated several more times, the attackers dying shortly after they picked up the ladder. But with each group, the ladders advanced a few meters.

The situation changed dramatically once the riflemen were in place. Gunshots rang out in the air, striking fear into the attackers. The faster riflemen could fire six shots a minute, and the wooden shields were no protection against iron bullets traveling two hundred meters per second. Half the ladder men now fell before they even reached the ladders.

It didn't take long for the attackers to realize, though, that there were a limited number of riflemen. They began to send twice as many men to each ladder, hoping to overwhelm the defenders with sheer numbers. Unfortunately for them, the rifles weren't the only guns the defenders had.

Gabe and Reyes still had their pistols, and they'd taken all the remaining ammunition into the tower with him. They hadn't wanted to waste bullets on archers fifty meters away, but the men running toward him with ladders were making it easy for them. "Okay," he said. "We're up."

Reyes nodded, leveling her gun on the firing holes in the watchtower. Gabe did the same on the opposite side. They opened fire.

Gunshots rang out, one after another. Ladder carriers began to fall in droves, and the ladders fell to the dirt. The men coming behind them fell as well, targeted by the riflemen. Only three ladders reached the fence, and the men climbing them were killed as soon as they poked their head above the fence. Unprepared for such a brutally effective counterattack, the rest of the attackers held back. For now, the assault had stalled. Cheers went up from within the fort.

"Nice shooting," Gabe said.

Reyes smiled. "I'm a little rusty."

"You did great. Let's just hope they don't try that again. We're almost out of ammo."

Then something strange happened. There was some discussion among the leaders of the assault, after which the men began to move back around the perimeter of the fort and down the path toward the river. The attackers were retreating.

"What the hell?" Reyes asked. "That can't be it?"

Gabe frowned. "No," he said. "They're regrouping. What for, I couldn't tell you."

"What's going on?" O'Brien asked. "Are they leaving?"

"Looks that way," Gabe said. "Stay ready."

But the attackers' retreat didn't appear to be a feint. The entire force retreated back down the trail toward the river. Soon Gabe glimpsed men congregating again on the bank. They did not appear to be boarding their ships.

Squinting into the distance, Gabe could just make out the forms of men on the riverbank. Gabe wished they'd had time to manufacture lenses for a telescope, but other tasks had taken priority. "I don't think they're leaving," he said. "Looks like they're unloading something from one of the boats."

"What is it?" Reyes asked.

Gabe shook his head. "Hard to say. Several pieces, like wall sections. Looks like metal. Some kind of siege engine?" The men carrying the heavy objects disappeared behind the trees, and *Andrea Luhman* wouldn't have line on sight to them for at least another hour. "Sigurd, can you send somebody down there? We need to know what they're doing."

"Copy that," Sigurd said, in his thick Norse accent. They'd given him Slater's comm, and he had taken the responsibility very seriously, including adopting the spacemen's lingo. "I will send Njáll." Njáll was notorious for being able to move through the woods quietly enough to sneak up on a rabbit.

"O'Brien, keep your riflemen in position," Gabe said. "Sigurd, give the rest of your men five minutes to rest. Then put them to work collecting arrows. And send some men out to chop up those ladders."

*****

By the time Njáll reported back, *Andrea Luhman* had come back around. Carpenter and Njáll's reports agreed: Harald's men were putting something together on the riverbank. It was roughly cube-shaped, about two meters on a side, and assembled from metal wall sections that had apparently been prefabricated for this purpose. Njáll also reported that men were chopping down trees along the path to the fort, presumably to make way for whatever they were building. Njáll and Carpenter were equally baffled by the apparent quality of the metal panels.

"The surfaces are smooth," Njáll said, in his native tongue. "I couldn't see any seams. The forge required to make such a thing must be gigantic."

The spacemen exchanged worried glances. Gabe and Reyes had come down from the tower, leaving two of the riflemen in their place. Reyes filled Carpenter in on Njáll's assessment. Carpenter concurred.

"I'm afraid I don't have any other explanation," Carpenter said.

The spacemen knew exactly what he meant: with the lander destroyed, there was only one way Harald could have gotten his hands on metal of that quality.

"There's no way Harald's men dredged the Cho-ta'an ship up," Reyes said.

"Maybe a piece of debris that broke off when it hit the water?"

"I'm checking the video now," Carpenter said. "Give me a few minutes."

They waited anxiously for more information from Carpenter while the Norsemen collected arrows and tended to their wounded. Six men had been hit with arrows; another had fallen from a scaffold and broken his arm. So far there were no dead.

"The video is pretty blurry," Carpenter said at last. "But it does look like something broke off shortly before the crash."

"*Before* the crash?" Reyes said. "Like an escape pod?"

"Could be."

"And you're just noticing this now?"

"I never had any reason to look at the video recorded before the crash. I was trying to figure out where the ship was. Anyway, it's almost impossible to see. At ninety frames per second, it only shows up in three frames. I'm going to try to figure out where it would have ended up based on its trajectory."

"Be quick about it," Reyes said. She turned off her mic and turned to Gabe. "What do you think?"

"I think that those panels are of Cho-ta'an construction," Gabe said. "The real question, though, is what else survived that crash."

"You mean the Cho-ta'an themselves," O'Brien said.

"Cho-ta'an and Cho-ta'an weapons. If those guys have a railgun, we're in trouble. Njáll, did you see any... strange-looking men? Very tall, probably wearing cloaks to disguise their appearance."

Njáll shook his head. "I did not see," he said in broken English. "I look at metal thing."

There wasn't much they could do but wait. A pre-emptive assault on the riverbank would be suicidal. They might be able to slow down the process of widening the path by having archers harass the men cutting down trees, but that would be at best a delaying tactic, and they couldn't afford to leave their archers exposed. Whatever Harald's men were building, they would find out soon enough.

CHAPTER FORTY

The work on the cube continued until after dark. Njáll went out twice more to spy on the men's progress, but was unable to get close enough to gather any additional information. Carpenter's surveillance was similarly unhelpful, but he did discover another clue as to the object's origin.

"If I draw a line following the trajectory of the object that left the Cho-ta'an ship, it intersects northern Denmark. There's a gash in a field about forty meters long that could have been caused by some kind of craft, but whatever made the gash is gone."

Gabe and Reyes exchanged glances.

"That's all you've got?" Reyes asked, reading Gabe's thoughts.

"You know," Carpenter said, "you went from 'Thank God you're still here' to 'What have you done for me lately' in record time."

"Sorry, Carpenter," Reyes said. "We're getting a little antsy down here. We thought we were going to be fighting Vikings with spears and axes. Not space aliens with... whatever's in that box."

"Understood," Carpenter replied. "I'll let you know if I find out anything else."

The night wore on, and still there was no sign of activity from the attackers. Clouds had come over the Moon, making surveillance difficult. Some time after midnight, Carpenter reported Harald's men were on the move. They'd attached long wooden poles to the cube, allowing it to be carried by a dozen men. They advanced slowly up the path, proceeded by a score of men with bows and spears.

"Any idea what's in that thing yet, Carpenter?" Gabe asked. He and Reyes continued to watch from the tower.

"Sorry," Carpenter replied. "No radiation, no heat signature. It's just a big fucking metal box. It could be filled with dead cats for all I know."

"Jesus, Carpenter."

Two men emerged from the woods bearing torches and shields. Immediately behind them followed another score of men with spears, and then two more torch-bearers. These were followed by the dozen men bearing the metal box. They set it down about twenty meters from the dirt rampart as more men continued to pour out from the woods. All of the men carried shields and either spears or axes. About one in twenty also had a torch. None of them seemed to have bows. The men in front formed two rows, staggering their shields to create an impenetrable wall.

"I don't like this," O'Brien said. "Not at all."

"Should we start shooting?" Reyes asked.

Gabe hesitated. "No. Arrows won't get through that wall, and we don't want to waste bullets until we know what we're dealing with. O'Brien, get all your riflemen to this side. Be ready to fire on command. Sigurd, can you get me some light on that thing?"

"Copy," Sigurd replied. He barked orders to several nearby archers, who ran to collect arrows from a chest near the watchtower. They climbed onto a scaffold against the east wall and nocked their arrows. Braggi moved from one archer to the next, lighting the wicks hanging off the arrows. The arrows streaked across the sky, their wicks tracing wide arcs that ended near the metal box. Most of them struck shields; some bounced off the top of the box; a few stuck in the ground. Then, one by one, the magnesium charges on the arrows caught fire, flooding the area with light. Harald's men shifted nervously but didn't panic. After a few seconds, the flares died out. The light showed them little that they didn't already know, but it revealed one aspect of the box they'd missed.

"What's that slot in the front?" Reyes asked.

"Gun," Sigurd replied. He'd climbed onto the platform with the archers.

Gabe nodded grimly. "It looks like a casemate for some kind of weapon. An automatic rifle or a railgun, probably."

"So what do we do?" O'Brien asked.

"Take it out," Gabe said. "Sigurd, I need a pair of men with magnesium arrows. Hit that thing every five seconds. If we can't see it, we can't hit it. O'Brien, I want every rifleman on this side of the fort. Aim for that slit. Archers too. Fill that goddamn thing with arrows."

The Norsemen were in position within a minute. The first magnesium arrow plinked off the top of the box, showering the area with light, and a deafening roar of gunshots rang out. This was followed by a cacophony of bullets and arrows striking metal. The fusillade had no noticeable effect. Gabe was almost certain one of the bullets from his pistol had gone through the slot, but it was impossible to know if it made any difference. "Keep shooting!" he yelled, as the men reloaded. He was going to feel very foolish if this was all an elaborate ruse to make them direct their fire at an empty box, but he couldn't take the chance. Even if they spent all their ammunition on the box, they'd still have a fighting chance against a Viking assault. But if there was a railgun in that box, destroying it was their only hope. Guns blasted again, and another volley of bullets and arrows bounced harmlessly off the box.

As he watched, one of the magnesium arrows hit the ground a meter or so to the left of the cube, momentarily illuminating a group of men who stood nearby, their shields raised. The brilliant light glimmered on their steel helmets and shin greaves. For a second, one of the shields dropped enough for Gabe to see a ruddy face framed by thick locks of strawberry blond hair. Gabe glanced to Sigurd, but Sigurd showed no sign of having seen Harald. The arrow burned out.

The gunners were reloading for the third time when one of the archers screamed. Gabe glanced down in time to see the man's left hand fall to the platform, severed cleanly from his wrist. The man dropped his bow, clutched the bloody stump that was left of his forearm, and fell backwards off the scaffold to the ground. Another man, who had turned to gawk at the fallen man, cried out—with good reason. In the lingering smoke from the gunfire, a narrow red beam could be seen, sizzling through the man's lower back.

"It's a laser!" Gabe shouted. "Get out of the way!"

The men on the scaffold stepped back, staring at the strange red beam that was barely visible in the smoke. It moved slowly downward, cutting one of the pine fence timbers neatly in half. Gabe watched as the beam sliced through the planks of the scaffold, barely able to believe his eyes. Breach-loaders and gunpowder bombs were one thing, but a laser! How the hell were they going to defend against a laser? If he'd had any idea Harald had a laser, he'd have built a mirror instead of working out the details of magnesium arrows. But it was too late for that now. The men were waiting for orders.

"Keep firing!" He shouted. "Aim for that slot!" Reyes stood next to him, silently watching. The laser continued to slice through the fence.

"Again!" Gabe yelled. The riflemen reloaded and the archers nocked their arrows. Gabe fired three more times with his pistol and then paused to glance down. The beam was just above ground level now, and had begun moving south, cutting crossways along the fence timbers. If they didn't stop that laser soon, it was going to cut a hole in the fence big enough for Harald's men to walk right through. With one man for every ten attackers, the defenders wouldn't hold the fort long. Harald's men would slaughter the occupants and drag the spacemen back to Norway.

But the bullets and arrows continued to have no effect. By this time, dozens of shots must have penetrated the slit, but it made no difference. There had to be another protective layer inside the box's outer shell. As the laser's path continued its sideways path, Gabe realized they had lost. There was no way to keep Harald's men from taking the fort. The cut was already a good two meters wide. The defenders would be overrun within minutes.

"Gabe," Reyes said, "we need to get out of here."

Gabe pounded his fist on the railing, not wanting to accept it. But there was no way around it: they had lost. "Everybody down!" he shouted. "Retreat!"

As Reyes started down the ladder, the Norsemen stared up at Gabe, uncomprehending. They understood the words, but retreating wasn't in their nature, and they'd never considered the possibility that they might lose a fight, particularly with the spacemen on their side. Several of them continued to reload their guns or pull arrows from their quivers.

"No!" Gabe shouted, climbing down the ladder after Reyes. "It's pointless! We're not getting through that armor. We need to run! Now!"

Still the men didn't move. Many ignored him and continued firing. Sigurd, who had just fired his last arrow at the cube, leaped down from the scaffold and began to scour the ground for more. Gabe and Reyes ran toward him, past men and women who were frantically gathering their possessions.

"Birgir, tell those men no chests," Reyes shouted. "Grab what they can carry and get down that tunnel. And keep people away from that beam!" The laser was cutting a path across the fort, slicing into the stones of the forge, which lay in its path. Gabe turned back toward the wall to see that O'Brien was the only rifleman who had moved.

Gabe approached Sigurd. "We need to get everybody out of here and into the tunnels."

"We cannot run, Gabe," Sigurd said. "This is our home. Everything we have—"

"Everything you have is going to be Harald's," Reyes said. "And you're going to be dead or tied up in the hold of a boat. You're not going to get your vengeance today."

Sigurd stared at her for a moment. "You saw him," he said at last. He looked at Gabe. "Both of you."

"Sigurd," Gabe said, "we don't have time for this. We've lost this battle. No good can come from staying here."

Sigurd turned to the watch the beam cutting horizontally across the fence timbers. On the scaffold above them, men continued to fire at the metal box. Around them, some men stood around in confusion while others ran into the lodge for their belongings. "I let him go once, because you begged me," Sigurd said. "And this is how you repay me? You knew he was here and you said nothing. My son deserves vengeance!" Sigurd drew his sword.

"Yngvi deserves vengeance," Reyes said, "but now is not the time."

"It will never be the time," Sigurd said bitterly. "I am not a fool. I hear you talk. You believe you see the future. You think my quest for vengeance is doomed to fail."

"I don't know anything for certain," Reyes said, "but if you stay here, you will die."

"Then I will die," Sigurd said. "Some must stay behind to fight, or you will not get away in time. Go. You have your quest. I have mine." He turned away from them and strode toward the section of fence that was being cut away.

"He's right, I'm afraid," Gabe said. "They'll be inside the fence before these people can get through the tunnel. Some of us are going to have to stay to buy you time." He turned toward the men on the scaffold. "Agnar, if you're going to stay up there, tell your men to save their ammo for the men coming through the gap!"

"Copy that," Agnar shouted.

Behind them, O'Brien and Birgir were doing their best to round people up and get them down the tunnel. Several men had joined Sigurd, weapons ready, watching the red beam cut through the palisade. They were willing to fight, even at ten to one odds. And they were going to die, every last one of them.

"What are you saying, Gabe?"

"You and O'Brien get out," Gabe said. "We'll slow them down."

"Don't be ridiculous, Gabe," Reyes said. "You're coming. That's an order."

"Damn it, Reyes, we won't make it. You can stand here arguing with me or you can take this chance to escape."

"No," Reyes said. "We stick together, no matter what."

"Then we die together."

Reyes shook her head. "I don't accept that. There's got to be another way. A way to slow them down. All this technology, everything we've accomplished—"

"It was all for nothing. We don't have a secret weapon to defend the fort against lasers. We lost, Reyes. I've got a few bullets left, but that's it. Maybe if we'd made more gunpowder instead of twenty kilograms of…"

As he trailed off, Reyes's eyes lit up.

Gabe smiled, realizing what Reyes was thinking. "Worth a try," he said. He turned and ran toward a barrel that stood under the eaves of the building they used as a workshop for making bullets. "Heimir! Eirik! Help me with this barrel!"

The two men, who were among those waiting for Harald's men to come through the gap, put down their spears and ran toward him. They tipped the barrel on its side and rolled it toward the fence just south of the beam. Reyes had already climbed onto the scaffold against the fence. Gabe climbed up after her. "Quickly!" Gabe shouted, as Heimir and Eirik hefted the barrel up to them. The beam was less than an arm's length from the bottom of the scaffold they were standing on. The Moon had come out from behind the clouds, and beyond the fence hundreds of men stood just beyond the dirt rampart, shields and spears up, ready to charge.

The barrel rolled onto the scaffold. Reyes and Gabe bent down to lift it. "Come on, Reyes!" Gabe said. "You must have built some muscles banging on that anvil for six months."

"Shut up, Gabe," Reyes grunted, as she lifted her end of the barrel to her chest.

"Agnar!" Gabe shouted. "Tell your gunmen to shut their eyes!"

Agnar, turning to see what they were doing, gaped for a moment and then gave the order. The men on the scaffold closed their eyes and turned away.

"On the count of three," Gabe said. "Up and over."

"Ready."

"One... two... *three!*"

As they heaved the barrel over the fence, the scaffold gave way. Reyes stumbled into Gabe and they fell together to the ground. A whoosh of air followed as the barrel split and the magnesium caught fire. Lying on his back, the wind knocked out of his lungs, Gabe looked up to see rays of brilliant white light pouring through every crack in the fence. Above, the dispersed smoke from the guns glowed like a fog illuminated by a spotlight. Beyond the fence, men grunted and screamed. Anyone who had been looking in the direction of the laser when the barrel of magnesium hit it would be blind for a good minute, probably more.

Reyes lay next to him, face-down and apparently unconscious. She must have hit her head on the way down. Gabe heard wood splintering and realized the fence was about to fall. He got to his feet, dragging Reyes with him. He had just enough time to push her out of the way before the fence came down on top of him, slamming to the ground. He was trapped, his legs caught beneath the timbers.

Pushing his upper body off the ground, he turned to see the gaping hole in the fence. The magnesium had burned out, but the fire had spread to the fence, and the men outside stood blinking and stumbling into each other in the flickering orange light. Following the sound of the crash, they pressed forward, stepping onto the fallen timbers, jabbing their spears at the air. Oblivious to Gabe, several defenders ran onto the fence to push them back, and Gabe groaned under the added weight. Gunshots rang out as the riflemen began to fire. Ahead of him, Reyes lay in the dirt, still not moving.

Heimir and Eirik, the two men who had helped lift the barrel, ran to Gabe and managed to lift the timbers enough for him to pull himself loose. Once he was free, they grabbed their spears and joined the fray. Gabe tried to get to his feet, but winced and fell to his knees as weight hit his right ankle. He'd twisted it when the fence landed on him. He crawled to Reyes, shaking her by the shoulder. She didn't stir.

To his left, Heimir, Eirik and the others did their best to stem the tide, but they were being pushed back by the sheer number of attackers. Somehow Gabe had to get Reyes out of here, even if he had to drag her through the tunnel on his knees. Gabe put his arms around Reyes and began to pull her away from the fight, but a looming shadow told him someone was approaching. He turned in time to see a man stumbling across the fence section toward them, swinging his axe wildly. Gabe had just enough time to put himself between Reyes and the axeman, hoping to protect her from a direct hit.

But as he crouched over her, he heard a grunt and suddenly the shadow was gone. Gabe looked up again to see a man standing over them with a sword. Sigurd. Behind him, the other defenders continued to hack at the half-blind attackers pushing their way into the fort. Sigurd slid the sword into its sheath.

"Move!" he growled.

When Gabe hesitated, he said it again. "Gabe, move!" Gabe rolled aside.

As Sigurd picked up Reyes, Gabe grabbed a fallen spear from the ground and pulled himself to his feet, using the spear to support his weight. Sigurd carried Reyes toward the shed, and Gabe did his best to follow. Everyone except the riflemen and the other dozen or so men who had stayed to fight had already fled.

Sigurd disappeared into the tunnel with Reyes, and Gabe turned on his cuff light and followed. The tunnel had taken a team of men six weeks to dig, using pattern-welded steel shovels and heat-tempered picks. The walls were raw dirt, reinforced every couple meters by spruce supports. Around a bend, Gabe could just see the flicker of the torches of the men ahead of them. He half-hopped down the tunnel as fast as he could after Sigurd. A hundred meters later, he came out inside one of the casemates overlooking the river. By the time Gabe exited the tunnel, Reyes was on her feet. Sigurd stood next to her with his hand on her shoulder.

"Hey, you okay?" Gabe asked.

"Think so," Reyes said, holding her hand to the back of her skull. "Just hit my head."

Gabe looked out the casemate door. The men ahead of them were hacking their way through the brush to get to the trail. Down below, a score or more men with torches stood on the bank: the invaders had left a contingent behind to guard their ships. As they spotted the people emerging onto the trail, they began moving toward the trailhead.

"Good," Gabe said. "Sigurd, stay with her."

"Gabe, where the hell...?" Reyes said.

But Gabe was already limping down the trail. If they didn't dispatch this group quickly, they were going to be caught fighting on two fronts. Once the attackers got past the riflemen, it wouldn't take them long to find the tunnel.

By the time Gabe caught up with the women at the back of the group, the melee had already begun. Birgir, Braggi and several others were trying to push their toward the riverbank, but most of the defenders remained trapped in the bottleneck of the trailhead. Only about ten of the defenders were currently engaged in the fight, and two men had already fallen.

Gabe pushed his way forward to the melee and then left the trail to get a clear shot. He dropped the spear, leaned against a tree to support his weight and drew his pistol. He had less than a full magazine left, but he was going to make it count. He fired at one attacker, hitting him in the forehead, then aimed again, knocking another to the ground with two shots in the chest. As Birgir sank his spear into the belly of one of the attackers, a second man approached him with an axe over his head. Gabe shot the man in the throat and again in the chest. Another man came at Braggi with a spear. Gabe aimed at the spearman's chest but realized the slide had locked back. He patted desperately at his flight suit, looking for another magazine, but he was out. Braggi tried to duck under the spear, but it sliced across his neck. Braggi yelped, stumbled backwards and fell to the ground. The blood spurting from his wound told Gabe that his jugular had been severed. As the attackers continued to crowd the defenders against the woods, Gabe holstered his gun and reached for his knife.

"Gabe!" cried a voice behind him. It was Reyes. Gabe turned. A flash of metal came at him through the darkness and Gabe got his hand up just in time to catch it. Feeling the soothing cold of machined metal, Gabe shifted the pistol in his hand and spun to face the enemy. The spearman who had hit Braggi came at him. Gabe fired three times at the spearman's midsection. The man took another step, dropped his spear, and fell face-down on the ground. Three more spearmen behind him advanced. Gabe put two bullets in each of them. As he aimed at a fourth man, the slide locked on the gun. Empty. Birgir stepped forward and plunged his spear into the man's throat. He fell to the ground. The battle was over.

"Move!" Birgir said, stepping aside to make way for the group to emerge from the trail. Gabe estimated about thirty heads, but a few stragglers were still coming up from behind.

"Gabe!" Reyes cried again. "Help!"

Reyes grabbed his spear and limped past the men and women emerging from the trail. Reyes was kneeling over one of the fallen: the girl called Inga. A stray spear had gone through her throat. Gabe crouched next to Reyes, shining his light on her, but it was clear there was nothing they could do. Inga, staring at them in horror, took a last wheezing breath and fell still.

"God damn this place," Reyes muttered.

"There's nothing we can do," Gabe said. "We have to go."

Sigurd began herding the others toward one of the smaller ships. But Reyes didn't move.

O'Brien came up from behind. "He's right, Reyes. She's gone. Harald's men will be here any second."

"No," Reyes said. "Wait."

"Reyes!" Gabe snapped. "Get it together!"

"Gabe, for the love of Odin, shut up for once," Reyes yelled. She stood up, removed her cloak and began unzipping her flight suit.

"Um," O'Brien said. "Reyes, what—?"

"Take off your clothes," Reyes said.

"Why the hell..."

"Do it, O'Brien," Gabe said, pulling off his cloak. "Those assholes are looking for spacemen. We'll give them spacemen."

Reyes switched clothes with Inga, and O'Brien located a man who'd died from an axe wound to the head. If Harald's men didn't look too closely, they might be fooled into thinking the spacemen had been killed. As Gabe searched for a man who'd been killed by a headwound, he saw that Braggi was still breathing. He knelt beside the man. Braggi struggled to speak, but choked on the blood in his throat. Gabe crouched behind him, holding up his head. Braggi reached out clumsily, holding something in his hand. Gabe found Braggi's hand with his own and Braggi pressed something into it. It was the lighter.

"Th-thank... you..." Braggi sputtered.

"Thank you, Fireman," Gabe said.

Braggi went limp in his arms.

*****

By the time Gabe had switched clothes with Braggi, they could see men coming down the path with torches. Harald's men hadn't bothered with the tunnel; they knew where it had to come out. There were shouts as the men spotted the three figures near the trailhead.

Reyes and O'Brien helped Gabe down the bank to the ship. It was a snekkja, similar to Ísbátr. There were just enough survivors to man the oars. The women and wounded men were already onboard, while Sigurd and a score of other men waited, standing knee-deep in river water. They had pushed the boat partway into the water already; they were just waiting for the spacemen to get aboard. The men helped Gabe aboard, and O'Brien and Reyes climbed in after him. The men on the bank gave the boat a heave. As it slid into the water, they climbed aboard.

"Ára!" cried Birgir, and the oars were pulled down and set in place. The crew, including the women, began to row the boat downriver. Arrows flew toward them from the shore, cracking against the hull or splashing in the water. Clouds had come over the Moon again, making it difficult for the archers to get a bead on them. The men on the shore didn't seem to be boarding their ships. Reyes breathed a sigh of relief: they were going to make it.

As they slid down the river, Reyes glimpsed a lanky, cloaked figure leaning over Inga's body, holding a torch. After studying the corpse for a moment, the figure straightened and looked down the river. A breeze picked up, momentarily blowing the figure's hood back. Reyes stood, letting out a gasp. The figure quickly secured the hood, but Reyes knew what she had seen.

The Cho-ta'an had survived.

CHAPTER FORTY-ONE

Of the seventy-five souls that had begun the day at the fort, thirty-eight had made it to the snekkja. Among those presumed dead were all twenty riflemen, including Agnar and Brynjarr. Njáll, who had fired at the attackers until he ran out of arrows, was the last man through the tunnel.

Andrea Luhman came back online as they left the mouth of the Rouen. Carpenter reported that several ships had gone after them, but were a good twenty minutes behind. Apparently the attackers had been so confident of success that they'd been unprepared to give chase. As the sky began to lighten in the east, a strong wind came up from the southwest.

"A good omen," Sigurd said, as Birgir directed the men to hoist the sails. Reyes marveled at Sigurd's spirit. He'd just lost his home and many good friends, and he was already looking to the future. Had he accepted the idea that he would never kill Harald? Or was he still dreaming of vengeance? Reyes put the question aside. Today it was enough that they were still alive.

"Where are we headed?" O'Brien asked. "We're running out of places in Europe where we haven't burned any bridges."

"England?" Gabe suggested. "Maybe the Shetlands?"

Sigurd shook his head. "Iceland."

"Well," O'Brien said. "That sounds... cold."

"I have family there," Sigurd said. "Many people have fled to Iceland to get away from Harald. They will welcome us there."

Reyes was skeptical about that, but they didn't have much choice but to trust Sigurd. "Did you get that, Carpenter?" she said. "Apparently we're going to Iceland."

"What the hell are you going to do in Iceland?"

"Same thing we did in Normandy, I suppose."

"Well, I'll have to talk the captain, but I expect we'll be able to see you through your voyage at least. After that, you're probably on your own."

"Captain's still thinking about trying to get back to IDL space?"

"That's the plan, unless you have a better idea."

Reyes squinted into the sun rising over the open sea. "Actually," she said, "I do."

"Raising that Cho-ta'an ship isn't going to happen, Reyes. It was probably a pipe dream even when I thought I could find the damn thing."

"That's... not what I was talking about." As Reyes turned over the idea in her head, she realized it had been lurking in the back of her head for some time—probably since the lander exploded. She'd needed something to hold onto, something to let her believe this wasn't all for nothing. The flight to Earth, defending the lander, the deaths of Slater and so many others... it couldn't all be for nothing. Even when they'd resorted to raiding poor villages for iron and copper, she'd needed to believe that it was for a reason. It wasn't enough that they had superior knowledge and firepower. There had to be a *reason* for them to win, to survive. A goal that was bigger than any of them.

"Okay, Reyes," Carpenter said. "So what's your idea?"

Reyes hesitated. Up to now the others had followed her and Gabe out of necessity, focused on nothing more than survival. But that wasn't going to cut it anymore. They'd reached a decision point, where they either had to embrace an impossible goal or admit they were just another band of bronze-age warriors scrabbling for a few more years on Earth. Reyes couldn't speak for the others, but she hadn't joined the IDL so she could lead a mundane existence, either in 2207 AD or in medieval Europe.

"What if we built our own ship?" she asked.

For a moment, the question hung in the air. Gabe and O'Brien turned to stare at her. Carpenter broke into laughter. When she didn't reply, he stopped.

"Holy shit, you're serious."

"Hear me out," Reyes said. "We've built firearms, bombs, a forge, a compass, a signaling system…"

"Okay," Carpenter said. "But—"

"Not finished," Reyes snapped. "We did all that in less than a *year*. We basically pulled a tribe of Vikings kicking and screaming into the eighteenth century, and we did most of it without your help, just the four of us. *Andrea Luhman*'s got terabytes of data on it. Historical, technological, geographical… You've probably got the specs for the Saturn V rockets in there somewhere. Tell me one good reason we couldn't build our own spaceship."

"Well, theoretically…" Carpenter said. "But it would take years. Decades."

"You got something better to do, Carpenter? As it is, you're going to show up two hundred years late for the war. Even if it takes us thirty years to build a ship, we'll have plenty of time to repair Andrea Luhman's thrusters and get to an IDL outpost before the war is over. Why not stick around and give it a try?"

No one spoke for some time. Finally Mallick's voice came over the comm: "Reyes, do you understand what you're saying? Building a craft capable of reaching orbit is no small feat, even for an advanced civilization. You're talking probably twenty years or more just for training and infrastructure development. You'll need mines, refineries, factories…."

"I'm aware of that, captain. It's an engineering problem."

Mallick laughed. "It's a bit more than that," he said. "You're going to need hundreds, maybe thousands of people. It takes the equivalent of a small city to build a spaceship."

"Then we'll build a city," Reyes said. "Start small, with the Norsemen in Iceland. Bring in people as we need them. Miners, mathematicians, whatever it takes."

"If you're going to go to those lengths, why not forget about repairing *Andrea Luhman*? Go all out and rewrite history from scratch?"

"Paradoxes don't exist," Reyes said. "Everything we've done so far could easily be lost in the noise of history. If we start actively trying to rewrite history, we'll fail. So we do it in secret. Find a remote location, someplace nobody will ever find. Cover our tracks. Do it in a way that doesn't contradict anything that's known to be known. After all, nobody knows a group of spacemen *didn't* help a tribe of Vikings build a spaceship."

Mallick laughed. "I honestly can't tell if you're a genius or if you've lost your mind completely, Reyes."

"It's a thin line," Reyes said, "but really, what do you have to lose?"

There was another long pause. "What do you think, Gabe?" Mallick asked.

Gabe stared over the prow of the ship, deep in thought. Reyes held her breath. She was still technically in charge of this mission, but it was mostly Gabe who had kept them alive so far. Building a spaceship was probably impossible anyway, but with Gabe on her side, she'd be willing to give it a shot. Without him on board, they were doomed from the beginning.

Gabe shook his head. "I think it's insane. I'm no engineer, but I have some idea of the kind of infrastructure it takes to build a spaceship. Airplanes had been flying for half a century by the time the U.S. started its space program, and it still took them years to put a man in orbit. That's in the wealthiest country on Earth, with twentieth century technology. Doing it here, now, in *secret*, no less… the idea is nuts."

Reyes's heart sank.

"That said," Gabe went on, "this whole *thing* is nuts. We shouldn't be here in the first place, and as for satisfying our original mission, we have zero options. I mean, we're seriously talking about sending a ship across the galaxy to rendezvous with humanity *two hundred years* after we've lost the war. It seems to me we're talking about degrees of insanity here."

"So you're on board with Reyes's plan?" Carpenter asked.

"Look," said Gabe. "We're the last hope for humanity, and Reyes is the reason we're all still here. She rescued me from Harald and she kept signaling you guys after I'd given up. To be perfectly honest, all I've been doing for the last year is trying to stay alive for another day, and it's fucking exhausting. We can't go on like this, just surviving. I've never been much for faith, but we've got to have something to believe in, some reason to keep going. So if Reyes wants to build a spaceship, I say we give it a go."

Reyes breathed a sigh of relief.

"Understood," Mallick said. "O'Brien, anything to add?"

"I'm with Gabe," O'Brien said. "These two are the only reason I'm still breathing. If Reyes tells me to build the tower of Babel, I'll start making bricks."

"Seems like we're all in agreement then," Mallick said. "We'll give it a shot. No guarantees, but we'll see where we are a year from now. God help me, we're going to teach the Vikings how to build a spaceship."

Ready for More?

The Dawn of the Iron Dragon is coming in May 2018!

The Dawn of the Iron Dragon follows the crew of _Andrea Luhman_ as they establish a secret facility in Iceland and then trade, negotiate and pillage their way across Europe, contending with power-hungry kings and devious Cho-ta'an agents, with one goal in mind: to build a ship capable of reaching space.

The Saga of the Iron Dragon will conclude with The Voyage of the Iron Dragon in December 2018.

Review This Book!

Did you enjoy _The Dream of the Iron Dragon_? Please take a moment to leave a review on Amazon.com! Reviews are very important for getting the word out to other readers, and it only takes a few seconds.

Acknowledgements

This book would not have been possible without the assistance of:

- **My technical advisors:** Dr. Lucy Rogers, author of *It's Only Rocket Science*, who helped me with the space travel stuff; Jackson Crawford, translator of the *Poetic Edda*, who kept me from mangling Old Norse too badly; Michael Carpenter, who checked my chemistry; Jake Steinman, who assisted with the sailing parts; and Charles Morello, who helped me with the railgun specs and combat tactics;

- **My beta readers:** Suzy Cilbrith, Bill Curtis, Mark Fitzgerald, Lauren Foley, Brian Galloway, Mike Hull, Scott Lavery, Christopher Majava, Viktor Nehring, Paul Alan Piatt and Mark Thompson;

- **And the *Saga of the Iron Dragon* Kickstarter supporters, including:** Tom Cannon, Chris DeBrusk, Rick DeVos, Christopher Finlan, Brian and Donna Hekman, Tom Hickok, Aaron James, Andrea Luhman, Arnie M., Matthew J McCormick, Steven Mentzel, Kristi Michels, Cara Miller, Kyle "Fiddy" Pinches, Chad and Denise Rogers, Justin Schumacher, Thomas James Slater, Johannes Stauffer, Christopher Turner, and Gabe Zuehlsdorf.

Any errors in this book are the fault of the author. I did my best.

Cover Art

Snowy mountains painting by Artur Zima:
http://arturzima.com/

Crashed spaceship image by Ricky Xie:
https://www.artstation.com/rickyxie

Titling by Steve Beaulieu:
https://beaulistic.wordpress.com/

Images used with permission.

More Books by Robert Kroese

The Starship Grifters Universe

Out of the Soylent Planet
Starship Grifters
Aye, Robot

The Mercury Series

Mercury Falls
Mercury Rises
Mercury Rests
Mercury Revolts
Mercury Shrugs

The Land of Dis

Distopia
Disenchanted
Disillusioned

Other Books

The Big Sheep
The Last Iota
Schrödinger's Gat
City of Sand
The Foreworld Saga: The Outcast
The Force is Middling in This One

Made in the USA
Middletown, DE
02 September 2021